Thomas C. DeRemigio
230 South Poplar Street
Gibbstown, N. J. 08027

W9-BFL-143

BENTON'S
ROW

Frank Yerby

BENTON'S ROW

THE DIAL PRESS · NEW YORK

Copyright, 1954, by Frank Yerby

MANUFACTURED IN THE UNITED STATES OF AMERICA

BENTON'S
ROW

Book One

BENTON'S ROW

1

Tom Benton, the man, himself, came into Louisiana in 1842, riding out of Texas, out of the sunset, out, in fact, of the myths and legends already enshrouding his past; becoming, by that simple act of appearing at the end of the San Antonio Trace, for the space of years, a man living, breathing, thinking like other men, differing from them only in the minor peculiarities by which each man differs from his fellows.

But only for a space of years. Because, given the opportunity, and having as one of his points of variation, a certain intensity, a driving force rather superior to that granted to the commonalty of men, he came to found a dynasty, becoming, as far as the back-country and bayou people were concerned, the first of that line of Bentons who were for so long to trouble their little portion of earth.

So it was that after his death, perhaps even before, he was to slide back again into myth and legend, his stature augmented in the minds of his progeny to that of a folk-hero, more, even into demigod, princely in his valor, sagelike in wisdom, strong beyond the possibility of mere humanity, fair with that commanding male beauty attributed always to the offspring of the dim, ancestral gods.

He, the man, himself, was none of these things. It was merely that he gave the legend shape, force, direction, by believing implicitly of himself all the things that were afterwards said of him. Thereby he convinced others of the verity of that which in actuality had little or no verity, being thus, in minuscule, the very type-form of the South, a region about which more lies have been solemnly told and believed than any other comparable section of earth.

But that spring afternoon when he appeared on the edge of the Tyler plantation in the back-bayou country near the Red River, he was not concerned with creating legends. His concerns were, at that moment, very simple: putting as many miles as possible between him and a determined group of Texans bent upon hanging him upon the nearest tree for the crimes of which he was indisputably guilty, finding food to fill a belly empty now for three days, discovering at last a place to hide—and rest. . . .

He pulled up the horse atop the little rise, and shifted his weight in the saddle, looking behind him. Looking back, westward toward Texas, had become a habit with him. But now, when he looked forward again, he saw the cabin.

Gray smoke plumed upward from the chimney. He smelled the smoke, and another smell, too: sidemeat and greens cooking; and the hunger inside his belly was a knife suddenly, twisting. He kicked in, touching the rowels of his spurs against the roan mustang's sides, and went on down the little slope until he came to the door.

The mustang's hoofs made a clatter on the hard clay of the yard; and hearing them, the woman came out. She stood there, gazing up at him. He pushed his hat back on his head and looked at her, his lips forming a soundless whistle, for this one was a woman, much woman, as the Greasers said, and the sight of her eased the torment of all the endless, sunbaked miles he had ridden, all the cold nights shivering, half asleep, his fingers clamped around the gunbutt, until, getting up in the morning, he had to force them open with his other hand—right out of him, and he smiled.

His face was teak colored from the sun; the jaw blurred with a week's growth of beard, so that the smile flashed like light out of darkness, and was gone.

"Howdy, Ma'am," he said.

She didn't answer him. She was a big girl, and her bones were big. She didn't have much flesh, but he liked them like that. Be a screeching wildcat in bed, I reckon, he thought; and the thought pleased him. Her hair was a dark, honey blonde; and her eyes were the gray of hickory woodsmoke, slow burning. Standing there, like that, she was something. Her eyes had no fear in them; but something else—curiosity, interest, appraisal, something more, something that she herself did not yet realize she had, a facet of her personality of which she was still unaware, a part, a basis of her being which would have horrified her had she recognized it. But he, being at the same time simpler than she, and more complicated, saw it at once, and smiled. He wondered how long she was going to stand there without saying anything; and he didn't know what to do about it; but, as it turned out, he didn't have to do anything at all. An old Negro appeared in the door behind the woman, a shotgun in his hands, pointing straight at the rider's chest, its muzzle shaking with fear and with fury.

"Git away from here, white man!" the Negro said. "Marse Bob done told me not to let no poorwhite menfolks light! You git, I tell you!"

Tom Benton grinned at him, and reined the mustang in closer.

"Now, Uncle . . ." he began.

"I said git!" the Negro shouted; but Tom Benton moved easily, smoothly, without any perceptible haste, swinging down from his horse, letting the reins trail downward over the beast's head, and starting toward the Negro with the calm deliberation of a man embarking upon a casual stroll. Except there was something else in it: a grimness almost tactile, a purpose so sure, final, confident, that the frail old man could stand but five seconds of it, the shaking growing like an ague all through him, until, while Tom was still two yards away from him, he dropped the gun and ran wildly back into the house.

Tom started after him; but the girl stretched her arm across the doorway, barring his way.

"Leave him be," she said.

"Mighty uppity for a nigger," Tom said. " 'Pears like I better learn him not to go round pointing guns at white men—specially not Texas white men. . . ."

"My husband told him to do that," the girl said.

"Then that makes somebody else I got to learn something," Tom said mildly. "Tell your nigger to come back out here. . . ."

"No," the girl said flatly.

He stared at her. Then, very slowly, he smiled.

"I won't hurt him," he said. "I promise."

She searched his face. Then, quite suddenly, she was sure.

"Jonas!" she called. "Come out here!"

"Miz Sarah!" the old Negro quavered, "I dasn't! I just naturally dasn't! I plumb scairt of that there white man. . . ."

"He won't bother you," Sarah said. "Come on. . . ."

Jonas put his head through the door, his black face ashen with fear.

"Come on out, Jonas," Tom Benton said.

Jonas slid sidewise half through the door. Tom moved then so fast that his arm stretching out, blurred with the speed of the motion, his big fingers closing into the front of Jonas' shirt, jerking the old man out of the door, holding him up so that only his toes trailed in the dirt.

"Please, suh, Cap'n," the old Negro wept, "don't. . . ."

"I promised your lady I wouldn't hurt you," Tom said. "And I won't. But get one thing through your thick skull, old nigger: Don't care what nobody tells you, don't you go pointing guns at no white men, you hear me?"

"Yassuh," Jonas quavered. "Please, suh, Cap'n . . ."

Tom released him.

"I don't aim to whip you," he said; "leas'ways long as you don't rile me. You and me's going to get along just fine, Jonas. I'm plumb, downright easy to get along with. I talk, and niggers jump. That way, I'm fine . . ."

"Yassuh, Cap'n," Jonas said.

Tom turned to the girl.

3

"He'll behave hisself from now on, I reckon," he said. "Now if it ain't putting you out, Ma'am, I'd shore appreciate a little hot water and the loan of one of your husband's razors—mighty tired of hiding under this brush. . . ."

"All right," the girl said. "Come this way."

"Ma'am," Tom chuckled, "I hope you won't think I'm pushing or forward, or anything like that; but I got a powerful hankering to know yore name. . . ."

"Sarah," the girl said. "Sarah Tyler."

"Mighty proud to make yore acquaintance, Miz Tyler," Tom said. "My handle's Tom Benton. But you just call me Tom. I don't believe in standing on ceremony. . . ."

"You sure Lord don't," Sarah said.

Tom sat in the kitchen and waited, watching her deft motions as she heated the water for him. Good-looking woman, he was thinking, moves so soft and easy like. Spirited, too; I kin tell that. Take a bit of gentling to git next to. . . .

"Here's your hot water," Sarah said.

She didn't go anywhere. She sat there, watching him hack off the wiry black beard, watching his face emerge out of concealment, her mind working slowly, maddeningly, the thoughts crackling slow like a brush fire starting.

Young—not old like Reverend Tyler. (She called her husband that, even in thinking.) Good-looking—bad, wicked good looks. Cruel, tormenting mouth. And those eyes . . .

He smiled at her, seeing her stare.

"What you looking at, Sary-gal?" he mocked her, laughing at her out of those eyes of his, crazily, impossibly blue in the burnt teak of his face.

"At fire 'n' brimstone," Sarah said, hearing her own voice far off, strange, a husky whisper in the oppressive stillness of the room.

He put the razor down carefully, and wiped his face before he came over to her. There was that about him too—the deliberation of his motions, the dreadful sureness with which he moved. Like a storm a-brewing, Sarah thought; like he knows there ain't nothin' or nobody what can stand agin him. . . .

But there wasn't any more time for thinking, because his dark face was above hers, blurring out of focus with the nearness, shutting out what was left of the light. When time came jangling back into existence again, she hung there still, staring at him.

"You hadn't ought to of done that," she said.

"Why not?" he mocked. " 'Cause you got a husband? The more fool he for runnin' off and leaving you alone like this. Finders, keepers, where I come from. . . ."

"I know where that is," Sarah whispered. "Out of night and darkness where the damned souls lie a-moaning and a-screeching, and even the fire what burns them don't give no light. . . ."

4

Tom laughed again, clearly.

"That's Bible talk," he said; "and you don't look like no Bible-reading woman. . . ."

"I am though," she said defiantly. "My husband's a preacher."

"And an old man," Tom added quietly.

She stared at him, her gray eyes opening wide.

"How'd you know that?" she got out.

"That kiss," Tom laughed. "That was a right pert hongry kiss for a woman what's properly wed and bed. . . ."

"Confound you!" Sarah flared; "I'll—"

"You'll kiss me some more when I git around to it," Tom said. "But right now you're looking at a starved and famished man. Don't tell me Louisiana folks ain't got no hospitality about them. . . ."

The food she had prepared for her own supper was still in the pan, pushed back a little from over the firepit of the clay firebrick stove the Reverend Tyler, her husband, had made for her, with his own strong, tender hands. She hadn't eaten it, not only because she hadn't had time to eat the greens and sidemeat—if only she had begun to eat as soon as it was cooked—but because she hadn't really felt like eating it at all.

She had put that down to loneliness, but it was more. It was true that the cabin was far out, just beyond the edge of the bayou country, on the beginning of the flatlands that stretched westward toward Texas and the setting sun, so that days ran together imperceptibly in the flux of time, melting into weeks, into months even, without her having seen another living soul except Jonas, and at rare intervals, her husband. There were times when she found herself talking to herself aloud, merely, she thought, to hear the sound of a human voice. That was bad enough. What was worse were the nagging doubts that came in the night to plague her.

He ain't really got the call. He stays away like this—circuit ain't really that big, he could come home more frequent—'cause he's afraid not to. . . . Good man, big, fine-lookin', but the strength's goin' out of him. . . . Younger man would give up this preaching foolishness and tend to his land—and—and his wife. Dear Lord, I'm sick of sleeping alone!

"All right," she said to Tom Benton, "I'll fix you some vittles. . . ."

She poked up the fire and brought the pan back over it. She could feel Tom Benton's eyes upon her, and then, unbidden, naked, a thought that she had often had, more than a thought really, a need, a hunger, transfixed her motionless, paralyzing her tall, good body under his eyes.

A child. A big, bawlin' young'un—wouldn't be so lonely then. Sing it to sleep at night. Tend to it. Only he's too old—too old—

It was then, at that moment, that the shaking got into her hands, so that she had to take them off the handle of the frying pan. She knew without turning that Tom had gotten up and come over to her, then his big hands closed over her shaking fingers.

"Bad bein' lonely, ain't it, Sary-gal?" he said, and his voice was curiously gentle.

5

"Yes," she said, "it's bad."

She sat there watching him eat. There was no hunger in her, at least not any such simple hunger. The way he ate, wolfing down the food, was enough to warm the cockles of any woman's heart. Reverend Bob Tyler merely picked at his food, too worn out tired to eat, really—the burdens of poverty, and of his scattered flock crushing down upon him so that his good, big, gentle mouth had forgotten how to smile.

Tom finished, and wiped his mouth with the back of his hand. Then he dug into his shirt pocket and came out with the battered stub of a cigar. She got a coal for him from the fire, and he lit it, sighing with satisfaction, rocking back in the rude chair, smiling.

Home, he told himself, I'm home. . . .

He didn't say anything. He just sat there, watching her clean up the kitchen, until looking through the window, he saw that the light had spilled out of the sky suddenly, so that the edges had blurred away off everything, the big oak near the gate a ghost shadow now, darkness upon darkness, and far off and dim, to the east, a single star.

He got up then, very slowly. He was not a man to hurry about anything. Seeing him coming toward her, Sarah got up, too.

"Come here, Sary-gal," Tom whispered.

She stood there, looking at him a long moment. Then, slowly, quietly, without any protest whatsoever, moving like a sleepwalker, she came to his waiting arms.

He was asleep now—now, at last that morning was graying the sky in the east, the light coming up so that she could see him lying there, the whole, lean, hard, clean-muscled length of him, one arm flung backward under his head, the black tuft of armpit hair showing, the silken mat of blackness covering his chest and belly, wideshouldered, slimhipped, hollow waisted, and she sitting up looking at him shamelessly, worshiping his male-god's body with her eyes, thinking:

It's done, and I'm damned to eternal hellfire the woman taken in adultery and no sweet Jesus nigh to stave off the flingin' stones. But Lord, God, it was good—right and natural and good, and this is what a man's like, a real man, mine!

She said his name, savoring it like a sweet, remembering how it had been, every detail, not even contrasting him with her husband, not even remembering her husband, out of mind, gone, longlost, forgotten, her body tingling still with the slow, endless, drawn out exquisite torment that was pain and pleasure so inexplicably commingled, that at the end the ecstasy was agony, so that she had bitten her lip, to keep from crying out, until even the remembering was too much, and she bent her head and flattened his sleeping mouth with her own, cruelly, fiercely, drawing him into wakefulness once more.

They lay in the full glare of the risen sun and talked. There was time for talking now.

6

"Yes, he's old," Sarah said. "Sixty-five, I reckon—maybe more. . . ."

"Why'd you marry him?" Tom said.

"He's good. Kindest, most gentle man you ever saw. And I was lonely. Maw 'n' Paw both died of the cholera in a single night, and I was left all alone. He come to bury them proper, then afterwards, he started stopping by right frequent to see after me—a girl eighteen years old and alone in the world, was mighty sweet of him, I thought. . . ."

Tom snorted.

"Horny old bastard like that."

"No, you're wrong, Tom. He never said a improper word. Even when he proposed to me, he give me a whole summer to think it over—never even tried to kiss me. We got married last fall. . . ."

"Then you ain't but nineteen! Great balls of fire!"

"It's hard out here, Tom. That's what makes me look so old. . . ."

"I'd reckoned you to be about twenty-five," Tom said.

"Don't matter," Sarah whispered. "The point is, what we gonna do now, Tom?"

"Do?" Tom yawned and stretched, "why we ain't a-going to do nothing, Sary-gal. . . ."

"But Tom, he'll be back in a week—two at most! Take me away from here—I'll leave him a note, I kin write pretty fair, and good as he is, he'll forgive me. . . ."

"Him and his forgiveness," Tom grinned. "We ain't going nowheres, Sary. I like it here—"

"But Tom!"

"I'll deal with him," Tom said calmly. "Don't you worry yore pretty head none a-tall. . . ."

But she did worry. In the daytime, while Tom Benton strode the few, pitiful, cleared acres and inspected them.

"Yore husband," he pronounced, "knows about as much about planting as the left side of my hindquarters. Less, cause my hindquarters knows a right smart bit about it. . . ."

"Don't do no plantin' in Texas," Sarah mocked; "that's cattle country."

"Sure, Honey-child," Tom laughed; "but I was born and raised in Mississippi, on the prettiest stretch of cotton land yore eyes could ever want to see."

"If you're such a planter, why'd you ever leave?"

Tom's eyes narrowed, then he smiled.

"Had to, Sary-gal. Got myself in a little game of draw-poker with a respected citizen, and found him with one ace too many. I kilt him. Didn't mean to—didn't even carry a gun in those days. We fought man to man, but I set him up good and let him have a goodun—trouble was his head hit a rock when he went down—never thought a big head like that could crack like a egg. . . ."

"Oh, Tom!" Sarah whispered.

"Had a bad reputation even then. Old man Benton's wild Tom, you know. Well them folks was planning a necktie party with me as the guest of honor, so any other place looked good to me—even Texas. . . ."

"What did you do out there?" Sarah said.

Tom looked at her.

"Sary-gal," he said mildly, "you got a awful bad habit of axin' too many questions. . . ."

"I'm sorry, Tom," Sarah said.

But his eyes were gone from her, retreating into a time and place in which she had no part. The buzzards circling above the arroyo, and the dust clouds still hanging, undrifted by any wind. That was what had made him cautious. That cloud was too big for just three horses. He had pulled the roan up, a mile from the arroyo, and made the rest of the way on foot. The last hundred yards he had crawled, making it from mesquite brush to Joshua tree cactus, to outcropping of bare rock, inch by painful inch under a sun that baked the juice out of his body clear down to the bitter bone. Lying there, panting, on the rock shelf above the arroyo, he saw at once there wasn't a chance.

There were fifteen Vigilantes down there in the arroyo, and in the middle of them Big Steve, and Dave Huntley, and Alvárez, the renegade Mexican. The three of them—the men he had led with rapacious impartiality against the trading posts of the Mexican government beyond the Rio Grande, against the lumbering postal stages of both Mexico and the Lone Star Republic, against even the ranch-houses of outlying American settlers in Texas, now since '36 free of Mexico, and a sovereign state in its own right—were already bound, sitting there on their horses, with the nooses looped about their necks.

Not even the weapon that had given him his ascendancy over them was enough—his beloved Patterson Colt, then in 1842 one of the far less than a thousand revolvers not only in the United States, but in the whole world. Experience had taught him that no hand gun would carry true over that distance, and even if he made every shot tell, there would still be nine Vigilantes charging him while he went about the slow and painful business of reloading, pouring powder, cutting patches, ramming home ball, and fitting caps. He would be dead, shot and sabred to death long before the task could be done.

He had taken the gun from the body of an ex-officer veteran of the Seminole wars, one of the fifty or sixty men Sam Colt had persuaded to buy his gun and thus furnish proof it was the best sidearm in the world. It was. But not against fifteen Texas Vigilantes under a hot Texas sun without enough cover to hide an armadillo, let alone a man.

So he lay there on his ledge of stone and watched them die. They didn't die well. By accident or design, the Vigilantes had made the nooses badly, so that instead of breaking the necks, bringing death in seconds, Big Steve and Dave and Alvárez kicked out their lives slowly, taking from four to eight minutes apiece to die, their faces purpling slowly in the sunglare, their eyes and tongues bulging out; and he, lying there, watching

8

it, sick to the pit of his soul, cold all over despite the heat, was unable to turn his gaze away from it for a second.

It did something to him. He didn't even stop to look for the gold, though he had seen at once the Vigilantes hadn't found it. Riding away from there, he knew at long last, and with awful certainty, that this was for him both an end, and a beginning. He had damaged a part of himself, a thing at once primitive and vital. What it was he had hurt, this core component of his being, did not exist for him in words, remaining actually below the conscious level of thought. Forced to explain it, he would have growled: "Hell, it's just a feeling I got. . . ."

And so it was, and more. A feeling, a belief, a conviction, a faith—that he, Tom Benton, was somehow different from the common run of men, that he stood taller in his boots and in his pride, that he shot straighter, laughed louder, ate heartier, loved more lustily, fought more fiercely—in short, that he was something special, one of God's chosen, so that everything, gold, land, women, pleasure, was his by almost divine right. More, having this feeling, he was far more touchy than other men, regarding any hint of opposition, anything remotely resembling an insult as a kind of blasphemy against one of the elect, at the very least a *lèse-majesté*; at most a profanation of the temple of his private holy of holies, where rested in all its splendor the divine object of his veneration: himself. And being what he was, a man of vast complications buried deep below the layers of consciousness, and of profound simplicity topping this complexity, hiding it, forcing it down, so that it could never rise to trouble him, he could see nothing wrong with his accustomed practice of playing judge, jury, and executioner, apportioning unto himself the functions of man, society, God.

But the deaths of his band had broken through the crust, made an exit through which the sensitivity he had all but killed in himself as a boy, all the doubts, confusions, questions that plague the lives of ordinary mortals, could from that day rise up to confound him. He was through with his old life. He was prepared now to go back into the world, to make peace with society, to submit, as far as it was possible for him to submit to anything, to the laws, practices, customs, which governed other men. Not that he thought about it in any such sweeping generalities; it would be years before he would be able to comprehend the existence of an abstraction, much less to think in abstract terms. The thoughts that jogged through his mind as he rode eastward, held bound in their simplicity all the complexities of life; but he did not know that then. He rode very quietly along, thinking:

No more of that. Aim to die in bed, with a passel of grandchildren brawling around me. Going to be a peaceable citizen, respected, on my own land, with the cotton blowing white as far as the eye can see. Ain't had no life, really. Money I took all gone, spent on hard liquor, and range-town *putas*. Want a woman now who ain't there for any man who's got the price. Want to live where I can see green things growing and smell the earth a-soaking up the rain. Back to the Delta country, to Mississippi—no. Too many folks there what still remembers. Louisiana—same kind of place, with New Orleans piled on top of all that for a man who wants to bust his traces once in a while. . . .

And now, after all the riding and baking and freezing, he was there. Home. Funny. Things never did fall out on the line the way a man planned. Here were the land and the woman, ahead of time, too damned soon really, before he was ready, and keeping them was going to take some doing, especially since he had to do it without killing. Couldn't afford that now. Had to get his roots in. And the Louisiana oaks were set up mighty fine for hanging folks on. He glanced up at one of them. Even a buzzard would have to do some tall flying to get to you up there.

His brow furrowed with thinking.

"What's the matter, Tom?" Sarah said.

"Problems, Sary-gal," he said. "To do justice to this here spread of land, we ought to have hands. And niggers come mighty dear these days. You got any money?"

"No, Tom," she whispered. Her voice made a caress, saying his name. "Anyhow . . ."

"It ain't my land," he growled. "But it's going to be, Sary-gal—it's going to be!"

He had no plan. Can't rightly make no plans till I see this Bible-pounder she's married to, he thought. Got to size him up. Might even have to leave here, and take Sary with me. Find land somewheres else. He's got the jump on me since I can't kill him, and he sure Lord can kill me. Never heard tell yet of a man being strung up in these parts for letting a little daylight into a hombre what's been pleasuring himself with his wife. In fact, all this Jesus-talker is got to do is to round up a few of his friends, and they'll help him do it—Still . . .

Still, he couldn't leave her. Not with what there was between them now. He had lost count long ago of the women he had had; but he knew with bedrock certainty that there had been no one like Sarah. He'd never give her up; he knew that. He'd give up breathing first. That would be easier.

The waiting was bad. They came together many times. At night. In the mornings. Under a noonday sun. He was walking the fields, for the hundredth time, looking things over, thinking, when he saw Sarah come over a little rise behind him. He stopped and waited, a little frown puckering his forehead, until she came up to him.

"What the devil do you want?" he spat at her.

"You," Sarah said, the one word coming up out of her throat half strangled. . . .

The first thing the Reverend Bob Tyler saw when he entered the empty kitchen was the table set for two, with the scraps of food still in the plates, and the stub of Tom Benton's cigar. His own razor lay open on the washstand, and the soap had dried in the shaving brush. A hundred things cried out the stranger's presence; things that a less solitary man might not have noticed, but which struck Bob Tyler one after the other like a rain of blows. He reeled out of the house, death in his eyes, and it was then that he saw them coming down the rise their arms locked about one another.

He stood there, waiting. Tom Benton studied him, not even bothering to glance at Sarah's stricken face, deciding at once what it was that must be done, until, coming closer, he dropped his arm from Sarah's waist, and shoved her toward the door, saying quietly, flatly, no emotion at all in his voice:

"Git in there, Sary-gal, and stay."

She went, leaving the two big men there, facing each other.

They didn't say anything. Tom's hand went down to the holster and came out with the Colt. Bob Tyler stared at him without fear and said evenly:

"I am a man of God. I don't bear arms."

"I know you don't," Tom said. "And I don't aim to use this—not lessen I hafta. You're an old man, Rev. You aimed a might further'n you could reach. You're too old, and you done stayed away too long. . . ."

"What do you mean?" Bob Tyler whispered.

"That I've jumped yore claim. I'm here, and I'm stayin' and Sary's staying too. 'Pears to me, about the only smart thing for you to do is git back up on that mule and ride away real quiet like—just the way you came."

"And if I don't?" the Reverend Tyler said.

Tom studied him.

"Then," he sighed; "I reckon I'm gonna hafta let a li'l' daylight into you, Rev. I don't want to. Done enough to you already. But what I done took is mine, 'cause it never rightly belonged to you. An' if I hafta kill you to keep Sary, I'll kill you. Real sorrowful like, but I'll do it."

Bob Tyler swayed there, death and hell in his eyes, so that Sarah, seeing him from the house, could read his thoughts, feel almost as if by touch the temptation that beset him.

Oh Lord, Oh Jesus, he's a-going to force Tom. . . . He wants to die now, easiest thing for him to do—what's he got left now, what reason is he got to go on livin'?

She came out of the house in a wild rush, and hurled herself between them.

"No, Tom!" she got out. "Ain't gonna be no killin'—not over me! Put up that there gun. You hear me, put it up!"

Slowly Tom let the muzzle of the revolver fall; then he jerked the whole gun upward and slammed it down into the holster. Sarah turned to her husband.

"Reverend Bob," she whispered, "listen to me. I ain't got no excuse. There ain't no excuse what makes any sense. I'm a bad woman, and you're too good for me. You always was, but I didn't know it then. So go 'way,

Reverend Bob, and let us be. I'll find some way to pay you for the land. . . ."

His eyes held hers. She wanted to turn away from them but she couldn't. She had to stand there and watch it—the death of a man's spirit, of his pride, his honor, his dignity, of everything there is inside of him, living, that raises him to the level of the angels, that separates him from the beasts. She had to watch it, being unable to turn away her eyes, this crumbling of the human spirit, this anguished splintering of a man's soul into the distorted planes and angles of pure grief. It was an ugly thing to watch; but she had to.

"All right, Sarah," he said, his voice so low that she felt, rather than heard the sound, "I'll go. . . ."

He climbed up onto the mule, so feebly that Tom had to help him mount. Then he moved off, his long legs sticking out grotesquely from the sides of the beast, his head bent far over on his chest. And Tom Benton, seeing it, threw back his head and laughed aloud.

Something exploded inside Sarah's mind at the sound of his laughter. She whirled upon him, her hands curving into talons, raking for his eyes. He moved aside, with a dancer's grace, and his hand came up, palm open, and smashed across her face with a noise like a pistol shot, sending her down to the earth at his feet.

"Git up," he said mildly. "You hadn't ought to of come out. Then there wouldn't of been all this trouble."

Sarah got up.

"You beast!" she whispered. "You mean, low-down, cruel, dirty beast!"

Tom took a step toward her.

"Git away from me!" she screamed. "You beast! You foul, dirty—"

"Beast," Tom finished for her, grinning, locking his arms about her so tightly she could not breathe. "Yep, reckon you're kind of right there. . . . I'm a beast-critter all right—but, Honey-child, you ain't no lily yoreself. Got your share o' bitch'n' bitters, too, as I remember. . . . 'Take me away, Tom!'" he mimicked; "'take me far away where he won't never find us. . . .' 'Pears to me I heard something like that somewheres. . . ."

"Oh damn you!" Sarah got out; "I hate you! I hate . . ."

"No you don't, Sary-gal," Tom murmured. "You love me. You love me with every living inch of that smooth 'n' silky hide o' yourn; and you ain't never gonna git shut o' me—'cause you can't!"

Then his big hand came up and caught her chin, imprisoning her face. To Sarah, his face coming down to hers was like night descending, so that there was no more light, not anywhere in the world. Then, as lightly as he would lift a child, Tom picked her up in his arms, and carried her into the house, kicking the door shut behind him. . . .

The old Negro, Jonas, stole around the house, and raced across the yard. They did not hear him. They were already, at that moment, incapable of hearing anything. So Jonas was able to stumble down to the stream a half mile beyond the house, and it was there he found the Reverend Tyler, kneeling beside a placid pool. Jonas stopped, held his breath, for the preacher had folded his hands and lifted his face toward the sky.

"God!" his voice rasped out, torn through with edges that ripped into the old black's heart; "I've been Thy faithful servant. I've tried always to do Thy will . . . and this cup Thou heapest upon me—my wife turned wanton, my land stolen, driven away from my own like a felon . . ."

His voice broke. From where he stood, ten yards away, Jonas could see his massive shoulders shake.

He stood up then, surged up rather, and raised his big fists against heaven.

"How, God?" he boomed; "I ask You—how? How could You let this happen to me? To me—Your servant."

He stood there, listening. Jonas crept closer. When he was very close, Reverend Tyler turned, and the Negro hung there, frozen, seeing his face. It was not that it was sick, and anguished and terrible; it was more; but how much more was beyond old Jonas' grasp. He saw, unbelievably, that his master was laughing.

"Jonas!" Bob Tyler roared, "we're free! You're free, and I'm free and every man on earth is free! Free to drink and fornicate and gamble! Free to lie, to steal, to kill, to do adultery before the House of God! You know why, Jonas? I ask you, you know why?"

"Nosuh, Marse Bob," Jonas croaked.

" 'Cause God is dead! Ain't no more God!"

"Marse Bob!" Jonas whispered.

"No God!" Bob Tyler thundered. "No God a-tall!"

Then he shoved Jonas out of his path, and went down the trail, into the deepening darkness. And Jonas, in his turn, crept like a scurrying thing of night, back to the house, pausing to listen fearfully for sound within.

They's sleepin', he thought; they kin sleep, them! But he was half wrong. Sarah lay propped up on one elbow, staring into the dark. Her mind worked slowly, clearly in the night: done sold my soul to the devil, an' brung down hellfire on my head. After what he done to Reverend Bob, my stomach ought to of been sick when he touched me. . . . But I come to him, all willin' like a setter bitch in season, and all my heart is saying is let Reverend Bob stay away—please God, don't let him come back. . . .

She sat up suddenly and said it aloud, flinging the words into the mindless night: "Stay away, Reverend Bob! Dear Lord, keep him away!"

"Huh?" Tom muttered sleepily, "whatcha say?"

"Nothing," Sarah whispered. "Nothing, nothing a-tall. . . ."

Then she put her face down in the darkness, and found his waiting mouth.

2

THE SUN was below the tree tops now. It caught the man and the mule in the last yellow wash of light, pinning them blackly against the sky, fixing them in space, in time, dwarfing them into minutiæ, crawling bug-like and diminutive out of, and into, nowhere. Behind them the woman and the old Negro came, scattering the seed, their motions stiff, ritualistic, themselves wedded to the earth in this oldest of all the rites of spring.

Even Tom Benton felt it. Something about this business of planting, he thought; but beyond that his mind would not go. He had a distaste for things he couldn't put his finger on. Obscure emotions, and vagrant thoughts which, like every man living, he occasionally had, baffled and annoyed him. He felt that they demeaned him somehow; softened his manhood into something—less.

He shook his big head to clear it of his mood, and looked behind him at the furrow he had turned. He could see Sarah and Jonas laying in the seed he had found, along with the mule—an animal so ancient that but for the fact it stood upright, he had been hard put to tell that it lived—in the ramshackle wreck which had served Reverend Bob Tyler as a barn. Nothing here was his: neither the mule, the plow, the land, the seed, the Negro, nor the woman. But he had to work as though they were, hoping that something—luck, a trick of fate, an unforeseen warping of the web of chance would make them so.

He had taken them and still they were not his. This wasn't the kind of loot a man could stuff into his saddlebags and ride off with. He had taken them; but equally and conversely they had taken him. He grinned wryly, thinking of it.

Any day now the old boy can come ridin' back headin' up a posse. An' I won't have a leg to stand on. Remember how old man Burke back home caught Miz Burke with that overseer? Put a double load of buckshot through the overseer's belly, holdin' so close it tore a hole in him big as my two fists put together, then after that hoss-whipped Sally Burke to a inch of her flighty life. . . . Never spent a hour in jail neither. Same thing as this. All I can expect, I reckon. . . .

He stared ahead of him and his thought changed. No point in dwelling on a thing a man couldn't help short of what he was already doing—keeping the Patterson Colt under his pillow. But what he was thinking now was scarcely more pleasant.

Be lucky to get two bales out of this. Not enough seed. Land could use a mite of fertilizer I reckon. Next year it'll be the same thing—if there is a next year. . . .

"Tom," Sarah called, "Oh, Tom—"

"Yep, Sary-gal?" he answered, turning.

"I'm plumb tuckered out. 'Sides it's gittin' too dark to see anyhow—an' Jonas is too old to keep up like this."

"All right," Tom said. "We'll finish this here row and call it quits for today."

He drove the mule on. Damn fine land, he thought. Was mine, I could go to the land office and get a loan on the strength of what any fool could see it would yield. Sary knows Hilton, the man in charge; but she's shamed to face anybody now, and Lord knows I can't. Hell! Even if the old boy don't come back, it'll be root hog or die for years. . . . Don't want to do that to Sary—nothin' ruins a woman's looks faster. . . .

She came up to him now and helped him unhitch the mule from the traces, leaving the plow at the furrow's end waiting for tomorrow's planting. They went back toward the cabin with their arms locked about each other. Even with all the work, the nights were still something between them; less than before perhaps, but very little less.

Any one of those upstate towns, Tom thought again, would be easy. Ain't had the practice guarding their banks and factors that they've had out Texas way. But I can't. I got this thing over my head now, and I'm done with runnin' and hidin'. Wonder if I went to Preacher Tyler and axed him outright to give Sary a divorce would he do it? Find some way to buy him out then—or move on to a new place where folks don't know us. . . .

"Tom," Sarah said; "it's funny. . . ."

"What's funny, Sary-gal?"

"Thought I was gonna die of shame at first. But you know what, Tom-love? I ain't shamed no more. I ain't got time. I'm just too busy being plumb, downright happy."

"I'm glad," Tom said. "I ain't too bad a cuss, once you git used to me—"

"You," Sarah whispered, "are the best, absolutely the best in the whole wide world!"

"How you know that, Sary?" Tom mocked her; "how many you done tested out to prove that?"

"Was to tell you," Sarah teased, "you'd be mighty mad. . . ."

"Sure Lord would," Tom laughed. "Mess up my plowing right smart. Hafta take time out then to kill 'em—every living one!"

Sarah looked at him and her gray eyes were wide.

"Would you do that, Tom?" she breathed. "Would you kill a man what tetched me?"

"Kill him for lookin', let alone tetching," Tom said. He sighed wearily. "Hog meat and greens again, I reckon? Lord God, I'll be glad when we can afford somethin' else."

"That'll be soon, Tom-love," Sarah said; "I know it's gonna be mighty soon."

But it wasn't. The days blurred into weeks, lost in sunglare and the ache of labor. The work went on, the seed sown now, the young shoots coming up; the warfare against the weeds enslaving them in the ceaseless day-long round of hoeing. There were nights now when they fell into bed like logs, asleep as soon as their heads touched the pillows. Tom had a hard time waking Sarah in the mornings. Often she was near tears when she dragged herself upright and began to dress. How long, he asked himself, is it gonna be like this? How long before she learns to hate me?

He worried it over in his head watching her lying there in a swarth of moonlight, moaning a little in her sleep from the ache in her limbs. He got his mind into it and shook it this way and that; but he could get nothing out of it—nothing at all.

It was half a minute later, it seemed to him, when he heard her call him. But when he straightened up he saw the dawn haze blowing through the window and he knew he had slept the night through. He could see Sarah standing beside the bed. Something was wrong with her face. It was white, too white, her mouth slack and trembling. He saw her double over suddenly, and the sounds came over to him, the ugly, racking spasms of nausea.

He jumped from the bed, got water, cloths. The retching passed. Sarah lay upon the bed, crying.

"I knew," she whispered; "oh, Tom, I knew! But I tried to tell myself it wasn't so—Oh, Tom-love, what we gonna do now?"

"Do?" Tom growled. "Damned if I know, Sary. Have the little maverick and tend to it, I reckon, like we got to. . . ."

Sarah straightened up and faced him.

"But Tom," she got out; "the other children'll torment it—they—they'll call him bastard!"

"So?" Tom muttered. "Words don't hurt nothin', I reckon—"

She looked at him. She didn't say anything. She just looked at him. Seeing her gray eyes minded him of a long time ago, fifteen years it was, he reckoned, when he had lain on the ground with the blood all over his face and looked up at the man who had beaten him. Nobody had ever whipped him since. Nobody—up to now.

He watched her moving about, gathering her clothes, putting them on.

"Where you goin'?" he growled.

Sarah turned and her face was still.

"To see him," she said.

"Sary, Name of God—" Tom got out. Then he stopped. It was bluster, and he knew it.

She came over and put her hand on his arm.

"Tom, this young'un's gonna be our'n—" Her voice held him. Something in it shut off his protests before he had half-formed them.

"Told you yesterday I ain't ashamed—of us. I ain't, Tom. I'm proud—mighty proud. You're mine and I'm yours, an' that's good and natural and right. What I had before was wrong—a mistake, Tom. I should of waited knowing some day you'd come along. But I didn't wait. . . ."

16

"Sary-gal," Tom muttered.

"Hush! I'm doin' the talkin'. Look, Tom, I been with you, God knows how many times. And ain't nobody or nothin' gonna cast no shame on this child I been a-hankering for—God, God, how long! Your child, Tom —that makes it better yet—your'n an' mine. . . ."

"So you gonna talk to the old boy," Tom said. "What d'you aim to say?"

Sarah turned her face aside for a moment. When she turned back again, her eyes were still and calm.

"Ax him to divorce me—charge me in public for what I done. Good man, Tom. Don't want him to take nothing on hisself, pretend the fault was his'n. I don't care 'bout me. My child's got to have a honest name. Let 'em call me whore, I don't care. They don't understand, Tom, they don't . . ."

"You kinda wrought up, Sary," Tom said. " 'Pears to me hit's my place to . . ."

"No, Tom. He wouldn't listen to you. You're a man—would you listen to him in a thing like this?"

"No," Tom said honestly.

She stood there a long time, looking at him.

"I'm going, Tom," she said.

"All right," Tom said wearily.

She tied her bonnet under her chin, and went down toward the creek. It was a long way to the Rudgers', where the Reverend Bob Tyler was staying, and already it was getting hot. The land lay before her in a shimmering wash of heat, the lines of everything vague, blurred by the heat waves rising from the sunbaked earth, and in the air the flies hung, droning blue motes suspended in the light.

Under the oaks it was cooler. She went on slowly, moving from shade to shade, scarcely feeling her discomfort, feeling only the muted tumult going on inside her mind.

Got to face him. Got to. Got to say: forgive me Reverend Bob. I'm wrong forgive me an' let me go an' forget me 'cause I ain't sorry. What you gonna do with a sin, Lord God, you ain't sorry for? How kin you help a damnation you can't give up? Say to him, I'm gonna have a child the child he wanted and couldn't have say I got this child from another man more man than he is say that to him and stand there watching his heart die inside his eyes stand there watchin' his face. . . . Don't want to hurt you no more Reverend Bob done hurt you more'n enough. But this one more time I got to. Just this once, please God. 'Cause you ain't important and I ain't and Tom ain't. Just the child comin' not axin' to be born just so's he won't suffer none a-tall for something that ain't his fault nohow. . . .

She went on, pushing the weary miles backward under feet unaware of their going until she came to the edge of the bayou and saw the Rudgers' house—a wisp of smoke trailing lazily upward from the chimney.

They home. That's bad. Have to ax him to walk me a little ways off, so's we kin talk. Dear Lord, what Nelly Rudgers going to say when she sees me? Likely show me the door. And I can't blame her. I ain't fittin' to keep company with decent folks no more. . . .

But she moved on until she came to the cabin. The door was open and Reverend Bob Tyler sat before the fireplace—alone.

She drew in a breath, held it. He had been burning something in the fireplace—something that smelled like leather. It hadn't burned very well, and he was poking it now, trying to make it fall to pieces. She came up behind him very quietly, and when she was close, she saw what it was. The covers of that book had been made of good stout leather, and the flames, which had destroyed the pages already, had been able to do no more to those covers, than make them curl a little so that the words, "Holy Bible" gleamed stubbornly up at her, the gold embossment dulled by the fire.

The breath she was holding came out in a rasp of sound.

"Oh, no!" she breathed; "no, Reverend Bob, no!"

He turned and she saw his eyes.

"Howdy, Sarah," he said quietly.

"Reverend Bob," she moaned, "that's a sin—that's a terrible sin! You're a good man, you can't—"

"I've done it," he said; "I burnt that pack o' lies—"

"But why, Reverend Bob, why?"

He looked at her.

"You ask me why, Sarah? You?"

She stood there so still that only when he looked at her face did he see she was crying. Reverend Bob sighed.

"Sit down, Sarah," he said. "I'll make you some tea. . . ."

"No, please don't, Reverend. I—I ain't got time. I come to talk to you. I got to ax you somethin'. I hate worse'n anything to have to, but I just got to. . . ."

"Then ask me," Bob Tyler said.

"Give me a divorce," Sarah whispered. "Please, Reverend Bob—"

"So's you can marry him?"

"Yes." He had to lean forward to hear the word.

" 'Pears to me you took yore time gettin' around to considering what you been doin', Sarah," Bob Tyler said.

"No, I wanted to ax you right from the first. But I couldn't, Reverend Bob—I'd hurt you enough. I—I was shamed to face you. . . ."

"Was?" Bob Tyler said.

"I still am. But now I got to. Can't put it off no longer. Now I can ax you to do it, 'cause it ain't for my sake no more, not even for his'n. . . ."

Bob Tyler's face grayed.

"I—I can't do it, Sarah," he whispered. "I can't go before a judge and brand you a harlot. . . ."

"I am a harlot," Sarah wept, "an' worse—I done earned hellfire. . . ."

18

"No. Ain't no hell, Sarah—nor no heaven, 'cept what folks makes for themselves right here. When I was young, I was a mighty big sinner—and now it's caught up with me. I wonder what it's going to be like for you. . . ."

"Awful," Sarah said; "but Reverend Bob—please—"

"You're with child, ain't you, Sarah? That's why you come to me now?"

"Yes," Sarah whispered.

He didn't say anything. He turned and looked into the dead fire a long, slow time. When he looked at her again, his face was calm.

"All right, Sarah," he said; "I'm gonna free you. Wait here a minute." He walked into the bedroom. When he came back, he had a heavy envelope in his hand. In his other hand, he carried a slim stick, freshly cut, the bark peeled off. The end of it was forked.

"Here," he said, "take these here papers down to Hilton at the land office. Give them to him. Tell him not to open 'em till tomorrow morning. By that time you'll be free."

"But—but Reverend Bob," she got out, "I always thought that it took a tolerable long time to git a divorce. . . ."

"Not the way I'm going to free you," he said gently. "That don't take no time a-tall."

She took the papers. She stood there staring at him, until, finally, the stick in his left hand caught her attention.

"What's that stick for, Reverend Bob?" she said. "What you gonna do with it?"

He smiled at her.

"That," he said gently, "is the rod of your deliverance, Sarah."

He walked her to the door.

" 'Bye Sarah," he said. "Make sure you get them papers to Henry Hilton afore closing time. They're mighty important. An'—Sarah—"

"Yes?" she whispered; "yes, Reverend Bob?"

"I hope you're going to be happy," the Reverend Bob Tyler said.

Coming away from the land office, Sarah felt like stripping off her clothes and washing herself in the first creek she came to. The way Hilton had looked at her! Like—like I was dirt, she almost wept. And the things those men on the sidewalk had said—out loud, too, on purpose so she could hear. But the women had been the worst, crossing the street to keep from having to speak to her, or holding their skirts aside as though she would dirty them by a passing touch.

What else could I expect, she thought bitterly, I axed for it; I plumb downright axed for it. . . .

Tom was waiting at the cabin when she got back, his hoeing done.

"Well?" he growled at her.

"He's gonna do it," Sarah said tiredly. "He's done promised to set me free. . . ."

"Good," Tom grinned. "Told you wasn't nothing to worry about. Come on, I fixed some vittles for you."

"I—I ain't hongry, Tom," Sarah whispered; "I ain't hongry none a-tall. . . ."

"You better eat," Tom told her sternly. "You're eatin' for two now, remember."

"All right, Tom," Sarah said.

But that night she lay there unable to sleep. She turned it all over in her mind. But it didn't make sense. Unless they had changed the law, nobody could get a divorce outside of a court hearing, and that meant waiting three or four months till the circuit judge rode around to Cantonment Jesup to sit over all the cases that had piled up by then. A body was lucky to get a case heard before he had to ride on again. . . .

There was no sense to it at all. Reverend Bob couldn't free her. It wasn't that easy or that quick. Yet he had said he could. She remembered the Bible burning suddenly and sat bolt upright in bed. Out of his mind! she thought wildly; poor man's been drove plumb loco by what I done to him—me who he was good to an' loved and trusted—that's it—course that's it! Oh, my Lord—I—

There was a moon caught in the oak trees, silvering the night. From the bayou, a night bird screamed—harsh and out of tune. Then it was still, so still she could hear Tom's breathing and the beating of her heart. She couldn't stand it. She couldn't bear the silence. She was afraid, suddenly. Something's happening, she told herself, something bad's happening. . . .

The swamp bird screamed again, nightlost, starcrazed. Sarah sat there, ghostly fingers crawling over her skin. Then, far off, a dog howled—just once, the sound hanging quaveringly on the night.

"Tom!" Sarah shrieked. "Oh, Tom!"

"Yeah?" Tom muttered, "whatcha want, Sary?"

She bent her head down, suddenly, wildly, and ground her mouth into his; her fingers tore at him.

I'm tired, Tom thought, dog-tired and this fool woman . . .

She writhed against him, moaning.

"Hell," Tom grinned, "reckon I ain't so tired after all. . . ."

It was high noon when Henry Hilton reached the plantation. Tom Benton took one hand off the plow handle, and mopped the sweat from his brow with his bandanna. Sarah moved in close to him, her eyes very big. Only Jonas went on working.

"Howdy, Mister Hilton," Tom said.

Hilton didn't answer him. He just sat there on his horse staring at the two of them with an expression on his face that Tom couldn't define. Then he spat copiously into the dust at his horse's feet.

"What's on your mind?" Tom growled.

"Reckon you know what's on my mind," Hilton said dryly, "since it was you who sent Miz Tyler to ask him to do it."

"Hold on now," Tom said. "I don't get you, Mister Hilton. I sent Sary to ask who to do what?"

Hilton studied him.

"You mean to stand there, Tom Benton," he drawled, "and tell me you don't know what I'm talking about?"

" 'Fore God, I don't," Tom said quietly.

"All right. Maybe you didn't send her. Anyhow you must know that your—that Miz Tyler went to her husband and asked him to free her so she could marry you. So he did—the quick way. . . ."

Sarah caught Tom's arm, her fingers digging in, working.

Tom looked at the land agent.

"What do you mean, 'the quick way'?" he said.

"He," the land agent said slowly, clearly, "put Jim Rudgers' shotgun betwixt his feet, with the muzzles of both barrels rammed into his mouth. Then he pushed down on the triggers with a forked stick. Kind of messy. They had to scrape his brains off the—"

"No!" Sarah got out. "Oh Lord, oh Jesus, no!" She bent double, her whole body shaking, the sobs tearing out of her, her own arms wrapped about herself, holding hard against grief and pain.

"That's enough!" Tom spat. "Sary, come on up to the house; you ain't in no condition to take on so." He took her by the arm and led her away from the field. A few yards away, he looked back. "Wait for me, Mister Hilton," he said; "you and me's got some more talking to do."

Sarah moved beside him like a broken thing, unalive, but moving, slowly, terribly moving.

"Come on," Tom said; "come on, Sary-gal. Don't take on so. . . . Ain't your fault. Ain't your fault none a-tall."

She didn't answer him, but allowed him to lead her up to the cabin. She lay down on the bed and turned her face to the wall. It was no good trying to talk to her and Tom knew it. So he went outside and stood in the yard, peering up into the heavens with the noonday sun in his eyes. And it was there that Henry Hilton came upon him.

He got down from his horse and stood there, looking at Tom.

"Ain't my place to pass judgment," he said slowly. "Ain't nobody's business, I reckon, except God's. But you, Tom Benton, have taken a man's woman, his fields, and—his life. Damnedest part about it is, the law can't touch you. Reckon you feel mighty proud. . . ."

Tom didn't answer him. He looked at Hilton, and his face didn't change.

"The will's valid and legal. Had any relatives, they might make a case on the grounds of undue influence while in a state of unsound mind. But Reverend Tyler was alone in the world. So this place goes to Sarah and her heirs—forever. Reckon when you get around to marrying her, that makes it yours. Anything I can do, you let me know."

"I," Tom said, "am going to need a loan. . . ."

Hilton looked him up and down, silently.

"Wish I could refuse you," he said dryly; "but my instructions are to grant loans according to the need of the planter, the value of the land, and the man's ability as a farmer. You need the money, the land's valuable; and I looked the place over on my way up here. What you've done with damn near nothing is a miracle. I have to admit you're the best god-damned planter I ever did see. And since the instructions don't say anything about refusing a man because he's an ornery cuss, a skunk and a polecat, I have to let you have the money. You come to my office to-morrow, Tom Benton."

"Thank you," Tom Benton said. Then: "When they burying the preacher?"

"Done buried him. Eleven o'clock this morning in a closed pine box, so nobody could see wasn't no top to his head. . . ." He paused, staring at Tom. "On second thought, I'll come out here tomorrow to talk about that loan. Folks down in town are pretty riled up. Might not be safe for you to come in. Anyhow, see you tomorrow, Benton."

Tom didn't answer him, or even watch him go. Instead, he walked out over his fields. I'll build the barn here, I reckon, he thought; and after that, a decent house for Sary. Buy me some niggers, and get ready for a big crop next year. Young'un's going to have something to start with, yessirree. . . .

But something eluded him. He dropped down on one knee, and ran his fingers through the rich, black loam. His land now, his. He should have been happy, but he wasn't. He was, he realized suddenly, plumb, downright miserable.

God damn him! he thought, he beat me! I drove him off his land, took his woman, and still he beat me. And I don't know how he done it. I got everything, but still I feel whipped. Why the devil do I feel like that?

It wasn't a mood he could support very long. A slow, black anger descended upon him. He wanted to strike out, to smash his fist against—whom? Can't whip no dead man, God damn it! he thought. Got to get shut of this—got to, or by hell, I'll bust!

Then it came to him in a savage burst of feeling that was very like triumph:

Them mangy polecats down in town. Riled up, are they? Sending that hossfaced land agent with his store-boughten teeth up here to warn me to stay out of town. Reckon they could do with a mite of learning—reckon they could, at that!

He turned back to the house. When he reached it, he was almost running.

Sarah lay on the bed with her face to the wall. She didn't turn over as he came in. She lay very still until she heard him pull the bureau drawer, and after that, the sound the Colt made when he cocked it, spinning

22

the chamber with his thumb. Then she whirled and stared at him, wild-eyed.

"Tom," she got out, "what you going to do?"

"Don't worry about it, Sary-gal," he said; "I'm just going to take me a little walk, right slap-dab down the middle of main street down in town. Heard tell there's a bunch of folks down there what don't cotton to me and the things they think I done. 'Pears to me they could do with a mite of learning—time they found out who Tom Benton is—yep, time they found out for good and all!"

"Tom," Sarah whispered. "For God's Love—Tom . . ."

"Be back in a little while, Sary," he said. "Don't worry your pretty head none a-tall."

She sat up in bed, facing him.

"I ain't worrying about you," she said savagely. "It's your child I'm worrying about, Tom Benton! Go on—go get yourself killed! Leave me helpless with your child—go on, I tell you!"

He thrust the revolver into his belt and came over to her; but as he put out his arms to her, she whirled away, crying:

"Don't you touch me, Tom Benton! Don't you dare!"

He straightened up, his face darkening.

"All right, Sary," he said. "I'm going now. See you when I get back."

Then he went out and closed the door very quietly behind him.

When he dismounted, and tied his horse up at the hitching rail on the main street, a silence moved before him. From man to man the silence went, words dying in midphrase, falling down into bottomless pools of quiet, so that the dry little wind that ran along the street grew by contrast in volume, and all the slight, usually unheard sounds augmented themselves into small thunder—a bough scraping against another, a horse's whinny, a dog's bark, far out beyond the town's limits sounding clearly, hard against the stillness. Women snatched their children and hurried off the street, banging the doors shut behind them, and most of the men bethought themselves hastily of pressing affairs far from that part of town.

He stood there, tall and grim, the butt of the Colt showing in his belt, there in the very vortex of that silence, feeling in his bones neither fear nor excitement, but a rockbed surety, a conviction that no one living could stand against him that armored him against fear, even against wonder. More, he felt down deep at the very core of his being, a profound and savage joy. He moved and the measure of his tread sounded loud in the silent street, coming slowly, steadily forward, through that roadway emptied suddenly of life, of movement, even the men held there by their shame at their own cowardice frozen into grotesque caricatures of the elaborately casual attitudes they had assumed upon learning of his coming.

He did not even look at them. He walked on, his big arms swinging at his sides, his hands not touching the gun butt, not even coming near it, as though he were unaware of its presence, his gaze straight forward, his eyes quiet, speculative, almost peaceful, twinkling a little as from some secret amusement, some cosmic joke which he shared only with the universe itself, with God.

He pushed open the door to Tim's place. The noisy babble inside continued for a half-second longer, during which he heard his name spoken, combined with picturesque invectives, until the nods, nudges, gestures had run from man to man; and then the silence was there before him after the words had run down a tinkling little glissando into stillness. Tim was pouring whiskey into a shotglass for a client. He went on pouring, not seeing the whiskey brim over the edge and gather around the bottom of the glass in a red pool, thickening, spreading until it ran over the sides of the bar and dripped onto the floor.

Then Tom Benton spoke:

"Damned shame to waste good liquor like that, Tim," he said; "s'pose you pour me a snort, stead of watering the floor with it."

Tim gulped, his brick-red face paling into pink.

"We don't want no trouble in here, Mister Benton," he got out.

"Ain't going to be none," Tom said mildly. "Pour me that snort, Tim."

He took the whiskey, holding the glass in his hand, studying the liquor as though it were the most important, the loveliest thing in the world, his eyes sober, calm, peaceful. Then he lifted it to his lips. By the time he set it back on the bar, the saloon was empty of all but one other man.

Henry Hilton came over and stood next to him.

"If there's any one thing I do admire," he said quietly, "it's simon-pure guts. And you got 'em. Have another on me, Tom."

"Don't mind if I do," Tom Benton said.

And that was the end of it, the lynch mob that was never formed, the talk of whipping, of tar and feathers, of riding him out of the parish on a rail. He stood there, drinking and talking easily, slowly, with Henry Hilton for a long time. Then he got back on his horse and rode once more out to his fields where Jonas and the mule waited, and the cotton stood—waist high.

3

TOM BENTON looked at Sarah and his eyes were somber. She was very big with child now, sitting there placidly in the rocking chair, sewing the things she would need for the baby. Tom swore savagely under his breath.

Can't live alone in back country, he thought for the hundredth time. What I'm going to do when it comes to the birthing? Need the neighboring wimmen then—need them damned bad. I don't know what to do—ain't never seen a young'un come into this world. And ain't no wimmenfolks hereabouts who'd cross my threshold for all that Sary 'n' me's hitched now, legal and proper. Reckon I crowded these here Louisiana folks a mite too far. . . . Lord God, but they're proud!

Got to git th' barn up. That's another thing. No proper place to store the crop. Need help for a barn raising. . . . Once I git a crop in an' buy some niggers, I'll be independent of these folks. But till then it's nip an' tuck. Got to do something to change these folks' minds about us. . . . Just got to. . . .

He stood up. Sarah looked at him questioningly.

"Going somewheres, Tom?" she said.

"Yep. Think I'll ride down to the settlement and kind of spy out the lay of the land. Maybe if I was to talk to folks a little—act friendly like . . ."

"Tom," Sarah said, "Tom-love, it won't do no good. I know these folks. They're plumb mule-stubborn. Ain't nothing going to change their minds—nothing short of a miracle."

"Then," Tom said, "reckon I'll have to kind of arrange a miracle, Sary-gal. 'Cause we sure Lord can't keep on like this."

"All right, Tom," Sarah said. "But please don't let them git you riled up. Lose your temper and git into a fight be about the worst thing you could do, I reckon."

"Sure Lord would," Tom sighed. "All right, Hon, I'll be careful."

He bent down and kissed her quickly. Then he marched out into the yard.

But once he had reached the little, unnamed settlement, consisting merely of a few feed and general stores, a saloon; and now, brand new, built since his arrival in Louisiana, a small white church, he could think of no way out of his problem. He went into the saloon, but the men there ignored him with elaborate casualness. He thought of ordering a round of drinks for everyone present, but he decided against it almost at once. If any man refused his offer, he'd be honor bound to fight. He was certain-sure he could lick the tar out of any man there; but win or lose, fighting wasn't going to help matters.

He had two quick snorts of bourbon and walked out, frowning. He wasn't getting anywhere and he knew it. He moved aimlessly down the wooden sidewalk, stepping into the dusty street now and again to avoid bumping into anyone, because Sarah's warning that he must keep away from trouble clung like a burr in his mind. Idly he stopped before the white Baptist church. There was a signboard placed in front of it. Painfully, Tom spelled out the words:

"Great Protracted Meeting! The Reverend Silas Boone of Kentucky will conduct a fourteen day Protracted Meeting for the Salvation of Sinners! Monster tent on the shores of the Bayou Pierre. Come and give Rev. Boone your hand, and God your heart! Accept Jesus Christ, Your Lord and Savior!"

Tom stood there, staring at the crudely lettered poster a long time. Something stirred inside his mind.

Protracted meetin', eh? Ain't been to one since I was a green young'un. 'Member how old Preacher Curtwright used to make a body dang near smell the brimstone. And all the sinners crowding up to the mourner's bench to confess their sins. Funny—Good Lord! Many's the man had to listen while his wife confessed what she done and who with—and him honor bound not to do a living thing on account of she done repented. . . . People taking sinners to their bosoms and forgiving thieving, drunkenness, pleasuring round about, even killin's! Funny what folks will forgive when they's worked up and think a body's seen the light. . . .

He stiffened suddenly.

Jehosophat! Sary said we'd need a miracle. Well, Sary-gal, here's yore miracle all made to order! I can see it now—me down on my knees a-crying —new onion shoot in my bandanna'll produce some mighty convincing tears. And Sary, big like she is now, calling for forgiveness so's damnation won't fall on th' head of an innocent child!

His grin faded. Sary won't go along with no trick like that, he thought morosely. She's good all the way through. Be so easy, though, wasn't for that. . . .

He moved on down the street, frowning. Midway down the block he stopped dead.

Lord God, how big a fool can a body be! Sary's been grieving her heart out thinking she caused old Preacher Bob's death. Wasn't for the baby coming, she might of gone out of her mind by now. Put it to her straight— say something like:

'Well, Hon, maybe we can't fix things up with the neighbors; but leaseways we got a chance to git right with God . . .' Have to pretty it up a bit, else she won't believe me. Tell her the baby's coming done give me a change of heart. Being a father, got to live right so my child can respect me. . . . That'll do it! That'll do it, sure!

He was almost running now, toward the hitching rail where he had left his horse. He was almost there when he saw Hilton coming toward him. He stopped, his brain racing.

Luck! The one man in town I kin talk to. Lay in a seed right now. . . .

He moved toward Hilton, his face grave.

"Howdy, Benton," Hilton said, "how's things out yore way?"

"Awright, I reckon," Tom sighed. "Only . . ."

"Only what?" Hilton said.

"Mighty lonesome out there. A body's got too much time for thinking."

"That so? And with all that time, Tom Benton," the land agent grinned, "I'd sure Lord like to hear just what you've thought up now . . ."

"Don't know as how you'd believe it," Tom said gravely. "It's the baby coming that put some strange ideas in my head. Strange for me—that is. Helpless little mite—won't have nobody to look up to me—his paw. Now I ain't never been nothing much. I'll admit that. But with my boy on the way, I'll tell you, Hilton—for the first time I got a hankering to live decent. Sary 'n' me's married now; but that ain't enough. Got to do something to pay back for the sin I led her into. Wasn't her fault none a-tall. . . ."

Hilton stared at him.

"That's why I was glad," Tom went on, "when I read that there notice of the Protracted Meeting. I'm gonna come to that meeting, Hilton. I'm gonna come every night till I feel the burden of sin lifted off my shoulders. A married man with children's got to be right with God."

"Well I'll be double damned!" Hilton swore; "who ever would of believed it!"

"'Tis a fact," Tom said. "You don't know how it is. Sitting there with Sary after the work's all done and sayin' to yourself real quiet-like: Tom Benton, you're a liar and a thief and maybe even a murderer. Tom Benton, there's hellfire awaiting you; there's evil on yore soul."

Hilton studied his face shrewdly.

"You need wimmenfolks to help with the birthing," he said dryly. "By now you ought to be considering raising a barn. Need menfolks around to help with that. That's it, ain't it, Tom? Win them over with your faked repentance."

"Why, Mister Hilton!" Tom's tone was genuinely grieved, "I never thought . . ."

"The hell you didn't!" Hilton laughed. "Damn my soul but you're a cunning cuss, Benton! And the funny part about it is I like you. Some folks takes a day off now 'n' then from being a bastard; but you work at it all the time."

Tom stared at him, thinking: Awright I owe you money. But the day I pay it back I'm gonna push yore store-boughten teeth right down yore craw, and I hope you choke!

"Don't worry," Hilton said, "I don't aim to let on. Wouldn't spoil this here show for nothing in the world. I'm going to be there front and center to see you do yore play-acting, Tom. Besides, I got to protect my investment. You can't pay me back lessen you git your crop in. . . . By God, this is going to be something! I'll spread the word around. Reverend Silas is going to be mighty grateful—biggest drawing card he ever had."

He put out his hand. Tom grinned, and took it.

"One thing, Tom. Don't give in too quick. Wrestle with the devil a long time. Give 'em a good show. Keep coming back night after night, letting 'em see you suffer. By the time the second week is out, you'll have the whole parish on your side. Get yourself more friends than you can shake a stick at, by the time you do give in!"

"I'll remember," Tom Benton said.

With Sarah, it was pitifully easy. Listening to his slow, hesitating words, dragged up, it seemed to her, from the depths of his tortured soul, she wept tears of joy.

"Knowed you was good, Tom-love," she sobbed; "knowed all the time you was a real good man!"

They set out for the meeting dressed in their Sunday best. For Sarah, it was an ordeal. But Tom looked into the sea of faces around the tent under the Spanish moss, with secret joy. Reverend Boone had already raised a hymn; but as Tom and Sarah entered the tent, it died.

The preacher stared at the newcomers. Then he glanced at Hilton. Slowly, theatrically, the land agent nodded. Silas Boone rushed forward, his big hands outstretched.

"Welcome, my children!" he boomed. "Come right here up front and set down!" Then leaning closer, he whispered: "Heard all about you folks. Mighty glad to see you here; yessir, mighty glad! 'There's more rejoicing in heaven over one sinner saved—' you know. . . ."

"Yessir," Tom said humbly. "Reckon we've got a powerful lot to atone for, Reverend."

The preacher turned to the congregation.

"Friends!" he roared, "this here is a joyous moment! That these folks have come here, braving your righteous scorn, shows their hearts are in the right place! Now's the time to display some Christian charity—not to mention the fact that I ain't yet found out how many of the rest of you's got hands clean enough to be flingin' stones! Yessir—a joyous moment! Friends, let's sing: *Washed in the Blood of the Lamb!*"

The hymn soared forth, the congregation shaking the tent with their fervor.

Like all good revivalists, Reverend Boone had intended to pace himself; but the unexpected opportunity to work upon two such first-class sinners inspired him. He outdid himself. Taking his text from the story of the woman caught in adultery, he set out upon a mighty effort to leave not one dry eye in the tent. He succeeded. Even Tom scarcely needed his hidden onion shoot.

Sinners came forward in droves, weeping and confessing their sins. Only shame and fear kept Sarah back. But listening to some of the other women, she came to the astonished realization that her sin was not unique or even unusual. What she had lacked was the cunning to conceal it. Back-county morals, she learned that night, certainly weren't anything to brag about.

She stole a glance at Tom. He was concealing a grin behind his bandanna, as they listened to a recital by a rather ill-favored country woman which named four of the men present in the tent as her partners in sin.

"She's braggin'," Tom whispered, "or dreaming. Even the popskull they make in these here swamps ain't gonna drive a man to pleasuring hisself with that scrawny old witch!"

"Tom!" Sarah was scandalized; "you hush!"

"Sorry, Hon," Tom grinned.

The country woman's confession diverted the Reverend Boone's efforts toward bringing the four men the woman had named forward. Three of them came sheepishly to the mourner's bench at last, more, Tom was sure, out of their Southern-bred unwillingness to deny a woman's word than for any other reason. But the fourth was made of stouter stuff.

"She's lying, Reverend," he said flatly; "I'll take my Bible oath that ain't nary a word of what she said the truth!"

The uproar that followed gave Tom a chance to lead Sarah away from the meeting.

"Won't do to over-tax yourself, Sary," he said. "We got plenty of time. . . ."

But the very next night, Sarah gave in. She went forward and started confessing her sin in such a low voice that the people in the back of the tent started calling:

"Speak louder, sister! We can't hear you! Don't be shamed to speak out before the Lord!"

Sarah spoke out clearly, but Tom caught only snatches of it. He was too busy watching the faces of the women around him. Fury worked in his veins.

Look at 'em! he thought angrily. Just look! Mouth hanging open half-panting like a pack o' bitches in heat. Look at their nostrils a-quivering! This what they call goodness. This is supposed to do their souls good. Hell! Every living one of 'em's got a cesspool for a mind, and what they're exercising right now sure Lord ain't goodness. Give their husbands a hard time tonight when they git home, them what's got husbands. And half the rest of 'em will be easy marks for any man what's got a mind to. . . .

He sat there clenching and unclenching his big hands. Someone touched his shoulder. He whirled.

"Easy, son," the old man behind him said. "We see your sufferin' and we respects it. Just keep a tight rein on—yore time will come."

"Thank you, sir," Tom said humbly, "but it's mighty hard. . . ."

Can't do that, he thought quickly. Almost give myself away that time. Like he says, got to keep a rein on, but not for the reasons he thinks. Hilton said it would call for play-actin'—Well, from now on, I'm gonna give 'em a real show!

Of them all, only Hilton was able to appreciate what a show it was. At times, during those two weeks, Tom was dangerously close to over-doing it; but he always caught himself in time. He reached the stage where he could produce tears without the aid of an onion. Near the end of the second week, he had learned to start up as though about to rush forward, then he would sit down again with a sad shake of his head.

Friday night, he took five steps down the aisle before turning back. Willing hands seized him to drag him forward.

"I can't, brothers!" he sobbed. "I just can't. Old Satan's still too strong!"

"Let him be, brothers!" Reverend Silas cried. "Can't you see there's warfare going on in his soul?"

The thing itself had its own definite rhythm—its own throbbing, orgiastic pace. They, the back-country people, had come from ancestors whose faiths had grown pale and quiet in their ancient, tired lands. But now, here, in the back-bayou country, they had reverted easily to type, slipping backward over the centuries to the blond barbarians who dyed their beards blue and worshiped cruel vengeful gods in sound and fury. That was part of it, but there was more. Being Protestant, they had inherited a religion their stiff-necked, logical reformer forebears had robbed of pageantry, of beauty, and of joy, holding these things rightly to be pagan, but forgetting in their righteousness that man, living, is forever pagan, that civilization is the old age of a people, that the loss of naïveté, barbarism, color, is a symptom of approaching senility, a foretaste of racial death.

Here in their new home of bayous over which the morning haze brooded, of fields shimmering in the wash of sun, under the blue immensity of sky, they had had to go back again, to break out of their prison of puritanism, give vent to the passion, force, joy boiling within them, take away, in fact the religion from gentle Jesus who had never suited them, and give it back to Astarte, who did; putting it once more upon its true, ancient basis of carnal lusts, reviving the voluptuous joys wisely retained by the Mother Church of reliving the cherished sin once more in the telling, combining it with back-country brag, to the tune of hammering chants having all the beat and cadence of tomtoms, to the staccato of handclapping, the pounding of two hundred feet in tune upon the earthen floor, punctuated by the shuddering cries of women caught up in an ecstasy truly sexual, set off by the contrapuntal bass thunder of male shouting.

So it was. And by that final Saturday, it had reached almost its peak, the point of near-explosion, so that afterwards there would be nothing left for them to do but to go back again to their empty lives which made these semiannual descents into barbarism necessary, lolling in a lethargy as complete—being, in fact, the same—as that which follows love. But not yet. There remained the mounting tension, the terrible upsurge of passion which this one last night must release.

Coming up to the tent, Tom Benton could feel it throbbing through the very air. A hundred pairs of eyes were upon them, glowing with savage anticipation, so that Sarah, feeling it, clung fearfully to his arm. Eager men and women opened a path for them with great ceremony. Tom felt Sarah trembling, her fingers working convulsively on his arm.

"You got to, tonight, Tom," she whispered. "You just naturally got to. I can't stand it no more."

"Don't worry yore pretty head, Sary-gal," Tom said. "Tonight I feel the spirit moving—I sure Lord do!"

"Thank the Lord for that," Sarah murmured.

Tom glanced aside just before they entered the tent. A group of young girls stood on the little rise, close to the bayou's edge, staring at him. Meeting his gaze, they giggled a little, but their eyes didn't waver.

I'll be a son of a maverick! Tom thought happily. Always a few like that hanging around a camp meeting. Religion affects them thataway, warms their sweet little veins up, and sets the juices a-jangling. My paw always said you could pretty nigh reckon the time of the last protracted meeting by the bumper crop of nameless brats that showed up nine months later—heap of 'em looking mighty like the preacher hisself!

He looked at the girls once more. And it was then that he saw her. She stood a little apart from the others—physically; but ages and aeons and unbridgeable chasms apart in spirit. She was dark, with great masses of black hair spilling about her shoulders, and enormous brown eyes, soft and velvety like the eyes of a startled fawn. She was as young as the blonde poorwhites, but she seemed at the same time younger, and older. She stood there looking at him gravely, without the self-consciousness of the others, studying his face as though she meant to memorize every line of it, looking at him in wonder, and interest, so that he, feeling her gaze, slowed his pace.

Cajun or Creole one, he thought; and mine for the axin'. Lord, God, but she's a pretty thing! Just you wait right there until after I gets converted. Don't you go nowheres, you sweet little half-wild critter. I'll be back—and I'll have the power, the glory and the holy spirit to share with you then, Baby-doll!

He was still staring at her as he passed through the tied back flap of the big tent. But at the last possible moment, he was rewarded: the full, wine-red lips drew upward at the corners in the slightest possible suggestion of a smile.

Doggone my miserable wicked soul! he laughed inside his mind. This getting religion business ain't a-tall bad, come to think of it!

He looked quickly at Sarah to see whether she had noticed anything. But Sarah was looking ahead, her underlip caught hard between her teeth.

Tom felt a rush of something as close to shame as he was capable of. It's like this, Sary-gal, he explained wordlessly, 'taint like you'll ever find out—even like it means something. It's just that I'm a hot-blooded man, you know that, and whilst you're like this we can't—Lord God, Sary, you can't expect a man to go all these months without . . .

"Praise God from Whom all blessings flow!" the Reverend Silas Boone roared; and the thunder of the hymn drowned Tom Benton's thoughts.

It would be a long time before anybody there forgot that last night. Reverend Boone started with a prayer for this lost, poor, sinful brother, who had a man's life and maybe the loss of that man's immortal soul upon his conscience. The preacher had a good voice, big and deep and rich, and he used it now like an organ, making dark thunder. Before he was halfway through, everyone there was moaning and stamping his feet.

"Tom Benton!" the preacher thundered, "you stand up!"

Tom got to his feet sheepishly, hanging his head.

"Tom Benton," Silas moaned, "the devil's got aholt on yore soul! Got to git him out! Got to trip him up; got to throw him! Brothers and sisters, I'm a-gonna wrastle that old Devil for the possession of this man's soul!"

He straightened up, tore off his frockcoat, hurled it to the ground. His fingers yanked at his string tie. It followed the coat to the hard-packed earth. Then the preacher rolled up his shirt sleeves, and fell into a crouch.

"Come on, old Satan!" he bellowed, "show some fight! Can't win, you know! Can't, 'cause the Good Lord's on my side!"

He pranced about, seizing imaginary holds.

"Slippery old Devil!" he panted. "Feel him weakening yet, brother?"

"Not yet, Reverend," Tom Benton groaned.

He stood there, trembling for ten long minutes, his brain working swiftly, surely, well. He could see the preacher's shirt was sweat soaked. All the women moaned.

Then, very slowly, Tom let his body jerk.

"You're a-gittin' him, Reverend!" he gasped; "you're a-gittin' aholt on him now!"

"Good!" Reverend Boone roared out. "Gonna git him now, brother—gonna git him shore!"

Tom let the jerks increase. Big tears rolled down his lean cheeks. Then he threw back his head.

"Glory hallelujah!" he cried; "I feel the spirit! God bless you, Reverend, you got him! I'm free! You hear me, friends! I'm free!"

Then, gasping and sobbing, he plunged forward and fell full length before the mourner's bench.

"Praise God from Whom all blessings flow!" Silas Boone thundered.

The whole tent was a crashing bedlam of sound. Men shouted; women shrieked; children, frightened by the uproar, cried.

Henry Hilton sat there, wiping his forehead.

Damn my soul, he thought, told you to give them a show; but you outdid yourself, Tom Benton! By God, if I didn't know you, I'd think you meant it!

Two of the women were seized with convulsive spasms. The shouting boomed, the shrieks were edged. Hilton saw Sarah slip quietly to the ground in a dead faint. He bent down and picked her up.

"Some of you wimmen go 'long with Brother Hilton," the preacher commanded. "Brother Benton'll be home later—he's still got to confess his sins and be received into the fellowship of the righteous."

After it was done, after Tom had publicly wept and told how he had suffered for his crimes, he found himself surrounded. He frowned, thinking of the swamp girl.

Got to git shut of them, he thought; got to. Keep up like this, won't be no way for me to claim the rewards of righteousness. . . .

He let his big body slump.

"Lemme go, brothers," he said; "I want to walk in the darkness alone and meditate. I want to commune with God in quiet. Been too much excitement now. Got to calm my soul afore I kin go home to the sweet gal I led so close to damnation. . . ."

"Let him go," Silas Boone said. "Tomorrow, friends, at eleven o'clock we're going to baptize all the sinners in the bayou. For though their sins be as scarlet, yet they shall be whiter than snow, once they've been washed in the blood of the Lamb!"

Tom staggered out of the tent. He seemed drunk with weariness. But he didn't go toward the oak grove. Instead, he walked southward, toward Natchitoches. When he was sure that no one was following him, he struck off across the fields, in a long, looping circle, until he was safely past the tent once more.

A little way beyond it, he saw the group of pine-barren, poorwhite girls who had attracted his attention before. They were already occupied, all of them except one, with several men much older than they. The one exception, a thin, colorless girl, whose pale blonde hair looked white in the glow of the risen moon, looked up at his approach, something like hope showing in her eyes. But Tom plunged on past, swearing under his breath, because the one he sought, the object of his pursuit, for whose sake he had planned and carried out this elaborate deception, was no longer there. He wanted to ask about her; but in the presence of these men, newly confessed and shriven sinners like himself, he did not dare. His mood was almost savage, driving him along toward home, the last place on earth he wanted to go. What it was that caused him to turn, to look back, he did not know; his trained ear, perhaps, which after years of existence as a fugitive had become so attuned that it registered the crackle of a twig broken by a footstep, the rustle of a leaf brushed aside in passing, the faintest whispered ghost of sound. But regardless of what impulse moved him, the fact was that he did turn, and saw a little way behind him the pale girl coming like a wraith in the moonlight, going home by the same path he was walking, or perhaps even following him.

He stopped, waited. She came on more slowly now; but she did not stop. When she was close, she looked at him a little fearfully, and whispered:

"Howdy, Mister Benton."

"Howdy, Honeybunch," Tom grinned. "Howcome you know my name?"

"Reckon everybody does, mostly," she said; "leaseways hereabouts. Mine's Rachel—Rachel Radley."

"Mighty proud to make your acquaintance, Miss Radley," Tom said. "'Pears like we're going the same way. Reckon I'll walk along with you for a spell."

"Be glad if you do," Rachel said. "I don't like the dark much. Gives me a sort of creepy feeling. . . ."

Tom walked beside her, watching her out of the corner of his eye. She wasn't hard to look at; but she didn't interest him—she was too pale, too colorless—even the blue of her eyes a mere shade darker than the whites, her hair white blonde, her lashes and brows almost invisible against her skin. Freeze a man to death in bed, Tom thought. Then suddenly, his original idea came to him.

33

"'Scuse me, Miss Radley," he said politely; "but I want to ask you something. . . . You remember afore the meeting, there was another girl with you-all—a kind of a little black-haired girl—a mighty heap different from the rest of you. . . ."

"You mean Lolette Dupré?" Rachel said.

"Could be—I don't know her name. Just noticed her 'cause she was so different, sort of . . ."

"That would be Lolette, all right," Rachel said. "She's a friend of mine. She just come down out of curiosity, 'cause she's Catholic, like all them Cajun folks. Don't tell me you're stuck on *her*, Mister Benton!"

"I'm a married man, remember," Tom said sternly. "I ain't stuck on no young girls. But she got me kind of curious. And now you're getting me more curious. What would be wrong with being stuck on her, allowing, for argument's sake, that I was free?"

"A right smart," Rachel said. "In the first place, she's educated. Her paw sent her down to N'Orleans to study. She talks so fine—like a book, sort of. She talks French and English the same proper way. What I mean is even her French is mighty different from Cajun talk—even I can tell that. So it would take a real gentleman to please her. That's one thing. Then she always stays home taking care of her paw and her baby sister, Babs—that's short for Babette, 'cause her maw is dead. And then there's her paw. . . ."

"What about her paw?" Tom said.

"That there Louis Dupré is a wild man," Rachel said. "Everybody down on the bayou scairt of him. One time a boy name Pierre Tanquier got smart with Lolette—tried to drag her off into the woods. Louis heard her screaming and came a-flying. They fought with knives—you know how them Cajun folks love to cut. Took Pierre six months to git out of bed after that, and he's twice Louis' size. Only reason Louis didn't kill him was because he didn't really want to. If Pierre had of got away with what he was trying to do, Louis would have cut his liver out and ate it raw. But as it was, he shore messed him up proper."

"Sounds like a man to steer clear of all right," Tom said. "Where they live?"

"Down near us. I turn off at the next fork and after that if you follow the path almost to the bayou, you come to our house. A little further on, you can see theirs. It's out in the bayou, standing up on stilts over the water."

"Thank you kindly, Miss Radley," Tom said. "I got a kind of hankering to meet this Louis Dupré. . . ."

"Well, now you know where he lives," Rachel said. "This is where I turn off. And Mister Benton . . ."

"Yes, Rachel?"

"Maybe you got a chance after all. 'Cause Lolette been coming down to that meeting for a week now—every single night. And every time she sure Lord looked at you mighty hard. . . ."

34

"Thank you," Tom laughed. "If I can ever do you a favor, Honey-bunch, just you let me know."

She stood there a moment. Then she grinned, impishly.

"Ain't but one thing you could do for me, Mister Tom Benton," she said; "and that ain't very likely—now. . . ."

"And what might that be, Miss Rachel?"

"If Lolette turns you down," she laughed, "you can rally round my way —now that you know where I live!" Then she was gone in a rustle of petticoats, down the little path.

Well, I'll be damned, Tom thought happily; I'll be double damned!

Being what he was, a man little given to contemplation when action was necessary, Tom Benton went the very next evening out to the Dupré place. And once more the thing that he depended upon far more than most men, luck, chance, the fickle goddess, to him at least so constant that it had never occurred to him to question her fidelity, was with him. On the trail leading down to the bayou he passed a small man, so wiry and panther-like, wraith thin, that he guessed at once who it was. And when he greeted the man, and saw his eyes, light brown with a light behind them like live coals burning, he was sure. Her paw, he mused; I'm in luck again. . . .

He stood on the edge of the bayou and gazed out at the house. But the problem of getting out to it had already been solved for him. Louis Dupré, in coming ashore, had tied his pirogue up at the bayou's edge, so all Tom had to do was to appropriate it, a thing any man who knew Louis would have thought about twice before doing. But Tom did not know Louis Dupré, and with his bland and overwhelming self-confidence, he would not have cared if he had. He poled awkwardly out to the house, perched on its pilings above the bayou, and tied the boat up next to the ladder.

He climbed up, knocked at the door. It flew open, and the girl stood there, holding her tiny sister by the hand.

"Oh!" she said; "it's you. . . ."

"Yep," Tom said. "Didn't you expect me?"

"No," she said quietly, "I didn't. Any reason why I should have?"

"I don't know," Tom said; "but the other night at the meeting, I saw you. And I got a mighty powerful hankering to see some more of you. When I get a hankering, I don't just let it lie—I do something about it."

"I see," Lolette said.

"Ain't you gonna ask me in?"

"No," Lolette said.

"Why not?" Tom demanded.

"For one thing, Papa wouldn't like it. For another, I'm not sure I would either."

"Well, I'll be damned," Tom said helplessly. "Would you mind telling me why?"

"I'd rather not. I'm afraid you wouldn't appreciate it."

"Why don't you try and see?" Tom said.

"All right. But remember you asked me. You've got an awful bad reputation hereabouts, Mister Benton—"

"So you *do* know my name."

"Of course; everybody does. I went down to that silly circus you folks call a religious meeting—out of curiosity. It was amusing—it's always funny to see people making fools of themselves—and rather pitiful, too. . . . Then you came with—with your wife. She's sweet. I felt so sorry for her. . . ."

"Well, I'll be—"

"I'd heard a lot about you," the girl said quickly, "so I was curious. I thought that you'd be different, handsomer, maybe. The first time I saw you, I thought you were downright ugly. . . ."

"But now you don't?"

"Now—I—I don't know. You're interesting. I guess you're just about the most interesting man I ever did see. . . ."

"Thank you kindly," Tom grinned.

"You'd better hear me out. You're interesting all right, but in all the wrong ways. First off, I couldn't see what that poor, sweet girl saw in you. You're big and strapping and fine, but so are a lot of other men. Then I saw. If a woman has an ounce of wickedness in her, you'd appeal to that. You'd bring it out, build it up, until you made her all wicked—or finished her. First human face I've ever seen with no goodness in it— no goodness at all. . . ."

"But I'm converted now, remember," Tom said.

"Don't know why you did that," Lolette said quietly; "but I knew sure as I'm standing here that that was faked. You had an axe to grind. All right, you asked me, and I told you. So now you'd better go."

Tom stared at her shrewdly.

"There's more to it than that," he said. "You came back seven nights in a row, and each night you watched me—now, didn't you?"

Lolette stared down at her feet. Then she raised her eyes.

"Yes," she said, "I did."

"Why?" Tom said.

"That, Mister Benton, is one thing you aren't ever going to find out. Good-bye."

"Reckon I am a-gonna find out," Tom said slowly. "Could be you got a mite of that wickedness you been talking about, yourself. You're a proud little filly and no mistake; but even the proudest can be gentled. . . ."

"I said good-bye," Lolette whispered.

"I know," Tom said, "I heard you." Then he bent down and kissed her—a long, slow, searching kiss, until, in the end, in spite of all her efforts, he had his answer.

When he released her, finally, her eyes were the eyes of a trapped animal, a small and gentle wild creature gazing up at its captor, not asking anything, neither mercy, nor death, just waiting, like that, in the purest agony of terror. Then that lessened, changed, became something else, a thing that another, a more sensitive man would have found insupportable: a shame absolutely naked and pitiful and complete.

But Tom Benton, seeing it, threw back his head and laughed aloud. "Dangblast my wicked soul!" he roared. "I was right! Now I know!"

At the bass boom of his laughter, the child started to cry—a high, thin, wailing sound. Lolette tightened her grip on her sister's hand.

"Please go," she whispered; "you're scaring Babs. . . ."

"Sorry," Tom chuckled; "but I am right, ain't I?"

The slow tears gathered behind the girl's lashes, hung there, spilled over.

"Yes," she said. "You're right. But it's not a thing I'm proud of, Mister Benton. And it's not going to do you any good. . . ."

"We'll see about that," Tom said, and started forward again.

She put her free hand up against his chest.

"Wait," she said. "If you do that again, I'll tell Papa. And he'll kill you. There isn't a man alive he couldn't kill. You've got your wife to think about—and your child's coming. . . ."

"I got you to think about now," Tom growled.

"No," she said, "you'd better forget about me. I can never be anything to you. . . ."

"Don't you," Tom said gravely, "want to be?"

She studied his face.

"Yes," she said honestly, "I suppose I do. . . . It's like my mother told me before she died. She said I was like her—that there'd be only one man in all the world for me—that when I saw him, I'd know. She was right—as far as she went. I saw you—and I knew. Only she didn't tell me all of it—I don't suppose she could. How was she to know that the one man in the world for me would be a bad, wicked scoundrel, already married, and his wife great with child?"

"When am I going to see you?" Tom said.

"You aren't. Not ever. . . ."

"You're wrong. Tell me one thing, Lolette. You love me, don't you?"

"Yes." The word was so low he had to bend forward to hear it.

"Then you don't want me dead. And if you don't meet me somewheres, I'll come here—paw or no paw. You want that?"

Lolette shuddered. The child went on whimpering.

"No," she whispered, "I don't want that. . . ."

"Then when—and where?"

"I'll send you word. You know anybody I know?"

"Rachel," Tom said. "Can you trust her?"

"Oh, yes. Only trouble is she's crazy about you herself. That's how I found out about you. She'd seen you down in town and—"

"Sure you can trust her?" Tom growled.

"Yes. She'd do anything for me."

"Then send me word tomorrow. Not at my place. I'll be in town about four o'clock. Tell her to kind of bump into me in the street." He grinned at her. "Don't look so scairt," he said quietly, "I ain't a-going to hurt you. I ain't nothing to be scairt of. You know why, Baby-doll? Because I'm too blamed proud to be troublesome the way you're thinking. I ain't never forced a woman—never in my life. Never had to. And I don't aim to begin now."

He kissed her again with the expertness of long practice.

" 'Bye now," he said.

She didn't move. She stood there watching him as he went down the ladder into the pirogue. When he reached the bank and went ashore, she was watching him still, her eyes great and dark and troubled.

Sarah caught a cold from the baptism and had to stay abed for two weeks. The women came in droves and took care of her. But Tom's barn-raising was delayed by the fact that he did not dare ask for help so soon after his conversion, as well as his twice weekly meetings with Lolette Dupré, in a remote spot on the river. She had come to accept these meetings, in fact to look forward to them, especially since Tom scrupulously kept his word about not making her do anything she did not want to. That he did so, that the promise given so lightly had somehow become binding surprised him much more than it did her. He had had no intention of abiding by his pledge but now he found it impossible to break.

The reason, had he been capable of self-exploration, would have astonished him—it was, actually, that Lolette was wrong: Tom Benton had, like all men living, a streak of decency about him, suppressed since his childhood, a tiny, almost extinguished spark of tenderness. And this, Lolette, with her shy, gentle ways, could reach. With all his cruelty, the timid Acadian girl could manage him; she moved him, touched long-unused chords of feeling he had forgotten he had; weaker than Sarah, she controlled him better; her yielding, her softness were barriers against which no weapons of his spirit availed him.

So he worked hard, aided by Jonas, driven by a balked, savage misery of mood, upon the walls of his barn, building them flat on the ground, hoping by the time they had them done, the men would help them raise them into place.

But time was running out on him. He had to get his barn up. He was so baffled by the problem that he was driven to do a thing almost unthinkable for him: he discussed the problem with his wife. And Sarah, with her instinctive practicality of mind, came up almost at once with a solution.

"Why don't you kind of pull them up with ropes?" she said calmly. "You got Jonas and the animals to help you. My paw used to raise heavy things that way. You know: you peel the bark off a log, and wrap the rope around it and . . ."

"Dangblast my stupid hide!" Tom said. "Knowed there was some reason I married you, Sary-gal! Damned if you ain't got brains in that head of yourn." Then he kissed her, hard, and ran out of the house, roaring for

Jonas. They spent the rest of the day making the winch, and working it into place.

But the next day, when he tried the experiment of raising his barn with the use of beasts instead of men, it proved to be harder than he had thought. Part of the trouble was the weather: the day was overcast, too still, and hot with a humid, sticky heat. Tom looked over to where old Jonas sat on the mule and frowned. He pushed back his hat and mopped his forehead with a bandanna; then he mopped his chest and belly too, sweat soaked from the sickening, oppressive heat. The clouds hung low, so that the tops of the oaks were shrouded in mist; but it was hot just the same—that bad, wet heat that didn't dry off a man's sweat, and left him feeling poison-mean and miserable.

He gazed at his crude winch, made of peeled log, with stout rope wound around it, and hitched from there to his horse and the mule that Jonas rode. Behind them, on the ground, lay the four huge walls of timber, with window openings framed, and a place for the doors. It was the only way he knew how to build a barn. In the back country, people often built them that way, the walls lying on the ground, waiting for the willing hands of friends and neighbors to push them into place. A barn-raising was something folks looked forward to—what with good liquor flowing, and the womenfolks on hand with cornpone hot enough to burn a man's fingers and sweet potato pies and candied yams and collard greens and any kind of game the men had been able to bring down. Back-country folks didn't mind helping. Out here, a man needed help, and a body never knew when he'd have to call for it in his turn. So a man went and worked all day and half the night helping a neighbor get his barn up and drank his home-made mash, and danced to the fiddler's tune afterwards and sparked all the girls.

But Tom didn't dare risk calling on them—not yet.

"All right, Jonas," he said; "let's git started. . . ."

The two animals moved forward, straining. The ropes tightened, creaked. The lower ends of the wall jammed hard against the stakes he had driven into the earth. The wall began to tilt, slanting up into the ominous gray of the sky.

The beasts dug their hoofs in. Sweat glistened on their coats. Their muscles bunched, straining. The wall groaned upward, still tilting.

"There!" Tom roared; "hold it, Jonas!"

He jumped from the saddle. He picked up some timbers and pegs, hammering the pegs home in holes he had already bored, so that the timbers angled out, making temporary braces to hold the wall upright. It had been guesswork, but his eye was good. Another long, steady pull, and the wall stood solidly enough, only a few degrees out of plumb.

True it up later, Tom decided; got to get the other three up. Don't like this here weather. It looks like it's gettin' set to blow. . . .

Jonas sat on the mule, sniffing the air, his broad nostrils flaring.

"Gwine to blow, Marse Tom," he said. "Us better hurry. Don't git them all up'n' braced, wind mash 'em right back down agin."

"Don't I know it!" Tom growled. "Pay out them ropes, Jonas."

The second side was easier, because they had gotten the hang of it by then; and because it butted against the side already standing. Tom climbed up, hammering wooden pegs into the holes he had painfully drilled with a brace and bit. He hadn't used nails, because they were too expensive. In those days they were still made one at a time by hand, which made them hard to come by, and dear. Besides, pegs were better. They didn't rust, and they expanded and contracted like the rest of the wood with the changes of weather, making a building hold snugly together. But it was much slower work, because he had had to bore a hole every place he wanted to put in a peg.

He was hammering the pegs near the top of the walls when he felt them shake a little. He raised his head and felt the wind. It came in short gusts, with long periods of quiet in between. Tom worked faster. He had made many holes for the pegs, because he had wanted his barn to be strong. And now that was what slowed him. Still, if he didn't put in enough, the wind might tear the walls down anyway. This was hurricane country, and even a tornado or two, twisting in from the Gulf, was not unknown.

He looked down into Jonas' worried face.

"Take the animals home!" he roared; "I'll make it afoot!"

Jonas' mouth shaped the words, "Yassuh," but Tom didn't hear him. A long, steady gust snatched the sound away, pushing against the walls so hard that Tom had to cling to them to keep from falling off. When it died, Tom saw Jonas moving away, riding the mule and leading the horse behind him.

The gusts were harder now, the times between them shorter. Each time they hit, Tom had to loop his arm over the top of the wall, clinging to it, and holding onto his big wooden-headed mallet at the same time. Jonas was already out of sight, beyond the oaks. Tom banged in another peg; then there weren't any more gusts, but the wind itself, coming in from the Gulf, steady and strong, with a note in it like a woman's crying. The cry rose. It was shrill now, with an edge in it. Tom dropped both the mallet and the pegs and clung with his big hands, digging his fingers into the wood.

A flight of gulls swept across the sky at an angle, hopelessly fighting the gale. A pelican crashed into the oak tops, and dropped, stunned, to the ground. Here, where he was, in the wild country between the Bayous San Patrice and Pierre, north of the San Antonio Trace, the old El Camino Real, miles from the Gulf, these sea birds were unknown. Seeing them, Tom realized how bad the wind was.

He worked his way downward. The walls were swaying like living things. Fifteen feet from the ground, he heard one of the braces let go with a noise like a pistol shot, so he jumped. He landed on his feet and started running until he was clear of the walls. He heard the crash as the second wall went down, and, as he turned, he saw the wind lift the first wall as though it were a leaf and sail it over the tops of the highest oaks, like a gigantic raft, plunging through the invisible rapids of the air, on and out of sight.

He swore, feelingly. But the wind snatched his oaths from his lips, so that he could only bend over before it and start to work his way toward the house. The quickest way was through the cheniere, the oak grove, but he knew better than that. Already the giant oaks were bending over like birch saplings, and even as he watched, one of them broke off, halfway up the trunk, making a noise like a fieldpiece, then came crashing down. He skirted the cheniere. His hat was gone, and his face stung from the flying earth. By now there ought to be rain, he thought. Then, almost as if in answer to his thought, the rain came. It came down in sheets, no lines showing, slanted hard by the wind, smashing against his unprotected body. In seconds, he was soaked to the skin, and the whole world disappeared in a hissing, roaring maelstrom of water.

He fought on, doggedly, toward the house. When he reached it at last, and shouldered the door open, he was ready to drop. But he couldn't, not yet.

The house had a cellar, dug by Reverend Tyler to store foodstuffs. Quickly Tom picked Sarah up, and went down the stairs.

"It's bad, ain't it, Tom?" Sarah whispered.

"Bad enough if the bayous and the river don't rise," Tom said. "But we're safe from the water here. This here is high ground. What worries me is the wind."

He set about making her comfortable, putting the feather mattress on the floor, and covering her with blankets. He brought the lantern down and some water. When he went back upstairs, he found Jonas in the house, quaking with fright.

"Lemme stay here, Marse Tom," the old Negro begged. "Wind done took my lean-to plumb away. I'm soaked, and it ain't fit for man nor beast outside noways."

"All right," Tom growled. "Wonder when it's going to let up?"

After two hours, the wind died down again to intermittent gusts, but there was no change in the pounding of the rain. It made a drumroll on the roof, so loud that the hammering on the door seemed a part of it.

"That's somebody knocking," Jonas said.

Tom listened.

"Damned if you ain't right," he said. "See who it is, Jonas."

Jonas opened the door a crack, but a gust tore it from his grasp, and the rain whined in past the huddled forms before the door.

Tom recognized the Rudgerses, the people who lived closest to them, and in whose house Reverend Tyler had . . . died.

"Come in, folks!" he said cheerfully. "Trouble down yore way?"

Jonas shut the door behind them, bolting it against the wind.

"Trouble," Jim Rudgers groaned, "more like ruination, Mister Benton. Wind smashed the house to smithereens—and after that the bayou backed up. Red River's rising a foot every twenty minutes—and in this storm, God knows how many folks gonna git drowned. . . ."

Nelly Rudgers stared at Tom Benton. There was a mixture of things in her eyes: fear, disgust, puzzlement—and fascination.

"Where's Sary?" she whispered.

"Down in the cellar," Tom said. "Safer down there. Even if the house blows down, a body'd be safe there. You go down there, Ma'am. Sary be mighty glad to see you. I'll send you down some of her clothes by Jonas so's you can change afore you git the grippe or something. . . . Me'n' yore husband'll stay here an' talk things over."

Nelly slipped gratefully down the steps as Jonas held the trap door open.

"Got some spare duds, Jim," Tom said. "You'd better git into 'em. I don't reckon the Good Lord'll mind if we backslide a little and have ourselves a snort under th' circumstances."

"Be mighty grateful—Tom," Jim Rudgers said; and in spite of that little pause before his first name, Tom Benton knew he had won another round of his battle.

Looking out of the window, Tom saw the first yellow swirl of the water creep across the lowlands below. He put his empty glass down on the table and turned back to Jim.

"Them folks down on the bayou and along the river gonna need help," he said. "Feel up to it, Jim?"

"Yep," Rudgers said gravely; "but seeing as how we ain't ducks, how the devil kin we . . . ?"

"Got a side of a barn," Tom said. "I was trying to git the barn up by myself when the wind hit. It—or a part of it, would make a mighty handy raft, Jim."

"All right," Rudgers said, "let's go find it."

They went down into the cellar and told the women what they were going to do.

Sarah clutched at Tom's hand.

"Be careful, Tom-love," she whispered. "Know you can't let them folks drown, wouldn't be Christian, but please don't git yoreself kilt, you can't leave me all alone with the baby coming. . . ."

"I'll be careful, Hon," Tom said.

They went out into the rain, carrying axes. The barnside was already afloat in the field below the house, and the wind had jammed it against the oak trees. It was much too big for two men to handle; but to two expert woodsmen, cutting it down to one-quarter size was easy. Then, using the timber braces for poles, they pushed it out into the swift running current.

I'm coming, Lolette-baby, Tom thought. You're a mighty sweet little creature, and I ain't got nowheres with you yet. But I'm going to. Can't let you drown, Baby-doll—not before then.

Even this here storm's got its advantages, he mused. Save enough folks, and ain't nobody gonna hold the past agin me no more. . . .

But it wasn't easy to get to Louis Dupré's place. He lived far upstream, and there were too many washed-out families between. Tom was perfectly willing to pass them up, and go after Lolette first, but he couldn't think of any convincing lie he could tell Jim Rudgers.

Oh well, he thought, she won't drown. That there Louis Dupré was born in a boat, 'pears like. Bet they're already on high ground. Still he felt uneasy about it. He had to go there, had to see. . . .

By early evening, he and Jim had transferred twenty-seven people to higher ground. They were greatly helped by the fact that during the afternoon the wind stopped completely. Jim Rudgers straightened up against his pole and sniffed the air.

"Don't like this, Tom," he said. "If that dadblamed wind had died down gradual like, I wouldn't be worried. But it's plumb, downright quit. That's bad. . . ."

"Why?" Tom said.

"You ain't lived around here long," Jim Rudgers said. "These here winds move in a circle, building up all the time—then they quit, which means they've moved away from this section. 'Bout three hours from now, they'll come back, or I miss my guess. And they'll be blowin' twicet as hard as they was this morning."

"Then we got three hours, Jim," Tom said. "Let's git busy!"

They got another ten people to safety in those three hours. But it was harder now, because the remaining families were more scattered. Darkness came early—just before Tom had worked the raft upstream until the Radleys' cabin was almost in sight.

"Them no-count Radleys!" Jim Rudgers spat. "Reckon we got to, though. . . ."

"We got to," Tom said.

Even in the failing light, he could see that the cabin was half under water. Something fluttered from the roof. The Radleys were up there, waving.

Tom and Jim forced the raft against the side of the cabin. Jonathan Radley, his wife, and his daughter, scrambled down.

"Thankee folks," Jonathan got out; " mighty glad . . ."

"It's all right," Tom growled. "Know whether the Duprés got away from their house?"

"I dunno," Jonathan said. "Likely they did. Louis is a mighty good man with a pirogue. . . ."

But Jim Rudgers caught Tom's arm, pointing. Then Tom saw it: the pirogue, upside down, jammed hard into the reeds at the bayou's edge.

"Dear Lord!" Tom whispered. "Come on, Jim—push!"

When they were close to the little shack on the pilings, Tom could see that some of the supports were already broken, causing the house to slant over crazily.

"Mister Dupré!" Tom bellowed. "You folks in there?"

Louis Dupré appeared in the window.

"Yes," he said calmly. "Come up under the window and I hand you down my girls, me."

They worked the raft below the windows. Tom stood up and caught the baby, Babette, in his arms; then passed her over to Mrs. Radley. Then Louis swung Lolette down without apparent effort although she was taller than he and almost as heavy. Tom eased her down gently; but at the last moment she clung to him, her mouth close to his ear.

"I knew you'd come," she whispered. "I prayed it would be you. . . ."

Then she turned him loose and stepped back.

"Move away," Louis Dupré called; "I'm gonna jump now, me. . . ."

Tom moved. Louis sprang from the window and landed on his feet on the raft for all the world like a great cat, giving with the impact so that he made no sound, the whole leap indescribably perfect, graceful, sure.

Tom stared at him. This one was something. Now for the first time he believed Rachel's story of the unfortunate Pierre. He could take a big man, Tom realized, quick like he is, a man's strength wouldn't mean nothing. Rip you open whilst you was getting set. This kind you hafta shoot and at no closer than fifty yards.

"Thank you, M'sieu," Louis said politely. "Now I gonna give you a hand with the poles."

"How come you didn't git out, Mister Dupré?" Tom said. "Folks always say you're the best boatman in the bayou country."

"Wind took my boat right off," Louis explained. "Broke the rope. I can swim, me—but Lolette can't, and water was too rough for me to carry them. So I waited. Now we better go, us. That wind, he coming back."

With Louis' expert help, they made the Red River before the wind hit. But when it struck it was like all the cataclysms in mortal memory rolled into one. The current caught the raft and whirled it downstream like a chip. Rachel Radley clung to Tom, moaning.

"Mister Benton," she wept, "don't let me drown! Please don't let me drown! I'll do anything you say afterwards only . . ."

"Shut up!" Tom snapped. "What you want to talk like that for?"

But in that hissing, roaring waste of water, no one had heard her. The raft pounded on, gathering speed all the time. Then in the pitch blackness, it slammed into the rocks, throwing them all flat on their faces. The raft hung against the boulders, grinding.

"It's gonna break up!" Jim Rudgers shouted.

Tom stood there. In that torrent, swimming was out of the question. But there was one chance. Here, at the beginning of the Red River rapids, there was a barrier of stones all the way across the river. In the daytime, it was possible to walk across, stepping from stone to stone—if you were sure-footed. But at night, with the stones under water . . .

One of the timbers tore free from the raft.

"Gimme a pole, Jim," Tom said.

"Whatcha gonna do?" Jim demanded.

"Gonna feel for the rocks with the pole, carrying the wimmen ashore one at a time. . . ."

"What shore?" Jim snapped; "ain't no more shore, Tom!"

"Well, to them trees, then," Tom said. "You come along behind me with one of the girls or the old woman. Louis'll bring the baby. Radley'll just have to follow us, hisself."

"Mighty risky," Jim Rudgers said.

"Staying here ain't risky," Tom growled; "it's sure death."

"All right," Jim Rudgers said. Then, to Tom's bottomless disgust, he turned and picked up Lolette, the action unpremeditated, natural, because Lolette happened to be closer to him. Tom started to protest, but then he saw Louis Dupré's eyes. Swearing under his breath, he picked up Rachel Radley.

They started out, Louis Dupré leading the way, carrying both Mrs. Radley and little Babette, balancing himself with the pole in his one free hand, cradling the child in his left arm, while the old woman rode pig-a-back on his shoulders. He moved off, as sure-footed as though he were on dry land. Seeing him, Tom and Jim shifted the girls to the same position in order to leave their arms free for balancing. Halfway across, Tom felt Rachel's fist pounding his back. He looked up.

"Paw!" she screamed.

Tom looked back. Jonathan Radley still sat, a hunched-up silhouette against the white waters, on what was left of the raft.

"Damn!" Tom swore. "Stupid old bastard! Now I'll hafta . . ."

But before he had the words out, he missed his footing and plunged into the water. Rachel hung on, her grip almost strangling him. The current slammed them into the rocks, cutting and bruising them in half-a-dozen places. Tom fought his way to his feet. He could stand up because of the rocks, and his head remained above water. He could hear Rachel whimpering at intervals between the gusts.

"Shut up, damn it!" he roared, and began to splash and paddle his way to the place where the east bank had been. He made it, and handed Rachel up to Louis who had climbed into a tree with Mrs. Radley and little Babette. Leaving the four of them there, he turned back in time to pull Jim and Lolette from the water. They had fallen in, too. The footing was impossible.

"Paw," Rachel quavered.

"Oh hell!" Tom groaned, and started back. When he was a few yards out, he saw it was no good. The raft was gone. He stood there, staring at the raging waters. But there was no sign of Jonathan Radley at all.

He came back and climbed into the tree beside Lolette.

"Mister Radley?" she whispered.

"Gone," Tom said gruffly.

She put her arms around his neck, and sobbed a little.

"Poor Rachel," she wept, "what's going to become of her now?"

"Don't know," Tom growled. "Don't take on so, Baby-doll—couldn't of been helped. . . ."

After a time, she quieted. They sat in the fork of two great boughs, hanging on while the wind tore at them. The tree groaned like a living thing. Other trees gave way, falling into the stream and being piled up against the rocky barrier by the torrent. After two hours, the wind died.

"You all right, Tom?" Jim Rudgers called from a nearby tree.

"Just fine and dandy," Tom called back. "But it 'pears like we'll have to roost up here till morning. . . ."

Lolette snuggled up against him, shivering. She kissed his throat, his face, his mouth, in a perfect agony of tenderness.

"Tarnation, Lolette!" Tom whispered; "yore paw's right over there in the next tree."

"It's dark," Lolette said. "He can't see or hear us."

"I know that," Tom growled, "but I'd give a pretty penny to know what he's thinking right now!"

"Tom," Lolette whispered. "I heard you and that Mister Rudgers talking on the raft. What you did was very brave and fine. I think maybe I was wrong. You do have some goodness in you."

"Thank you," Tom said shortly.

"Don't talk like that. I love you, Tom—you know that. And now I'm beginning to see why. . . ."

"Just because I saved folks? Hell, Baby, that's only natural."

"No. Because you can be kind—really kind." She raised up a little and kissed him—a long, slow time, very softly and sweetly and tenderly.

"Tom," she said quietly, "the next time you ask me—that—I—I don't think I'll say—no. . . ."

"Because you're grateful?" Tom said angrily. "Hell's bells, Lolette, I don't want no damned gratitude."

"No, Tom," she whispered; "only because now I want you, too—that's all."

"Well, I'll be—" Tom began; but she stopped his profane words, with her warm and yielding mouth.

First in the morning, the sun fought its way through the clouds. The countryside was still flooded; but the current had slowed. When they climbed down they found that the water was no more than waist high.

Tom and Jim set out, leading the women, and behind them Louis Dupré came, carrying the sleeping child. Tom could feel the Cajun's eyes boring two small, precise holes between his shoulder blades.

Got his suspicions now, he thought morosely. That's going to make it hard—mighty hard. . . .

But Louis said nothing. He recognized, with his Gallic practicality, the unlikeliness of his daughter's honor being compromised in the high branches of a storm-whipped tree.

Lolette did not talk either. She waded along beside Tom, looking at

him from time to time out of eyes filled with an odd mixture of speculation, awe, and tenderness. But no fear—no longer any fear.

They came at last to the little hilltop, become an island now, where
they had left the first victims of the flash flood.

"Water's going down fast," Tom announced. "You folks stay here a few
more hours and you'll be able to make it home afoot. Me 'n' Jim's got to
leave you now—got to go and see after our wives."

"You go right ahead, Mister Benton," Nancy Cattlet said. "You sure
Lord done enough for us."

Her husband, Hunt, gave her their baby son, Ron, and stood up. He
put out his hand.

"Tom Benton," he said, "I swore my solemn oath never to take the
hand of any man what could do what you done to Bob Tyler. But right
now, in the presence of these folks, I want to take back that vow. Mighty
white what you done, Tom, yessir, mighty white!"

Tom took his hand.

"No hard feelings, Hunt?" he said. "I'm sorry about what happened to
the Reverend—and I said so in public. I thought everybody understood
how bad I felt about that. Well, if you don't, I'll say it again: I'm most
humbly sorry I caused the good Reverend's death—and hope you folks can
find it in your hearts to forgive me."

"Forgive you?" Hunt Cattlet snorted; "you expect us to hold a grudge
against the man who's just saved half the parish?"

"God bless you, Tom Benton!" a woman cried.

"Thank you, Ma'am," Tom said. "Thank you all, mighty kindly.
Reckon I'll be going now. . . ."

He and Jim still had to wade in places, but the water was going down
fast. An hour later, they reached the edge of Tom's place; but they stopped
there, staring.

"Where in hellfire's the house?" Jim got out. Then they started to run.
They scrambled up the muddy rise, and when they were close, they saw
it: a jumble of timbers, piled in a low mound where the house had been,
and smashed against the trees fifty yards further on, all that was left of
the roof.

Dear Lord, Tom prayed, let her be safe and I won't never look at another woman agin—not even so much as look!

They tore at the timbers with frantic hands, prying the heavier beams
up with ridge poles used as levers. Then the trap door of the cellar came
in sight—untouched. The two men stared at it, panting. Then they stiffened. The sound came again—a thin, plaintive wail, rising from beneath
the cellar door.

"The young'un!" Tom breathed; "Name of God, Jim—come on!"

They yanked at the trap door, hurled it open. Nelly Rudgers looked up
at them, her fingers across her lips.

"Shhh!" she hissed. "Sary's sleeping. She's all tuckered out, poor thing!"

Tom gulped twice before he found his voice.

"And the young'un?" he croaked.

"Fine and dandy! You've got yoreself a mighty pretty daughter, Tom—"

"A daughter!" Tom gasped. "Well, I'll be damned!"

He swung into the opening and eased his way down the stairs.

Nelly held up the little bundle for him to see. His daughter was a tiny, red-faced mite with great masses of inky black hair covering her head. She looked like all new babies, red and wrinkled and ugly; but Tom stood there staring at her in breathgone fascination.

"Don't you want to hold her?" Nelly said.

"Hell no!" Tom exploded; "my big paws would bust something sure!"

Sarah stirred.

"Tom?" she got out.

Tom dropped on his knees beside the mattress.

"Sorry it wasn't a boy," Sarah whispered.

"Hell'sfire, Sary-gal!" Tom laughed; "this ain't th' last—besides hit's the prettiest little thing I ever did see! What we gonna call it?"

"I—I named her Stormy," Sarah smiled weakly. "You see, she come right after the roof blew off. . . ."

"Stormy, eh?" Tom savored the name. Then he grinned. "Stormy! Now there's a name what's fitting for a Benton if I ever heard one!"

He turned toward where Jim and Jonas were looking at the baby, still cradled in Nelly Rudgers' arms.

"Bring her over here, Miz Rudgers! Lemme hold her—I'll be careful."

He took the infant, holding her as though she were made of delicate crystal.

"Well, Stormy Benton," he laughed; "how you like yore paw?"

The baby set up an anguished howl.

"Never you mind," Tom grinned, "we gonna git acquainted real good, ain't we, Missy?"

He knelt there a long time, holding his daughter, his blue eyes really gentle for the first time in his life.

And the last.

4

Tom Benton sat on a rail fence and watched Jim Rudgers driving the Negroes. He had to watch Jim occasionally, because, as an overseer, Jim was a mite too ready with the whip. Not that a nigger didn't need a taste of leather on his black hide ever so often; but Jim, out of his disappointment at losing his own poor, marginal lands the year after the big storm, was inclined to vent his towering, impotent fury against man, the universe, fate, upon the helpless backs of the slaves.

Tom understood that. He had a hard core of practical understanding when it came to what made people tick. He knew, and grinned at the thought, that deep down, Jim Rudgers hated him.

Reckon he thought I should of given him back his place when I bought it off of Hilton last year. But that wouldn't of done no good. Ain't fitten for nothing but to grow corn for the niggers and fodder for the animals. It gripes his ornery guts to be beholden to me. I give him the job and a house to live in. Pay him good, too—more'n any other overseer in the parish. And I don't even make him call me Mister Benton, excepting when there's folks around. . . . But I can't have him crippling my niggers 'cause he's mad with me and the world. Give a nigger a few good ones to git some life into him, show him who's boss; but you don't beat him bloody any more than you do a good riding hoss—for the simple reason that a fieldhand costs just about as much as the best hoss nowadays and is gonna cost more soon, or I miss my guess. . . .

He sat there like that, dreaming. His hand moved, smacking his expensive, polished boots with his crop. He wore a frock coat now, a brocaded waistcoat, a string tie. His shirt was ruffled, and a heavy gold chain crossed his waistcoat front to the massive gold watch in his pocket. He was fine, every inch the great planter and he knew it. He was extraordinarily pleased with himself. He had managed everything very well indeed.

Hilton had renewed the loan, of course, and granted him another after the hurricane and flood had wiped out all Tom's chances as it had the chances of so many other small planters. He hadn't done that for many other people; but Tom's double coup: his faked conversion, and his quite genuine heroism during the flood had put public opinion solidly on his side. There was nothing else for Hilton to do.

It was a day made for dreaming. The Negroes moved down the rows with the sacks slung from their shoulders, picking the cotton with easy, rhythmical motion in tune to the lead hand's song. The fields stretched out before Tom Benton clear to nowhere and beyond, washed in the yellow afternoon light, shimmering with the rising heat waves, so sunfilled, broad, lovely, that Tom remembered again the name he had given his place: Broad Acres. He said the name aloud, savoring the sound.

His now—his. All this. And in two short years. The land was his, and the blue heavens above the land, and the fantastic spires and cathedrals of cloud towering up into them. He half-listened to the boom of the lead hand's belly-deep bass, and beyond that, far off and faint, the sound of coon-hounds mourning through the pine wood. It was cool here where he sat in the blue shade under the cheniere, cool, and a little dark, so that the sunfilled fields glowed even brighter before his eyes—hazed over a bit from dreaming.

He had worked for it, and it was his. Been lucky, too, he thought. Everything's turned out just fine. . . . He was seeing again, vividly, more real than the shimmering wash of sun over his fields, the day the whole population of the parish had descended upon his land, two days after the last of the floodwaters had gone down. He had been in the lean-to he had built for temporary shelter, tending to Sarah, alone, because the Rudgerses were gone, grubbing through the wreckage of their own place, when he had heard the shouting:

"Come on out, Tom! Come out of there and greet your friends!"

He had come out, blinking. All the men of the parish were there with their sons and wives and daughters. The men had axes, saws, hammers. Tom stared at them, open mouthed.

"We're aiming to build you a house," Hunt Cattlet said, "and a barn. The wimmenfolks done brought vittles, and we got a fiddler here, not to mention a drop or two of the best bust-head your lips ever did taste. Now tell us, Tom—where you want your house?"

Tom looked from one of them to the other. And it was then that he saw that Louis and Lolette Dupré were among them. He stared at Lolette, seeing again how lovely she was. He had never believed a Cajun girl could look like that. Usually—he tore away his gaze.

"Why—same place the old one was, I reckon," he said. "And thank you, Hunt; thank you all. Mighty white of you folks to do this for me. Yessir, mighty white. . . ."

In three days they had the house up. The house and the barn. Tom and Sarah lived in that house still, and it now had eight rooms instead of the original four. Tom had added the others, as the need, more fancied than real, arose. It was a typical planter's cottage, low and rambling with verandas, called galleries in that Cajun country, all around it; all of it built on one floor. The following spring, Tom had painted it white, more to satisfy Sarah than for any other reason. On a shopping trip to New Orleans, she had seen one of the neo-Grecian great houses the very richest planters were building, thereby creating one of the dearest-held and most undying of all Southern legends—that planters lived like this, grandly, in these huge, chaste temples of domesticity; but legend it was, and near-myth, and would remain no more.

"What in hellfire would I do with a house like that?" Tom said; "a body couldn't put his feet on the bannisters!"

Tom knew he wouldn't have felt at ease in such a house. And most planters, great or small, shared his opinion; shared it, that is, whenever they had even so much as seen a neo-Grecian house. Since there were never even a thousand of them, and perhaps, more truly, not even half that number, scattered across the vast length and breadth of the Southland, among the eight million of her inhabitants, this was seldom indeed.

Besides the house and the barn, Tom owned his own gin now, and over fifty slaves. He was moving eastward, toward the river, buying land, snapping up mortgages. Git that last parcel of land off of Davin Henderson, he thought grandly, and I'm gonna have my own steamboat landing, too. . . .

He was, of course, up to his neck in debt. But to the great planters, debt was the accustomed mode of life. To the day he died, he would continue to spend and borrow, treating his creditors with regal contempt, throwing them a payment now and again as a sop to their fawning but insistent demands, precisely as one throws a bone to a starving dog.

He did not even think of his debts. His mind was on other, more pleasant things: His daughter, Stormy, beautiful as a cherub at two, with his own black hair and startlingly blue eyes; and Wade, his year-old son. My two sons, he corrected himself, and a grin of pure deviltry lighted his eyes.

Louis would cut my heart out if he knew, he thought wryly. Thank God little Clint ain't got blue eyes!

He remembered now, again, his shock when the Cajun guide he went duck-shooting with had told him:

"That Lolette, she done made her dirt, her! Belly this big, yes! Old Louis, he mighty mad, him; he done beat her so bad she like to die."

He had gone at once to see her, having himself poled through the twisting wastes of the bayous, whose ramifications he could never remember. And when he reached the shack, perched upon pilings above the stinking marsh with muskrat skins nailed to its walls for drying, Louis Dupré was there.

"I heard you beat Lolette, Louis," he said quietly. "That was a mighty mean thing, my friend."

"She lucky I don't kill her," Louis said. "She turn whore on me, her. I give her everything—sent her down to the convent in New Orleans, me. She read good, write good—speak good French, good English, her. Was gonna find her nice Creole boy, *bon famille,* to marry her. Now look what she done!"

"Can I see her?" Tom asked.

Louis paused, staring at him. His eyes were brown coals, suddenly.

"Wasn't you, was it, M'sieu Tom?" he whispered. "You been good friend to Louis. Bring me good likker, new traps. But t'ink it was you, I cut yore heart out, me. I cut it out an' eat it raw, yes!"

Tom looked back at him, steadily.

"No, Louis," he lied; "it wasn't me."

"All right," Louis grunted. "I don't t'ink you lie to me. I don't t'ink. You got black hair, you. An' Lolette got black hair. But M'sieu Tom, you better pray your *Bon Dieu* that *bébé* don't have blue eyes!"

Tom turned to the boatman who had brought him to the shack.

"Hand me up that jug, Antoine," he said. He took the jug and turned back to Louis.

"Here, Louis," he said, "this'll take yore mind off yore troubles a mite—"

"Thank you," Louis said. Tom paused long enough to see that the trapper had sat down on the gallery, the jug cradled in his arms. A few drinks of that pop-skull and he could forget about any more trouble from Louis Dupré. He opened the door and entered the cabin. He saw at first only little Babette playing in the corner with a homemade doll. Then, as his eyes grew accustomed to the dimness, he saw Lolette.

She lay upon the bed moaning softly to herself. Even in the smoky lamplight, Tom could see the blue-green welts on her thin arms. He stood there, staring at her, seeing her again, as though this were for the first time, with wonder, with awe, caught by her soft loveliness. For hers was such a quiet beauty, a velvety, violet beauty that shunned the sunlight, soft and simple and sweet, but night blooming only. Her hair was midnight, blacker than midnight, the very negation and absence of light; and her eyes were animal brown, soft and frightened and shy, like the eyes of the little furry creatures, or like doe's eyes, staring at him out of the thickets of her fears—until almost he took pity on her, almost he would let her go. . . . Her skin was brown, too; paler than her father's; but a golden tint so definite, that Tom, who knew how she hated daylight, was inclined to think she had Houma or Tangipahoa or even Choctaw blood. More than likely Choctaw, he mused; she's too gentle and sweet to come down from them murdering Houma bastards. . . .

He stood there, looking at her.

"How you feel, Lolette?" he murmured.

"Just awful, Tom," she whispered. "I want to die. At least, I would want to—if—if it wasn't yours. . . ."

"Sure about that?" Tom said.

Her brown eyes were enormous, suddenly.

"That's what you think of me?" she said. "Now I *do* want to die!"

"Sorry," Tom said. "I didn't mean it thataway. Lolette, you know I got a wife and a kid."

She looked at him. It was so still, he could hear the child babbling to her doll in the corner. Tom felt something close around his heart. He couldn't breathe. He hadn't the words for it. He didn't know how to describe this dignity as simple, profound, and deep as time itself. He didn't even know what it was. All he knew was how it felt to have to face it.

"I told you I knew that the first time you came here," she said quietly. "Why do you mention it now? It's not important. What counts is the way you are. I thought the day you saved us that you'd changed, that in spite of all the bad things you'd done, you were at heart a good man. But now I know I was wrong then—that the feeling I had about you the first time I saw you was right: A brave man, yes. Strong, yes. As beautiful as Thoume Kene, the Great Spirit my mother used to talk about. She was Indian, you know—Chitimacha. But bad really—a bad, wicked man with a cruel, laughing mouth, and the devil's own blue eyes. . . ."

"Then why on earth?" Tom began.

"Did I stay with you?" Lolette whispered. "Because, by then, even knowing what you're like didn't do any good. I'm a woman, Tom. All right I'm much younger than you; but I'm still a woman. And nobody has ever figured out the way to measure the distance between a woman's mind and her heart. You can only measure it in years, in centuries, not in anything so puny as miles. . . ."

"Cut his black heart out!" Louis roared from the gallery, "and eat it, yes!"

"Papa mad!" Babette said suddenly, clearly.

"You'd better go," Lolette whispered.

"I'll see you?" Tom said.

"Yes. Funny you need to ask. I could no more do without seeing you than I could do without drinking water or breathing air."

"I'll send you money for the kid," Tom said.

"If you like," Lolette said indifferently. "Now kiss me quick, and go."

A rail fence was a wonderful place for sitting and dreaming back over the good, lost years. Sitting there, that early fall day of 1844, a few days past his thirty-fourth birthday, Tom Benton was almost drunken with content. The hounds still mourned through the pine wood, fainter now; amid the topmost branches of the oaks, the doves cried out, far off and sad. He could smell his favorite opiates, hot earth and pine wood and the sweet overpowering perfume of Magnolia Grandiflor. He had no will to move away, to go back to the house where Sarah waited with the babies, surrounded by the house servants, busy, happy.

He frowned. Funny about Sarah, he thought. Never heard tell that having children made so much change in a woman. First met her, she was panting wild; wanted it more than I did, never gave me no rest— but now . . .

His frown deepened. How long has it been since we been together? 'Pears to me every time I make a move in her direction I hear something like: "Tom-love, I'm so tired" or: "Tom, be good! You want to wake the children?" Damn! And I can't get to see Lolette oftener than once a month. That Louis is too damned suspicious. . . .

There were, he decided, no unmixed blessings. He sat there a little longer, but the mood had passed. He felt cramped now, uncomfortable. So he got down at last and mounted the black stallion which had replaced the roan mustang, and turned back in the direction of the house.

The next day, he rode down to see Davin Henderson about the last parcel of land that lay between Broad Acres and the river. He had already bypassed the town, surrounded it, swallowed it; but he permitted it to stand there as a reminder of his magnanimity. He had given it a school, enlarged the church. Already men were beginning to speak of it as Benton's Town, or more simply, because of its straight narrowness, having no really long cross streets, giving it the name that was to cling to it all down the years: Benton's Row. He was on his way to making his ownership of the town, which, mistakenly men assumed already, a reality. His lusts consumed him, and of them, none was stronger than his passion for possession, for ownership, carrying as it did, in its very essence, the implication of mastery over time, over men. His hungers were gigantic: he wanted to drink all the whiskey, bed with all the women, master all the men. He could have now, if he had been willing to slow his pace, freed himself of debt within five years. More, he could have acquired many of the things he wanted; the half, perhaps, even three-quarters, free of liens, mortgages, the dead weight of money borrowed, the slow leakage of interest charges, if only he could have waited, acccumulating the sums with which to buy them outright. He could have, that is, in the sense that such a possibility existed; but given his temperament, being inflexibly and unalterably himself, actually, he could not. He had to have it all—and now.

Nothing rankled him more than his failure to gain the thing which in reality he actually needed: land fronting on the river, where he could build a steamboat landing, and thus freight with ease his crops down to New Orleans. The only available acreage was high-bluff land, useless for growing either cane or cotton since it always escaped the floods, and was thus never enriched by the river silt. It might afford a meager growth of foodstuffs, vegetables, potatoes, corn; but beyond that, it had little value. Yet the man who held it, hung onto it stubbornly, resisting all Tom's blandishments, resisting even offers of five times what the land was conceivably worth.

In this, indeed, there was something else again: there was Davin Henderson, himself. From the outset, Tom had disliked Henderson intensely; now he hated him with that towering passion he brought to all his emotions. The man bilked him, tormented him, defeated him by the mere fact of his existence. It was, had Tom Benton been capable of analyzing it, all very simple: Davin Henderson was what Tom wanted to be, could not, in simple fact, ever be: an aristocrat, and a gentleman. And this to such a degree that he could reduce Tom to impotent, speechless fury by a tone, a gesture, a tiny, negligent wave of his exquisitely slim hand.

He was a Virginian, a younger son, crowded out of lands grown too poor to support so many; plowed over, cut over, bled of their strength and substance by the rapacious, devouring root tendrils of tobacco and cotton; so that he, Davin, had come here; and as the slim, exquisite, beautifully mannered Virginian gentlemen usually did on the frontier, he had failed. A frontier is no place for gentlemen. It was made for horsetraders, sharp dealers, hard, violent men, thieves. In short, it was made for Tom Benton, and men like him, who would provide the beginnings, pile up the money gouged out, stolen, gained by chicanery, by fraud, by force, and at bottom from the sweat of black men's faces, to the tune of the whiplash, and in the cabins, the sorrow songs. It would be left for their descendants then to whitewash them into gentlemen, invest them with the polish they never had, make affairs of honor of their drunken brawls, and bloom their unpainted pine and cypress cottages, with saddles, ploughs, drying corn, the impedimenta of rural living cluttering up the verandas, the galleries—into white Grecian mansions, silver in the moonlight, serene under the magnolia trees.

But Davin Henderson complicated matters by being a little more than a Virginia aristocrat, by retaining some of the toughness of fiber of his own debtor-prison, impressed-children, indentured-servant ancestors (for, being of a realistic turn of mind, he had been known to laugh at the Cavalier theory of Virginia's forebears, knowing well that landed, wealthy lordlings don't come to starve, freeze, and be slaughtered by savages in a new land, that even when driven out by Roundheads, they go by choice to nearby, civilized France . . . "Your pioneer," he was fond of saying, "is always born of starvelings, or of criminal scum. . . ." which is to say, that though he failed, he did not fail completely. He managed to scratch enough poor, short-fibered cotton out of his bluff lands to pay a creditor or two with sufficient frequency to keep them off his back. He operated then, on a lesser scale, precisely as Tom Benton did on a greater, by ceaseless borrowing. And Tom, who knew from his own experience how the system worked, knew too that Davin could go on forever upon it, neither rising nor sinking, growing older and shabbier, but keeping his lands, and above all, his pride. It was questionable which of the two things Tom Benton wanted most to accomplish: to take Davin Henderson's lands, or to destroy his pride.

"Damned uppity Virginia bastard!" he thought as he rode toward the shotgun cabin, but little better than those occupied by the Negroes, which served the Hendersons as a home. "Be damned if I'll let him git under my skin this time. . . ."

He saw, as he came closer, that Davin was sitting on the gallery fanning himself. He had only five Negroes, but he didn't believe in killing himself with work. His wife Griselda was in the kitchen, Tom guessed, supervising the cooking, and at the thought of her slim figure and red-gold hair, Tom smiled. That's another thing I'm gonna take off'n him, one day, he thought. He rode up to the gallery, dismounted. Davin Henderson stood up with languid grace. He was a tall, thin man with hair so blond it was almost white, a long, bony face, out of which his blue eyes perpetually twinkled in quiet mockery.

"Mister Benton," he drawled; "my poor house is honored—again. . . ."

And Tom felt the veins at his temples stand up and beat with his blood. That 'again' so negligently added, with absolute lack of expression, so that the mockery in it was almost completely hidden; this was perfection itself, the essence and refinement of baiting, and Tom Benton seeing it, knowing it, was helpless to reply in kind.

"Yep," he growled, "I'm here again and you know why, Davin. I want to buy this here place of your'n. A body would think I was trying to cheat you or something. Why don't you face facts? The land ain't worth nothing much to you, an' it's worth a good bit to me."

"Why?" Davin Henderson said.

"Because it ain't really cotton land," Tom snorted, "as any fool can plainly see."

"Then why do you want it?" Davin asked.

Tom looked at him. All right, you finicky bastard, I'll have to tell you the truth this time—even if it means you'll jack up the price on me.

"Because yore place fronts on the river," he said slowly. "The land itself don't interest me much, except in so far as I could grow corn on it for the niggers and fodder for the animals. But you got deep water right out in front of you—steamboat water, Davin. Build myself a landing right there. Float my bales down to New Orleans, sell stuff as far north as Shreveport, now that the channel's been cleared that far. Save myself a mint of money in transportation, warehousing and the like. . . . Now do you see?"

"A snort of bourbon, Mister Benton?" Davin Henderson said.

"You mean you ain't a-going to sell?" Tom roared. "Why look here, Davin—with what I'll pay you for this here homestead, you could buy yoreself a decent spread of land—good land, somewheres else."

"How about the bourbon, Mister Benton?" Davin smiled.

"Oh, all right, don't mind if I do," Tom said. "But I must say you're the most peculiar cuss I ever run across. . . ."

"Hardly that," Davin said calmly. "I'm just a Virginian, Benton. Our land is more to us than just a means of gaining a livelihood. My attachment to this place has nothing to do with its commercial advantages or lack of them. As you say, I could buy better lands. But I like the view here. Notice how the sunlight falls through the Spanish moss on the oaks by the bluff? And there's the river flowing beyond that—a rather imposing vista, don't you think? I find it immensely satisfying—one of the good things of life. And then I haven't any particular desire to become rich. Odd, isn't it?"

"Odd!" Tom snapped. "Mister, you're as crazy as a bedbug!"

"Perhaps," Davin smiled. "Another?"

"Don't mind if I do," Tom said automatically. "Look, Davin, if it's a question of price . . ."

"It is not," Davin said firmly. "I've had a good season this year. In that barn there—" he pointed with his fan—"is enough to tide me over until next year. Of course, I'll admit that that crop is the only thing standing between me and bankruptcy. But God has been kind. And, as I said before, there's the matter of my view. I find it priceless. You haven't enough money to buy that from me, Mister Benton. I doubt if there's that much money in the world."

"Well, I'll be damned," Tom said helplessly.

"I rather think you are," Davin said. "Any man so blind to beauty, so driven by his acquisitive instincts is most apt to be damned. Don't you ever think of anything but getting, Benton? After all, the hog is hardly the handsomest of animals. . . ."

Tom stood up, his eyes blue ice.

"You callin' me a hog, Davin?" he said.

"No. The simile was rather overdrawn. I withdraw it—and apologize—largely because I consider it beneath me to insult a guest in my own house. Sit down and stop looking so fierce. It's tiresome." He smiled. "You know, Benton, if I compared you to any animal, it wouldn't be a hog. A painter, perhaps—a black one. Or a tiger . . ."

Slowly Tom Benton grinned.

"A tiger, eh?" he said. "That's better—that's much better."

"I thought you'd like it," Davin said. "By the way, since you're so bent upon having your own steamboat landing, why don't you buy a piece of ground from one of those Cajun families north of here, from some of the white-trash squatters? There are plenty of other spots on the river."

"Not like this one," Tom said. "In the first place, you're directly in front of me. In the second, this is the first really clear stretch of water on the Red. Even though old Henry Shreve's been butting away at the logs and debris in the river with those steamboat rams of his for more'n five years, the stretch north of here is pretty tough going. From here on down to where the Red runs into the Mississippi just above the State line, it's clear sailing. If you had any sense, you'd build a landing yoreself."

"Or any money," Davin said; "that's the principal thing, isn't it?"

"Look, Davin," Tom said eagerly, "let me build a landing for you. Advance you the money, I mean—all I'd want out of it would be the right to cross yore place and use the landing with you. I wouldn't press you. Hell, man, you could pay me back when you got around to it. . . ."

"No," Davin said quietly.

"Of all the mule-stubborn! Would you mind telling me why not?"

"Not at all. I just don't like being beholden to any man. That's one thing. Another is that I'd have scant use of the landing, while your wagons would come rumbling through here all the time. I wouldn't like that. I like quiet."

Tom stood up.

"I reckon there's nothing more to be said," he growled.

"No," Davin said, "I don't suppose there is. But don't deprive us of the pleasure of your company just because we can't do business. Come and sup with us some evening and bring your good wife. Griselda has been pining to meet her. She's heard so much about her. . . ."

I'll bet she has, Tom thought angrily; but I'll see the both of you in hell afore I'll bring Sary over to be eyed by no uppity Virginia woman. . . . But he didn't say that. All he did say, mustering up the best show of manners he was capable of, was:

"Thank you kindly; I'll tell Sary." Then he mounted Prince Rupert and rode away.

There the matter might have rested, but for two things: Tom's stubbornness, and Griselda Henderson. Tom brooded over the state of affairs for a week, probing deep into his own consciousness to try to discover what Davin Henderson's real motives were, and how he might surmount them.

That Henderson had told him the truth, as he had; that there were men on earth uninterested in money, to whom the sweep of sky, a shaft of sunlight shredded by the moss, the river slow coiling like a golden snake in the distance, were beyond price, he was incapable of believing. More, he was incapable of even grasping the existence of such a frame of mind. He loved his own broad, sunlit fields with a total passion; but he would never admit to himself, did not in fact realize, that their lilting beauty had something to do with it. And if it had ever been forced upon his conscious mind that he, too, like every man living, was at least to a certain extent a worshiper of beauty, he would have been ashamed.

One of the things that troubled him most about his relationship with Lolette Dupré was that based as it was upon this subtlest of all hungers —the hunger for loveliness—he didn't understand it. "Damned if I know what I see in her," he told himself time after time. For Lolette lacked his prime requisite in a woman: she was not passionate. The savage, torrential, volcanic passion he was able to awake from time to time in Sarah, simply did not exist in Lolette. She submitted to his embraces; but more, he was sure, as a means to hold him than from any specific enjoyment of the act itself. She did not, of course, find it repugnant; she accepted it, as she accepted all of life, with gentle resignation. He wore himself into exhaustion trying to bring her to the moaning, sobbing state of ecstasy he was accustomed to triumphantly inflict upon Sarah and upon the other women he had known. When he could not, he accused her of being cold.

"But I am not cold," she protested; "I love you very much. I—I even like—this—very much. . . ."

"Why?" he demanded brutally. "You don't feel anything."

"Ah, but I do," she whispered; "the most lovely, wonderful feeling—like far-off music, sort of sacred, Tom—like—like tiny little bells. . . ."

"Damn!" he exploded; but he continued to meet her just the same. Her elfin, nightshade beauty held him, her gentle sweetness. But he didn't understand that. He couldn't.

On the other hand, Griselda Henderson, Davin Henderson's wife, was, he was sure, his kind of a woman. A mite bitchy, he thought with pleasure, the way a woman ought to be. . . . What he meant was that the relationship between a man and a woman was to him, in its essence, battle, conflict, war. A war, of course, which after several interesting preliminary skirmishes, the man inevitably won. "The wilder they are, the better I like 'em," he was fond of saying. He was, of course, not nearly so uncomplicated a man as he thought of himself as being; even his lusts were no simple hungers, but carried with them other facets of his being: his acquisitiveness, for he thought of a woman first and foremost as a possession, in much the same way that the Negroes were his possessions; his need for domination, for even in embracing a woman, he was conscious of the need for making her submit, of bending her to his will; and, perhaps most of all his cruelty, making the act of love for him a combat, in which the woman was beaten, ridden, broken in will and spirit, humiliated into an open

58

avowal of her animalism. . . . It was this that he could never find in Lolette. He could never make her cry out, look torn, exhausted, disheveled.

"Damn!" he said, "her hair don't even git out of place!"

But Griselda Henderson was another matter. He thought of her often now, his mind working on its highest level—which amounted to no more than instinctive, animal-like cunning. Git next to her, and I'll have that landing. Ain't nothing like a woman for pressuring her husband into something he don't want to do. . . .

So the next time he visited the Henderson plantation, if their few pitiful acres could be dignified by such a name, he was careful to choose a time when Davin would be away from the house, out in the fields, supervising his Negroes, since he could not afford to hire an overseer.

Griselda greeted him with frigid politeness.

"Come in, Mister Benton," she said. "I'll send one of the girls out for Davin."

"No, don't," Tom said quickly; "I'd like to talk to you a spell, Ma'am, if I may."

"Well," Griselda hesitated; "I can't imagine what you'd want to talk to me about; still . . ."

"The same thing I been talking to your husband about, Ma'am," Tom said. "I kind of thought that maybe I could swing you over to my side. When a woman sets her mind to persuading—a poor man ain't got a chance. . . ."

"I see," Griselda said flatly. "You want me to persuade Davin to sell you this place. My God, but you're a stubborn man, Mister Benton. How many times do you have to be told we like it here?"

"You'd like it somewheres else just as well, Ma'am," Tom said patiently; "a mite better to my way of reckoning. 'Cause with the money I'm willing to pay yore husband, you could git yoreselves some really good land. Afford to dress in silks and satins, then, Ma'am. Wear the kind of clothes that'll do justice to yore beauty. For if you don't mind my saying so, Ma'am, you're one mighty pretty woman."

"As a matter of fact," Griselda said icily, "I do mind your saying so. I like compliments—every woman does. But coming from you, it's no compliment—it's an insult!"

"Well, I'll be damned!" Tom said in pure amazement.

"Nor do I like your language," Griselda snapped. "I'm afraid, Mister Benton, I shall have to ask you to go—now!"

Tom stood there, grinning.

"High 'n' mighty, ain't you?" he said. "Thought you'd take a bit of gentling. And there ain't nothing I like better—nothing a-tall!"

Then he moved forward and seized her, pinning her arms to her sides with his left arm, raising his right hand to imprison her face, to stop the wild thrashing of her head. She didn't say anything, she just went on fighting like a wild woman, like a thing possessed, until he held her helpless, bending his big head down to find her mouth. It was then that she did the thing that was to him inconceivable, impossible, for already he was quite sure of himself. He had had women fight him before, but always before the very ones who fought the hardest became in the space of half an hour, less than half an hour, usually, the moaning, disheveled, female-smelling she-things, used and broken, which always awoke in him a faint feeling of disgust. So it was that he was savoring in anticipation his triumph, when Griselda Henderson opened her mouth and spat full into his face.

He released her at once, and stepped back, groping for his handkerchief. He wiped his face and stood there staring at her, unaware of the fact that he was trembling.

"I shan't tell my husband," Griselda said quietly, "because he'd want to fight you, and he might be killed. But I'll say this, Tom Benton—I hope you've learned something. I know all your experience has been with these river-basin whores; but now, you've met a Virginian. We don't shame our husbands. The vows we take are sacred. So go home now to the kind you're used to, go home to the woman you whored with, whose husband you killed, and . . ."

Her figure wavered, blurred before his sight. His head was surrounded by intolerable heat; he was suffocating, stifling. Her voice was an indistinct babble in his ears.

"Shut up!" he roared at her. "Don't you foul my Sary with your lying, filthy mouth! Don't you dare!"

"Chivalrous, aren't you?" she mocked. "Or are you just afraid? You have a right to be—for the time will come when she'll serve you the same way she did her first husband. Adultery gets to be a habit, I'm told. . . ."

Something burst inside Tom's brain at her words. He saw with curious detachment his big hand fly out; he heard it explode open-palmed against her face with a noise like a pistol shot, and her going down in a crumpled heap before him, lying there. Then the rage was all gone, and there was nothing in his veins but ice. He bent down to pick her up, shaking all over from the reaction and the chill.

"Don't touch me!" she snarled at him. "Don't put your dirty hands on me!" She came up into a sitting position. "Unbelievable!" she whispered; "they told me there were men like you. . . ." Then in a sudden, renewed surge of fury she screamed at him: "Get out! And if ever you come back again, I shall shoot you, myself—through the belly like a dog! Get out, you hear me! Get!"

And Tom Benton went.

He did not go home. He was in no state to face Sarah. Instead, he went to the little saloon in Benton's Row where he often spent his evenings, basking in the warm approval of the poorwhites, buying them drinks, pontificating a little before them—the great man before his inferiors, the Patron surrounded by his Clients. Not that they realized they were being patronized. Rather they thought Mister Benton a hell of a

60

fine fellow, a slashing *beau sabreur*, but with no pretenses: "Nothing grand about him, no sirreebobtail! Stands right up there and drinks his pop-skull with the next man passin' the jug from mouth to mouth and swapping yarns with the best!"

But tonight, he was too quiet, and after a time they noticed it. They were about their usual pleasures, the less violent ones at least, for the usual pleasures of the poorwhite included such niceties as biting off the nose or gouging out the eye of a favorite enemy, or beguiling the tedium of a hot afternoon by soaking a woolly dog in turpentine, setting him afire, and turning him loose to run to the vast amusement of all the spectators. Tonight they were confining themselves to their quieter amusements. At the end of the bar, one of them was standing on his head while his fellows timed him with the big watch they had borrowed from the saloonkeeper. Two or three scraggly, unkempt pine-barren men were having a whiskey-drinking contest, seeing how much they could down at a gulp, without taking the bottle from their lips, the loser to pay for all the liquor consumed. In the middle of the floor, several others were vying with each other for the tobacco-spitting championship of the parish—the target a row of spittoons, aimed at with deadly precision from chalk marks drawn on the floor; at each round the distance between the marks and the spittoons being increased until the weaker practitioners of the back-country art of expectoration began to fall by the wayside. Outside, an iron-jawed countryman had just taken the loose silver of all and sundry by lifting a hogshead of flour clear of the banquette with his teeth.

Tom, but lately escaped from their ranks himself, always felt at home among them. He enjoyed their simple pleasures hugely. And if he now felt it beneath his new-found dignity as a planter to indulge in them, he none the less spurred the poorwhites on, encouraging them, and buying them drinks, first for the winners, for having won, then for the losers, as consolation for having lost, and ultimately for the whole house, for the hell of it. They accepted him, not as one of themselves, but as something more: a father-image, actually, clan chieftain; regarding him as *primus inter pares*, they fell quite naturally into the habit of honoring him, deferring to his knowledge and judgment, consulting him on every occasion, and looking to him for leadership and opinion—all of which warmed the cockles of Tom's heart.

And not only Tom. They felt that way about most of the planters, knowing them intimately, hunting with them, eating from time to time at the big house, not infrequently sleeping there; for the planters, instinctively realizing that in the coming struggle with the Yankee they were going to need the common white, were sagacious enough to make the social lines most elastic. More, in the sparsely settled back country the poorwhites were often related to the big planter by blood, no further removed, at times, than the first or second degree of cousinship, so that the planters' attempt in the presence of Yankee guests to explain them as a different breed, children of redemptioners, bondsmen, debtor-prison scourings, was, in part at least, a lie. But only in part. Such were some of their ancestors; but, on the other hand, such were some of his. And to complicate matters the more, not too rarely, a lank, scraggly, clay-eating countryman could claim in truth a lineage to put the best of theirs to shame. Men rise. Men fall. It was as simple as that.

But it had not occurred to Tom Benton consciously, any more than it occurred consciously to the other great planters to actually use the poor-white. His morose mood that night was genuine. He had been wounded in his tenderest, his most vulnerable part: his pride. A woman had scorned him, and he was unaccustomed to being scorned. A man had balked his dearest ambition, and there was nothing he could do about it —absolutely nothing at all.

They noticed it, finally. Zeke Hawkins shifted his chaw of tobacco from one side of his cavernous jaw to the other and nudged one of his fellows.

"Sumpin's bothering Mister Tom," he said. "Ain't never seed him look so down in the mouth before."

The others nodded in sage agreement.

"Go ax him, Zeke," Lem Toliver said: "maybe we kin help him out a bit."

Zeke walked over to where Tom sat, brooding over his glass of bourbon.

"What's the matter, Mister Tom?" he demanded with that perfect, idiot's gravity which was so much the mark of his breed.

"Oh—Zeke! Sit down and join me. Tim, another of the same for Zeke here. . . ."

"You're looking mighty poorly, Mister Tom," Zeke said. "Don't reckon I ever seed you looking so sad like afore."

"I've got troubles, Zeke," Tom sighed.

"Tell me about 'em," Zeke said promptly. "Maybe I kin figure something."

Tom's natural impulse was to laugh. But he did not. Instead, for no better reason than a very human need to get the whole thing off his chest, he told Zeke the story, omitting, of course, the tale of his encounter with Griselda.

"And the worst part about it," Tom finished, "is that the land is no good to him. He ain't no planter. Wasn't for a few miserable bales he's got in his barn, he'd be bankrupt right now. I wish to hell lightning would strike that barn o' his'n. . . ."

"Why?" Zeke said.

"Because then he'd have to sell, don't you see? Or else Hilton would take him over and I could buy the land from him. Damned Virginia bastard!"

"Hmmmn," Zeke said. "Thankee fur the snort, Mister Tom. Thankee mighty kindly."

So it was that Tom was entirely unprepared for Davin Henderson's descent upon him the next day. The Virginian came riding into Tom's lower acres, surrounded by all five of his blacks.

"There he is," he said coldly, as soon as he saw Tom. "Grab him!"

The five big Negroes swarmed all over Tom holding him with their big, work-hardened hands. For the second time in two days, Tom Benton was completely outraged. First a woman had spat in his face; and now a man had set his niggers upon him—niggers, by God!

"What in hell'sfire!" he roared. "Davin, you gonna pay for this!"

Davin sat on his horse, a smile lighting his pale, cynical face.

"I suppose you don't know," he said quietly, "that my barn was burned to the ground last night? I suppose you are completely disinterested in the fact that I am now a bankrupt—that I have no other recourse but to turn over my lands to your so very close friend, Mister Hilton?"

Tom stared at him, dawning comprehension showing in his face.

"Zeke!" he said aloud, the name escaping him before he had time to stifle the impulse.

"Ah, so you did know!" Davin smiled. Then very slowly he began to uncoil the big mule-skinner's whip he had coiled around the pommel of his saddle. "Under ordinary circumstances, considering your exalted position as a planter, I would challenge you, Mister Benton. But I won't dignify dirt by meeting it on the field of honor, no matter how high its pretensions. So, Mister Benton, I'm merely going to flay the living hide off of you. Perhaps, who knows? I might even be able to awake in you some small appreciation for the meaning of the words, honor, and decency. . . . Rufe, snatch that coat off of him!"

The command was a mistake. The removal of one pair of black hands from his arms was all Tom Benton needed. Veteran of a hundred barroom brawls, he was in his element now. The Negroes, big men, strong men that they were, knew nothing of the art of dirty fighting, and of that art Tom Benton was past master. He moved with sudden, savage violence, bringing his knee up between a black's thighs, and the man lay on the ground moaning, clutching the tenderest parts of his body; and Tom, still moving, the motion uninterrupted, unbroken, one blow flowing into the next, an elbow to the solar plexus, two fingers bridging a blunt nose, ramming hard into a field hand's eyes, a fist brought up almost from the ground to smash against a black jaw, and he was free, tugging at the shoulder holster where he kept his equalizer; but the shoulder holster, a concession to his new elegance, defeated him. The Colt stuck. Once more, Davin Henderson smiled.

"I regret to have to do this," he said, and shot Tom Benton through the body with the derringer he carried loose in his side pocket, firing through the pocket itself without even drawing the gun. He sat there on his horse, looking at the sprawling body of his foe. He sighed deeply.

"Come," he said to his Negroes, "I guess we'll have to get out of the State after this. . . ."

5

WHEN, HALF an hour later, Jim Rudgers and the Negroes brought Tom to the house, Sarah did not scream or faint. She simply stood there, and her face whitened to the roots of her hair.

"Is—is he—alive?" she whispered.

"Yes, Ma'am," Jim Rudgers said grimly; "but he ain't got long, I don't think. . . ."

"Bring him in," Sarah said.

They laid him down on the big bed, and Sarah began to loosen his clothes. She turned to one of the field hands.

"Take off his boots," she commanded. Then, to one of the house maids, who was standing goggle eyed in the doorway:

"Bring me my scissors. Tell Marie to put water on to boil—get some cloths—hurry, damn you!"

Jim stood there watching as she cut the blood-soaked clothing away from the wound. It was low on the left side, and it still bled sullenly.

Sarah looked up at Jim, her gray eyes questioning.

"If," Jim said, "it missed the big gut, and if you kin stop that there bleedin', and if I kin find that damned sawbones in time, and if he kin find the ball, and if he knows what the hell to do after he finds it. . . . A mighty heap of ifs, Miz Benton; but I'll try. . . ."

"Do," Sarah said.

Jim Rudgers hesitated.

"Ain't you even interested in who done it?" he said.

"No. I'd rather not know. Since it was some woman's husband—I'd rather not. . . ."

"Thought you'd think that," Jim said. "But it warn't that, Ma'am. It were Davin Henderson, and the quarrel was over land and a barn burning. . . ."

He could see some of the tension go out of her face.

"And Davin was wrong. Tom never sent nobody to burn no barn. That ain't his style. He's more straightforward like. So long, Ma'am; I'll be back directly."

Sarah didn't even hear him go. She was much too busy. It took a dozen cold compresses to stop the bleeding. After that, Sarah bandaged the wound, and sat down beside Tom to wait. There was nothing else she could do. If only I could get a little whiskey into him, she thought. But she knew she couldn't. To drink a man must be at least semiconscious. She could hear the grandfather clock in the hall ticking. The ticks got louder and louder and louder until they were crashing like thunderclaps

64

against her ears. Outside the window, a leaf drifted down from the oak, and whispered against the windowpane. She jumped at the sound. It was too still, so still that her ears ached from the thunderous noises of silence: the clock ticks, a board creaking as a servant tiptoed across it, the rustle of her own breathing, the drumroll of her heart.

"Dear Lord," she prayed; "he ain't a good man—I know that. He's a mean, wicked, cruel kind of a man; but he's all I got. And he's my children's paw. And—and God, You understand me; You made me with my blood hotter'n fire and no wits in my head. . . . What I'm tryin' to say is that I love him, God—You can't take him away from me! God, You can't!"

Then she put down her head and cried.

Two centuries later, Jim came back with Randy McGregor, the young doctor, having been unable to find old Doc Muller. Sarah did not know it then, but chance, fate, destiny, the unpredictable, the incalculable element, which, like most people, she ordinarily disregarded, had entered in. For Doc Muller was old, tired, and a good bit of a humbug; while young Doctor McGregor was fresh out of Edinburgh, where, above all else, they taught a man surgery. Hearing their footsteps in the hall, she ran to meet them, seeing in a flash of quiet astonishment by the grandfather clock that only a little over two hours had passed; then she saw the red, freckled face of the young doctor and stopped dead.

"Don't worry, Ma'am," Randy McGregor said; "I won't kill him—that is, if he isn't dead already. . . ."

"Come," Sarah said. Then, looking back over her shoulder, she saw the sway in his walk, and turned upon him, waiting until he was close enough so that the heavy whiskey fog of his breath enveloped her, and then she was sure.

"Why," she said, "you're drunk!"

"Wouldn't be surprised," Randy said. "I quite often am. . . ."

"But you can't!" she got out; "I won't let you touch . . ."

"Listen, Ma'am," Randy said quietly, "I happen to be the best damned surgeon in this State—drunk or sober. But if it bothers you, you can go make me a pot of black coffee—and you can boil some water, lots of water—that should keep you out of my way for a while. . . ."

He entered the bedroom and looked at Tom.

"Hmmnn," he said. "Bad. He's lost a good bit too much blood. Who dressed that wound?"

"I did," Sarah whispered.

"Damn good job—Now go get me that coffee and some hot water." He looked at Jim Rudgers.

"Help me to turn him over," he said.

Jim stared.

"That's where that ball is," Randy explained patiently. "If it didn't come out the back of him, it's still a hell of a lot closer to the back than the front. That was almost point-blank range—and even a derringer ball should have gone clean through, except, which God forbid, it hit bone. . . ."

Carefully, they rolled him over. Randy reached for his satchel. Then he saw Sarah standing in the doorway.

"I'd thank you to leave, Ma'am," he said; "this isn't going to be pretty."

"I can stand it," Sarah whispered.

"All right," Randy said; "but if you faint, by God I'm going to leave you lying there, and get on with my work."

"I won't faint," Sarah said.

The ball hadn't come out; Randy looked at the wound, squinting at it with one eye to observe the angle of penetration.

"Just about here," he said; "bet you this rib stopped it." He made a quick, neat incision, and pushed in the probes, turning them so that they were underneath the rib. The blood gushed out, dyeing his hands. Then he withdrew the probes and the bullet was in them. It was a little flattened, but not much. The thirteen grains of powder ordinarily loaded into a derringer hadn't that much force.

He worked very fast, bandaging the wounds. Then he straightened up, smiling. The whole thing had taken him a shade under seven minutes.

When Sarah came back with the coffee, he smiled at her.

"Thank you, Mrs. Benton," he said; "I'm all done with him, now."

"Will he—?" Sarah murmured.

"That's hard to say. He should live. He looks as strong as an ox. But infection might set in. I've packed the wounds with lint so they won't close too fast."

"What about his insides?" Jim Rudgers growled. "Reckon that ball hit the big gut?"

"That worries me, I must confess," Randy sighed. "And he's in no shape for me to do an exploratory. But there's one sure way of knowing."

"What's that?" Sarah said.

"I'm sorry, Mrs. Benton; but if the intestinal wall was pierced, he'll be dead by this time tomorrow night. If he isn't, he has a chance, a rather good chance, I'd say."

He downed the coffee in one gulp, hot as it was; then he stood up.

"If you'll allow me, Ma'am," he said, "I'll stay the night. I'm not too busy. Most people in these parts think a doctor has to be at least sixty before he's good."

"I'd be glad to," Sarah said; "I'll put you in the guest room."

"Excuse me," Randy said; "but if you have an extra bed, I'd rather you'd have some of the blacks move it in here. I'd like to be on hand. It might make a lot of difference. . . ."

"Is it that bad?" Jim Rudgers whispered after Sarah had gone to get the Negroes.

"Yes," Randy McGregor said; "it's that bad."

Later, when he was stretched out in the small bed, placed at the foot of the one in which Tom Benton lay, Randy McGregor thoughtfully extracted a bottle of bourbon from his satchel. As he opened it, he stared at his patient.

Strange, he thought. I'm a doctor. All my life I've worked toward an objective viewpoint. But I don't like this man. I don't understand it. I don't know him. I came here and did my work upon an inert hulk of flesh —not dead, but unliving in any real sense of the word—lacking everything, mannerisms, ideas, opinions, anything at all that should cause me to react to him. And I quite definitely don't like him.

He raised the bottle to his lips and took a good, long pull. Then he put the bottle down. He knew then that he wasn't going to drink any more. That, for the first time since he had fled Scotland, pursued Orestes-like by his private Furies, he had no desire for liquor. He considered Tom Benton gravely.

"It's not the stories I've heard," he mused. "I heard them long ago, and they didn't matter. I didn't know him then—and I don't know him now. Then why in hellfire do I have this feeling? And I can't even define the feeling itself—except to say I sense somehow that in saving this man's life, I'm doing the world a disservice—the world, and myself. That's it—that's the crux of it—there's something personal involved—but what?"

He worried it over in his mind, but he could make nothing of it. He had to give it up finally; but it kept him awake for a long time, and afterwards, it troubled his dreams.

It was not until two weeks later, after he had become an accepted member of the household, that he began to realize what his feeling was, and from what source it came. He had had to stay on, for Tom Benton did not die that next night, nor any of the nights that followed; but lingered on in a trancelike coma, between sleep and waking; between life and death.

Randy was sitting on the gallery, a glass in his hand as usual, puzzling the matter over once more in his mind, when Sarah came out. He got to his feet at once.

"No, sit right back down," she said; "I'll sit a spell with you. The girls have got the cleaning going right pert—and Tom seems all right. He looks stronger today."

She sat down in a big rocker, turning it so it faced him.

"Doctor McGregor," she said; "why do you drink so much? You're a young man and a good doctor—a heap better one to my way of thinking than old Doc Muller. So why do you have to drink?"

Suddenly, unaccountably, under the level gaze of her soft gray eyes, he found himself telling her. He could see her expressive face growing paler during his recital; but he could not stop. He had held it in too long, and it had to come out now—it had to.

"So I came back from Edinburgh," he finished; "and I found that she was gone from my house. She was living quite openly with her lover in a house a few streets away. There was even—a child. I went through hell. I thought of killing the man, killing her—and myself. But there was the child. In the end, I did nothing. Divorced her, of course, started drinking, drifted down to England, then to Canada, New York—and finally here—God knows why. Perhaps I'm looking for something. . . ."

He was aware then that she was crying.

"Oh, I say," he got out, "I'm so sorry. That was beastly of me. I'm sure I didn't mean to . . ."

"It's not yore story," she whispered. "Reckon I'm too selfish to cry over other folks' sorrows. It just reminded me too much. . . ."

She raised her eyes to his face.

"I did that to a man once," she said; "with—with Tom. I didn't know what I was doing, didn't care really—couldn't help myself. But my first husband, he was a preacher, and he lost his religion over what I done. In the end, he killed hisself; put the barrels of a shotgun in his mouth and—"

"I know," Randy said harshly.

"Oh!" she whispered and her eyes were very big. "I reckon you think I'm a mighty bad woman. . . ."

"I don't judge people," Randy said. "I'm a doctor, not God."

She sat there, staring at him. Then suddenly, impulsively, she put her hand over his where it rested on the arm of his chair.

"She was a fool," she said. "You're a nice man, Doctor. Nicest man I ever did meet, I reckon. . . ."

"Nicer than—Tom?" he said.

She stiffened a little, drew away her hand. He could see her considering the thought.

"Yes," she said at last, "ever so much nicer. But that ain't hard. Tom's a devil, kind of . . ." She looked down at the floor a moment, then back at him, steadily. "The only trouble is—I love him," she said. Then, abruptly, she stood up. "Reckon I'll be going now," she said; "don't do to leave them nigger gals alone too long."

He sat there very still after she had gone. He knew now. Then, at that moment, quite suddenly, and perfectly, he knew.

It was the day after that one that Tom Benton regained consciousness. Sarah came and told Randy about it. He didn't say anything; he just got up and went into the bedroom. When he came out again, he said:

"He's going to be all right now. Not much use in my staying around any more. I'll stop by once in a while to check. . . ."

But he did not finish his thought. Something in Sarah's eyes held him—something wild and deep and unfathomable.

"Don't go," she said; "not for a spell leaseways. S'posin' he was to take a turn for the worst? He's still so weak, Doctor. . . ."

Randy studied her.

"All right," he said quietly; "I'll stay."

He turned abruptly and walked away from her. Sarah stood there, looking after him.

"Now why on earth did I ax him to stay?" she thought. "I don't need him—I don't. I could manage Tom just as easy—Lord, Lord, what a mixed-up, foolish kind of a woman I am!"

But afterwards she was glad she had asked him; for, curiously, Tom's improvement was very slow. Sarah could not understand it, nor could Randy McGregor, because it was a thing beyond their times, beyond their knowledge, and even their instinctual sympathies: that the wound which held Tom Benton captive to his bed was not the fast-healing gunshot in his flesh, but the deeper, hidden, more abiding sore that festered in his spirit, was not, perhaps, beyond their powers of comprehension; it simply lay too far outside of ordinary experience for them to grasp it.

But lying there, silent, brooding, Tom, himself grasped it. He even understood it. And it was the very completeness and perfection of his understanding that defeated him. He had been scorned, doubly scorned, by a woman he had wanted; and by a man who had held him in such contempt as to set his Negroes upon him. More, given the opportunity to take his proper vengeance, he had failed, had been shot down like a dog, and his assailant had escaped, gotten clean away, fled to Mississippi or Texas, and rested there, savoring no doubt, the sweet memory of his victory.

And this, moreover, for a thing that he, Tom Benton, had not done; had not, in sober truth, even thought of doing. There was, of course, something else: deep down there remained a bitter confusion in Tom's soul. The idea clung that what he had been accused of was not totally lacking in justice; he was, he knew, quite capable of it, and worse. He would have, had the thought occurred to him, burned a hundred barns to get that land—and all this mingled with an acid tinge of regret that he had not thought of doing so. . . .

So he refused food, and lay there staring in morose distemper at the ceiling, speaking little if at all—until that day when a new idea penetrated the black morass of his obsessions. He was lying there, while Randy examined him. Sarah sat by the bedside, watching. Then, the examination finished, Randy raised his eyes to hers. He started to speak; but suddenly, startlingly, he could not. He passed his tongue over dry lips; but that was not where the failure lay. He was lost, drowned in the gray pools of her eyes. And she, too, sitting there looking at him was conscious of something —something she could not put into words, but that was infinitely deep, sad, disturbing. She had the feeling that if her life depended upon it, she could not turn her gaze from his. It was more than a feeling. It was fact. She could not.

And Tom Benton, lying there, saw that look that passed between them, and a legion of fiends waged warfare in his soul. He sank fathoms deep into icy terror; for Sarah was his world, his life. He was constantly unfaithful to her in the flesh; but he had never been unfaithful to her in spirit. He was disturbed by Lolette Dupré because the relationship between them was too like love, had too much of an element of tenderness in it; which was a thing he could not define.

Only with Lolette did he sometimes have the uneasy feeling that he was betraying Sarah; the others were nothing, a sport, a game to while away the idle hours. But Sarah, he loved; more, he honored her—falling easily into the Southern habit of venerating its womanhood to stifle the pangs of shame and self-loathing at the lusts that drove them even into the slave cabins to take their fill of the fiery and complaisant Negro women; until he came finally to almost believe his protestations, to think in the natural Southern haze of romantic revery that she was indeed something of a goddess, something to be enthroned, worshiped, held even above himself. And this Sarah aided by her lessening interest in pure passion; for she had three now to divide her heart among; growing older, she was also growing less simple, her emotions existing now on many levels, so that the early, basic need to have her man had grown weaker, though sometimes it surged back again. Now, finding her less carnal than himself, Tom came to think her better; as in fact, she was, and always had been, only the idea itself was new.

So, his first reaction was one of terror at the thought of losing her. But his second was rage, black murderous rage at this man who dared lay hands even in thought upon the temple and fount of his idolatry, the chiefest of all his possessions. But he lay there and did not show it; his mind was working coolly, clearly, soberly.

Got to get well now. Got to eat—going to need my strength. Been laying here brooding over what was done to me, and while I was wasting my time, I was running the risk of being done to some more. Sarah's good, but this red-haired bastard gets to her. Damn my soul if I ever thought to see . . .

Lucinda, Sarah's maid came silently into the doorway. She coughed discreetly; and it was by this, at last, that the spell was broken.

"Mister Hilton's outside," she said. "Says if Marse Tom is strong enough, he'd like to talk to him."

"I'm strong enough all right," Tom growled; "I'm a heap stronger than a lot of folks would think."

Randy and Sarah both stared at him. It was the first time since he had been wounded that his voice had risen above a croaking whisper. They were both conscious of something else in it—an edge, perhaps, or a rasp like a file being drawn across steel.

Randy stood up.

"I don't think you'll have any further need of me now," he said. "I'll drop in from time to time to check. But I think you've found what you needed."

"And what's that?" Tom said.

"Something to give you the will to live," Randy McGregor said.

"Know what it is?" Tom demanded.

"No," Randy said easily, "I can't say I do."

70

"A man crossed me and got away with it," Tom said slowly. "That's what's been keeping me down. But it comes to me that there's a few other polecats with ideas about crossing me some more in the back part of their heads. Crossing me in a way a mighty heap more serious than Davin Henderson did. . . . Reckon I better get up from here. My trigger finger's getting rusty. Kind of think I could do with a mite of target practice—if you get what I mean. . . ."

"No," Randy said, "I don't get what you mean—not that it interests me. But I agree with you: shooting polecats is a fine sport—big polecats, Mister Benton, as well as small ones. Good-bye now—I guess I'll be moving along."

Sarah got up.

"I—I'll help you get your things together," she said.

Tom started to protest, to say that one of the house servants could do that just as well; but he checked himself. Give them enough rope, he thought grimly; after all I'd better know just where Sary stands. Then, unbidden, Griselda Henderson's words came flooding back: 'Afraid? You have a right to be—for the time will come when she'll serve you the same way she did her first husband. Adultery gets to be a habit, I'm told. . . .' He lay very still; but his hands gripped the coverlet until the knuckles whitened from the strain.

"Howdy, Tom," Hilton said from the doorway. "Hell—you look all right to me. Told me down in town the devil was stoking up his number one pit; but I can see they're dead wrong."

"I," Tom said flatly, "am going to live to bury the lot of them. Sit down, Hilt, and tell me what's on your evil mind."

"Something that's going to please you right smart," Hilton grinned. "Got a letter yesterday from your dear friend, Davin Henderson. No return address of course; but posted somewheres in Mississippi. Says he won't be able to pay, and instructed me to take over his place. Told me I could sell however I wanted to, because he was certain sure your widow wouldn't have no interest in steamboat landings."

"The bastard," Tom chuckled. "Reckon I got him by the short hairs at last, even if I did have to get shot to do it."

"Tom," Hilton said, "tell me the truth. Did you send some of them clay-eating swampers to burn his barn?"

"'Fore God, no!" Tom said. "I never even thought of it. I was sitting in the saloon looking kind of down in the mouth, and one of them pine-barren boys came up to me and asked me what was the matter. So I told him. And when Davin came riding down here with his niggers aiming to horsewhip me, you could of knocked me over with a feather!"

"You mean they took it upon themselves to help you out?"

"Exactly. You know I'm always good to those boys. I stand for their drinks and go hunting with them and such like. Reckon they felt they owed me a favor. But I didn't even hint at it, let alone tell them to do it."

"I see," Hilton grinned. "You can still skirt closer to the edge of the law

71

than any other man I ever heard tell of and get away with it. . . . Feel up to talking details of that business?"

"No. Just transfer it over to me. Then bill my account. But stay within reason, won't you? That land ain't worth much."

"To you," Hilton said, "it's worth every penny I can stick you for. But considering what a hard time I have getting money out of you now, I'll be kind of considerate."

He stood up, put out his hand.

"Be seeing you, Tom," he said.

It took only a few minutes for Sarah to get Randy McGregor's things together. He stood there, silently, watching her, the two of them enveloped in a painful kind of constraint. Then he took up the saddlebag and his satchel and followed her out on the gallery.

"I've sent one of the boys after your horse," Sarah said.

Randy didn't answer. He stood there, looking at her.

"You can send us the bill," Sarah said, lamely.

"There's no charge," he said, harshly.

She brought her eyes up, wide with questioning.

"It was easy and simple," Randy said. "I did little for him. And—I don't like getting paid for something I did against my will."

"Against your will?" Sarah whispered.

"Yes," Randy snapped. "For since I've seen you, Sarah, I wish your husband were dead and in hell—where he belongs!"

Sarah stared at him.

"You oughtn't of said that," she said slowly. "That was a mighty ugly thing to say, Doctor McGregor—"

"Randy to you, please!"

"All right, Randy. But it was still an ugly thing to say."

"But true," Randy said. "Ugly as truth often is."

"You mustn't come back," Sarah said. "I'll tend to him. I—I think he knows—how you feel. . . ."

"And how you feel?"

She stiffened under his gaze. Then she looked away from him to the drive down which one of the Negro boys came now, leading his horse.

"I asked you a question," Randy McGregor said.

"I—I can't answer that, Randy."

"Afraid to?"

"No. I—I just don't know!"

"Then I'll help you find out," Randy said grimly, and stepping forward, took her in his arms. She didn't fight, she just stared up at him, her gray eyes slowly closing, as his face came down, shutting out line, feature, coloring by its nearness, shutting out the world, time, thought.

In the hallway, Henry Hilton came to a soundless halt.

When she could breathe again, when time itself came sighing back into existence, Sarah stepped back a little. She stood there in the circle of his arms, looking at him, and ever so slowly, the great tears spilled over her lashes, and made two bright tracks down her face.

"You'd better go," she said.

"All right," Randy said harshly; "but now you know."

"I know," Sarah got out, "just one thing: I mustn't never see you again —not never!"

"Why?" Randy whispered.

"Because now I am scairt. I wasn't before; but I sure Lord am now. And I've got more than enough sin on my soul. Go, Randy—please go!"

Randy stood there a long moment, a little smile lighting his eyes. Then he bowed to her, a little mockingly. He picked up his bags and marched down the stair.

In the hallway, Hilton hugged himself in pure delight. Well, I'll be damned, he thought happily; I'll be ring tailed, double damned! But if ever a man had that coming to him, it's you, Tom Benton!

He stepped out on the gallery. Sarah whirled, her eyes big with terror.

" 'Scuse me, Ma'am," Hilton said gallantly. "Didn't mean to frighten you. Didn't even know you was there, in fact. Reckon I'm getting kind of old. My sight ain't what it used to be—nor my hearing. . . . Well, so long now, Ma'am—be seeing you . . ."

" 'Bye, Mister Hilton," Sarah said. Then she turned, and fled, wildly, back into the house.

6

THE YEARS, going, were a kind of bleeding, draining the strength out of a man. Tom Benton knew that, now. He knew, thought about, accepted many things that he hadn't before: that life itself is a long, slow dying; that you couldn't ever win, really, even when you thought yourself conqueror, you were already slipping imperceptibly over the line into the ranks of the vanquished. There were the days that crept up out of the bayou mist, and stole into night going down in swamp haze to the sound of a whimpering wind; there were the days that came up in trumpet blasts of sun and flamed down a red sky into darkness heralded by the wild fowls' honking. There were the dreaming days with the coonhounds mourning through the pine wood, and turtledoves talking darkly in the oak tops, with the sunwash taking the edges off everything so that the difference between what was, and what was not, became unclear. But they all had one thing in common: they went.

They went, and with their going bled the strength out of a man—so slowly that he did not feel its loss, feeling himself the same, Tom Benton, rampaging over the earth, ravishing the world, fighting, loving, taking—

until he tried to do exactly and precisely the things he had done before; finding, indeed that he could do them still; but without his former ease: that battle lacked its savage joy, each victory leaving him a little more gasping-spent, a shade nearer to defeat; that love itself had lost its savor, so that women who formerly would have caused his eye to sparkle, his pulse to quicken, passed him by without awakening so much as a glance. More, he no longer wanted things so much. He was letting opportunities slide by, and cursing himself for so doing, yet not caring really, feeling in his bones, that he had enough, that—and this was the worst, the most damning thought of all—the things he had gotten at so much cost in time, in effort, in pain, were not really worth what they had cost, becoming himself the man encamped upon the mountain peak, gained by the most arduous and heartbreaking labor, knowing with absolute certainty and sorrow that all roads lead down, that the journey downward into night, defeat, death, is encompassed about with all the crevices, precipices, perils, struggles of the climb itself, and himself, enfeebled, facing that, with no incentive toward the struggle, with no rewards in the offing, except the final lassitude of surrender, the promise at long last of rest. And the rebellious spark within him still struggled against this—the unwillingness to give up life, the instinct to fight on, but growing dimmer now, the day of acceptance approaching. . . .

So it was that he sat now with Randy McGregor at a table in the saloon that fall day in 1854, thinking how only a few years before he had been certain that sooner or later he would have to kill the young Scotsman. Now, looking at Randy, he smiled dryly, because he not only no longer had any conceivable excuse for murder; but could not even imagine any circumstances where the thing would be necessary or feasible. Under his back-country code, you could only take action when your rival had committed some overt act, some open assault upon your honor; and Randy had done nothing, nor was he likely to.

Ought to blast him just the same, he thought with grim self-mockery; if a man is what he thinks, like the Good Book says, Randy McGregor ought to be dead. Ain't *you* what kept the horns off me, is it, boy? Neither you, nor Sary, but a man what's dead. Warn't for Preacher Tyler a-moldering in his grave, I wouldn't know now where the two of you had lit. 'Taint me what's prevented it, but Sary's shame at doing twicet a thing that cost so much the first time. . . .

Yet, the strange relationship amused him. He cultivated the younger man, sought his company, kept, in fact, an eye upon him. And Doctor McGregor knew it, playing in his turn, with the same grim amusement his part in the comedy that skimmed forever upon tragedy's very edge.

Even during the war they had been together; for Tom had not dared enlist until he had learned that Randy had already done so. At Buena Vista, that dress rehearsal for future glory, where Braxton Bragg had raked the Mexican forces with artillery fire, and old Zach Taylor's son-in-law, Jefferson Davis, had given the order to charge, getting a ball through his foot for his pains and thereby gaining national renown which was to lead him on to a darker immortality than even he had dreamed of, they had both distinguished themselves: Randy by the cool heroism with which he had tended the wounded under fire, and Tom by his reckless, roaring, full-throated courage.

And that, strangely, had formed the basis of their new relationship; for, after that, each of them respected the other with that profound respect that one brave man has for another. They were not friends, even now, nor were they enemies; they were something less, and something more; bound to each other by their love of the same woman, held in fragile equilibrium by tenuous, insubstantial things: Randy's honor, Sarah's fearful memories, Tom's allegiance to a code which could only take vengeance after the fact, never before, however certain he might be of both desire and contemplation. Somewhere, some time, something had to give way, had to break; but until then, they waited—and watched.

"Been a long time, ain't it, boy?" Tom said. And Randy, holding his glass almost level with his lips, nodded, then gulped the fiery liquor down.

"Too long," he said.

"Funny you ain't never married," Tom baited; "fine upstanding young fellow like you."

Randy studied him.

"I," he said evenly, "have never found a woman who suited me, and who was—free."

Tom grinned at him, but didn't answer. That was a part of the game, part of the slow, deadly duel they fought with each other, each time they met. They both knew the limits, and the rules. When one of them pushed it a little too far, as Randy had done now, the other retreated. For they could not bring it to a conclusion and they knew it; not by words, talk, a provoked quarrel. Only Sarah could do that—by making a choice; and the choice, actually, was not left with her: a dead man held it in his skeletal hands.

Funny about women, Tom thought. They're a mighty heap of trouble when they don't mean nothing to you—and when they do, they're worse. Lolette, now—didn't think she meant so much to me; but Gawddammit how it hurt when I came back and found her gone!

"What are you thinking about?" Randy demanded.

"Nothing. No—that ain't so. I was thinking about a girl I was in love with once. You brought her to mind when you said that about not being free. Sweetest little thing you ever did see—gentle-like and loving. Her folks warn't much, swampers and such like. But her paw brought her up to be a lady, educated and fine. Then she ran afoul of me. . . ."

"Poor thing," Randy mocked.

"Yep. Poor thing. Only she had grit in her craw. When you'n' me was off fighting the greasers, she kind of took stock of things. Ran off to N'Orleans, found work. . . . I'd of swore she'd of gone to hell in that there town; but she didn't. Married young Jules Metroyer. . . ."

75

"Lolette," Randy said. "Lolette Dupré. So it was *you* who fathered her child."

"I ain't a-saying," Tom grinned. "How come you know so much about it?"

"Delivered the little bastard," Randy said. "Fine-looking kid, too."

"Could be," Tom said. "All brats look alike to me. Anyhow, she married this here young Creole sprig. His family raised hell. She wouldn't lie about the child or give him up. So Jules took her, child and all. I can understand that. She was worth it."

"Where are they now?" Randy said.

"France. Couldn't live in N'Orleans under the circumstances. And there's a branch of the Metroyers still living in the old country. High mucker mucks over there, too. And they didn't know the story. So the two of them went there, carrying the kid. Hear they're doing all right, too—moving in the highest circles. . . ."

"Ever," Randy said evenly, "think of the child?"

Tom laughed.

"Just want me to give you a stick to beat me with, don't you? I ain't afraid. Yep, I think of that boy right smart. Hate like hell to have him growing up a dainty frog-eater with perfume behind his ears. Only they can't ruin him. He's got too much good stuff in him—from both sides. Look, Randy . . ."

"Yes?" Randy said.

"Sary ain't never heard tell of that. I hope she don't never. And right now the only way she ever could, would be from you. . . ."

Randy stared at him. Tom could see his face tighten.

"Ever know me to fight dirty, Tom?" he drawled.

"Naw," Tom said. "You ain't that kind, thank God—or else I would of let some daylight into you long before now."

"Don't let the kind you think I am stop you," Randy said grimly; "I'm perfectly willing."

Tom grinned at him.

"Now get down off of that high horse, boy," he said. "What the hell have you'n' me to fight over?"

"Nothing," Randy said disgustedly; "though I sometimes wish we had."

"Well we don't," Tom said flatly; "and what's more, we ain't never going to have. 'Cause the choice ain't left with us, and you know it. Come on now, drink up; I got to go."

They came out on the banquette together. As they did so, a woman came toward them. She was leading three small children by the hand, and her face was hidden by her poke-bonnet. But seeing them standing there under the street lantern, she stiffened; then she came on, more slowly.

Another one, Randy thought. Having a woman like Sarah, he still turns to creatures like this! Dear God. And I would give my life to sit near her for an hour, stretch out my hand and touch. . . .

76

But the woman had reached the place where the lantern light could illumine her face. It was weather-beaten, worn. She was not old, Randy saw; but if he had been called upon to guess her age, he would have erred by fifteen years too much—perhaps by twenty. I'm wrong, he thought grudgingly, not even Tom Benton would have . . .

Tom stood there looking at her, and the sadness inside of him was a weight, pressing intolerably against his lungs. He was seeing, feeling again that unutterable, lost, moonburning night of the Protracted Meeting, and contrasting it with now, looking nakedly into the face of time, into the slow decay by which living becomes dying, by which life eases into death. . . .

Rachel! he breathed inside his mind. Lord God, who would of thought it!

This wrinkled, sunwhipped, middle-aged woman. This creature bowed down by pain, by labor, by never having enough of anything, neither of time, nor leisure, nor even the simple necessities of life. Tom didn't know her husband, but he could have pictured him to the hair. A hound-dog man. A coon-hunting man. Sitting under the shade trees for days on end, communing with a jug of bust-head. Exploding into violence, into action only in the hunt, the square dance, the barroom brawl. Leaving his wife and scraggly, underfed brats to scratch a perilous living from a few acres of wornout, eroded, submarginal land.

Could of left her her looks, damn it! he thought savagely. But that's too much to hope for, I reckon. Even Sarah's fading a bit—and me. . . . He snorted with abysmal disgust, and spat the end of his cigar into the gutter.

"Another of your loves?" Randy mocked.

"No," Tom growled. "Just an old, old friend of mine. Many's the favors that there woman's done me in the old days, Randy. And damn my soul, you should have seen her years ago—she was pretty as a picture. . . ."

"If she was so all-fired pretty," Randy said, "why wasn't she one of your loves?"

" 'Cause she and Lolette was such good friends," Tom said honestly, "that I never could figure out how to manage it. But, Lord God, look at her now!"

"The faded rose," Randy said, and put out his hand. "Good night, Tom."

"Night," Tom said absently. "Drop by the place some time."

I'll see you in hell first, Randy thought. You know damned well that's the one thing I couldn't stand.

Riding homeward toward the white cottage, not yet a big house even in contemplation, Tom thought about tomorrow, and what he was thinking did not help the blackness of his mood.

Got to do something about that Wade, he thought bitterly. Never would have dreamed that a son of mine would of turned out like that. Fat, greasy little bastard—no wind, no strength, no guts. God in Heaven! Why wasn't Stormy the boy?

Thinking about his daughter, he smiled. Stormy did that to people. Even at eleven she was beautiful, darkly, vividly beautiful. Her eyes were Tom's own eyes, crazily, impossibly blue, flashing like summer lightning out of the sunburnt darkness of her face. More, she was his child with nothing of Sarah about her. She could ride anything that had four feet, and at an age when other small girls were lovingly dressing their dolls, she had asked for and gotten her dearest possession: a gun. Tom had had it made for her—a beautiful fowling piece, intricately engraved, fitted with a hand-carved walnut stock, cut to her measure. She delighted in banging away at trees, stones, small animals with remarkably accurate aim, while Wade stood by, both hands covering his ears, and a mingled expression of fear and acute disgust upon his round, porcine little face.

There was nothing new about the problem before Tom Benton. Like every other father living before or since, he found it simply impossible to contemplate his son as a being living, dreaming, thinking, suffering upon the face of earth. Wade was to him something more: an extension of his own personality, his gage against death, his personal guarantee of immortality. Therefore, Wade must be more than he himself had ever been; bigger, stronger, fiercer, more courageous. He must drink deeper, laugh louder, love more women more beautiful than any Tom had ever known. That the boy might have a different standard of values, that he might prefer quiet, a good meal, lazy contemplation instead of active participation had never entered Tom Benton's head. And now, confronted with the actuality of that difference, being incapable of doubting the virtues of his own concepts, Tom's reactions were conventional: he was both shocked and outraged.

He set about then upon what was indisputably the worst course of action possible: he was bent upon forcing Wade into his own semiheroic mold, upon making of the boy that, which, given the basic raw materials comprising Wade's sleepy, gentle being could not, in sober fact, ever be made, the result foredoomed, the whole course of action having its own dark inevitability.

The ground was gray with hoarfrost when he got Wade up that next morning, making even the oaks the same color as the Spanish moss that clung to them. From the river below the white haze rose slow and heavy, and thin columns of smoke stabbed the sky from the chimneys of the neighboring houses, more numerous now, giving Tom Benton the feeling that he was being hemmed in, the broad expanse of space, the immensity he subconsciously found necessary to move about in, to breathe, to have his being—the sweep of land commensurate with his own grandeur, his physical and spiritual giantism, limited by them, so that, although he was far and away the biggest landowner in the parish, he felt diminished, robbed.

Before his encounter with Davin Henderson, he would have done something about it, striking down without compunction all who dared invade his kingdom; but now he did nothing. It was not, as the parish dwellers whispered: "That there Davin Henderson done put the fear of God into him—he ain't been the same, since . . ." for he was no more afraid than before, had, if anything, even less respect for the rights, wishes, feelings of his fellows; but that he was pervaded with a cosmic fatigue, as big as his emotions always were. He was baffled into idleness by Sarah's indifference, by his involvement in a situation which could not be solved by force, by violence, not realizing that nothing in human history has ever been solved that way truly, nor ever will be, so that his roars fell upon deaf ears, and his blows smashed against the thin and yielding air.

And added to this—Wade, his son, growing up timid, placid, weak.

Tom looked at him, standing there before the fire, shivering and rubbing his eyes. He could see from the expression on the boy's face that Wade wanted to cry, and also that out of fear of him, Tom Benton, the child did not dare. The thing infuriated Tom, as complicated emotions, and glimpses of normal, human weaknesses always did.

"Get a move on, boy!" he roared. "We ain't got all day! Ducks be halfway to Canada before we get there, waiting on you!"

"Aw, don't be mean to Wade, Paw," Stormy said. "He ain't nothing but a little snot; and before you know it, you'll have him bawling his head off."

She, of course, was already dressed. She sat in the corner by the fireplace, lovingly polishing her gun.

Tom looked at her, and his gaze softened.

"Help him out, Missy," he said, "else we ain't never gonna get there . . ."

Stormy put the gun down and came over to her brother.

"Come on, you little snot," she laughed; "let me fix you."

She started to dress Wade, jerking him this way and that with considerable force. Tom stood there watching her, grinning at her unfeeling efficiency, until Sarah's voice came from the doorway, saying:

"That's enough, Stormy, I'll dress him." Then, looking at Tom: "Lord God, but she's your child!"

"Whose you expect her to be?" Tom growled. "Glad one of them's got grit in her craw."

"I'm not," Sarah snapped. "Call it grit if you like, Tom Benton; but that there's a streak of poison-meanness a yard wide—just like yourn. And you're going to live to weep over it yet, mind you!"

"Didn't bother you oncet," Tom said grimly; "but that was before . . ."

"Before what?" Sarah said, and her eyes were level and still.

"Before you found out that a man ought to talk real pretty like, and maybe carry a little satchel, and hold people's hands and look wise . . ."

"That," Sarah said quietly, "is more than enough, Tom Benton. Man who talks like that in front of his children, ain't much of a man to my way of thinking."

"To hell and tarnation with your way of thinking!" Tom roared. "Don't get me riled up, Sary! I can shoot other critters beside ducks—hunting polecats ain't a bad sport neither, if you understand me, rightly. . . ."

"I do," Sarah said. "Only you're forgetting one thing, Tom. Ducks can't shoot back. And this particular breed of polecat can—right smart good, too. There son, if it gets too cold, you tell your paw to bring you home."

"Yes'm," Wade sniffed, and wrapped his fat little arms about her neck. "I love you, Maw," he blurted. "You're nice, not mean like Paw and Stormy . . ."

"Come on, you sissified li'l' snot," Stormy railed. "Come on, cry-baby, Mama's boy, so me'n' Paw can feed you to the garfish for bait!"

"Stormy," Sarah said.

"Yes, Maw?" the girl's voice was sullen.

"Wade come home and tell me you been pestering him, there's gonna be trouble, you hear me?"

"Yes'm," Stormy said, and started for the door. But in the doorway, she whirled.

"No they won't neither!" she jeered, " 'cause Paw won't let you—so there!" Then she skipped out into the dark.

Sarah looked at Tom.

"You are going to teach that child to respect me," she said, "or there really is going to be trouble, Tom. More trouble than you ever heard tell of."

Tom looked at her; but her gaze met his, held it. He put out his big hand, and took Wade's.

"Come on, son," he growled. "We got to get going, now."

The reeds stood up out of the bayou, black against the reddening sky, like a forest of spears. The morning haze, a legion of tormented ghosts, moved over the gray silver water. When the first glow of light from the not-yet-risen sun struck the bayou, the water was blood colored. The pirogue moved toward where they waited, a black sliver on the blood-and-silver waters, a thing out of, beyond time, unheard, phantomlike, the silence of its coming robbing it of reality, making of it a thing out of man's darker dreams, out of his secret fears. . . .

It slid up to the bank and Louis Dupré looked up at them.

"Brung ma Babette along," he said flatly. "Didn't reckon you'd mind, M'sieu Tom, since you bringing your own kids, you."

"Fine," Tom said, "glad to have her along, Louis. She'll be company for Stormy. Here, take this here boy of mine."

He swung Wade out and over, and Louis took the boy in his iron grip. Stormy jumped at once into the pirogue, causing it to rock wildly, so that Louis had to steady it with the pole. When, in his turn, Tom had gotten into the boat, he looked at Louis' second daughter. He had not seen her since before Clinton's birth; because after that, Lolette had always managed to meet him far from her father's house—in Natchitoches on shopping trips, and from time to time, even in New Orleans. The last vivid memory he had of Babette was as a tot playing on the floor and disturbing his efforts to talk to her sister. Now his blue eyes widened. At fourteen, Babette was already prettier than Lolette had ever been, as pretty, almost, as Stormy, herself; delicate and fine, already budding into maturity. She had Lolette's soft, dark coloring; but there was something about her more earthy, something that smoldered out of her great, dark eyes, which Tom, with his roué's instincts, recognized at once.

But, for some obscure reason, it made him sad. He was conscious once more of the slow bleeding away of time: yesterday, a grimy tot playing on the floor, and himself that was, but gone now, a ghost and phantom out of yesteryear, sitting beside the pallet, holding Lolette's hand, seeing the great welts where Louis had beaten her; now, today, half a heartbeat later, this almost-woman sitting here in a pirogue on the frosty bayou, regarding him with smoldering eyes. He felt immensely old, unbearably weary. Ten years. What had happened to them? Where down the slow-rolling river of time had they gone?

He looked at Louis. This one, at least, had escaped time. Louis Dupré was ageless. Not by a whitened hair, or a single additional crease in his leathery skin, did he show change. He poled the pirogue with the same effortless certainty that he had before, skimming through the black clusters of reeds on and on towards—what?

A flock of ducks feeding in the marshes. Or toward time, eternity, man's fate, the answer to all the seeking, the stilling of all hungers, all lusts—the final quenching of all thirsts of the flesh, and of the spirit—this, too, perhaps.

Tom shook his head to clear it of these thoughts that plagued him, ideas, feelings, he hadn't the words for, could not, in fact define even to himself. Getting crazy, he told himself angrily, getting moonstruck, loony, mulling over silliness. I'm me. I'm big Tom Benton, a pizen wolf from Bitter Creek; I'm half hoss and half bull 'gator, and when I roars . . .

But it was no good and he knew it. Even this—tall talk, back-country brag, did not help. He was himself, a tired, aging man, beset by the feelings he had armed his heart against; defeated by all the tenuous, insubstantial things that bent before his blows, slipped aside, melted into air, leaving him baffled and sick with weary, impotent rage.

Louis stopped the pirogue before his shack and came back with the retrievers, black, shaggy dogs, at home almost in the water as on land, silent dogs who almost never barked, intelligence in every line of their broad, fine heads.

"Mighty late now," Louis said. "Sun's gonna be up 'fore long, yes. Kids held you up, I reckon, then."

"Yep," Tom growled, "but whatcha gonna do? Got to teach a boy to use a gun sooner or later."

"Sure, sure," Louis grinned. "He fine boy, him."

Tom snorted, but said nothing. He was thinking of Clint—tall and fine and manly even as a tiny child. Wonder what he looks like now? he mused. Hope they don't gentle the manhood right out of him. . . .

They moved through the marshes. Louis stopped poling and stood straight up, listening.

"Over ther'," he said, pointing.

Tom passed a light double-barreled shotgun to Wade.

"Cock it," he said.

Wade regarded the weapon with pure, undisguised terror.

"Cock it, I said!" Tom spat.

The boy picked up the gun. His pudgy fingers tugged at the hammers, slipped. He couldn't budge them. Great tears gathered in the corners of his eyes. He tugged at the hammers in a fury of desperation. Tom watched him in mounting, icy rage.

"Here," he snorted, "give me that gun!"

Wade passed it over, his hands trembling so he almost dropped it.

"Sissy!" Stormy laughed.

Tom cocked the gun and gave it back.

"When Louis tells you," he growled, "you shoot. And God help you if you miss!"

Babette looked from Stormy to her brother.

"Poor little boy," she murmured in Cajun French; "he has fear, him."

"Yes," Stormy mocked in English; "he has fear all right. He always has fear. He's a coward, and I hate him!"

"You're bad," Babette said. "You're a bad, bad girl. I would not hate my brother, me. I would be so glad to have a brother that I would always be good to him, yes!"

"*Tais toi!*" Louis spat. "Shut up, Babs!"

He took out a peculiar object, made of a section of reed, and pieces of leather. He put it to his lips, and a wild high honking came out, exactly the same sound that the ducks made, but higher, clearer.

It was Stormy who saw them first, coming in high over the marshes in a black vee, etched against the flaming sky.

"There!" she breathed, and lifted her gun.

"No!" Tom said, "Wade first."

The boy lifted the gun; then, without waiting until the ducks were near enough, or taking aim, he closed his eyes tight and fired both barrels at once. The gun kicked against his shoulder, hard. He cried out in pain and dropped it. It made a great splash in the water. When he opened his eyes again, the ducks were gone.

No one said anything. They all sat there staring at him. He looked from one face to another, his mouth slack with terror, crouching like a trapped animal, waiting. He saw his father's eyes, blazing like blue coals in his great, dark face. Then suddenly, wildly, hopelessly, the boy started to cry.

Babette worked her way forward toward where he sat. She put her arms around him and drew his head down upon her breast.

"Poor little boy," she crooned, "poor scairt little boy. Don't you cry, you. It's all right. Nothing wrong with being scairt. Everybody's scairt of something. . . ."

Louis shrugged.

"Leave him be, M'sieu Tom," he said. "Ain't your kind of a boy, him. Be professor maybe, fiddler, poet, something like that. . . . Takes all kinds to make a world. . . ."

"Aw hell!" Tom spat. "Come on, Louis, let's go find them ducks!"

But they couldn't. No matter how Louis honked, the wildfowl weren't coming back. They had fled that section of the marsh. And now the sun was up, the haze lifting, so that the hunters hadn't a chance, and they knew it.

"Thanks to him," Stormy said. "Paw, we gonna leave him home, next time, ain't we? We ain't a-going to bring him along to spoil things with his cry-baby self are we, Paw?"

Tom stared at his son.

"No, Stormy," he said. "We ain't a-going to leave him. He's my son. He's got to learn to ride and shoot and hold his liquor like a gentleman. He's got to, and I'm going to make him, or beat him to death a-trying!"

"Aw hell!" Stormy said clearly.

"Mind your language, Missy," Tom said mildly. "All right, Louis, reckon we better be getting back, now . . ."

In those next two years, between his tenth and his twelfth birthdays, Wade Benton went through pure, unmitigated hell. He managed finally to bring down a wild duck about every fifth or sixth time his father took him hunting. He learned to stay on a horse finally at the cost of a broken arm, two fractured ribs, endless beatings, shouts, silences, deprivations of supper, and of the minor pleasures dear to his boyish heart. He learned to tramp endless, aching miles without complaint, to work like a Negro in the fields, and never to contradict his father.

And he learned one thing more; and this, finally the saddest aspect of his personal tragedy: he learned to hate his father with a passion that was all consuming and bottomless and complete; thereby setting the pattern for all future generations of Bentons as yet unborn, as yet even unthought of—thereby, though nothing was further from his thoughts than this—dooming them.

7

HISTORY, the march of days, the muted clangor of far-off events, is usually, in a man's life, no more than bee-drone on a summer's day. Off-stage noises, a few spear-bearers in the wings clashing their counterfeit weapons to represent an army, the Greek chorus rolling ponderous antis-trophes about disasters unheard, unseen—these penetrate a man's con-sciousness dimly, if at all.

But there comes a time when the clangor becomes louder, more in-sistent; when the spear-bearers clash their wooden swords into present thunder, when the far-off disasters loom nearer, near until there is no longer any escaping them. Then, suddenly, cruelly, history becomes per-sonal, becomes, indeed, a matter of individual choices, which a man must make for himself, and by himself—alone.

So it was with the decade of disaster, 1850-1860. Tom Benton had seen young men he had known well sail away with Narciso López to die before Spanish firing squads in Cuba; he had read thirty pages of *Uncle Tom's Cabin*, before putting it down forever with a snort of abysmal disgust. And, having himself, in bandit days, raided frontier towns, the clash of arms and screams of dying men at Lawrence, Kansas, and John Brown's murderous vengeance at Pottowatomie Creek, were like tocsins sounding in his own blood.

He went abroad more, now; he talked to other men. He stood, a tall and graying man, heavier of build now, approaching his fifties, in the courthouse squares, and listened to the fervent roll and boom and bom-bast of Southern oratory. He made no speeches himself; talking was never his forte; but men, seeing him there, knew with absolute conviction, that here was one of the leaders, here was a Southern Captain, standing tall in chivalry, quiet and knightly in his pride.

They were not entirely wrong. That there was going to be a war, Tom Benton knew. And granted that one inescapable fact, the approach of what William Seward had already labeled the "Irrepressible Conflict," it followed that he must presently march out at the head of his cohorts, to blaze in glory before the eyes of his fellows, to come back in weary triumph after it was done, or to fall in honor upon the field, soaked in his imagination with the blood of heroes.

It had been a long time now since the Mexican War—more than ten years. In Tom Benton's mind, essentially Southern, and hence essentially unrealistic, romantic, inexact, the filth and boredom, the bad food, the flies, the heat, the weary marching, the unjust, bullying nature of that conflict, conceived in dishonor, and consummated in thievery, had long since died away. Even the battles themselves, instead of the disgraceful driving of an army outclassed, untrained, poorly armed, from a few fields won without cost and without honor, had augmented themselves in the warm distortions of his memory into heroic victories against overwhelming odds.

He would go again once the time came. He was in love with glory; he pictured in a thousand multicolored variations himself singlehandedly winning the day, saving the South, returning in triumph to the plaudits of the multitudes. That these dreams of his were basically adolescent, even puerile, troubled him not at all; because in no way did they make him less than his fellows. The Southern mind was, and, sadly, is, basically adolescent, puerile, infantile; the conditions of life under which it developed making it so: geographical isolation, rural living, the economic necessity of defending, of distorting into a virtue a thing totally without virtue, of inventing sophistries, syllogisms to justify the most nearly indefensible system ever invented upon the face of earth. And to this add the fact that this painful necessity of defending slavery, the South's "Peculiar Institution," made as a by-product, absolute conformity of thought an essential condition of living: to differ being to weaken the defense, to make a chink in the armor against a people, who, however wrong they might be in other things: their own wage-slavery, child labor, hellish working conditions, protective tariffs, business methods not even one cut above pure chicanery and fraud, were in this at least, absolutely, and indisputably right.

Even Tom Benton, hard as he was, dimly sensed this. There were times when gazing upon some magnificent physical specimen of a black—a fine physique being a thing he found easy to admire—he was vaguely troubled. It was true that in a rough way, he was kind to his slaves; but it was also true that no amount of kindness could make up to a man the soul-destroying indignity of being owned like a dog, or a horse. So, like most other Southerners, he put these disturbing thoughts quickly out of his mind, and settled back into that comfortable orthodoxy that was to cost the South so much, stifling as it necessarily must, every trace of boldness, of originality of mind, making of that vast and blooming land a cultural desert so arid, sterile, bare, that in those days, while the poets of bleak New England sang like angels, the South could boast but three very minor bards, not one novelist of stature, no painter, no composer, no instrumentalist even worthy of the name. More, for all the superficial sprouting of Greek and Latin tags by planters' sons, sent, for the most part to hated New England for their education, or in rarer instances, to England or France, a semi-illiteracy was the rule, extending in the vast majority of cases into the parlor of the Big House itself, so that they, the ruling classes, were themselves to leave behind them a host of papers, diaries, letters, whose spelling, grammatical constructions, incoherence, and almost total absence of logic would have disgraced a New England schoolboy, and which were to make the task of the historian as painful as it was boring.

Beyond this, there remained the Harvard, Princeton, occasionally Oxford or Sorbonne trained man; and from him, from whom the South expected and needed leadership, she got rhetoric, oratory. For in this haze-filled, sunwashed land, where everything lacked precision, clarity, even the outlines of the physical world itself, nothing was easier than to forget logic, sense, to believe that cotton was indeed King, that one lordly Southerner could in sober fact whip ten moneygrubbing Yankees, to seize upon lovely words, to roll them deep in the throat, to heap them in redundant thunder upon one another, until the last vestige of meaning

85

had disappeared, and nothing was left but the wild, sweet intoxication of sound, the tomtom beat of savage rhythms upon the hidden seat of feeling. So it was. The South talked herself into a suicidal war, which from the start she had no chance of winning, and men like Tom Benton, listening, nodded in sage agreement to the wildest outburst of windy bombast; the longest sustained outpouring of polysyllabic, high-blown nonsense that ever assaulted human intelligence. But the beast that lurks in the darker places of man's soul, has ever found intellect but a feeble foeman; in 1859-60, the beast had burst his chains and went rampaging through the land. . . .

On the platform, the speaker was announcing that if the Black Republicans won, Louisiana would leave the Union; that further, if the North dared use force, the South could whip the filthy traders to their knees with a handful of beardless boys armed with children's popguns. Tom shook his head a little at that. Many of the men he had fought alongside in Mexico had been Northerners, and they, some of them, had made damned fine soldiers. Others had been knaves and cowards. But, then, so had the Southern boys. He couldn't see where the section a body came from made much difference. A man was what he was. Brave men, North and South; cowards North and South. The speaker was a liar, and a fool.

He shook his head, and turned to leave the square. Then he saw Randy McGregor coming toward him. Randy was thinner than ever, and his eyes had a deeper, more somber fire.

They say he never looks at a woman, Tom mused; because of Sary, I reckon. Lord God, I couldn't do that—even at my age, I'd bust!

He could see that Randy's red hair was plentifully streaked with gray. There wasn't much difference in their ages, really, a year or two at most.

Must be forty-seven, or eight, Tom thought; and me, I'm fifty. Good Lord, who would of thought it? Time just kind of slips away from you, somehow, and afore you know it, you're . . .

"Howdy, Tom," Randy said.

"Howdy, boy," Tom said. "You been missing some mighty fine speechmaking."

"I mean to miss some more," Randy said. "It riles me to be taken for a fool. I heard the last thing that fat jackass said—about fighting the North with popguns. He may be right there. God knows we haven't anything else to fight with."

"Well now—" Tom drawled.

"Well now, nothing!" Randy snapped. "Where are our munition plants, Tom Benton? Our powder works? Damn it, man, we don't even have a textile mill to make uniforms, or even a shoe factory to make boots! Come to think of it, we couldn't even fight them with children's popguns. Every blasted toy gun I've ever seen was made in Boston, or New York."

"Easy, boy," Tom said. "Ain't going to be no fight. This here Abe Lincoln ain't elected yet. Soon as we put a good man up . . ."

"We won't," Randy said gloomily. "We never could agree on anything down here. Look what happened in Charleston last month—convention broke up without making a nomination. I'll tell you just what's going to happen, Tom: We're going to split and split again, and in the end there are going to be two or three men running against Lincoln, cutting the Southern vote into little pieces, and the Republicans are going to enter the White House by default."

"You may be right," Tom said. "But one thing I'm glad of, Randy. I notice that you keep saying 'we.'"

Randy stared at him. Then his lean face crinkled into a slow smile.

"Can't help that, Tom," he said. "I'm a Southerner—by adoption, I'll grant you; but I'm a Southerner all the way through. I don't like slavery. I think it's plain damned wrong. I've never owned a slave; don't aim to. But my roots are here. I've been very happy. I've brought half the younger generation of this town and this parish into the world. I've sat by the oldsters' beds and watched them die. This is my home, Tom. It's sort of like fighting for your family. Right or wrong, you fight for them."

"Good!" Tom said. "What's that you got there, boy—the *Picayune?*"

Randy looked down at the folded newspaper he had been slapping against his knee. Then he gave it to Tom.

"I brought it to you," he grinned. "Little item on Page three is going to interest you a lot, or I miss my guess."

Tom took the paper, thumbed through it.

"I don't see . . ." he growled.

"Bottom of the page," Randy said, "just a few lines."

He could see Tom's forehead crease with the effort of reading; then the big man straightened up, his blue eyes gazing out upon time, upon memory.

"So," he said at last, "Lolette's come back."

"Yes," Randy said, watching him.

"And her husband's dead," Tom muttered.

"But Sarah isn't," Randy said grimly. "Don't forget that, Tom."

"I won't," Tom said. "It's too late now, Randy-boy. Years and years too late. . . . Still . . ."

"You want to see her."

"Yep. Her and the boy. Hell, Randy, you realize that kid is sixteen years old, now—same age as Wade?"

"A good age—sixteen, no troubles then, no worries," Randy said. "How about a snort, Tom?"

"Don't mind if I do," Tom said automatically.

"All right then. Come on."

They crossed the square together, two tall men, so unlike that they seemed deliberately juxtaposed for contrast. Just before they entered Tim's place, Tom stopped.

"That boy of mine," he grinned, "looks like he's going to turn out all right after all."

Randy looked up in time to see Wade Benton passing in a smart little rig. Beside him Babette Dupré sat. The two of them were talking so earnestly that they didn't see either Tom or Randy.

"Louis knows about that?" Randy demanded.

"Yep. In fact, I told him. Wade's serious, Randy. Wants to marry the girl. I explained that to Louis. He ain't happy over it; but he's no fool. After all, my boy ain't the worst catch in the parish. And both them kids promised him they'd behave themselves. . . . Got to wait anyhow. Wade's still too young."

"Younger than Babette, isn't he?"

"By about three years. But heck, Randy, any kid of Louis' is bound to be all right—three years don't matter one way or another."

"Strange," Randy smiled.

"What's strange?" Tom demanded.

"How different a man's thoughts are about his son—and his daughter," Randy said.

Tom stopped dead.

"What do you mean about that, Randy?" he growled.

"Nothing—nothing at all," Randy said, and pushed open the swinging doors.

"But, Babette," Wade groaned, "I still don't see why . . ."

"Look, Wade," Babette said patiently, "I've told you a dozen times. I like you very much. You're a very nice boy. That's just the trouble: you're too nice—and too much a boy."

"Just because you're a little older. . . ."

"I'm a lot older. I'll soon be twenty, Wade. And you're sixteen. I feel like a fool being seen with you. All my friends are calling me 'cradle robber.' I wouldn't be seen with you but for two reasons: my papa rather likes the idea of my marrying the son of the richest man in the parish; and I don't like to hurt his feelings—or yours."

"It isn't like it's going to be right away," Wade argued. "By the time I'm twenty . . ."

"I'll be twenty-four. It's more than that. If you even looked a little older, more like your—"

"My father?" Wade snapped. "That's what you were going to say, wasn't it?"

"Yes," Babette smiled, and her eyes were soft. "There's a man for you! I used to think he was too stern, maybe even mean; but now . . ."

"But now you'd rather have him than me, wouldn't you?" Wade said.

"Yes," Babette said tartly. "Yes, I would. I reckon most any girl would who had the chance. He sure is something, him!"

"Don't talk that Cajun dialect to me!" Wade growled. "You know what, Babs? I wish my father was dead!"

"Wade!" Babette's voice was genuinely shocked.

"Well, I do," Wade said doggedly. "All my life he's been there, getting in my way. People never could see me for him. He can ride and shoot and spark the girls, and that's all right for a young man. Only he isn't young any more. He's fifty. Time he was getting out of the way, letting me take over. But he won't. He still talks and acts like a young man."

"And looks like a young man, too," Babette said. "No, I take that back. No young man could be that handsome. That white hair around his temples and streaking the top of his head, and the way his face looks windbeaten, and sunburnt—that takes time. You, for instance, are kind of a pretty little boy—soft and pink and white and golden; but your papa's a man, and the way he looks is better than just plain handsome: he looks strong and fine and—and . . ."

"And what?" Wade demanded.

"I can't explain it. I don't know how to say it. It's kind of a feeling. I just know that if he touched me, his fingertips would brand me; if he kissed me, I'd melt all over; and I'd do anything he wanted me to without even thinking about whether it was right or wrong."

"Oh, hell!" Wade half wept.

Babette stretched out her hand and touched his arm.

"I'm sorry, Wade," she whispered. "There'll be some nice girl for you, and . . ."

"But I don't want some nice girl!" Wade got out. "I want you!"

"You'll get over it," Babette said. "Now take me home, Wade. I've got to get packed."

"Packed?" Wade's voice had pure misery in it. "You're going away, Babs?"

"Only to New Orleans. You see, my sister Lolette has come back. Papa's just dying to see her. She always was his favorite."

"I didn't know you had a sister," Wade said wonderingly.

"Well, I do. She's much older than I am. She's thirty-six, about the same age as your mother. She's got a son as old as you are. . . ."

"Funny I never heard tell of her," Wade said.

"No, it's not. People don't mention her much because they're scared of Papa. There was a scandal about her. They say she had her baby before she was married. But that's not the main reason you never heard of her. . . ."

"No?" Wade gulped, "then why didn't I?"

"Folks say that her baby is—your brother—your half brother, Wade."

"You mean that my father—?"

"I don't know. I've heard that. Anyhow it's been a long time, and she's come up in the world since then. Her husband, he was a Metroyer, you know, died in France last year and left her rich. She's got a house on Royal Street, and fine clothes and servants, and all. I'm dying to see her, too. Papa says she's the most beautiful thing you ever laid eyes on."

"She couldn't be prettier than you," Wade said stubbornly.

"Thank you, Wade," Babs laughed; and, leaning over, she kissed his soft cheek. "Come on, now; drive me home."

"My father," Wade said bitterly. "Damn him, if he ever touches you, I'll kill him! I'll kill him dead!"

Babette smiled at him. She was all woman, and very complete—even to the fine bitchery, the instinctive, feline cruelty.

"How do you know he hasn't?" she said.

North and South, the land brooded. Men neglected their accustomed pursuits, stood long in public squares, listened, talked gravely, slowly among themselves, knowing the time out of joint, half conscious of the weight of silence, of waiting, so that it seemed in the chenieres no birds sang, no hound went sorrowing through the pine wood; the slave voices sadder now, the burden of sorrow deeper—intolerably, crushingly deeper in their songs, so that the white men, listening to the dark voices soaring up from the cabins in the night shivered and muttered:

"Damn them! Wish to hell they'd shut up!"

It was a fearsome time; a sorrowing time. Only the fools made merry. Only the little men, drunk with the bombast of their own oratory were sure; but the others—the Randy McGregors, the Tom Bentons and their like—were far from sure.

Which was why, perhaps, that Tom Benton was reluctant to leave Randy's company that afternoon, and Randy equally reluctant to have him go. They, the two of them, felt more at ease in each other's society than they did in that of any other person, and this despite the potential cause of conflict resting between them, unchanging over the years. They understood each other; they trusted each other; more, in sober truth, they were fond of each other, though both of them would have hotly denied it. So it was when Randy said:

"Come ride with me on a few calls, Tom. You don't have a damned thing to do, and you know it."

Tom replied gruffly:

"Don't mind if I do. . . ."

They rode through the bayou country, tying up their horses, and being poled out to the shacks of the trappers.

"Call this a civilized country?" Randy snorted. "Know what's wrong with most of these children, Tom? Plain filth, and bad food."

Tom looked at the tiny Cajun child, spotted all over with running sores, and having a particularly unlovely eye-sickness, which had crusted her lids so that she couldn't open them.

"*Les moustiques*, Docteur," the trapper said. "They're something fierce, them. They bite the bébé, and she scratches herself, yes—that's what makes them sores."

"I know," Randy growled. "But damn it, Jules, haven't you ever heard of mosquito netting? It doesn't cost much. . . ."

"We don't see much cash money, us," the trapper said sadly. "Takes it all for clothes and food, yes. Ain't like we was farming people. Can't grow no legumes in the bayou, Docteur."

"I'll send you over five yards of netting tomorrow," Randy said. "You keep this baby's bed covered, you hear me? As for those eyes—use this salve. And you've got to see that this child gets more green vegetables and more meat. Fish is fine food, but you've got to eat something else from time to time."

"Yessir, Docteur," Jules said; "I do my best, me."

Only he could not do any better, and both Randy and Tom knew it. As they got out of the pirogue and remounted, Randy turned upon Tom.

"There is your number one argument against slavery," he said angrily. "That child there!"

Tom stared at him.

"That there Cajun brat ain't no slave," he said; "I don't see what in hellfire you're talking about, Randy."

"Simple. That white child is not a slave—right. But she is, none the less, a direct victim of slavery. Ever see a Negro child look that bad?"

"No," Tom said, "still—"

"Still, nothing!" Randy spat. "You'll never see a black baby who looks like that, because a Negro child is worth something—has an economic value in the scale of things. That child has none. Her folks subsist, rather than live, on the fringes of our economy, because slavery keeps us from having any need of them, and they're reduced to making a living by a way that doesn't concern us, except the few of us that serve as middlemen and rob them blind in the process. We don't have to wear furs down here, so they depend entirely upon the Northern and foreign markets. And by the time the pelts of the animals they trap pass through half-a-dozen hands, they've precious little left . . ."

"That's true," Tom said heavily; "but all of it ain't our fault, Randy. If they're robbed, you can bet your bottom dollar the Yankees have got a finger in it."

"Right. I've never said the Northerners were saints. All I'm saying is that their sins are on their own consciences, and are no excuse for ours— the way we try to make them. Perhaps, to your mind, the Cajuns aren't a clean-cut example of what slavery does to white people. But I'm going to take you to visit some people who are. Come on."

Three hours, and five families later, the argument was still raging.

"All right! All right!" Tom Benton roared. "So them pine-barren crackers is starved into eating clay—and them swampers got skin disease from bad food; but whose fault is it? Their own, damn it! Look at 'em! They're halfwits one and all! Different stock, Randy. Their folks warn't nothing in the old country. Had any grit in their craws, it'd be different. I come from poor folks, and look at me. Only difference was my folks was sober Godfearing people with a mite of gumption, and a mighty heap of git up and git about them. Blood talks, Randy—you can't deny that. . . ."

Randy smiled at him a little mockingly.

"Like the Landsdownes, for instance?" he said. "Gerald Landsdowne would deny it on a stack of Bibles, but the fact remains that he and old

Pete Landsdowne who we just left under a tree whittling a pine stick with a jug of bust-head beside him, while his kids looked at us from behind their mother's exceedingly filthy skirts like wild creatures—are first cousins. Pete's father and Gerald's were brothers. What's more, Pete's mother was a Taylor of the Virginia Taylors. . . ."

"How the hell you know all that?" Tom demanded. "You ain't been in these parts long enough."

"Looked it up in the courthouse records. On purpose, because I'd gotten tired of that blood-will-tell nonsense. I picked those last five families out, Tom, just to show you. Every one of them, from the standpoint of blood, is from the very best aristocratic stock—every one of them is also related to some of our largest landowners, and I can prove it. The trouble with them is based on a difference in temperament no greater than often exists between two brothers. They just weren't hard enough, maybe not even mean enough. So they got pushed back into the submarginal lands, while the big boys, who had it in them to play rough and fight dirty, grabbed the best lands, dispensing with those nice, gentle folks because owning Negroes freed them in any way from having to depend in any way upon the lesser white man. So those families sank down the scale, their wits dimmed by bad liquor and worse food, by being shut off from any contact with anybody except people just like themselves. And they're a large part of our population, Tom—that's what slavery has done to the South."

"Done a lot of good, too," Tom growled. "Most white folks ain't like that. To my mind, folks like the Ransoms is more typical . . ."

"We have to go there," Randy said. "Jane Ransom wants me to look at her niece—thirteen-year-old kid from Mississippi, up Natchez way. And the Cattlets. Nice sampling of all kind of people in the parish. Hunt Cattlet is the largest landowner, next to you, that we have. Jim Ransom is a typical yeoman farmer—just as you said. And each of them has been victimized by the 'South's Peculiar Institution' to quote our windy orators —in different ways, of course; but definitely and seriously injured by it just the same. . . ."

"You talk like an abolitionist," Tom said.

"I am. The only difference between me and those noisy fools up North is that I have better reasons. They're right, of course; but only on moral grounds. And you can do damned little with a man by proving to him he's a polecat, Tom—or even attempting to prove it. Let's not delude ourselves: Nobody but God, Himself, has the moral right to own a human being; perhaps not even He. Because, if you accept the doctrine of free will, He set us free long ago. But I don't hammer away at the picture of the poor, downtrodden black, because as an argument it's ineffective as long as it runs counter to the much stronger argument of human self-interest. I'm way ahead of those reformers up North because I know that even the self-interest is an illusion. Slavery hurts everybody, even those who seem to benefit by it."

"That," Tom said grimly, "is going to take some proving to men like Hunt Cattlet and me."

"Come along then," Randy said, "and I'll show you."

Nancy Cattlet met them at the door, her serene patrician expression belied by the worry in her eyes.

"Don't know what's wrong with Hunt, Doctor," she said. "He ain't sick—I mean not like folks generally gets sick. But he can't sleep, don't half eat, and about half of what he does eat won't stay on his stomach."

Randy looked upward at the little fanlighted windows overlooking the small balcony that nestled high up under the roof of the veranda, behind the enormous two-story-tall Corinthian columns. The Cattlets had built the first and only neo-Grecian mansion in the entire parish. It had been completed in 1855, fully five years ago; and Randy strongly suspected that the root of Hunt Cattlet's illness was his growing recognition that neither he, nor his son, Ron, was ever going to be able to pay for it. It was an imposing house, huge and white and beautiful. But it was absolutely impossible to heat in winter, it leaked in every heavy rain, and shuddered and groaned whenever the wind rose. The insects of the bayou used it for a parade ground, so that even on the hottest nights, the Cattlets smothered under the thick mosquito netting hung over their canopied beds—without which sleep would have been impossible.

Not a half-bad design, Randy mused. But no matter how good a design is, you can't build a tight house with slave labor. The essence of craftsmanship is pride—and how much pride can a man take in work he's whipped to? Green lumber sawed on the place, with every joint coming open as it dries and shrinks. Homemade bricks too, crumbling before five years are out because the local clay is too sandy, and nobody knew how to really bake brick anyhow. The ironwork's good though—because it's a thing that whoever made it could take pride in. . . .

"Well, Doctor?" Nancy Cattlet said.

"Sorry," Randy sighed; "I was just looking at your house. . . ."

"I," Nancy Cattlet burst out, "hate this house!"

Tom stared at her.

"Why, Ma'am?" he demanded.

"Good and sufficient reasons, Mister Benton. There aren't but three of us: Hunt, Ron and me. A nice little cottage like you've got would be more than enough. But no, Hunt had to go saddle himself with debt to build this monstrosity! I drive myself till I'm half dead trying to keep it clean—and you know what it is to make nigger gals clean. Be easier to do it myself. Then, apart from the fact it's poorly built, we had to put it here because this is the only ground that's high and dry on the place. Two miles from the spring house and the creek. In summer milk sours on the way to the kitchen. Hunt had a well dug, and the water turned out bad tasting. So we have to send a couple of niggers two miles for every drop of water that anyone drinks, bathes in, or washes clothes and dishes with—and if that ain't a powerful encouragement toward slovenliness I don't know what is."

"I'd better look at Hunt now, Ma'am," Randy said.

Hunt Cattlet was stretched out on the big bed staring at the ceiling.

"Howdy, Tom," he said. "Evening, Doctor. Sorry Nancy called you. I ain't sick—leasewise I ain't got the kind of sickness a doctor can cure. My stomach's gone back on me 'cause a man just plain can't worry and digest his vittles at the same time."

"Tell me what's worrying you, Hunt?" Randy said.

"Everything. First off there's Ron who's turning out to be the wildest young sprig the Cattlets ever produced. Then there's forty thousand other things all of which you can lump under the heading of money. Funny thing it all grows out of owning too much: too many niggers, too much land, too many mules, too many expenses. . . .'"

"But," Tom growled, "cotton calls for bigness, Hunt. It ain't a crop for small farming."

"I know that. But you got to be both big and efficient. I got a Yankee first cousin on my ma's side. Farms a place up in Ohio. His place ain't half the size of this one. But he gets more work out of one hired white farmhand than anybody down here gets out of three niggers and that includes you, Tom Benton. If them abolitionists up there ever have their way, we're going to find out that it's us who're going to be freed 'cause be damned if we ain't the slaves of a passel of worthless, good-for-nothing, trifling, lazy niggers! If they even spent one-half the time working that they spends figgering out ways of getting out of work, I'd be rich."

"Hunt," Randy said quietly, "if a man put you to plowing and chopping cotton, with an overseer standing over you with a whip, how much ambition would you have? If you could look forward to wearing gunny sack trousers and eating fatback and collard greens the rest of your life—and beyond that the possibility that Ron could be sold down the river like a boar hog or a stallion, you'd take an interest in seeing that your master made money? Would you, now?"

Hunt Cattlet stared at him.

"That's strange talk, Doc," he said tiredly, "coming from you. First place, they're niggers, which means they don't think like us—if they think at all, which I doubt. They're happy. They sing all the time, and they're always laughing."

"They are the world's finest actors," Randy said. "And if you'd ever bother to listen to the words to their songs, you'd find they're the saddest things you've ever heard. You keep the patrols—the ones the Negroes call the paddy-rollers—scouring the woods all night every night because they're so damned contented, Hunt? That Fugitive Slave law we jammed through Congress—that was to impress the Yankees? And those advertisements in the papers: 'Runaway from Toliver, my plantation, my nigger man Brutus, tall, coal black with a scar on his left cheek,' and so forth. Hundreds of ads like that every issue, Hunt. Not to mention the shivers all you plantation owners get everytime anybody mentions Haiti, Santo Domingo, Nat Turner and John Brown. . . ."

"You ain't making him any easier in mind, Randy," Tom pointed out.

"Right," Randy smiled. "Sorry, Hunt. I'm going to give you a little something to make you sleep. Then I'd suggest that you'd better cut down on your holdings and arrange things so that they can be managed. If you don't, you're really going to be a sick man, and that's not going to do anyone any good."

"Not much hope of that, Doctor," Hunt Cattlet said.

The Ransoms lived on a small farm just north of the Cattlet plantation. Riding toward it, they were both silent, encompassed round about by that private world into which each man must from time to time retreat, communing there with himself and by himself, alone.

Another thing, Randy thought, where else in America or perhaps in all the world would a great landowner express himself in a language scarcely more polished than the dialect of his field hands? I'd wager my last copper that neither Hunt Cattlet nor Tom here has ever read a book except perhaps the Bible, in all their lives. But I can't offend them by saying that. Even the ones who do occasionally read, subsist on a mental diet of that romantic idiocy that Scott turned out by the ream. They've identified themselves with the notion of chivalry. I guess a man must have some ideal to cling to—but God help the land whose leaders deliberately choose to retreat out of logic into hazy romanticism—Gerald Landsdowne solemnly showed me a genealogical chart tracing his family back to Ivanhoe. And when I pointed out to him that Ivanhoe was a figment of Walter Scott's imagination, he was furious—not with the charlatan who'd robbed him with that elaborate nonsense; but with me for destroying his dream.

I love this damned, stupid, highflown wrong-headed land; but it's an anachronism—the whole South is nothing but an anachronism; an entire nation, for they are that, too—marching backward into the past on the double—

He looked at Tom Benton.

And you, my friend, he mused, are the type-form of that anachronism—a man who exists in two separate entities: the man you are, and the man you believe yourself to be. But the man you are: the big, fine animalistic brute; the thief and scoundrel; the seducer and rake; is, after all, in process of becoming the man you dreamed up: the knightly Southern gentleman, courtly for all your ignorance, dignified for all your lack of anything valid upon which to base that dignity—except perhaps your courage. That I will grant you, especially now since it too is becoming something else—not merely the ferocity of a beast; but something strangely like moral courage—the bravery of a man who chooses, makes decisions upon the basis of good and evil—and sticks by them. However you started, Tom Benton, you will end as something very fine—and it is that which defeats me—that and my own honor, if I can be Southerner enough to use the word—

Tom stared straight ahead. Thinking for him was a painful process, since he had none of Randy's facility of language; and language being after all the tool of thought, he had to grope for images on which to flash his ideas.

Randy's right. And he's wrong. I can't explain howcome; but he's right and wrong both. Reckon it is wrong to own a man, nigger or not. But it's the way we live, it makes possible a kind of living that's just plumb gracious. Right or wrong, we can't give it up. It's like having a wife and a mistress. No question that keeping a gal on the side is wrong; but Lord God, when she twines her little arms about you in the dark, it's mighty sweet! That's the trouble. What folks like Randy is asking us is to give up the sweet, slow living—the riding out over the fields at Broad Acres, so pretty with the sunlight on them—the fact of being somebody, being looked up to. Hell, I like that. I like it when lesser folks comes to me for help and advice. I like it all—all the good mighty fine things about the way I live. And to ask me to give it up because it ain't just to pine-barren crackers and a passel of black burr-headed savages, is asking too much.

They rode into the yard at Jim Ransom's place. Except for size it was very nearly identical with Broad Acres, which was not strange since practically all rural Southerners lived much the same way. From Virginia to Texas, it was rare to find a painted house outside the cities, whitewash being employed in a minority of cases, and in the majority nothing at all. Once you left the tidewater counties of Virginia, and the delta of the Mississippi, the imposing planters' mansions all but disappeared; even the rice growers of the Carolinas lived in a much simpler fashion.

Randy himself, in his brief sojourn in the North had seen the sketches of the romantic idea of plantation life, a legend believed with some justification in Yankeeland because the Northerners had Virginia on their doorstep to mislead them but believed, strangely enough, with even more fervor by the Southerners themselves in spite of their daily contact with the reality.

And, Randy mused now, it makes little difference how rich they are—they build these one-story unpainted pine cottages bigger and with more rooms if they can afford it; but they all keep saddles, guns and sometimes grain in the halls, dry corn and okra on the veranda, and hang bridles, harnesses and whips up over the doors. Even the big ones like Tom here only dress up once in a while—and they all talk alike except those planters who are also politicians or preachers. Men like Jim Ransom are better off. He has only three or four Negroes, and is therefore less enslaved by the system. Hunt's right—economically speaking Negro slavery is the most wasteful, inefficient system ever invented by men. And not because the Negro is naturally unintelligent; but because he is both docile and subtle— what he does really is to quietly resist and evade the demands put upon him until the whole slave economy becomes economically self-defeating.

And he does it so damned well that the white man doesn't know he is doing it. . . .

Jane Ransom came to the door. She was a plump, pretty woman in her thirties, of the type, Tom saw at once, who accepted responsibility only under protest, and then shrugged it off as fast as was humanly possible.

"I do declare," she said at once, "this here child's got me beat! 'Taint like she were my own child, Doctor. Never had no brats, so I reckon I just ain't used to them."

"What seems to be the trouble, Mrs. Ransom?" Randy said.

"I'll be blessed if I know. I gave her sulphur and molasses; but it's more'n spring fever. She won't eat—won't hardly talk to nobody; just sits and mopes the live-long day. I'm mightily a-feared, Mister Benton, that I'm gonna have this here child on my hands the rest of my natural life."

"Why?" Tom said shortly.

"She ain't pretty—won't never be, I reckon. And she ain't got much sparkle to her. Be a mighty poor type of man who'll ever want to get hitched with Mary Ann."

"She's only thirteen, isn't she?" Randy said. "Appears to me you're concerning yourself prematurely about marrying her off . . ."

"Reckon I am," Jane Ransom said; "but I kind of have to think that way. Seeing as how we didn't have no children it's kind of hard to be saddled with one this late in life."

"May I see her please?" Randy said, and his tone was edged.

"I'll send her out here," Jane Ransom said. "She's up and about and I've my chores to attend to."

"You run right along and attend to them," Randy said quickly. "We'll wait here."

"Reckon I know what's wrong with that child," Tom said seriously. "Woman like that would drive a mule mad."

"It's more than that," Randy said tiredly; "though that's part of it—wait now, here she comes."

The little girl came shyly out on the veranda. She was as thin as a lath, and her penny-brown eyes were wide and frightened. She was a plain child, with her small face covered with freckles, and a trembling mouth that was far too big for the rest of it. Only her hair was truly lovely. It was a soft auburn shade with red-gold highlights, and fell in heavy waves down to her waist.

Randy took her hand.

"Tell me about it, Missy," he said.

"About what, Doctor?" Mary Ann whispered.

"About things. Just anything—aren't you happy here?"

"No sir," Mary Ann said.

"She mean to you?" Tom growled; jerking his head toward the door.

"No sir. She fusses a whole lot, but she ain't mean. I—I don't know, Mister. . . . I reckon I just don't know how to be happy."

"Homesick?" Randy suggested gently.

"Yes, Doctor," Mary Ann said, and both of them could see the rush of tears in her eyes.

"Tell me about home," Randy said.

"It—it was nice," the child said, blinking against her tears. "Wasn't much different from here; but nicer. We had lots more darkies. Used to play with me, and sing to me, and make me things. Wasn't no white children around to play with. But here, I ain't got nobody—not even niggers to play with. . . ."

"Why'd you leave there, Missy?" Tom said.

"Had to. My pa—my pa—he . . ."

But she couldn't finish it. She rocked back on her heels, her arms wrapped fiercely about her small body, holding hard against her pain and her grief.

"He met with an accident," Randy put in quickly. "He was cleaning his gun. And Mary lost her mother shortly thereafter—so now we've a nice new neighbor, eh Tom?"

"Yep," Tom said quietly. "Tell you what, Missy—you come visit my kids. 'Course they're older than you. Stormy's seventeen, and Wade's a year younger; but we'd be mighty glad to have you. Wade specially. He's nearer your age, and I 'spect he's a mite lonesome hisself. What you say, Missy?"

She stood there staring at this big man.

He's kind, she thought; I ain't afraid of him no more. And there was a small glow of joy, slow stealing somewhere behind her eyes.

"Yessir," she murmured, "I'd like that. But you'll have to ask my aunt— if she'll let me come, I mean."

"You go tell her to come back out here," Tom said heartily; "I'm a-fixing to ask her right now."

"Thanks, Tom," Randy said after Mary Ann had gone back in the house. "That's the best medicine anyone could have given her."

Riding away from there, after it had all been arranged, Randy told Tom the story.

"So this Randolph Perry challenged Jed Barker to a duel. Over that damned foolishness, a difference of opinion, no more. Not a woman, or a gambling debt or any of the usual excuses—just the political question of secession. They met early in the morning under the oaks, and Perry shot that child's father dead because Jed Barker didn't believe, and said so, that the Southern States have any right to leave the Union. Olive Barker, this poor child's mother, had a weak heart. The shock killed her."

"Hell of a thing," Tom said heavily.

"It is. And it's a thing that could only happen today in this barbaric section we live in. They've stopped that obscene nonsense of dueling up North. So since Jane Ransom was Jed's sister, the child was sent here. You saw what kind of woman Jane is. That's why I say you've done a fine thing, Tom."

98

"Wasn't much," Tom grunted. "She believes that story about her pa cleaning his gun?"

"Yes," Randy said. "Better that way. . . ."

"I'll tell my kids that, then," Tom said.

It was night when they got back to town. Even so, they sat over a bottle of bourbon at Tim's until midnight.

Tom stood up.

"Got to be going," he said. "Sary'll be worried."

"Right," Randy said. "See you tomorrow, Tom."

But, riding homeward, Tom Benton was morosely sure that Sarah would not be worried, that she wouldn't care much one way or the other if he never came home at all. For that, too, was another casualty of the years: her love for him. He tried now, stubbornly, to win her back again, bringing her presents, behaving at times like a lovesick schoolboy, paying her compliments, admiring her dress, the way she did her hair. But Sarah only looked at him coolly, and said:

"Oh, get along with you, Tom, and stop your fooling!"

He could not win her back again, and in his secret heart, he knew why. It was because love was dead within him, too—love and the capacity for loving. He had all but forgotten how his youthful body had screamed with the most powerful of all hungers; he could not recall how it was to rove the land nightlong searching for surcease from the awful need that drove him. Physically, he was still capable of love; actually, the years which had cooled the fires within him, had made him better controlled, and hence, from the woman's point of view the better lover; but increasingly the whole thing seemed scarcely worth the bother.

Yet, he needed Sarah—not her still fair and slender body; but as a person, living, breathing, feeling upon the face of earth. He needed to have her to talk to—about things, and in ways he could never talk to Randy; and it was here, chiefly, that she failed him. She did not, would not, could not listen. Her awakened mind, racing ahead of his slow pondering, found him heavy, dull. It may be that secretly she contrasted him with Randy to his detriment; but this he could not prove with any certainty, for she never mentioned Randy's name. He was a stranger and alone in the house that he had built; he wandered an alien ghost across the sweep of fields he had stolen, bought, acquired. He belonged to no time, and to no people; his belief in his superiority, his difference, had marked him, for by now other men had come to believe it too.

There were those who admired him, and they were few. There were many who respected him, deferred to him, sought counsel of him; but there were times when he was painfully aware that among the ranks of those who loved him, he could not number with any degree of conviction, a single human soul.

Not even Stormy. She was too much like him for their stubborn personalities and powerful wills not to clash. She knew, as surely as he had known the same thing in his own youth, that right was what she wanted to do, that all the rest of the world was composed of fools, knaves, and cowards, bent upon thwarting her—him alone she paid the supreme compliment of exemption from their numbers. Rules, laws, the conventions of morality were perhaps necessary to govern the human cattle lowing and stumbling through life, with her, the elect, the superior, shining one they had nothing at all to do.

He roared at her, threatened to beat her; but in sober fact he could not control her. For like him, she possessed the fearful Benton force, the iron will. She could never be bent; she could only be broken; she could never be defeated—only destroyed.

And he loved her too much to contemplate breaking her, destroying her. To kill the thing she was, was in a strange way suicide, for Stormy was the himself that had been in a way and to an extent that Wade could never be.

She balked him, teased him, irritated him, and he was powerless. He suspected dully that only the fact that no one dared speak of it to him had prevented his learning that some kind of scandal had already attached itself to her name. He contemplated the idea in slow misery, but beyond that he would not go. He preferred not knowing; to find out the actuality of ill fame would necessitate his taking steps, and what steps could anyone take against Stormy Benton?

Scold her, you have to beat her, he mused painfully; beat her, you have to kill her—and I couldn't do that—I couldn't. . . .

He rode into the courtyard and saw to his astonishment that the light was still on in the master bedroom. He pulled the bell cord to awaken the slave who slept in the loft above the stable, and went into the house without waiting to see whether or not the Negro had come for his horse.

Sarah was waiting for him, her gray eyes dull with misery, her face drawn, tired, old.

"What is it, Sary?" he growled. "Something wrong with Wade?"

"Not Wade," Sarah said grimly. "Stormy. I told you, Tom Benton, you'd live to weep over . . ."

"What's she done?" Tom croaked.

"She's not home yet!" Sarah said, "and here it is after midnight. Lord God, the times I've tried to reason with her about . . ."

"About what?" Tom Benton said.

"Ron Cattlet," Sarah whispered.

"That wild young bastard!" Tom growled. "And you never told me! Sary, in the name of hellfire, why?"

"What good would it have done?" Sarah said tiredly. "She always could wind you around her little finger. I've tried to reason with her but she won't listen. It's an open scandal how she rides over to the Cattlet place to seek him out. Nancy Cattlet had words with me about it—told me to keep my little hussy of a daughter off her place. . . ."

"Damn my soul!" Tom roared.

Sarah was crying now, an ugly, noisy sound.

"They've been seen kissing in public places. Folks have come up on them sitting in Ron's buckboard after dark in deserted lanes. That uppity Jim Rudgers said to Hunt Cattlet right in front of my face: 'Hunt, I hear that boy of yourn has been putting in a crop afore he's built a fence!'"

"Jesus!" Tom cried out, naked anguish in his voice.

"She ain't never stayed out this late before; but you don't have to stay out late to get into mischief. And when I try to talk to her, she looks me in my face and says: 'You should talk, Maw. At least I ain't cheating on my husband; and ain't nobody killed hisself over me yet!'"

Sarah covered her face with her hands and gave way to a storm of weeping.

"It's true, Tom!" she sobbed; "it's true! What can I say to my own child? What right have I to say anything a-tall?"

Tom put out his big hand and patted her shoulder with awkward tenderness.

"Don't take on so, Sary," he said; "ain't your fault—ain't your fault none a-tall."

"Oh, but it is!" Sarah wept. "You're a man and folks don't expect much of a man. But a woman's different. She's supposed to uphold the decency of her house—and now look what's happened. . . ."

"I think you've been doing that all these years," Tom said heavily; "you made one bad slip, and that one was my fault. And you repented of it and kept your word ever since—so don't take on so. Now I've got to go. I'll be back as soon as I can. . . ."

Sarah looked up at him, then, her gray eyes big with terror.

"Tom," she whispered.

"Yes, Sary?"

"Don't use your gun. He ain't nothing but a boy, and . . ."

Tom drew his revolver and handed it to her, butt first.

"You keep it," he said quietly. "Don't need a gun to handle that young sprig. Besides, the Cattlets are pretty decent folks—and if this thing has been going on long enough . . ."

"Thanks, Tom," Sarah said.

Then he went back into the yard, finding Prince Rupert still at the rail, for Caleb, the groom, snoring blissfully in his loft above the stable, had not even heard the brazen clangor of the bell.

At last he rode out of the big gates into the impenetrable darkness, that was around him and inside him, too; there being, for him, at that moment, no light anywhere in the world.

He rode the lonely road beside the river, and the lonelier lanes that curved into the woodlands, and skirted the edges of the bayous. He heard the soft, secret night noises: the scurrying of the small furry beasts, the beat of predatory wings. The demented screaming of the marsh heron slashed against his ears, and all the mourning sounds, too: owls hooting in the tree tops, the sad, far-off howling of the watchdogs crying the absent moon.

But though he could not find his daughter, he came very close to finding himself: what he was, living, the essence of his being. Night and brooding darkness have their uses; they can drive a man inward upon himself, until he is face to face with the actuality of his mind, soul, spirit. But being what he was, Tom Benton recoiled in anger and in fear. He could not accept himself yet; that required further humbling. So he rode the whole night through on the edge of the discovery that might have saved him. But of Stormy he saw no sign.

He came, finally, as dawn was graying the east, when trees, buildings, fences were taking on their first faint shapes of unreality in the process of becoming the things they were by day, when witchery dies before the slow-creeping light, and the world is itself again, commonplace and comfortable, known, seen, believed—to the outbuildings on the very edge of the vast Cattlet plantation. He had not looked there before, because it seemed to him incredible that Stormy and Ron would have had the nerve to go there; but considering the matter from the standpoint of how closely his daughter resembled himself, even in her habits of thought, he came to the conclusion it was precisely the sort of thing that would appeal to her habitual audacity.

So he dismounted, and walked quietly among the buildings, a secondary group, placed for convenience in servicing the plantation's outlying acres, more than a mile from the big house. He saw then with the weary recognition of one who has found precisely what he expected, the two horses, tied up behind one of the barns, well enough hidden to keep them entirely out of sight of the road. He pushed against the small door cut into one of the huge doors. It was bolted from the inside. He tested it with his shoulder, noting the amount of give. Then he stepped back a few paces, and slammed his body against it with all his force. It gave way at once with a splintering crash as the cross-bar broke, and he half fell into the barn.

He stood there, blinking against the darkness; when he heard the rustle of their movements, and Stormy's voice saying coldly, clearly, filled with abysmal disgust:

"Oh, my God, it's Paw. . . ."

He took a step forward, and his eyes began to adjust themselves to the gloom. Then he saw Ron Cattlet, on his feet now, shivering a little from fear, and from his nakedness.

Tom stood there, waiting. When the boy was close enough, he slapped him, open handed, to the ground. Ron came up again, wild with fury, driven by the insult of being struck thus like a woman or a child. This time, Tom did not knock him down again at once, but slapped him right and left, jerking his head from side to side on his slender neck, jetting the tears out of his eyes, still striking, his own big hand making a blur moving, the explosion of the blows like a fusillade of small-arms fire, and the boy hanging there, taking it, unable to reach Tom Benton with his own wild swings until finally the big man ended it, slashing the youth down with one hard blow, and stepped back, leaving the boy there sobbing and retching, the blood trickles from his broken mouth penciling his chin.

Tom looked at his daughter. Stormy didn't move or speak; but there was no fear in her eyes.

"Get up," Tom said, and his voice was curiously mild. "Get your things on, I'm taking you home."

She didn't answer him, but stood up at once, and Tom turned away from the aching loveliness of this nakedness that was his own nakedness, flesh of his flesh, blood of his blood. He lit a cigar and stood there, smoking quietly, listening to the silken rustle of her clothing, the ugly hoarse rasp of the boy's sobbing. Then she came up to him and touched his arm. He took her by the elbow and started toward the door. Then he felt her stop.

" 'Bye, Ron," she said.

"Stormy!" The boy's voice was a near-scream, edged with death and hell.

"I said good-bye," Stormy said flatly. "For good, Ron. You're no man. And I can't stand anyone who isn't."

Then she walked on, a little ahead of her father, and stepped through the door.

On the ride home, neither of them spoke. Stormy looked straight ahead, her blue eyes staring into dark and secret places, a little smile hovering about the corners of her mouth. It got to him almost at once, that smile. And all the way home that slow, secret smile worked in his blood, taunting him into fury, into black and murderous rage.

They rode into the stableyard at Broad Acres. Tom swung down and stood there, looking at her.

"Get down," he said harshly.

Stormy got down. She said:

"You're going to beat me." It was a statement, not a question.

"Go into the barn," Tom said. "Wait for me there. Don't try any tricks."

He went into the stable and came back with the mule-skinner's whip. Then he went into the barn after her.

She didn't weep, or even cry out. He couldn't stand that. He slashed harder, cutting the stuff of her dress to ribbons, cutting through the tender flesh beneath it, bringing blood. Still she didn't cry out. Fire exploded behind Tom Benton's eyes. A black hood closed down over his head. He brought the whip whining whistling down, not even hearing the sick, wet smashing sound it made biting into her, but from Stormy no cry, no sound at all.

Then, suddenly, the rage went out of him, leaving him sick and trembling, icy sweat beading his forehead, the sour taste of nausea in his throat, and bending down beside her, he saw that it had been a long time since she could have cried out; the handful of straw she had thrust into her own mouth to prevent the sound's escaping bitten through, her tongue itself bitten through, her mouth half filled with blood.

He picked her up. She lolled in his arms like a rag doll, limp and boneless. He marched into the house with her, shouldered open the door to the bedroom, and stood there in the doorway, holding her.

"Here," he said harshly, "take your daughter."

Then he put Stormy down on the bed and walked out.

Four hours later he was on a steamboat headed downstream to New Orleans. He never afterwards remembered going ashore. For before the *Bayou Belle* had passed Natchitoches, he was already coldly, blindly, completely drunk. Two weeks later he came to his senses in a whorehouse run by an enormous German woman called Big Gertie, down on Gallatin Street.

He lay very still, not even looking at the blowsy, ill-favored wench who snored beside him, and tried to think of what he would do next.

It took him a long time to think of it; but in the end it was very simple. He would pay a call on Lolette Dupré.

8

STORMY LAY very quietly in the big bed and stared at the ceiling. It was almost two weeks since Tom had beaten her, and during all that time, no one in the household, not even the slaves, had heard a word pass her lips. She was perfectly capable of talking; moreover, she could have left her bed days ago if she had wanted to; but it suited both her nature and her plans to lie there and subtly put the whole household on the defensive in their relationships with her.

She had had ten days, more or less, for thinking; and she had thought everything out very carefully and well. Her mind was an astounding mixture of complete maturity and utter childishness; it was to remain so in varying proportions all the rest of her life. What she proposed to do was a schoolgirl's daydream: she was going to run away from home, go to New York, and become a glittering luminary of the metropolitan stage. The simple realities of the matter: that she had absolutely no talent for acting, that she had never even so much as read a play, not to mention having seen one, that her diction was but little better than that of the Negro slaves from whom she had unconsciously absorbed it; her ideas of enunciation, pronunciation, grammatical speech practically nonexistent—these troubled her not at all because she was unaware of her defects. And, since she was her father's daughter, they would have troubled her no more had she known of them.

One asset she had, and that was rendered ineffective by being itself a commonplace in the theatrical world: she was truly beautiful. She knew this very well; but she attached no special importance to it. Her vanity was beyond that; when anyone mentioned it, she dismissed the compliment with a shrug. She was Stormy Benton—of course she was prettier than anyone else, just as she was smarter, a better horsewoman, a better shot, superior in every way; all this was implicit in her being herself—a part of the very nature of things; and the result of her deep, overwhelming, convinced, utterly complacent vanity was strangely like modesty. She had absolutely nothing to prove; so she never primped, put on airs, or talked about herself, never dreaming that anyone ever saw her in any other fashion than the way she saw herself: a shining goddess set down for a little while among vastly inferior beings whose sole reason for existence was to serve her.

But if her final goal existed truly in a dreamer's never-never land, her methods of accomplishing it were coldly, brilliantly precise and practical. Smiling that slow and secret smile that had goaded her father into almost killing her, she got up from the bed and began to dress without any haste whatsoever. She knew exactly where every member of the household was at that minute: her mother in the big kitchen, built for safety's sake behind the house and apart from it, supervising the preparation of the midday meal; Wade mooning off by himself, down by the river, bemourning his lost Babette; and her father away since the day he had beaten her, in New Orleans, more than likely, drinking and consorting with those dreadful creatures down on Gallatin Street. She did not consider the Negroes at all, except to take a few simple precautions against their eternal tale-bearing.

Her toilette finished, she walked calmly across the hall and entered her father's study. She opened the drawer of his secretary and took out his checkbook. What she was going to do, Tom Benton himself had made possible. A firm believer in practical education, he had long ago started teaching his children something about financial management. To this end, he had often sent Wade, and even occasionally Stormy, down to the bank to draw money for operating expenses. Stormy had already become official bookkeeper for the plantation, for she was very good with figures. More, about six months ago, she had entirely replaced Wade as her father's messenger; a thing that had come about very simply and naturally as a result of Wade's having lost a packet of bills containing more than five hundred dollars on the way home from the bank.

"From now on, you stay home!" Tom had raged; "I'll send Stormy— she's twice the man you are, anyhow!"

She sat there a long moment, her brow furrowed with thinking. At that moment her resemblance to her father was startling. Slowly she picked up the pen and began to write, imitating fairly well her father's heavy strokes and painful penmanship. She wrote four checks for five hundred dollars each, forging her father's name at the bottom of them. Her work, of course, would not have supported detailed scrutiny; but she had little fear of that. The clerks at the bank would not look at the checks too carefully; after all, they were accustomed to having her come in and draw large sums in her father's behalf.

It was a measure of her craft that she wrote four small checks instead of one large one. Tom seldom drew more than five to seven hundred dollars at a time. Even though they were all made out to cash, Stormy reasoned that they would arouse less questioning than a single check for two thousand dollars. With her healthy contempt for the reasoning powers of ordinary humans, she was sure that the teller, already accustomed to cashing checks of that particular sum, would give her the money without a qualm.

She sanded the checks, folded them, and put them in her handbag. Then she got up and walked slowly and thoughtfully out of the house, having made absolutely no mistakes at all—not even the normal one of packing her things and attempting to leave the house with a valise. She knew that the Negroes would have run to her mother with that information before she could have passed the big gate. Besides, she consoled herself, my clothes are too countrified anyhow. I can buy much prettier things in New Orleans. . . .

But before she had reached town, she had modified her plan in light of the fact that the voyage downstream to New Orleans was far too long for anyone coming aboard without luggage, without even a hat or a parasol, not to arouse suspicion, particularly a young, unescorted woman. So, she decided, I'll buy a ticket to Alexandria, get myself just a few things and a valise there, then go on to New Orleans, and then to New York. . . .

She had it all clear, all firmly fixed in mind when she came out of the bank with the money. Then she walked on down to the landing, and went aboard the *Bayou Belle*, smiling a little to herself.

The whistle jetted its plume into the sky, screaming. The paddlewheels turned over, bit water. The steamboat moved downstream, gathering speed. And Stormy Benton, sitting on the foredeck, did not even look back.

9

THERE WAS one thing that could be truthfully said of Big Gertie: she ran an honest house. Tom Benton was able to leave it with almost as much money as he had when he went in, and that was a sizable amount, for his pride made him keep his pockets well filled. But he was in no condition to visit anyone, and he knew it. He was bleary eyed, unshaven, his clothes stained, unpressed, his shoes muddy, his handkerchief, hat and cane all lost somewhere en route during his homeric bout of drunkenness.

It was fortunate for him that he had always stayed at the Saint Louis

Hotel, and was, therefore, well known there, both as a bon vivant and a free-spender; it is extremely doubtful that otherwise the management of that august establishment would have let him in. As it was, they conducted him upstairs to his room in considerable haste, even going so far as to send the register up for his signature instead of having him sign it in the lobby, which might have caused his coming to the attention of too many of their distinguished clientele while in his present sadly disreputable state.

But once safely in his room, Tom gave a convincing demonstration of the man from whom Stormy had gotten her traits. Within a half-hour, he had bathed, been shaved and clipped by the hotel's barber, had a manicure, sent a bellboy out armed with his size numbers to purchase a new hat, fresh underwear, new shirts, a new cravat and a cane, had sent also his suit down to be sponged off and pressed, and his boots to be shined.

Then he sat down, grotesquely wrapped in towels, and forced down a fairish portion of the meal he had ordered, no mean feat after two weeks of steady drinking. By midafternoon, he was able to smoke a cigar. By six o'clock, all his purchases having arrived, and his other clothing having been returned in an entirely presentable state, he was able to make such an appearance as he descended into the lobby as to bring all the hotel's functionaries out to greet him, all smiles and respectful attention.

He walked slowly up Royal Street, swinging his new cane. He felt, strangely enough, at peace with the world. He let his gaze wander over the old street, studying again the ironwork balustrades on the galleries, like filigrees of fine old lace, moving very slowly, allowing the sights, sounds, smells of this his favorite city to wash over him in a sensuous wave. It was as if he were seeing New Orleans for the first time, or—the thought tugged insistently at his consciousness—the last. Either way, it was good. He had had it all: joy, victory, bitterness, defeat; and having had all this, he found that he had grown very quiet inside, that his hungers no longer gnawed at his vitals, that the rage for living had gone out of him, so that now, at last, he was very quiet, and very complete.

Some time during his two weeks of drunken stupor, it had all burned out of him: the rage, the furor, the lingering hungers, the need to impress his stamp upon men and events, upon time itself. Things of tremendous importance to him before, his daughter's shame, Sarah's indifference to him, his son's weakness, diminished before his dreaming eyes into their proper place in the scheme of things, becoming part of life's inevitabilities, part of that slow reduction that time worked upon the spirit of a man, grinding down the prickly edges of his pride, until he could accept, believe, bear all things with equanimity, with only the faintest, sighing respect for the honor, pride, intractability of his youth.

I'm a tired old man, he thought, nothing more. I want to do two things: see Lolette again, and meet my son—find out for good and all if I ever had it in me to sire a man—that's all. After that, maybe the

Yankees will ease me out of it. Had enough—Lord God, I'm tired. . . .

The house on Royal Street was a fine old courtyard house, hidden by walls with shuttered windows, frowning doors from the street, but flowering and gracious within. A Negro in spotless livery took his hat and cane, and said with a trace of Gumbo-French accent:

"Who I tell Madame is calling, M'sieu?"

"Benton," Tom growled. "Mr. Thomas Benton."

"Yessir," the Negro said. Then he was gone, and Tom sat there a long time in the anteroom, unconscious of the passing of time, the flower scents from the garden stealing around him, coaxing him into lassitude, into drowsiness, until the click of her heels upon the stairs drew him out of it, awakening him into life again, into consciousness.

She stood in the doorway, smiling at him.

"Tom!" she breathed. "So good of you to come!"

He got clumsily to his feet and stood there, staring at her. She was exquisite. He stood there looking at her, and the sadness pressed down upon his heart like a weight. She was exquisite—not lovely any more. She had lost that look of a wild woods creature, frightened and shy, become something else, something that troubled him because he did not know how to deal with it, or even exactly what it was. She was perfumed, coiffeured, lacquered, polished, dressed with a taste that reflected the summit of the art of an artful people; but her eyes had hardened, lost their fawnlike softness, considering him now with interest, but coolly, with faint amusement, but without the things that had endeared them to him before: either fear, or respect, or tenderness.

"Well," she said, and her voice held the ripple of barely concealed laughter in it, "aren't you going to greet me?"

"Ain't sure I know you, Ma'am," Tom said. "Lord God, but you've changed!"

She came up to him and kissed him, her lips clinging warmly, softly, expertly; then she drew back and laughed aloud.

"But you haven't," she said. "Oh, you've gotten older and heavier. Grayer, too. But you haven't changed. Not in the essentials. You're still you—and that would be funny, if it weren't so sad. . . ."

"What do you mean by that?" Tom growled.

"Everything—nothing," she said coquettishly. "Come on, don't you want to see Clinton?"

"One of the reasons I came, Ma'am—I mean Lolette. Where is the boy?"

"Upstairs," she said. "He'll please you. He's your image. Come—"

They went up the stairs together, without haste. And walking close to her, Tom saw the threads of gray in her own dark hair, the tiny web of lines at the corners of her eyes, the ravishments of time that her skillful use of cosmetics concealed very well at a distance, but showed close up. She was a year younger than Sarah, but he was aware suddenly that stripped of her artifices she would have looked ten years older; and he knew with something like conviction from her face, the history of her years.

Time leaves no face unscarred, but pain and bitterness, loneliness and terror leave crueler marks. And that kind of pleasure born—he guessed, in this case at least—of the desire for vengeance, the abandonment of self into the mindless, soulless delights of voluptuousness, of lust and venery, droops the corners of the mouth, dulls the eyes, and twists the face in ways peculiar to itself.

Had a hard life, ain't you, Baby-doll? Tom thought as they paused upon the landing, and the weariness was upon him, resting like a mountain upon his chest.

"What are you looking at?" she said.

"At how different you are," Tom said heavily.

"You expected me not to be? I've grown up, Tom. Apparently you haven't."

"You mean you've gotten hard," Tom said. "There's more than one way of growing up, Lolette. Some folks kind of mellow down into wine, and others sharpen up into vinegar."

"And I'm vinegar," Lolette said quietly. "You want to know why, Tom?"

"Reckon I kind of know already. I started it. . . ."

"And others finished it. My husband. My lovers—my many, many lovers. You see, it took me a long time to grow up, Tom. I kept looking for something that wasn't there. Finally I learned that men at heart are either beasts, or children; some needing the whip, and the rest, a mother. Doesn't leave much for a woman, does it? A real woman wanting one sole thing: a man who is master of himself, and hence, of his world. But he doesn't exist, does he, Tom? A whining, weakling infant, wanting to be comforted or fed, or a snarling beast to be whipped back on his haunches— that's all the choice a woman has. You find me hard—well, I am. I know now that men are there to be used, and to give one's heart into their keeping is to toss it to a savage dog to tear. . . ."

Tom stood there on the landing, looking at her.

"Well," she said, "shall we go in?"

"After you," he said tiredly.

He saw, as he entered the room, that the boy was not alone. He was talking to his grandfather, Louis Dupré, a flood of rapid French pouring from his lips. Babette sat on the arm of her father's chair, gazing at this tall nephew of hers, only three years her junior, in awe and wonder.

Seeing them, young Clinton stood up. At sixteen, he was already almost as tall as his father; but lacking Tom's great breadth and enormous strength. Beyond that, as Lolette had said, he was his father's image; but refined, somehow, softened by his mother's beauty into a brooding handsomeness that Tom had never had. Still, seeing them together like that, anyone not blind or a fool could see instantly that here were father and son; and Louis Dupré was neither.

"*Espèce d'un cochon!*" he got out. "Species of a pig! I should have known then, me! *Par la Sainte Vierge*, I should have known!"

"Howdy, Clint," Tom Benton said, and put out his hand.

Slowly, hesitantly, the boy took it. His hands were slender, but his grip was iron beneath velvet, and Tom Benton smiled.

"This is Mister Benton," Lolette said evenly. "I've told you about him, Clinton. . . ."

Tom could see the blaze kindle in the boy's dark eyes.

"Then he is—?" he whispered.

"Your father—yes," Lolette said.

Louis was on his feet then, like a cat.

"I think I kill you now, me!" he roared. "I think you done lived now sixteen years too long!"

"Oh, don't be a fool, Papa," Lolette said calmly. "That was a long time ago, and there's too much water under the bridge by now. Besides, if you kill all the men who've shared my bed, you'd need half the Federal Army to help you—"

"*Maman!*" Clint said, "have you no shame?"

"None," Lolette mocked. "Men are such sentimental fools, Clinton, *mon fils*. I've tried to train you differently. Look, Papa, if you had killed Tom Benton sixteen years ago, I'd have wept my heart out. Today, I'd yawn. What are you trying to prove? That you can slice the liver out of this overdressed country bumpkin, middle aged as he is, and running to fat? Of course you can—this is nothing, you comprehend? Or are you still defending your daughter's honor? Then I must decline the defense—I haven't any of your peculiar, provincial honor left; I haven't had for a long time—since, *cher* Papa, long before I met Tom Benton. If you like the pleasures of prison life, or the thrill of being hanged, go ahead—I won't stop you. Well, Papa, what are you waiting for?"

Louis stood there, looking at her. Then, very slowly, he reached for his hat.

"Come, Babette," he said; "we go home now, us. You're my daughter—my only daughter now. Come—"

Babette turned to her sister.

"I think," she said, "you're perfectly horrible!"

Lolette smiled.

"And I think you're a dear," she said pleasantly. "But I think also that you will learn—and that's a pity. . . ."

After they had gone, Tom stood there still, making no effort to sit down.

"Well, Tom?" Lolette said.

Tom didn't answer her.

"Clint-boy," he said heavily, "I've been a bad father, maybe even a bad man—I don't know. But I got a place up the country, nice spread of land. Any time you want to come there and live, I'd be mighty proud to have you. Make up for some of the time we lost. Even if you just come to visit, I'd be glad—what you say, boy?"

Clint glanced at his mother.

"I—I'd like very much to visit you, sir," he said, "but I cannot live with you. I couldn't leave my mother for so long—she's not very well, and she needs me."

"Oh, you can visit him if you like," Lolette said. "It would do you good. Tom would certainly toughen you up a bit, and you need that. But I haven't any intention of giving you up forever to a man who ignored your existence for sixteen years. Well, Tom, aren't you going to sit down?"

"No," Tom said; "I'm going now. When can the boy come?"

"Next month," Lolette said. "Give my love to your dear Sarah, won't you, Tom?"

" 'Bye, Clint," Tom said, and put out his hand. "We're going to have fun, boy. Mighty good hunting and fishing out at Broad Acres."

"Good-bye, sir," Clinton said; "I shall be very pleased to come."

Lolette walked with Tom down the stairs and into the courtyard.

"Strange," she said quietly; "I've been looking forward to seeing you again, but it was no good—was it? I'd told myself that I'd given up for tinsel, for dross, the one real man I'd known. And I was right; but I've changed too much. One can never go back again, can one?"

"No," Tom said. "Reckon life is a one-way street, Lolette. 'Bye now."

Then he put his hat firmly atop his head, and moved off, down the street.

Watching him stride away, Lolette had a feeling he did not go alone. A brightness moved before him; but behind him darkness came, growing, spreading, shutting off the light.

She felt very strange suddenly: cold and weak and tired.

I don't understand it, she thought; what a crazy way to feel.

Then she went back into the courtyard, closing very quietly the door between her and the world.

10

FIRST IN the morning, Wade Benton mounted the gray gelding, and rode out to the Duprés' cabin. But he was spared the trouble of poling a pirogue out into the bayou to reach it, for when he got there, he met Babette and Louis coming ashore.

"Good morning, sir," he said politely, then: "Babs—"

But Louis cut him off.

"You stay away from my daughter, you," he said. "Don't want to have nothing to do with no more Bentons, yes. See her in a convent before I let her marry Tom Benton's whelp. Know what's good for you, you keep away."

"You don't have to worry about that, Papa," Babette laughed. "I wouldn't have that sniveling little puppy for a Christmas gift. I've told him that, me. Don't know why he keeps on hanging around."

"Babs," Wade got out.

"Don't call me Babs," she said cruelly. "When I marry, I want myself a man, and that's one thing you'll never be!"

"No," Wade said acidly, "if you mean that I'll never be like my father, you're right. Don't even want to be. All right, Mister Dupré, you won't have no more trouble out of me. Not that you ever had. You been barking up the wrong tree all the time. It ain't me you have to watch out for—it's my pa."

"What you mean by that, boy?" Louis said quietly.

"Ask Babs," Wade spat. He was beyond all caution now. "She told me herself she was in love with him!"

"Why, you dirty little sneak!" Babs said.

"Dirty? I don't go fooling around with other folks' wives. And my pa's my ma's husband. Who's dirty, Babs? I ask you! And right now I want to see you turn round and look your father in the face and tell him it ain't so. Go on, I dare you!"

"Babette," Louis said, and his voice was a blade half drawn from its sheath.

"It ain't so, Papa!" Babette said desperately. "Why, I ain't never so much as talked to Mister Benton alone!"

"That ain't the point," Wade persisted. "Tell him you didn't say you love my pa!"

Babette opened her mouth to speak, but then she saw her father's eyes, and closed it again, without saying anything at all.

"I see," Louis whispered. Then: "You tell your father, you—that if I ever hear tell of his even saying 'Howdy' to *ma Babette*, I cut his liver out. Tell him that. And you, little fool, I take care of you when we get back from town! Pity I got to go there, yes; but I stripe you all over soon as we get back. Come on, now!"

"Now see what you've done!" Babette wailed.

"Go home, boy," Louis said. "I don't feel like looking at no Bentons too long!"

Wade turned and rode off, then, out of the clearing. He was careful not to ride too fast. Like every Benton born, he had his pride.

He did not ride directly home, but made a long, circular detour, as if to cherish the savage misery that tore him. On the edge of the Ransom place, he saw the small, forlorn figure of Mary Ann Barker. He knew her already, for during his father's absence Jane Ransom had brought her to visit. They hadn't been able to introduce her to Stormy, because at that time his sister had still been abed as a result of a savage beating Tom had dealt her.

Wade didn't even like to remember that visit, for despite Sarah's magnificent efforts at concealment, the strain under which they labored hovered over them all like a suspended blade. Mrs. Ransom had not come back, perhaps attributing the strange atmosphere she had sensed at Broad Acres to a lack of friendliness—even to a degree of hostility on Sarah's part. She was wrong, of course; but it wasn't a thing anybody could explain.

Mary Ann came forward, smiling her shy, childish smile.

"Howdy, Wade," she murmured.

"Oh, git out of my way!" Wade snarled; "I ain't got no time for the likes of you!"

The child stepped back, her brown eyes wide with astonishment and pain.

"All right, Wade," she choked, "if that's the way you feel. . . ."

"That's the way I feel all right!" Wade snapped, and put spurs to his mount. But five minutes later, he was sorry.

Why'd I do that? he thought miserably. Mary Ann's a sweet little thing. She ain't much to look at, but she's nice. Be a heap better to be interested in somebody like her than that wicked, no good Babette. Oh Lord, I just naturally always say the wrong thing at the wrong time. . .

He rode into the yard at Broad Acres, and tossed the reins to Caleb. Then he went into the house, thinking: Pa's home by now for sure. Ma got that letter four days ago. . . . In his present state of mind, nothing would have suited him better than to hurl Louis' message into his father's teeth. He put his hand on the knob; but at the last moment, he did not turn it. For his mother's voice came through, muffled a little by the wooden door, but speaking slowly, clearly.

"Yes, Tom," she said; "I moved your things into the guest room. If I had anywheres to go, I'd leave you. But I haven't. Still you can't expect me to go on sleeping in the same bed with you, knowing where you've been and what you've been doing."

"How do you know?" Tom said.

"I know, and that's enough. If you think you can spend your time whoring around in New Orleans, and come back to me like nothing's happened, you're crazy. Visiting your woman and your unlawful brat . . ."

"How the devil did you know that?" Tom roared. "Randy! Why damn his miserable hide—"

"Randy McGregor ain't never let your name pass his lips. He don't care that much about you. Besides, he's a gentleman—lucky for you he is—Tom Benton!"

Tom let that pass.

"Then how did you know?" he growled.

Wade moved closer to the door, shaking, all his muscles tensed for flight. "Don't tell him, Ma!" he breathed silently; "for God's sake don't tell him it was me who told you!"

"None of your business," Sarah said. "Anyhow, I'm finished. First you get me in trouble. Then Lolette Dupré. God knows how many others. And now, to top it off, you've drove your only daughter away with your poison-meanness. . . ."

"Stormy's gone?" Tom said. Even through the door, Wade could hear the pain in his father's voice.

"Yes," Sarah said. "Drew two thousand dollars out of your account and disappeared—took not a stitch of clothes with her. I hired a New Orleans detective. He found out she bought things there—that's how smart she was. Didn't want folks to see her leaving with a bag. That detective traced everything she did. Seems she sailed North on a boat bound for Boston. . . ."

Wade heard the scrape of his father's chair.

"Tom," Sarah said, "where're you going?"

"Boston, where else?" Tom Benton said. "You get some of my things packed, Sary. I'll go down to Alexandria to see about tickets and such like. I'll be back tomorrow. . . ."

"All right," Sarah said. "Time you did something what makes sense."

Wade moved fast, then—away from the door, rushing into his own room, leaving the door ajar so that he could see. He saw his father come out, his face frowning and intent, and go out on the veranda. A moment later, he heard him call:

"Caleb! Saddle Prince Rupert for me. And hurry, damn your lazy black hide!"

Wade closed the door very quietly. He was free, now—for a little while longer. For the time being, at least, he had escaped.

When the groom came with the horse, Tom vaulted into the saddle and started off at a hard gallop toward the town. At that time, the telegraph lines had not yet reached Benton's Row. While it was possible to board a steamboat there, the village having already become an established stop, and pay one's fare aboard for any distance as far north as Shreveport, and as far south as New Orleans, Tom was obliged to go to Alexandria to wire ahead for accommodations aboard one of the coastal steamers which plied between New Orleans and the Northern ports. In 1860, the only way to reach any major city in the United States from Louisiana was by water; exactly thirty-five miles of railways existed in that State.

It was only the tumult within him that caused Tom Benton to gallop the stallion; in actuality, he had plenty of time. The downstream boat would not stop at Benton's Row for another three hours, and no amount of haste would get him to Alexandria before the telegraph office closed for the night. He would, he knew, have to stay overnight there, get his message off as early as possible in the morning, and wait around for his reply.

So it was that he reached Benton's Row with more than two hours to spare. Once there, he followed his accustomed habits: he went at once to Randy's office to invite the doctor to have a drink with him. But Randy was away, out on calls. He was always busy, now. More, since that day, five years before, that Doctor Muller had been gathered to whatever rewards that awaited his ignorance and his bungling, Randy McGregor had been overworked to the point of exhaustion.

Frowning, Tom set out for Tim's place alone. He had wanted very badly to talk with Randy. He's my friend, he thought soberly. Reckon him and Hilton are just about the only two real friends I've got. Funny thing to be friends with a man who's in love with your wife, but there it is. And, damn it all, it's because Randy's my friend—really my friend—that I don't even have to worry about that. Level headed, too. I could talk to him, and he'd give me some good advice. Randy ain't often wrong. . . .

He saw, as he came up to Tim's, that Babette Dupré stood on the sidewalk a few paces from the door. He knew at once what she was doing there. Louis had gone inside for a drink, and since females weren't allowed in saloons, Babette had to wait outside for her father. He came up to her before she saw him.

"Howdy, Babette," he said, "how's everything? Had any more news from that there sister of your'n?"

She turned and all the color drained out of her face.

"Mister Benton!" she got out. "Go away! Get away from me! Mister Benton—please!"

Tom stood there, staring at her.

"Now looka here, little lady," he said. "Always thought that you and me was friends. . . ."

"It's not that," Babette said, the edge of hysteria getting into her voice. "It's papa! Wade told him some awful lies, and—please, Mister Benton, I can't stand here talking to you—I just can't! That would be all papa would need. . . ."

He saw the shape of the words she had intended to speak on her lips; but the sound of them died somewhere deep in her throat, so all that was left was her lips moving, her face graying under its natural tan, and the look of utter terror in her eyes.

Tom turned slowly, half knowing what he would see. Louis Dupré was not a drinking man. He had had his one tall glass of sour red wine, and now he came out again through the swinging doors of Tim's saloon.

He stopped dead, a yard from Tom.

"So," he said. "Told that boy of yours to tell you to stay way from *ma Babette*. Told him I'd kill you if you didn't. Didn't listen, did you, Tom Benton? Going to kill you now, me. Going to kill you and get it over with!"

"What in hellfire are you talking about, Louis?" Tom growled. "You out of your mind?"

"Your own boy told me," Louis said. "You been after *ma Babette*, too. One of my daughers wasn't enough, eh? You got to ruin 'em both, you! Pray your *bon Dieu*, Tom Benton, 'cause I'm going to kill you now!"

Tom saw then, incredibly, that Louis meant it. The small man fell into a crouch and brought his knife out, gleaming dull blue in the sunlight. Tom fell back and reached for his gun. But his hand came out of his coat empty. After years of peace, he had finally gotten out of the habit of carrying a gun.

Louis came in fast, in the instinctive crouch of the born knife fighter. Tom stood there, then, with a roar, he charged the smaller man.

But Louis made no mistakes. He did not lift his knife, and swing it downward, making it easy for his opponent to catch his wrist. Instead, he held it low, the razor sharp edge upward, waiting for an opening.

Tom hadn't a chance, and he knew it; but he came on in, driven by the one thing in him that was really splendid, a courage bigger than he himself was, a profound, deep-seated conviction that it was better to die than to run away, and afterwards have to remember the fleeing. So it was that he smashed his left fist hard against Louis' face, spinning him half around with the blow, and Louis, shaking his head, came out of the crouch, the blade flashing up and forward, one hundred thirty pounds of wildcat bone, muscle and sinew behind the thrust.

Tom felt something hot and searing deep in his vitals. Then Louis stepped back, and the blade came out, leaving only the terrible burning, the hot gushing, the flooding warm wetness, and the awful weakness spreading. He pushed against himself hard, hanging there, seeing Louis' yellow-brown eyes glaring into his, waiting for him to go down, to fall.

Then Babette started screaming. And Tom Benton stood there, hearing the sound of it, formless and wild, tearing the fabric of heaven itself apart, shrill, demented, terrible.

The doors of the saloon burst open, spilling a horde of men out into the street. They saw the bloody knife in Louis Dupré's hand, and recoiled away from him in two waves on both sides, making a semicircle, frozen into immobility, death-struck, silent.

They stood there, all of them, watching it. Babette was past even screaming now. And standing there, like that, they saw the only true miracle that humanity is ever privileged to witness: the shining steel of a man's will, standing up tall amid the rags of his flesh, moving him, one awful step after another, this man beyond human help, beyond even compassion, dying there very slowly before their eyes, still on his feet, still moving.

They saw him unhitch the reins with his left hand; but to mount, he had to use both, and the red tide of his life pumped out of him faster. But he got incredibly, miraculously into the saddle, using almost the last of his gigantic strength in the doing, driven by his unshakable belief in himself, his refusal to accept even death, and held up by these things and his iron will, he rode away from there, down the street toward the plantation.

Babette started screaming again, seeing that. Louis wiped the knife on his trouser leg and thrust it back into the scabbard. Then he came over to her and slapped her five or six times very hard across the face until she stopped screaming.

He did not look at the men who had come out of the saloon. Instead, he walked diagonally across the street and into the courthouse where Sheriff Brighton's office was. No one moved, no one followed him.

John Brighton was sitting in his big chair, his feet on his desk, reading a three-day-old *Picayune*. He looked up when Louis entered and smiled.

"Howdy, Louis," he said. "Got troubles, old man?"

Louis took out his knife and dropped it on the desk.

"Came to give myself up," he said quietly. "Done killed Tom Benton, me. You find him 'bout halfway 'twixt here and his place, yes. Sorry I had to do it; but I had to. Well, John, reckon you better lock me up, now."

Louis had underestimated Tom Benton. For when Prince Rupert the black stallion came into the gates at Broad Acres at two o'clock that afternoon, Tom was still in the saddle. The horse moved slowly up to the hitching rail, and stood there, trembling. And Tom Benton sat there upon him, and made no move to dismount.

Seeing him lolling there in the saddle like a drunken man, Caleb, the groom, came running. When he was close, he stopped dead, his jaw dropping open, staring.

"Closer, boy," Tom muttered through clenched teeth, "come closer, give me a hand. . . ."

Caleb put up his arms, and his master slumped out of the saddle, loosening all over suddenly, falling into the Negro's arms.

"Miz Sarah!" Caleb screamed. "For God's sake, Miz Sarah, come out here! Somebody done 'most kilt Marse Tom!"

Sarah came out of the house with Wade at her heels.

"What ails you, Caleb?" she snapped, "yelling that way! Wade's got an awful headache and . . ."

Then she saw what Caleb held in his arms.

"Oh Good Lord Jesus!" she whispered. "Not again!" Then, very quietly: "Bring him inside, Caleb. Wade—go get Jim Rudgers. He's down in the south section. I'll send Caleb for Doctor McGregor. Careful, Caleb! Don't drop him—now. . . ."

When Wade got back with Jim Rudgers, she had already dressed the wound. The three of them stood by the bedside, looking at him. His eyes were closed, and his breathing was labored, with now and again, an ugly, gurgling sound.

"He's dying," Sarah said, her voice taut against the hysteria rising within her. "I asked him why he didn't stay in town—get help. He said— he said—he had to come home—to me. . . ."

She turned to her son.

"He asked for you, Wade. Said there was something he wanted to tell you—something he had to say—"

At the sound of his son's name, Tom Benton's eyes came open.

"Wade," he got out; but then his voice failed him. But he didn't need to speak. His eyes held steady, filled with icy fire, and Wade, standing there, whiter than death, heard inside his own heart, the rolling, thunderous, measured curses, his own consignment to eternal damnation that his father's lips formed but which he had no strength to say.

When, a few minutes later, Sheriff Brighton and Randy McGregor reached the house, he was lying there, still staring at his son. Wade was powerless to move; he had to stand there, had to take it.

Randy came over to the bed. He kneeled very quietly beside the big man, but he did not open his satchel. Instead, he put up his hand, and, as tenderly as a woman, drew down the lids over the bright blue eyes. He stayed there a long moment, saying something, his words so low, that not even Sarah, who stood beside him, could hear what they were.

"What are you saying, Randy?" she said.

"'He was my friend, faithful and just to me,'" Randy said harshly. "A quotation, Sarah—from Shakespeare. . . ."

Something in his tone caught her, and it was then, that peering closer, she saw the tears, hot and bright and sudden, in his eyes.

"Why, Randy!" she whispered; "you're crying! For him—you're crying!"

She did not need to say the rest of it: How strange it is, my love, that you should weep for him, who all these years has been the stone in our path, the wall, the barred gate, the locked door. . . .

"Yes, Goddamnit!" Randy said. "He was a man, Sarah. With all his faults you have to give him that. The way he was, he couldn't help, any more than I can help being what I am, or you. . . ."

He got up then, and turned to the Sheriff.

"You can charge Louis Dupré with murder, now, John," he said.

The case of The People of the State of Louisiana Versus Louis Dupré was heard three weeks later, when circuit Judge Neal Hanley got back to Benton's Row. The trial was over in six minutes less than one hour. And five days after that, they hanged Louis Dupré from the tall gallows behind the jail. He died very well and bravely, as he had lived.

The Cajun people hired a mason, and put a stone bearing these words above his grave: "*Louis Dupré, né 1802, decédé le 25 Juin, 1860. Victime de son honneur, il mourut pour garder intact le nom de famille. Passants priez pour lui.*"

They might better have invoked the prayers of passers-by for the immortal soul of Wade Benton. He had the greater need of prayer. For life is a harder thing than death for one like Wade, with private horrors in him: his dread of life made hopeless by his greater dread of death, and, now—having no place to throw his thirty pieces down, nor the strength of will to seek his final tree—the necessity of living with that which no man can in any comfort live, or any peace: a self-contempt grown now into loathing, a hatred for the thing he knew himself to be, utter and final and complete.

Such men have need of prayer.

Book Two

INCIDENT AT BRIAR CREEK

1

SARAH SAT on the veranda at Broad Acres, holding the pan of peas in her lap. She was shelling them, but without haste, because they were for her own dinner, and after nearly five years of eating alone, her meal times had become very irregular. She was seldom if ever hungry. Being alone did that.

Maybe now, she thought, I won't be lonely no more. Thank you, Lord, for sparing Randy. Reckon You do look after Your own. . . .

She stared out into the desolation of the yard. The weeds had mounted, all but hiding the fences, because ever since the Union armies under General Banks had devastated the Red River parishes, last year, the Negroes had fled.

It had been something to see, that flight. It had been and was, because largely it was still going on, although the war had been over for weeks now. Sitting there on the porch, her hands moving with listless inattention over the peas, Sarah could see the wall of dust rising above the river road. She knew what was beneath it: a crowd of Negroes, men, women, children; grandsires and babes in arms, moving forward at a slow shuffle, their kinky wool white with the dust, their brows and lashes filled with it, even their black faces whitened by it, except where the penciling of their sweat had drawn traces. They weren't going anywhere; they hadn't anywhere to go. They were simply moving, following some dim, instinctual migratory drive, their eyes glassy, staring straight ahead; moving like that, not even speaking, in the dust-filled vortex of that silence, except when they broke into their weird, chantlike singing. It would take them hours to pass, there were so many of them; and afterwards anyone walking that road would find those who had fallen, the ones too old, too tired, too sick to keep it up; they, the others, not even turning their heads to watch them fall, shuffling forward in that blinding heat, moving, going on.

She had tried to prevent the Benton Negroes from joining that sense-less, directionless, all but purposeless wandering; but she had failed. Old Caleb, speaking for the rest, told her:

"Got to go, Miz Sarah—just nacherly got to. Don't go, how us ever going to feel like us is free?"

And they had gone—to 'cross over Jordan,' as they put it; to explore this formless, dimensionless thing they had hoped for, dreamed of, prayed for—so many, many years.

Randy'd been here, he could have stopped them, she thought; and, as always, her face relaxed into warmth and beauty, remembering him.

He waited so long, she mused. Thought for sure I was going to have to ask him to marry me. 'Course, it wasn't no more than right to wait. A body's got to have a decent amount of respect for the dead—And Tom and Randy was such good friends. Reckon hadn't been for the war, he never would of got around to asking me. . . .

Her fingers were not even moving now. She sat there, surrendering to the warm lassitude of memory, sliding back into time, finding that moment again, recapturing it.

Randy McGregor had stayed away from her with such tortured self-control after Tom Benton's death that she had been moved finally, to send him a note:

"Folks ain't that concerned," it read, in part; "they've got other things on their minds—things a heap more important than you and me, Randy. I'm too lonely, and I'm pining to see you. Tom's dead. He's been dead nigh onto a year now—and it's been a whole lot longer than that since I ceased to really care for him. So come to see me, please. It would do me right smart good to sit a spell and talk with you—even to look at you, Randy, if you will excuse the boldness. So please come. You and Tom was friends. He liked you and respected you; and you never gave him cause not to. I kind of think that wherever he is, he really don't mind."

He had come the very day he received her note, dismounting and lop-ing up the stairs with wonder and pain and pity and joy and hope com-mingled in his eyes. He had stood there, like that, looking at her, trying to get it out, trying to put it into words, all of it: the wonder, the pain, the pity, the joy and the hope; but he could not. Too many years of wait-ing had crowded it down too far.

"Sarah," he whispered, "Sarah. . . ."

And she had stepped forward, her hands outstretched in welcome, and drawn him very simply and naturally and peacefully into her arms.

They were married the very next day, April 12, 1861, at Broad Acres, with only the minister, Wade, fourteen-year-old Mary Ann Barker, whom Wade had invited, and the servants present. By the time they reached the landing to embark on the downstream boat for their honeymoon in New Orleans, the northbound boat, the one coming upstream from Alexandria where there was a telegraph office, had already brought the news of the bombardment of Fort Sumter.

Randy McGregor stopped then and there, but Sarah caught at his arm whispering:

"It ain't going to be over in four or five days, Randy. You can enlist after our honeymoon just as well as before. . . ."

Randy looked at her and smiled.

"Right," he said; "I might as well know exactly what it is I will be fighting for."

And after those five brief days of magic, he had gone, swallowed up in the flame-shot mists, and echoing thunder to the north. Tales had come back of him—of his kindness, his patience, his valor. For this Scotsman, this convinced abolitionist became, like Lee, a hero in a cause he did not truly believe in, fighting with matchless devotion for the land whose sins he wept over, because at bottom, he loved it with all his heart.

Well, it was over now, and she was glad. Randy would come back to her, and life would start again. There would be the long years ahead; many of them, barring accident, because, aside from her own mother and father, who had fallen victim to a cholera epidemic, all of her family had been exceedingly long lived, not one of them to her certain knowledge ever having failed to reach their seventies; and not a few persisting on into their eighties and nineties. Besides, thirty-seven wasn't really so old, come to think of it. She knew women who were still bearing children at her present age. Even Randy, past fifty, could expect to bring her many more years of happiness and peace.

She needed that, the peace, anyhow, for it was the one thing she had never really had. She had known great happiness with Tom Benton, but absolutely no peace at all. And certainly her children hadn't helped matters.

Poor Wade. He certainly had never been anything much; but, in the end, he had proved himself a Benton—and a man. She had long since given up hope for him, for even in the wording of the military communiqué, there had been small grounds for it. "Missing in action," it had read, "under such circumstances that his death must be presumed. . . ."

For Wade Benton, after trying every trick of evasion his normal cunning sharpened by his cowardice could dream up, had gone off to war, finally; and when events had demanded it of him, he had risen to the occasion, and conducted himself with a gallantry that even Tom Benton could have been proud of.

But it was not that she was remembering. Though she had seen war itself, here on the very outlying fields of her own plantation, or even, perhaps, because she had seen it, her mother's heart rebelled against picturing in imagination the scene of her son's presumable and indisputably heroic death. What she went back to, with almost painful honesty she could not control, was Wade's boyhood, and how she had pitied him.

She had not loved her son. Wade Benton had never been a person anyone could love, not even a mother, wanting and needing to. She could picture him now, porcine and fat, his sleepy little eyes staring out upon vacuity, with mindless fatuousness.

Not that he couldn't think, she mused bitterly. He just plain didn't want to. He never did want to do anything but eat. Lord God, what a hog he was at the table! And every time Tom pushed him into something, he would come a-whining to me . . . Reckon he was just plumb, downright womanish. Not—not strange like them curious kind of menfolks what loves other men; but just too delicate and weak with a girlish way of doing things. Like the Good Lord meant to make a female of him and then changed His mind. I remember the time . . .

That Wade had broken his arm, after Tom had forced him to mount a not too spirited horse. He hated horses because he was afraid of them. He was afraid of nearly everything that drew breath. He lay in the bed and cried for three whole days without stopping except for the times he slept.

"It hurts, Ma!" he quavered; "aw, Ma, it hurts so damned bad!"

"Look Wade," Sarah told him, "you're a boy—and one day you're going to be a man. For the Lord's sake, try to act like one! 'Course it hurts, but a-weeping and a-wailing ain't a-going to help it none a-tall. Menfolks got more pride than to lay there blubbering because something pains 'em a mite. Buck up, boy—show me what you're made of."

"Can't, Ma!" Wade sobbed. "It just naturally hurts too much—and Pa was a mean old bastard to make me do it! Don't need to ride no hoss. I can walk, can't I?"

"Oh, my Lord!" Sarah said; but Stormy came into the room and stood there looking at her brother, her lips curled in purest contempt.

"Tired of listening to him, Ma?" she said. "Sick of hearing that sissy little old snot whine?"

Sarah looked at her daughter, darkly.

"To tell the truth," she said; "I am. But I don't see what you think you can do about it."

"I can though," Stormy said. "Just leave it to me, Ma."

Half an hour later, the blubbering coming from the bedroom ceased. When Sarah entered it to see what had happened, she found Wade sleeping peacefully, his round, red face covered with a sticky mess, and a huge stick of peppermint candy in his hand. At that time, he had been all of fourteen years old.

Sarah called Stormy and pointed.

"Did you give him that?" she said.

"Yes, Ma," Stormy answered calmly. "Only way to deal with him. He ain't nothing but a baby—and what's more he's gonna stay a baby all his

life. Some folks grow up, and some don't. Wade's the kind what
don't. . . ."

And you, Sarah thought, looking at her, are the kind that will never
know what it is to grow up—how kind of wonderful it is being young,
because, bless my soul, you was just born old!

Her hands moved again, shelling the peas, but she was not conscious
of it. She stared out into the weed-filled yard.

I wonder where she is now, she thought; five years—and not a word
from her. . . .

She did not for a moment think that Stormy was dead. What she did
think was something else: She's leading a shameful life—and that's why
she don't dare write. . . .

In this, she was both right and wrong. Stormy Benton, by her mother's
standards, was indeed leading a shameful life: in the five years since she'd
run away from Benton's Row, she had been the mistress of three men in
succession, each richer than the last, and all of whom she had despised.
She was at the moment contemplating marriage to the last of them, old
General Rafflin, a man who could have been not only her grandfather, but
even her great-grandfather, if age were the only consideration. But the
wrongness of Sarah's conception lay in the fact that being both a Benton
and a female, Stormy was almost absolutely incapable of shame. To her,
then, her life was not shameful, but eminently practical.

She had soon found that her original idea of becoming an actress was
completely impractical. And since she was as ignorant as a field hand and
twice as lazy, she soon found that she could live only by capitalizing upon
the rather remarkable assets which nature and her Benton heritage had
given her: stunning good looks, keen intelligence, and remorseless will.
The combination saved her from the usual fate of a young girl alone in a
big city—saved her, that is, if one is prepared to accept that curiously
feminine genius for rationalization which makes the difference between
prostitution and respectability a question of price. Stormy's luxurious instincts made her from the start such an expensive proposition that she
could only be an old man's darling, few young men possessing the means
to afford her.

The old men she allowed to keep her, she betrayed flagrantly, constantly,
with younger men who amused her. There was in this, the curious circumstance that Stormy was one of those not too rare women who feel
almost nothing but contempt for men. Subconsciously, the heroic father-
image of Tom Benton made all other men seem weaklings, cowards, and
fools to her; and this very real difficulty was augmented by the fact that
being immensely, formidably strong herself, her feminine need for a man
himself strong enough for her to rely upon, lean upon, was almost always
thwarted by the curious psychological mystery which inevitably attracts
weaklings, little boys in search of a mother, and other male aberrations to
such women as her.

She was almost completely honest. As she belonged to the great race of predators, the male idea of the promiscuous female as a warmhearted, rather stupid little creature constantly victimized by ruthless men, made her laugh wholeheartedly, knowing, as she did, that in her case, at least, the shoe was completely upon the other foot. Actually, two rather completely contradictory pictures of herself reposed with blissful lack of conflict in her head: In one of them, she was of the great tradition of courtesans, Pompadour, du Barry—and this was conscious, because after the initial humiliation of having her almost purely Negroid dialect laughed at, Stormy had set about refining both her speech and manners, until, given her acute native intelligence to begin with, in a remarkably short time she had achieved that polished perfection of diction and behavior that is never found in the duchesses to whom the public attributes it, but almost always in those glittering, expensive ladies of the evening which Stormy herself now was. In the other, quite contradictory mental image, she pictured herself as the heroine of a great romance; and it was here alone that her basic honesty failed her.

Or rather, it was here that her intense femininity defeated her honesty, for the two things are mutually incompatible. Since her feminine mind was not only subjective and illogical, but actively, fiercely hostile to both objectivity and logic, it followed that that kind of honesty in the masculine sense which makes a man admit: "All right I was a skunk to do that, but she was such a cute little trick . . ." was a trait even more incomprehensible to her than it is to most women. Stormy, then, regarded her casual, continual promiscuity as part of her search for the great love of her life. But her honesty did save her from the supreme rationalization that almost results from this peculiarly feminine quest: She was incapable of taking some shoddy specimen of masculinity, and dreaming him into her prince, closing her mind and eyes to the actuality of what he was. What her feminine instincts did do, however, was to prevent her from ever recognizing that her habitual behavior was exactly the same as that of women whom she herself dismissed as being 'cheap little tarts,' and that the fact that she was not paid for her favors—at least not directly by the old men who kept her, and not at all by her occasional younger lovers, was a rather complete irrelevancy, all things being considered. Why she behaved as she did, finally, had the same relative importance to the men she betrayed as the nice question of whether a gun was fired in anger or by accident has to the man whom the bullet has killed.

It was, therefore, all to the good, that Sarah knew nothing of Stormy's life in New York; though, knowing her daughter, it could not be said that she could not imagine with rather painful accuracy. Nearly all of her memories of her daughter were painful.

Like that time, she mused, I tried to teach her to cook . . .

Stormy had come into the kitchen and stood there sullenly without touching anything.

"You get the skillet real hot," Sarah said; "then you dip the pieces of chicken into the batter—" She stopped short, glaring at Stormy. "You ain't heard a living word I said!" she snorted.

"Right, Ma," Stormy yawned; "and what's more I ain't going to. Don't see why I need know how anyways, since I'm always going to have a passel of niggers to do it for me."

"There's folks what ain't got niggers," Sarah pointed out. "And all men ain't rich. What you gonna do if your husband's a poor man?"

"My husband," Stormy said flatly, "ain't going to be no poor man."

"You're mighty sure, ain't you, Missy?" Sarah snapped. "The human heart's a funny thing. What guarantee you got you won't fall in love with some nice boy who ain't got a picayune?"

"None," Stormy smiled; "but I've every guarantee in the world I wouldn't marry him, Ma. To marry a man just because you love him is stupid—and that's one thing I ain't . . ."

"You mean you'd turn a poor boy down because he didn't have no money?" she demanded.

"Of course not," Stormy said. "Who said anything about turning him down? I just wouldn't marry him—that's all. . . ."

Sarah stood there, letting the meaning of this sink in.

"Lord God, Stormy!" she gasped. "You don't mean . . ."

"That I'd copy after you, in your younger days, Ma?" Stormy mocked. "Not exactly. I'm smarter than you ever was. Never would of married an old fool like Preacher Tyler in the first place lessen he had a pile of cash. What I would of done in your place would of been to marry some rich old jackass, and just kind of keep a fine young stallion like pa sort of rallying round. You wasn't smart. You had to play it according to the rules. And even when you broke 'em, being young and having blood in your veins, you suffered. But I'm a Benton, and we make our own rules. And we sure Lord don't suffer. So Ma, I don't aim to cook and do nigger work and get myself tied down with a passel of brats. You better understand that right now, Ma—that way, you'n' me can live together real peaceful like . . ."

She had yawned, then, and walked out of there, leaving Sarah in helpless silence, wondering what she should have said to her, recognizing finally, with the bitterness of total defeat, that there was absolutely nothing to be said.

A passel of niggers to work for her, Sarah thought, her fingers flying now, shelling the peas, moving from the twin compulsions of anger and bitterness, not from any increase in hunger. Well, that's one thing that's done, and I'm glad. I always hated slavery after I got to know what it was. Made white people spend a lifetime controlling niggers and losing their own self-control in the bargain. Young men getting themselves ruined, 'changing their luck,' as they called it, down in the cabins. People getting so proud 'cause they had niggers to do everything for 'em that their minds shut tight and they never learned nothing at all. And women going crazy in the big houses having to manage a passel of worthless, trifling nigger wenches. . . . No we're free, not the niggers. They'll never be free lessen somebody ships 'em back to Africa where they can be amongst their own kind. They're just too different to fit in—leaseways not in a white man's world. But it's us who've been freed; 'cause just like Nancy Cattlet said: "Before the war, the only two really free things in the South was a nigger woman—and a white man. . . ."

She saw the two men, far off, coming up the river road. But she didn't pay any attention to them. That spring of 'Sixty-five, returning Confederate veterans were too commonplace a sight.

2

EVERY DAY for weeks, that spring and summer of 'Sixty-five, you could see them coming back. Sometimes alone, but more often by twos and threes, they came very slowly over the desolate land, walking tiredly through the roads, lanes, traces; those of them who had their own two feet supporting the others who had but one, and sometimes not even that, hobbling on hand-cut canes, swinging along on rude crutches, filthy, bearded, vermin infested, an army of specters on the march, moving through a countryside so broken, stripped, devastated, that they said of it with wry humor:

"Hell, even a crow flying 'cross these parts have to carry his own rations."

Begging at farmhouses, sleeping in haylofts, moving half fearfully toward what had been home, not knowing what they would find when they got there, what manner and species of horrors: the big house gone, burnt, perhaps, the stock run off, the Negroes fled, wandering themselves, like gypsies over the endless expanse of devastation, driven by some blind instinct to try the dimensions of this thing called freedom, to go to the ultimate ends of it, see how far it extended, north, south, east, west. . . .

And the women. They dared not think of that. Marauding bands in all the land the last few months of the war. Confederate deserters, skulkers, even Negroes.

"By God, if they laid a hand on her—I'll—"

But even the threats were left unfinished, swallowed deep in the throats of men too worn out, hungry, desolate of heart to even utter them. So came home the South's tall sons, too tired to scratch the vermin that devoured them, their nostrils blunted by long habit to their bodies' unwashed stench, their hound-lean bellies so accustomed to hunger that they looked at food placed before them and ate very little, and that little very slowly, staring at each morsel in wonder and in awe.

Then off to sleep in one more hayloft, hearing the day noises dying away into silence, and the quiet little night sounds, the rustle and creaking, the hoof stamp of the beasts below, the whippoorwill's cry, rising to take their place. Then, tomorrow . . .

"Ain't far now, is it, Wade?" Oren Bascomb said.

Wade glared at him.

"Be there tomorrow," he growled. "I told you that already."

"I know. Kind of like to hear it agin. Lord God, it's been so damn long since I slept in a bed! Tell me, Wade-boy, 'scuse me, Lieutenant, sir! Tell me—"

"Mister Benton," Wade said dryly. "You promised, Oren."

"Mister Benton," Oren mocked; "yessir, Cap'n, sir, I won't forget!"

"You know why," Wade said. "You come from these parts. Be mighty funny if my overseer was to call me Wade. Or, Wade-boy, like you do, mostly. People'll think something. And it's mighty important that they don't."

"Sure thing, Mister Benton," Oren laughed. "Can't have them thinking anything funny about the Hero of Briar Creek. You're going to be mighty big back home, Lieutenant. Don't worry about that—"

"I got a heap more to worry about than being big," Wade burst out. "How do I know I can trust you, Oren? How in hellfire do I know that?"

"Now, now, Lieutenant, don't take on. Going to be plumb, downright easy. In the first place, there's your honorable scars—"

"A Minie ball through the knee," Wade said; "just enough so I'll have to limp the rest of my life and carry a cane. What the hell is honorable about that?"

"Then there were that charge. Remember, I saw it. Here you come, at the head of your boys, jumping your hoss over Briar Creek, riding hell for leather toward the dam the Yankees was building to float their gunboats over the shallows. Then all hell busting loose! Your boys surrounded, but fighting like tigers. No surrender. Yankees going down in droves and—"

"Oh, for God's sake!" Wade said disgustedly.

"All right, Mister Benton," Oren Bascomb said. "See, I got it down pat, now. Tell me, Mister Benton, are the girls pretty up your way?"

"Yes," Wade said quietly.

Oren looked at the young lieutenant. At that moment his face held something infinitely dark and disturbing, but lighted with an inner joy— a malicious glee that made it worse, that heightened it.

"Any one of them you specially interested in?" he said.

"What you want to know that for?" Wade demanded.

"Struck me funny," Oren grinned. "You and me been down there on Ship Island for more than a year. In all that time, I never heard you mention a single filly by name. 'Tain't natural. Young fellow like you, son of the richest man in the parish, good-looking to boot—'pears to me there must of been gals round you in droves. You been hiding something from me, Mister Lieutenant Wade Benton?"

"No," Wade said. He looked at Oren. Can't call him good-looking, he thought again. Matter of fact, he's a homely cuss. Then what am I scared of? Never mentioned Mary Ann to him because—because, the remorseless honesty of his private thoughts insisted miserably, I'm always scared of something. 'Cause I wasn't born with what fellows like Oren have. Lord God, the minute those New Orleans girls who came to visit us with food and stuff looked at him, you could see their eyes sparkle. It ain't looks. Looks don't matter. I reckon men like Oren were just plain born exciting. A woman looks at me and yawns. Let her see him and she starts wondering about all sorts of things, most of which she ain't supposed to think about a-tall, if she's decent. . . .

"Well, sir," Oren mocked, "what's her name?"

"What's whose name?" Wade countered.

"This here very special filly you been hiding out on me," Oren said.

Got to tell him, Wade thought. He'll meet her anyhow. Can't be helped. Lord God, what's the matter with me? Sweet girl like Mary Ann, and you'd think I couldn't trust—

But there was more in it than that, and with the sad, half instinctive wisdom of all dull little men, all those born without the spark, the fire, the lilting, magic quality of desirability, Wade knew it. He knew deep down that Mary Ann did not love him, although she thought she did, for the simple reason that he was not lovable, or exciting, or strong, or interesting, or, indeed, anything that draws a woman to a man. Beyond that, on another level of consciousness, he sensed what he did not permit himself to think: that no woman is ever faithful to a man because the conventions of morality tell her she must be. He had known Babette Dupré too well to believe that. He had also, early in his teens, been all but destroyed inside the very core of his being, when he was told by his sister, Stormy, with vicious exactitude of corroborating detail, the story of his own mother's misdeeds. And he had learned more of Lolette Dupré, had met her in New Orleans, and had been fascinated by her with that curious fascination that causes small beasts to stand motionless before a cottonmouth moccasin. Women, he dimly realized, are faithful to those men who please them, satisfy their basic physical and spiritual needs, who combine charm with force, tenderness with a kind of quiet, unobtrusive mastery. And when a woman is physically faithful to a man lacking these qualities, it is only because of fear, absence of opportunity, or her own want of sufficient desirability in the eyes of other men. Women, he knew even then, have a great respect for the laws of society when applied to little things: manners, modes of dress, the niceties of social intercourse; in great things, they have absolutely none. He reasoned it out, painfully: reckon it's because they're just more personal than men. Men are bigger sinners, but they always know they're sinning. A woman don't. A sin to her is always what the other woman does. What she does is damn near always right, because it's her who's doing it, and she's always got what's to her good and sufficient reasons. Lord God, you can't understand them no-how. . . .

Knowing all this, without realizing how he knew it, or by what precise method he had arrived at it, he had instinctively concealed the name of his fiancée from Oren. For this pine-barren poorwhite, tall, rawboned, ugly in a curiously Lincolnesque fashion, had it all: the spark, the fire, the magic. He charmed all manner, classes, and conditions of women with effortless ease; and Wade Benton, enrolled forever in the legion of the pitifully damned: the eternally unwanted, unloved, rejected of this world, both feared and hated him.

"Yes," he said at last, "there is someone special. A girl named Barker—Mary Ann Barker."

"Lieutenant," Oren said with mock gravity, "why didn't you tell me this before?"

"Because," Wade said, "a man doesn't go around spouting about a girl who means that much to him. The way you talk and think about women, Oren—I just didn't like to bring it up—"

"Lord God!" Oren laughed. "You thought I'd go fooling around your gal, Lieutenant? Reason I asked you was to know which one to leave alone."

"You mean that, Oren?" Wade said.

"Bible oath. Tell me about her, Mister Benton, sir. She pretty?"

"No," Wade said honestly. "She's got a funny little turned up nose, and a mouth that's wide and always smiling, mostly. Scads of freckles, and penny-brown eyes. Her hair's sort of auburn. But she's not pretty. She's little and neat and trim, and kind of ugly cute. What she is, I reckon, is just plain sweet. Anyhow, I love her, Oren. And if I have any trouble out of you . . ."

"You won't, Lieutenant. Known her long?"

"No, I haven't. She came down our way a little before the war. Her pa was killed in a duel, though she doesn't even know that, yet. They told her it was by accident while he was cleaning his gun. The shock killed her ma. They lived on a place in Mississippi. But old man Ransom, her pa's brother-in-law, has a little place north of the Cattlets, and after she lost her folks, Mary Ann came there to live. That's where I met her."

"Sounds like the girl for you all right. Planning to get hitched right away, are you, sir?"

"Soon as I get back," Wade said, "if she'll have me."

"Oh, she'll have you all right. After I get through spreading your distinguished war record all over the place, won't be a filly what wouldn't jump at the chance to . . ."

"Aw, shut up!" Wade said.

"I'm serious, Lieutenant. And you don't have nothing to worry about. I'll take my Bible oath on that. You don't for the best damn reason in the world: the bigger you are, the bigger I'll get to be. And I aim to be mighty damned big!"

"Couldn't you," Wade suggested tiredly, "get there by yourself?"

"No. Look at the odds agin me. My folks warn't much: white trash, swampers and suchlike. No war record. Course I fought like hell, but I fought Rebs as much as I did Feds. Fought for me. What did I care if folks kept their niggers or not? Never owned no niggers. Got caught, either side would of hung me out of hand for robbing the dead, bushwhacking, foraging and stealing. But all that's finished. Everything's plumb busted to pieces. Man like me's got a chance now, if he's smart. And damned if this thing on my shoulders don't work right pert good."

"I'll grant you that," Wade Benton said.

"But, coming from nowheres, I got to have somebody big to latch onto. Your pa was the biggest man in that there parish. That gives you a head start. 'Course you're flat busted like everybody else. But, hell, man you're still a Benton. And a hero. That makes a mighty heap of difference. Me and you are going to be rich. Your position and my brains. You couldn't do it alone; you ain't hard enough. I couldn't neither; ain't got the position. But together—"

Wade stared at him, bleakly.

"I'd like to go to sleep now, Oren, if you don't mind," he said.

They came up to the house at midmorning. Sarah put down the pan of peas and stood up, doubting her own eyes. But they came on until she could see them clearly: Wade limping along on his cane, his wispy blond beard framing a face that had lost its childish roundness, his body wraith-thin, now, so that he looked much older, and with him, the tall, rawboned man, moving along beside him, helping him, with an inscrutable, indefinable expression upon his bony face. An expression oddly like triumph, as though he had won through limitless and unimaginable hardships, through difficulties and struggles that would have broken a lesser man, the goal shining before him now, at this moment, the victory in sight.

Seeing her son coming thus, almost literally back from the dead, Sarah was conscious of mixed emotions. She hoped, suddenly, that Wade wouldn't spoil things now; for his supposed death, in a wild charge to cut off the Yankee retreat above Alexandria, at that nameless little stream the bayou people called Briar Creek, had been, in its essence, a vindication of all she had suffered for his sake. For no one had expected Wade to make a soldier; she, who knew him best, even less than anyone else.

She came down the steps, running. When she was close, she stopped.

"Howdy, son," she whispered.

"Howdy, Ma," he said. Then he leaned forward, and kissed her cheek.

She got the smell of him, then, full in her nostrils, but her control was superb. She straightened up, slowly.

"Come on up to the house, boys," she said. "I'll fix you something to eat."

"Ma," Wade said, "this is Oren Bascomb. He saved my life."

Sarah put out her hand.

"Thank you, sir," she said simply.

"Lord God!" Oren got out, in a tone anyone would have sworn was sincerity itself, "can't get over it! I do declare I can't. . . . You're Miz Benton—his ma? 'Tain't possible!"

"I'm his ma, all right," Sarah said, "but I'm Mrs. McGregor. Wade's father was my first husband. Come on, now."

"His sister," Oren persisted; "I'd of sworn my Bible oath. His younger sister at that."

"Please, Mister Bascomb," Sarah said.

"Mister Benton told me there was some mighty pretty girls in these here parts; but I sure Lord didn't expect to find his ma the prettiest of the lot."

"Mister Bascomb, please!" Sarah said, and her voice was ice.

"Sorry, Ma'am. Only we ain't seen no pretty women in so damn long— Lord Jesus, how I do talk! Forgive me, Ma'am. Comes of being shut in so long. Me and the Lieutenant been prisoners of war since last April. My compliments, Ma'am. You sure got yourself a boy to be proud of."

"Ma," Wade said, "we aren't hungry. We had breakfast this morning at the Cattlets. What we'd appreciate right now would be a bath. A haircut, too, and a shave. Could you fix all that up? Reckon all the niggers have skedaddled."

"There're a few of them left," Sarah said. "I'll trim your hair myself. I know how—been trimming hair for boys for weeks now."

She did know, especially the essential part of it, which was to shrivel the locks on a shovelful of hot coals the instant they fell. Out in the kitchen, the sole remaining housemaid heated water on the clay firebrick stove.

"Give me your clothes," Sarah said; "I'll burn them, or bury them. You've got some of your things from before the war, Wade. As for Mister Bascomb, some of your father's things will fit him as far as height goes. Reckon he'll have to wrap them around him twice in spots."

"Please Ma'am," Oren said quickly, "don't git rid of our uniforms. Have them boiled, cause we're right pert proud of our country's duds. Sort of like to keep them—to remind us, kind of. . . ."

"I can understand that," Sarah said. "All right, I'll have Luella boil them."

After they had bathed, they sat in the kitchen, and Sarah listened while Oren told the story. She noticed that Wade kept squirming while he told it.

"It were like this," Oren said. "Them Yankees under Genr'l Banks come up from Bayou Teche and took Alexandria. Then they sat around for nigh onto three weeks, fussing among themselves till our ol' Dick Taylor—there was a genr'l, Ma'am!—got all the reinforcements he needed: them Germans from Texas under Colonel Buchell—dear Lord how they loved to cut! Kept their sabers after every other calvary regiment in our army had give 'em up for pistols; and all them Cajun and Creole Louisiana French folks under Alfred Mouton, whose pa used to be Governor. Then there was that cowboy regiment from Texas under Prince Polignac

—a real prince, Ma'am—his folks was the Bourbons, the royal house of France, but he come over here to fight for us. And he was one first-class fighting man. . . ."

Wade stared at Oren in real admiration. Now he knew why his unwanted companion had spent so many hours in prison poring over those old newspapers—going to any length to get them, begging them of the guards, imploring the Confederate women visitors who came to cheer up the poor devils locked up on Ship Island to bring them to him. He had needed a frame in which to set himself, a substantial background upon which to base his future; and he had it now, all of it. The ill-starred Red River campaign was to be his frame of reference, the bulwark of his defense when men asked, as they would: "And you, Mister Bascomb, what did you do in the war?"

"Anyhow," he went on, "them Yanks come up toward Natchitoches, marching along the banks, alongside of them thirteen gunboats and thirty transports they was steaming up the river, and just barely gitting across them there shallows above Alexandria. Bet there wasn't more than a inch of water between their bottoms and the rocks. . . ."

"I know," Sarah said; "I saw them."

"Did you now, Ma'am? Fearful sight, wasn't it? Anyhow, ol' Dick sent us in at Mansfield, and we whupped them Yankees good and proper. Next day, at Pleasant Hill, it was their turn. Fought us off right smart like. But they'd seen the handwriting on the wall. Went a-steaming back to Grand Écore, and then down to the shallows. . . .

"But the river had done fell a foot or more. And we had 'em! Believe me, Ma'am, what with them gunboats and transports bottled up north of the shallows, we could of cut the Yankee army into pieces, and captured their whole blamed fleet, wasn't for Genr'l Kirby Smith being such a damn fool!"

"Mind your language, Oren," Wade growled.

"I'm most humbly sorry, Ma'am," Oren said; "but he was. Took all Genr'l Taylor's men 'cepting a few, and sent 'em chasing after that Yankee Genr'l Steele on the Saline. That was when it happened. Genr'l Taylor sent a few of us"—he grinned at Wade as he uttered this barefaced and monstrous lie, he whose very uniform, in all probability, had been stripped in ghoulish secrecy from the dead body of a man honorably fallen in defense of the land which he, and those like him, had only preyed upon— "out to scout, and the Yankees cut us up. Couldn't even git back with the news of how that there Yankee engineer, Lieutenant Colonel Joe Bailey of Wisconsin was using blamed near the whole Federal army to build the finest set up of wing dams, cribs, and chutes I ever did see. He was one smart engineer that Yankee. Right away I could see what he aimed to do— make the whole river flow through a li'l' gate just wider than a gunboat, forcing all that there water through so's you could of sailed a ocean-going Baltimore clipper through, let alone a gunboat—

"After we couldn't git back, Genr'l Taylor sent your son, Ma'am, out to search for us with a few cavalry scouts. I was lost—been separated from my regiment nigh onto four days. Yankees ever' which a where, building them dams. Then Mister Benton come crashing through the underbrush, jumping that sorrel right over Briar Creek, and a-sounding the prettiest Rebel Yell these old ears ever did hear. . . ."

"I don't think I made a sound," Wade said sullenly.

" 'Deed you did! Felt my back hair stand straight up. Then them Yankees was all around him and his boys, shooting. They had Enfields, and our boys didn't have nothing but Colt pistols; but they give a good account of themselves, Ma'am. Must of kilt nigh onto a hundred Yanks afore . . ."

Sarah let his voice fade out of her conscious hearing. She was remembering the rest of it, the time before, the terrible, shameful time that contradicted every word he was saying.

It hadn't been so bad before the Conscription Act. But by the time it was passed, Wade was already eighteen and liable for service. He had hid for a while behind the provision exempting the owners of twenty or more slaves from service, on the intelligent assumption that the large slaveowner was more valuable to the Confederacy producing supplies for the army than fighting in the ranks.

But all the yeomen farmers and poorwhites had set up the cry of "A rich man's war, and a poor man's fight!" until that provision had been repealed. And since his stepfather Randy McGregor had already gone to war, and there was no other doctor in the parish, he could not, as hundreds of other Southern cowards had already done, buy a certificate of physical unfitness from a venial physician—not that Randy would have countenanced such a thing in the first place.

Then he had tried to hire a substitute, which the law also permitted. But the parish was already bled white of its younger men of all classes, and he hadn't been able to find one. His keen fear of ridicule prevented him from suddenly becoming an evangelist, and thus escaping service on religious grounds; but he actually tried that other favorite device of Southern draft-dodgers: he bought a supply of snake oil, roots, powders and quack nostrums and set up shop as an apothecary. Being laughed out of that profession, he opened a school, for teachers, too, were listed among the exempt classes. But the widows of men already dead on the field of honor, and the mothers of younger children whose brothers, uncles, fathers were already engaging the Yankee on the far-flung fronts were understandably reluctant to entrust their offspring to his care. He never had even one pupil.

The women of the parish came to call on Sarah. They sat around her in a circle, chanting: "Why doesn't your son go to war? Why doesn't your son go to war?" until she had fled weeping from their presence.

That night, Wade ran away from the plantation. He hid out in the woods two weeks before the cold and the wet, and his abiding horror of snakes drove him home again. When he got back, he found Mary Ann there.

"Wade," she said quietly, "I'll never marry a man who won't do his duty by his country."

And Wade Benton, trembling all over, his usually pink face as white as death, had gone down to headquarters and enlisted. Three weeks later, he went AWOL in New Orleans, and spent two hundred dollars on Babette Dupré, who was by then number-one girl at Big Gertie's. They had dragged him back and put him in the guardhouse. But Randy, home on leave, intervened for him, and got him out. After that, he became a model conscientious soldier. Then, a year later, came the news of his heroic death.

Sarah had found it hard to believe. There's some mistake, she thought; they got somebody else mixed up with Wade. But now, hearing it from an eyewitness, she had to believe it:

"Yessir, they kept right on fighting till wasn't a man of 'em left. Wade was shot in the leg, a-sitting there on his hoss, milling about and a-crying and a-cussing and fighting like a wildcat-devil. Then the Yanks shot the horse from under him, and he was throwed so hard it knocked him cold. Rest of them boys, warn't more'n five or six left by then, kept on shooting till they was out of ammunition, and after that they chunked their pistols at the Yankees, and stood there chunking rocks and sticks till the Feds charged in and bayoneted them. What saved Wade was the hoss. He was part the way under him, and them Yanks thought he was crushed. But they was in so much of a hurry with them dams and suchlike to git the gunboats across the shallows that they couldn't take time out even for a burial detail. So they left them there, and I come out of the woods and found that Wade was alive. Nursed him for four days. On the fifth, a Yankee patrol caught us, and they put us in one of them transports, went through that there flood gate with feet to spare and took us down to N'Awleans."

Oren grinned wryly.

"That's howcome we spent the rest of the war in jail," he said. "Got to be fast friends, there—me'n' Mister Benton. He promised me a job up here when we got out. Sure hope you don't object, Ma'am—'cause I ain't got no folks, nor nowheres to go . . ."

Sarah looked at him steadily.

He's a conniving skunk, and a scheming polecat, she thought. He'd use anybody comes his way. But with poor Jim Rudgers gone—and he was good to Wade. . . .

She stood up.

"No," she said, "no objections at all."

"Heard anything from Randy?" Wade said.

Sarah's gray eyes softened. There was a glow in them.

"He came out of it alive and unhurt, thank God," she said. "Should be home any day, now."

"I'm glad," Wade said, and he meant it. His stepfather had been good to him. In the few months they had had together before and after Sumter,

Wade had had more fatherly companionship from Randy than his own father had given him in all his life.

Sarah stood there, looking at him quizzically.

"Aren't you," she said, "even going to ask after Mary Ann?"

Wade gulped, and glanced quickly at Oren.

"Yes," he got out, "how is she, Ma?"

"Just fine. Prettier than ever. A mite thin, though—like everybody these days. Reckon nobody's had enough to eat. . . ."

"That's sure Lord the truth!" Oren said.

"She brought every one of your letters over here and read them to me," Sarah said. "When they told her you were dead, she took to her bed for a week. I went to see her. She swore she'd never marry anyone else."

"Fine girl," Oren said.

"A mite foolish," Sarah said flatly. "She didn't know Wade that well. What she was grieving over was the idea of him she had sort of fixed up for herself in her mind. But all girls do that in wartime. I understand that. And she is a sweet little creature; I couldn't ask for a nicer daughter-in-law. If I was you, Wade, I'd go over to see her today."

"Yes'm," Wade said; "I'm going, right now."

Riding over to the Ransoms on a tired old mule—all the horses having been seized at one time or another by both the armies—one nagging fear clung like a burr to Wade's consciousness: Lord God, he prayed, hope she never found out about Babette. . . .

The thing he referred to, the very pit and nadir of his personal humiliation, was his New Orleans debacle, when, on pretense of renewed interest in him, Babette Dupré had encouraged him to spend every cent he had and all he could borrow, and then very thoroughly revenged herself upon him for his part in her father's death, by refusing him, in her new professional capacity, the very favors for which he had—at least by the current market values along Gallatin Street in the 'Sixties—very amply paid her.

But he couldn't turn back now. He rode on, comforting himself with the thought that only his stepfather knew that story, and Randy wasn't the sort of man to go about talking.

It was James Ransom who saw him first. Wade's route up to the house led him through the south section of the Ransom farm, and Jim Ransom was there plowing, with Mary Ann scattering the seed behind him, all the Negroes having fled in the wake of the Yankee armies.

Jim Ransom let out a whoop.

"Lord God!" he cried, "if it ain't Wade Benton! Mary Ann, it's Wade! Bless my soul, boy! Bless my living soul but I'm mighty glad to see you! They told us—"

Wade slid down from the mule and hobbled forward, his hand outstretched.

"I know," he said; "they told you I was dead. They were about halfway right, Mister Ransom."

Jim Ransom took his hand and shook it, fiercely.

"You're a sight for sore eyes, boy," he chuckled, "and no mistake! Why this here filly has been grieving her heart out. Won't eat, can't sleep—been such a pest I started to give her to the Yankees for counterband. . . ."

Mary Ann had come up to them now. She stood there, staring at Wade, and her plain, sweet face was white under the freckles.

"You've been hurt," she whispered; "you've been bad hurt!" Then very softly, she started to cry.

"Go on, boy," Jim Ransom laughed, "give her a buss! Don't stand on ceremony. Don't you know nothing about wimmin? They always bust out a-crying when they're plumb, downright happy."

Wade smiled and drew the girl to him. Then he kissed her, very gently.

"Call that a kiss?" Jim Ransom hooted. "Hell, boy, we done better than that when I was young! Come on up to the house. Jane's going to be right smart surprised. Reckon we can rustle up another plate of vittles, can't we, Mary Ann? This here young'un look like he ain't had enough to eat in a coon's age."

"No, thank you, sir," Wade said quickly. "Ma fixed me a bite before I come over. I'll come up to the house though. I want to pay my respects to Miz Jane."

"That the truth, boy?" Jim said, trying to keep the relief out of his voice; "you really had your grub?"

"Yessir," Wade smiled. "Ma laid down the law—told me folks don't go dropping in 'round mealtimes these days. Hard enough to scrape up enough for the family, let alone outsiders."

"But you're family, now, Wade," Mary Ann said. "You don't have to go home real soon, do you, Hon? I've got a million things I want to ask you."

"And I got just one thing to ask you," Wade said; "and I don't need but one little word to ask it with: When?"

Mary Ann's face was the color of a sunset.

"Oh, Wade!" she breathed. Then she looked at her uncle.

Jim Ransom frowned, thoughtfully.

"I tell you, boy," he said; "that's going to require a mite of thinking. It ain't that I've got any objections—far from it. Be happy to see this poor little orphan hitched up with a fine, upstanding young man like you. But there's problems. Your ma's been running that big place of yourn without a man to help her. Done pretty good, too; I tell you—"

"Thank you, sir," Wade said.

"You young'uns listen to me. Love is fine. But there's a thing called money what's mighty helpful when it comes to smoothing out hardships. Now I ain't got none. And neither, my boy, have you. What we both got is the chance to make some. How 'bout you love birds waiting till after we both gets in a crop? Be cash on hand then. Have a nice splicing: veil and white dress and a big whoop-te-do afterwards—cake and stuff. That's how I'd like to see it done."

136

"Sir," Wade said, "don't you have any bales laid by? Ma has. Right smart, too. And the way prices are going up—why Mister Ransom, the whole blamed world is starved for cotton!"

"Yep," Jim Ransom said, "I sure Lord have. Got me between five and ten thousand dollars worth, hid out in shacks I built in the woods. Your ma's is hid good, too. I talked her into hiding it. That's why we both got it, and the Yankees ain't. But, Lord God, Wade, now ain't the time to bring it out!"

"Why not, sir?" Wade said.

Jim Ransom spread his work-gnarled hands, and counted off the reasons on his fingers. "Number one, the Government done put a tax of twenty-five per cent of its value on all cotton raised by slave labor—and what cotton ain't? Number two: revenue tax of two'n' a half cents per pound on all cotton raised by anybody, loyal to the United States or not; Number three, a shipping fee of four cents per pound for the privilege of sending it to market—that don't include what rates you pay to ship it, boy—that means you got to pay 'em for turning it loose! Number four: and this here is the real hitch, boy—they confiscates all cotton sold to the Confederacy, paid to the C.S.A. as tithes or taxes, set aside for such payment, or pledged to our late, lamented government as a loan, or in any way fixed up to give aid and comfort to Jeff Davis and his boys."

"Lord God!" Wade whispered, "that means—"

"Damn near all the cotton there is—specially since it's them who decides whether or not your bales come under that heading. And with the stuff selling for close to a dollar a pound, how much you think them Yankee thieves is going to let go on the open market, and how much is they going to confiscate?"

Wade groaned.

"That's why we got to wait on a crop. That there cotton will be raised by paid labor, though where in hellfire we going to get the money to pay the niggers with, or how we going to git them lazy black bastards back to work even if we do pay 'em, is a couple of other questions. . . ."

Wade turned to Mary Ann.

"Looks like we've got ourselves a long wait, Honeybunch," he said.

"I won't wait!" Mary Ann burst out. "Wasn't so bad when I thought you were dead. But you're alive now, and crippled up like that you need me to take care of you. Besides, folks ought to have their children while they're young, so—"

"Mary Ann!" Jim Ransom said. He was genuinely shocked.

"Sorry, Uncle," Mary Ann said; "but I love him. I'll make my veil out of old lace curtains if I have to, and we can eat that cake on our golden wedding anniversary with our grandchildren helping us enjoy it!"

"Let's go talk to your auntie," Wade said. "Maybe between us all, we can figure out something. . . ."

But they couldn't. Neither they, nor Sarah, with whom the young couple discussed the problem the next night, when Wade brought Mary Ann home for supper.

Oren Bascomb sat there listening to all the talk, a smile lighting his dark, sardonic face. He pushed back his chair and stood up.

"You young folks plan that there wedding for Sunday, two weeks from now," he said, "and leave the rest to me. That gives me two whole weeks. In that there two weeks, I'm going to git your cotton sold, Ma'am, have your niggers back on the place, and hard at work, round up some draft animals, and git most of the repairs done. Wade'll have to help me. Sorry, sir, but you got to give up your sparking for two whole weeks. You'll forgive me, Miss Mary Ann? After all, you'll have him all to yourself after that."

"I'll do anything," Mary Ann said fervently, "just so's we can get married and start living like folks."

"Thank you kindly, Ma'am. Now, Mister Benton, sir, I humbly beg you to excuse yourself and come with me."

Consternation flooded Wade's face.

"Tonight?" he gasped.

"Yessir, tonight. Time's a-wasting, sir. You want to git married, or you want to sit around holding hands?"

"Go with him, Wade," Mary Ann said sharply. "Me'n' your mother will sit here a spell and talk."

"All right, then," Wade said.

An hour later, they stood at the bar at Tim's with the Federal cotton agent. Oren did all of the talking.

"Look at it this way, sir," he said quietly, "suppose I was to put you onto some Reb cotton—not that I could, really; but just for argument's sake. . . ."

"Where is it?" the cotton agent growled.

"I don't rightly know. But I can find out, if you'll use your head a little bit. Send it up to Cincinnati, and what do you git out of it? A pat on the back and a nice letter commending you for your valiant services to the United States. Fine. But can your kids eat that?"

Wade stared at his overseer, lost in pure admiration.

The Federal agent considered the idea. Greed showed in his small blue eyes.

"What do you suggest, Mister Bascomb?" he muttered.

"A little arrangement. I'll cut you in for one-third of the profits if I git from you beforehand a stamped seizure order and a signed, official release with the Grand Seal of the Republic at the bottom of it, stating over your prettiest signature that this here cotton is untainted with any smell of Reb. . . ."

"One-half," the agent snapped.

"Nosir! I got the cotton and you ain't. Where I got it, you ain't got a ghost of a chance to git at it. I'm paying everything: taxes, fees, freight. Give you half, what's left ain't worth my while. I'll just sit on the stuff till hell freezes over and the devil throws a skating party. Take it or leave it!"

To Wade's vast amazement and relief, the agent took it.

Four days later, nineteen thousand dollars, all that was left of the profits from bales which would have brought them more than fifty thousand in the open market, was deposited to the accounts of Mrs. Randy McGregor, and her son, Wade Benton.

"What do you want out of it?" Wade asked Oren.

"Tell you later," Oren Bascomb grinned.

With the Negroes, his tactics were different.

"So you're free," he said. "You been wandering about all over. How you like your freedom?"

"Just fine, boss," one of the younger Negroes said.

"Had enough to eat?" Oren demanded, looking at Caleb and the other older Negroes.

"Nawsuh," Caleb said mournfully. "But just as soon as we gits that there forty acres and a mule them folks up Nawth done promised us . . ."

"Just you wait, Uncle!" Oren laughed. "Guarantee your backbone be asking your belly if your throat's done been cut by then! Now, you niggers listen to me! I don't believe nobody's going to give you nothing, but even if they was to, you still got to eat till they do. You ain't slaves no more, and 'fore God, ain't nobody trying to take away your freedom. But I got a little proposition to make to you all. Come on back to Broad Acres, go to work for Miz Benton, who you know and love. We'll give you your cabins, and the ground around 'em to grow your vittles. You can keep chickens and pigs long as you stay with us. . . ."

"Where us going to git them chickens and pigs?" Caleb's son, Buford, demanded.

"Got it all figgered, boy," Oren said. "You pay us rent for the land, out of the stuff you raise. We furnish everything you need against a credit at our store. And I do mean everything: Land, seed, implements, work stock, food and supplies for your families, fodder for the animals. You pays us seven bales out of every ten you makes, keeping the three for yourself for your cash crop—that covers the rent for the land and your cabins. . . ."

"And them other things, suh?" Buford said suspiciously.

"I'm going to write them down in a book at the store. End of the year, you settles with me. Don't worry, it won't be much. You'll still have cash on hand."

They sat there a long time, thinking about it. It was all there, the shape of it, the form and the texture of the new slavery that was to replace the old. But they couldn't see it then. They hadn't the knowledge, nor the experience.

"All right, suh," Buford said at last; "we be there tomorrow early."

"Fine, boy!" Oren said. But in his mind, he guarded the thought: Have to watch that young nigger. He's smart, and uppity. Going to have to take him down a peg or two. . . .

By the Friday before the day set for the wedding, Oren had made a sizable hole in Wade's nineteen thousand dollars. But Broad Acres had mules, plows, seed, fertilizer, axes, saws, new wagons and feed for the beasts. The labor contracts had been filed with, and approved by the Bureau, and for the first time in four years, Broad Acres was beginning to look as it had under Tom Benton's firm hand.

Oren had divided his labor force. Two-thirds of the Negroes he put to work at once about the usual business of plowing, for most of the plantation's vast spread of land had been untouched by war; but the remaining third had other things to do. The section near the river and touching on the bayou had been marched over, fought over, and here the fences had fueled the campfires of the armies, the barns had been burned, and the gins smashed with that savage vindictiveness that the Yankee troops brought to bear upon anything having to do with cotton, holding it the very root of this hateful conflict which kept them marching in heat and dust and cold, and dying, too, far from their own cornfields and the girls they had left behind them. There hadn't been much they could do with the fields themselves, but there were the gins, symbols, in wood and iron, of everything that had cost them so much in weariness and boredom, blood and pain. So they had burned them, after taking sledgehammers and axes, and more rarely gunpowder to the machinery. Sometimes, caught in their looting of silver, and feminine finery from the big houses, and fired upon, they had burned them, too. Tom Benton's house, however, had escaped burning or pillage, because it was built so far from the river, a circumstance determined by chance, itself, because when the bayou people had built it for him, he had owned no land on the river, his conquest of Davin Henderson having come after that time.

The house, actually, had been in greater danger from Confederate skulkers, that savage and cowardly crew, most of whom had avoided service for their country for four long years, and the rest, unwilling patriots from the first, who had deserted from her armies. Three times Sarah had had to stand off marauders with the big Walker Colt Tom had brought back from the Mexican War. Of all the Southern legends, the one most nearly true is the belief that had her soldiers been as indomitable, unconquerable as her women, the South would have won her war. . . .

So the house stood, but the fences were out for miles in every direction, and gangs of Negroes worked all day and far into the night rebuilding them, while others pulled down the charred wreckage of barns and gins to make room for the new ones they would presently build. The very old and the very young among the blacks had still another occupation: collecting the bones of dead horses and mules left after the skirmishes to be sold to the fertilizer factory near Natchitoches, and the Minie balls, broken muskets, and occasionally even saber blades to be sold to the ironmongers.

In such fashion life came back to Broad Acres, in general conformity, with minute variations, to the pattern being established all over the South. Dressing, that Sunday morning, for his wedding, in his patched and faded uniform, with the brass buttons decently covered with cloth—

for to wear anything bearing the Confederate insignia was now a crime, the epaulets stripped off, the stripes of rank traced in sad fidelity by the unfaded cloth beneath them, guarding thus, proud and unconquerable, the marks of their having been, Wade could see Oren driving the Negroes, nothing about the scene below his window differing one jot from before the war, the new overseer (for Jim Rudgers had died, a Yankee bayonet through his guts at Shiloh Church) from habit having forgotten he was now dealing with freemen, the freemen from the same habits having almost forgotten they were free.

Sarah had baked a cake, a poor thing, unworthy of her usual standards, but good enough considering the scarcity of eggs, the total absence of butter, the use of a sugar brownish, lumpy, but half refined. She had almost cried over it; but it would have to do. The house was spotless, for the Negro girls, who dearly loved both their mistress and a wedding, had worked harder than ever before in their lives.

Dressed at last, Wade and Sarah mounted the buckboard and drove down to Benton's Row, to the little white church, where Wade's guard of honor, more than half of them crippled, waited to erect an arch of sabers over the wedded pair.

It went smoothly, almost to the end. But standing before the pulpit to receive the blessing of Reverend Benbow, clad still in his uniform of a Confederate chaplain, Wade was aware of the rustle in the audience, and finally, in spite of himself, he too turned to see the tall thin man in the faded garb of a Lieutenant Colonel, standing in the doorway, looking upon them with eyes benign and thoughtful, filled with peace.

"Randy!" Sarah got out. "Lord God, it's Randy!" Then she left her place next to her son, and went down the aisle, all the illumination of heaven poured into her face.

Randy's hair was snow white now, not a trace of its former red showing. He had grown a military mustache and goatee, which became his lean, aquiline countenance wonderfully well. He stood there, smiling, the very epitome and idealization of all the South believed her men to be; then he bent and kissed his wife in full sight of the congregation, so that they, forgetting for the moment the purpose for which they had come, made the very rafters ring with their cheers.

Randy turned to them, smiling. Then he took Sarah's arm.

"Come, mother," he said, "we mustn't break up the wedding."

The two of them came back down the aisle together. When they passed Nancy Cattlet, sitting there in her widow's weeds, which never again in her life would she put off, in faithful mourning for both husband and son, dead at Fredericksburg, and before Atlanta, she looked up at them, and whispered in a voice which in the silence after the cheering, carried better than any shout:

"Lord God, a body'd be hard pushed to tell Sarah ain't the bride. . . ."

3

I'M GOING to tell him, Mary Ann thought; I'm going to tell him now. I won't wait until he comes home for supper—I'll go down to the store right now, this minute!

She picked up her bonnet and tied it firmly under her chin. Then she went out on the veranda and called Caleb.

"Yes'm, Miz Mary Ann," Caleb said; "I'm a-coming."

"No," Mary Ann said sharply. "Stay where you are, Caleb, and hitch Nellie to the buckboard. I'm going to town."

"Yes'm," Caleb said. After a quarter of an hour, which was the absolute minimum it took him to do anything whatsoever, Caleb came around the side of the house leading the mare.

"You wants me to drive, Miz Mary Ann?" he said.

"No," Mary Ann said. "For God's sake, Caleb! You know I can handle Nellie. She hasn't even enough life to bolt at a gunshot."

"Yes'm," Caleb said. "But it don't look proper, Miz Mary Ann, for you to be driving yourself. You's a Benton. Folks kind of expect Benton ladies to have they niggers drive for 'em. 'Sides—"

"Besides what, Caleb?" Mary Ann said.

"Sure Lord would like to take a little drive. Ain't been nowheres in so long. . . ."

Slowly Mary Ann shook her head.

"Not today, Caleb," she said. "Today I want to be alone."

"Yes'm," Caleb said sadly, and helped her to mount.

I'm going to put a stop to it, she thought. I'd rather starve than to live on the misery of poor people this way. It's all Oren's fault. He put Wade up to opening that store. Cheating those pine-barren folks out of their last red penny. Time rates forty, fifty, sixty per cent. He and Wade have foreclosed on half the small farms in the parish, and then rented them back to those poor devils on share rates so high they can't never get out of debt. Lord God, how I hate that store! I can't help what Randy says about not getting Wade excited. I'm going to fix that. I'm going to fix it, right now!

But she wasn't sure she could. In the first place, there was the matter of those attacks that Wade had been having for more than a year. He suffered frequently from nose bleeds, ringing in the ears, and even dizziness. Once or twice he had fainted. When, upon her insistence, he had gone to Randy, he had been found to have an alarmingly high blood pressure.

"You've got to make him diet," Randy said sternly. "It's his weight, mostly. And above all, he mustn't get excited. He's just the type to have a stroke. . . ."

She had tried. But dieting was one of the many things that Wade Benton simply could not do. He realized dimly that his gluttony was itself a species of illness, a symptom of the malaise of soul into which his private furies had driven him; but he would not, could not do anything about it. He had neither the character, nor the will.

But, beyond her husband's illness, there was still another obstacle blocking her desire to change the shameful methods by which they lived: something dark, deep rooted, powerful, that she would have to overcome. She had learned that the first year of her marriage; even now, in the fall of 1869, thinking about it brought her bolt upright against the seat of the buckboard, white about the corners of her mouth, her nails digging into the palms of her hands. It was a thing that escaped time, that existed for her now and here and living and vivid as it had then and there.

She had been in the kitchen when Oren came in. He stood or rather lounged there, watching her out of those dark eyes of his that were the epitome and intensification of malice, always laughing, but without mirth, having in them that expression of mockery, of contempt for man and all his works that always made her feel cold and faintly sick.

"What do you want, Oren?" she said.

"You," he grinned. " 'Pears to me I done held off a sight too long. Damn it all, Honeybunch, you're as cute as a speckled setter pup."

"I have a husband, Mister Bascomb," she said tartly. "Or have you forgotten that?"

"Nope," he said. "But that's only about halfway true. Maybe less than that. You been married to that shoat-hog more than a year now. Time enough to find out he ain't no man—not even by half. . . ."

And the barb in the slow-spoken, lazy words, the hook twisting in her flesh was that he was right. She had listened enough to the Negro women when they didn't know she was within earshot to know that. This thing a woman did with a man, had more in it than the mere begetting in the dark, in shame, in secret, in disgust, of a child.

"Lord—Lord!" Luella had laughed; "then the roof fell in and the stars kind of reeled around crazy like, and when the bed broke down, we never even noticed it! That there Tim! Lord God Almighty!"

But for her, there was—nothing. The faint disgust, the unwilling, dutiful submission. Thank God, she thought, he doesn't even bother me much that way. . . .

She looked at Oren speculatively. In her innocence, she did not know how she was looking at him, or how he would interpret it. How precisely, correctly he would understand her curiosity, her quite impersonal longing, that had nothing to do with him as a man, living, just the quiet, half-formulated desire to find out, to know. . . .

But the next instant, he had taken her in his arms. She fought him then with cold, controlled, savage fury—but silently. But Oren was all bone and sinew, he prevailed finally, found her mouth, holding her like that, so bound, helpless, captive that neither of them heard Wade when he came into the kitchen.

"That'll do now," he said, and his voice made splinters of ice, tinkling against the floor.

Oren turned her loose. He stood there; then slowly, insolently, he grinned.

"Reckon I'll be getting back to work now," he said. He walked straight toward Wade. And at the last possible instant, Wade stood aside and let him pass.

"Wade!" Mary Ann got out, her voice high, taut, strangling. "How could you?"

Wade started toward her then. When he was close enough, he drew back his hand and slapped her, hard across the mouth. Then he turned and went out again without another word.

That should have been the end of it, but it wasn't. Although Wade had never again come upon them, there had been many occasions in the last three years when she had had to deal with Oren—to lash him off with words, most of the time, but not infrequently to hold him off with the tiny, silver-mounted derringer she had bought in New Orleans, called the "virgin's pistol," and designed expressly, in those lawless years, for the exact use to which she put it. Beyond this, there was another thing: the belief that she had, slowly deepening into certainty, that Wade knew Oren hadn't ceased his attempts upon her, and knowing, incredibly said nothing, did nothing about them. She had dug into the why of it in a silent fury of concentration, but she had come up with nothing. Either Wade was afraid of Oren Bascomb, or he simply did not care. She dismissed the first idea as unworthy of consideration: a man who had fought the whole Yankee army almost singlehanded, and this by Oren's own corroboration as an eyewitness, was scarcely likely to be terrorized by one man. The second was almost equally unacceptable: she knew with a certainty granted to few women, that Wade did not so much as look at anyone else; she had seen his blue eyes upon her with the sad, hopeless adoration of a faithful dog in them. Then they would change, and there would be fury in them, blank, mindless rage.

The thing that was gone from them was tenderness. To her hurt, puzzled astonishment, every time Wade spoke to her now, his words were barbed. He had an almost feminine genius for the cruel, the cutting, the devastatingly unexpected disparagement. He continually belittled her looks, the same combination of line, feature, coloring which had intrigued him enough before to make him propose to her, her abilities as a housekeeper, which were more than considerable, being on a plane approaching even Sarah's matchless skill; and her inability to present him still, after four years of marriage with an heir.

Mary Ann grimly suspected that at least part of the blame in this last regard was his. She was wrong; all of it was. That his infrequent seizures of a wife half asleep, unaroused, without preliminaries, without even a spoken word, being in itself a species of rapine, leaving her sleepless, tormented, sick to the point, that now, at the first touch of his groping hands, she had to fight back the nausea, armed all her spirit and perhaps even the very chemistry of her body against him, becoming thus in its essence a rejection of his seed, he never even dreamed, not to mention thought of.

Now, jolting along in the light rig, a queasy remnant of the slight discomfort she had been feeling every morning for two weeks rose to trouble her.

I'd better see Randy, she thought. Lord God, wouldn't it be awful, if—

She stiffened in her seat, and stared straight ahead. She had it, then, the very completion of all that had happened to her. She had been very close to it for a long time now. Sitting there in the buckboard, she remembered the last time that Wade, inspired by having Sarah and his stepfather as an audience, had grown expansive on the well-worn subject of her defects.

I didn't even listen to him, she realized suddenly. I didn't feel hurt or mad, or any way at all. I just didn't care. It's been a long time now since I cared about anything he said or did, or thought. . . .

Then, very slowly, she shaped the thing that was in her mind, putting it into words at last, clear, exact, and terrible:

I don't love him. I don't even like him any more. Oren's right. He's a hog. Sitting there bolting his food like somebody was going to take it away from him. Getting fatter, and fatter . . . and Doctor Randy says that fat is going to kill him one of these fine days. . . .

She stiffened against the seat. I mustn't think that! she told herself, I mustn't! It's wicked and ugly to think that way. . . .

But she was nothing if not honest. It would be his own fault if he did, she thought bitterly. I'm doing my best to save him, so it would be all his own fault. And I—I would be free of him . . . or would I? Can I ever be freed of him now—can I?

She could see the town now, in the river bottom. The cluster of houses, the tavern, the white church, the store—the hated, unspeakable store.

Then she completed her unbidden thought: For three years I've been praying for a child; and now, maybe, I've got one. Women get sick like this in the mornings at first. Only now I don't want it. I don't want Wade's child. Her lips moved, shaping the words, just below the level of audible sound: "Lord God, wouldn't it be awful if I am!"

When she came up to the lovely, gracious house that Randy McGregor had built for his belated bride, Sarah was sitting on the veranda. She got up at once and came to the gate.

"Come in, child," she said kindly. "My but you look kind of peaky."

"I haven't been well lately," Mary Ann said. "Randy's home? I want to talk to him about something. . . ."

Sarah opened the gate, and put one arm around her daughter-in-law's waist.

145

"I can guess," she said. "Getting strange hankerings in the middle of the night? Been kind of sickish mornings?"

"Yes," Mary Ann whispered. "Oh, Mother Sarah, you don't think . . . ?"

"Yes, child, I do. Heck, I know. You got the look. But talk to Randy anyhow. He'll hem and haw and say maybe till you're twice as big as you are now; then he'll swear he was sure all the time. I really don't see how he saves anybody now that I'm married to him and have found out just how much he knows and how much is humbug."

"Randy is a mighty good doctor, Mother Sarah," Mary Ann said. "He's the best these folks down here have ever had."

"Which ain't saying much," Sarah laughed. "Oh, he can cut all right. Anything what needs cutting, sawing and stitching, he can fix up just fine. But he really don't know what makes folks tick. I think he just sits beside 'em and suffers so much worse than they do, that they get well out of sympathy for him."

Mary Ann looked at her mother-in-law and smiled.

"You love him very much, don't you?" she said.

"Reckon I do," Sarah said. "But I'll allow that about half of it's pure relief. It's kind of good to be married to a real nice man after Tom—"

"Mother Sarah," Mary Ann said, "is Wade anything like—his pa?"

Sarah pushed a rocker forward, and stood there, considering the question.

"Yes," she said. "He's got that same Benton streak of poison-meanness, only it shows in different ways. Lots of times I was happy, married to Tom. In all the years we was married, he never said as much pure, low-down ugliness to me as I've heard Wade say to you in one half-hour. Wade's my son, but I have to admit he ain't the man his pa was. Even if a man's mean, he don't have to let it out if he's strong. Wade's kind of weak and he knows it. Reckon that's why he has to take it out on you. . . ."

"But he is brave," Mary Ann said uncertainly. "Everybody says that what he did at Briar Creek—"

"Ever hear tell of anything else he done in the war?" Sarah said flatly. "Mind you, I ain't running down my own child; but even a cat will fight if he's cornered. Wade had good luck that time, Mary Ann. The Yankees had him surrounded, so he got his back up, and fought—he had that much of his pa in him. And he happened to have done it before a witness. Folks believe that Oren Bascomb because they know he ain't the kind of man to say nothing good about anybody else lessen he has to—sit down, child. I'll go call Randy."

The examination took barely five minutes.

"Hard to say for certain this early in the game," Randy said; "but I'm pretty sure that in nine months you're going to make me a grandpa, young lady. Damned if I don't like the idea! Me, a grandpa! Have you told Sarah?"

146

"Didn't have to, Doctor Randy. She gave one look at me and she knew. . . ."

"Then it's a sure thing. When it comes to babies, Sarah's the damned best diagnostician I ever did see. Come on back out on the porch. Wade won't be going home for yet a while."

"All right, Doctor Randy," Mary Ann said.

They sat on the porch.

"Mother Sarah," Mary Ann said, "I've got troubles—"

"You sure Lord have," Sarah said; "but you'll do all right. I did."

"Oh, I wasn't thinking about that. It's—it's that Oren Bascomb. . . ."

"What's he done now?" Randy growled; "I'll be blessed if five minutes of him is just about all I can stand!"

"Two," Sarah said flatly.

"He's always leading Wade into things. You know about the store—how it works, I mean?"

"Yes," Randy said. "Pure, unadulterated robbery! By God, the war was supposed to free the Negroes. Maybe it did; but it certainly has enslaved the white man. Damn it all, Sarah! You know those McPhersons? Went out there yesterday, and helled and bedamned the place down, trying to get that McPherson woman to understand that children need milk and eggs and vegetables. Know what she told me?"

"Yes," Sarah said; "told you they couldn't afford it because they owe so much at the store. . . ."

"I'm going to talk to Wade!" Randy thundered. "If that boy's got a spark of decency left in him, he'll see—"

"He'll see all right," Sarah said grimly; "but he won't do a blamed thing, Randy. That black-hearted scoundrel's got him completely under his thumb."

"They even cheat the Negroes," Mary Ann whispered. "No matter how many bales a tenant makes, with Oren keeping the books, he ends up in debt. Those poor creatures can't read or write, so he cheats them something awful. I stuck my nose in that, and Oren told me point-blank to tend to the big house, and let him manage the place like he was hired to. . . ."

"And Wade backed him up?" Randy asked.

"Yes," Mary Ann whispered. "But that's not the worst of it. Oren's a member of the Knights of the White Camellia, and I'm not sure that—that Wade isn't, too. . . ."

"He is," Sarah said grimly.

"I'm still not sure, Mother Sarah," Mary Ann said. "I know he goes out a mighty heap at night. . . ."

"I am," Sarah said. "They've got to go on playing heroes, all those boys. They've got to swill their likker and ride a-whooping and a-hollering down on some nigger's cabin. And after they whip him 'most to death and burn his shack, they feel real brave—it's Gettysburg and Shiloh

Church, and Antietam rolled into one all over for them. Lord God, it's enough to make a body puking sick!"

"But, Mother Sarah—all those carpetbaggers and scalawags stirring the colored folks up. . . ."

"Don't get touched—or rarely," Randy said in his deep, still voice. "No, it's the black who's the victim. They know, they must know, Mary Ann, that the Negro is no more than the stick in the hand of the bully who beats us. The thing to do is to strike at the men who hold the stick, the Republicans themselves—by patience, by endurance, by quiet courage, which are the things we haven't got. . . .

"No, the black man is the victim made to order, because his Republican bosses, who herd him, fete him, drill him to the polls, give him liquor and barbecues, excite him with promises of land, tickle his childish vanity with letting him play at lawmaking, don't give a damn about him truly, any further than they can use him. But the others, the Kluxers, the Innocents, the White Camellias, hiding under their dirty bedsheets, are, I submit, the most despicable band of criminal scum that ever disgraced a land capable of producing a Lee, a Stuart, a Jackson!"

"You're speaking of Wade, too, remember," Mary Ann said.

"I am. And I regret to speak so. They, our home-grown, night-riding heroes, have their excuses: They say we are damnably misgoverned, robbed, maltreated—and we are. But we were damnably misgoverned, robbed, maltreated long before the carpetbag became a symbol of dishonor. I soberly beg the young blades of our irregular, buffonic cavalry to consider the record of the Know-Nothings in New Orleans in the 'Fifties —of the endless procession of embezzlers, cheats, thieves, who have held office in Louisiana since the day we took over from the French. I ask you, is it the thievery we object to, or merely its preservation as the *droit de seigneur* of the local talent?"

"Still, Doctor Randy," Mary Ann said, "we can't permit black Republicans and Yankees to treat us the way they do. Most decent white people can't vote, while all those ignorant darkies can. I haven't anything against black people. You know that. I'm always taking up for them. But they just don't know enough; they haven't had the experience. They're like children."

"I grant you that. That's not the point, child. It's not objectives I'm talking about, but methods. Any end is inevitably dirtied by dirty means —and I tremble to think of what the white Southerner is going to be like after thirty years of night riding, unbridled violence, and mass slaughter of the helpless. We've learned to spit on due process of law down here —we have come to condone, here in Louisiana, more—to uphold, to boast of, a savagery that would disgrace a Sioux. Last year, A.D. 1868, was election year; and we, under various provocations, none of which, I insist, justified the sickening barbarity of our actions, engaged in a Negro hunt in Bossier Parish, chasing black men into the swamps, running them before the dogs, whether they had had anything to do with the killing of those two white men or not. When it was over, we had killed forty Negroes, if you accept the Democratic estimate, or one hundred twenty, if you take the Republican. It doesn't matter which. Perhaps, in the scales of God, the lives of two white men balance those of forty or even of a hundred and twenty blacks. I can't measure human souls, add up, and balance lives. . . .

"In St. Landry, it was worse: four Negroes killed in the first skirmish, eight arrested and subsequently lynched, and a mass manhunt lasting two weeks, organized like a grand turkey shoot, with an even bigger difference in the tally according to which source you take it from. Thirty, say the Democrats, three hundred, the Republicans. Again it doesn't matter how many hunks of human meat were left after the shooting, stabbing, knocking out of brains—"

"Randy, for the love of God!" Sarah said.

"And even burning. We've come to that. We've gone back that many centuries into human barbarism. It doesn't matter. Do not count them. Them nor the forty-odd those Sicilian savages who call themselves the Innocents killed in St. Bernard. And this, ladies, in one year, in one State, in defense of your sacred honor. How do you like possessing an honor of such magnitude, of such shining purity; yet, by definition, of such manifest feebleness that it requires rivers of blood to uphold it? Dear God! We left you alone, on outlying farms, surrounded by young and lusty Negro men for four years—and I have yet to learn of one authentic case of rape in all that time. But now it becomes the issue; we must have a stalking horse. We cannot admit we butcher Negroes because it suits our conception of political expediency at the moment—or more truly, because there's a sickness of cruelty in us, coupled with a cowardice that dares not touch the real authors of our misfortunes—since, unfortunately, if we kill them, the windy thieves who herd the blacks to the polls in pursuit of plunder, we, ourselves, are in danger of hanging. No—rather this slaughter of innocents, this shooting of tame and tethered ducks, until butchery becomes a way of life, until we reverse the decision lost upon the field of honor—and in this dirty fashion we shall win. . . ."

"You think so, Doctor Randy?" Mary Ann said.

"I know it, child. We shall win our ignoble victory. But in the end we shall go down, sink down out of the bonds of civilized men, retreat out of decency, kindliness and honor, bring up generations of young men who will accept the abuse of the helpless, injustice, cruelty, the nasty, stinking business of mankilling as the normal way of life. We will do it. And may God have mercy upon our souls!"

They sat there in the silence, feeling the afternoon heat dying a little, the first coolness of the evening stealing in.

"The Knights asked Randy to join," Sarah said. "Did you know that, child?"

"No," Mary Ann said; "but I'd have given a pretty penny to hear what he told them!"

"I rather disgraced myself," Randy said. "Kicked the scoundrel down the flight of stairs from my office. Then I went over to their headquarters and told them I'd pistol the next blackguard who had the temerity to cross my threshold. They haven't bothered me since."

He turned to Mary Ann, his face gentle and grave.

"You want me to talk to Wade, Mary?" he said.

"No," Mary Ann said, and stood up. "I'm going over there and have it out with Wade. Maybe I can get him to see the light. . . ."

"You do that, child," Sarah said.

The first thing she heard when she entered the store was Wade's high-pitched, nasal voice storming at a client.

"Damn it to hell, Murphy! You think I'm made out of money? I have to pay dear for this stuff. Folks I buy it from don't wait. I advanced you fertilizer last season; plowlines, seed, God knows what else! You was to pay for it out of the crop. Now you tell me you didn't make no crop! Howcome, Murphy? Name of God, man, I ain't no charitable institution!"

"Mister Wade," the poorwhite's voice quavered, "Listen to me! I ain't got no field hands. Can't afford to hire help. And my old woman ain't been right since the last kid. He was born queer—don't think he's ever going to walk or talk or anything. . . ."

"What in hellfire that got to do with me? I want my money!"

"Mister Wade, Mister Wade—you ain't going to sit there and tell me that a man with a sick wife—Mollie's got a misery in the chest and hit's mighty bad; she done took to spitting blood—and with my wife like that and a flock of kids to feed you ain't going to let me have a little more credit? Why Doctor Randy says—"

"To hell with my precious pa-in-law and what he says! If he wants to tote the whole parish on his shoulders, let him! But as for me—"

There's nothing worse, Mary Ann thought, than putting a sniveling coward in a position of power. Takes out everything what's eating him on everybody else. Look at him! That's my husband, the man I married, the man who's going to be the father of my child. Sitting there slobbering and spitting, so blamed fat you can't half see his mean little eyes. Ugh! By the living God this is the last child I'll ever have for you, Wade Benton! Come nigh me again, I'll take that derringer to you.

She waited, very quietly.

"Lord God, Mister Wade," Tim Murphy half wept; "you really mean you won't?"

"I won't," Wade said; "and that's my last word, Murphy. Now get out of here and let me be!"

Mary Ann stood aside and let Tim Murphy stumble past; then she stepped forward.

"Wade," she said evenly, "you've got to quit this. You're going to close up this store. And you're going to kick that Oren Bascomb plumb off our place. I'm not asking you—I'm telling you."

"I can't close it," Wade said; "you know that, Mary Ann. The plantation don't bring in enough for us to live on. Wasn't for the store, we'd starve sure!"

"Then you got to give these folks better terms. You can do that. You hear me, Wade?"

"I hear you all right. But if you think I'm going to start giving away my hard-earned profits—"

"Hard-earned?" Mary Ann snorted. "At sixty per cent? And you and Oren call the Yankees thieves! You listen to me, Wade Benton. You've been complaining that you have no son. Well, now you've got one—or maybe a daughter—I can't guarantee which—"

Joy flooded Wade's round face.

"You're sure, Mary Ann?" he breathed; "you're really sure?"

"Certain sure. But if you don't start treating these poor folks better, I'm going to leave you. I'll go so far away you'll never find me—and a sweet lot of good it'll do you to have a son you'll never see!"

"You wouldn't!" Wade got out.

"Just try me," Mary Ann said. "And Bascomb goes, too!"

"I can't, Mary Ann!" Wade croaked; "I just purely can't!"

"Why not?" Mary Ann demanded.

"No reason. But I can't. You got to take my word for it, Mary Ann."

"He goes," Mary Ann said flatly, and walked to the doorway. In it, she turned.

"You know one thing, hero," she said, "I think Oren's lying about Briar Creek. I think you ran like hell!"

Then very quietly, she went out into the sunwashed street.

And Wade Benton, alone in his store, sat turning the pages of the big ledgers, which held in tenuous, fading ink, the black and white tenants of the entire parish in thralldom, having here, in its essence, the new slavery of debt, and poor men's honor—and this, and more, the measure, the record of his own dishonor, his greed, and the sickness of mind and soul which drove his breed to gorge in vulturish rapacity upon men made defenseless by ignorance and poverty. Then, suddenly, he put his head down upon the ledger, and cried.

"Dear Lord!" he wept, "dear Lord! Dear Lord! Dear Lord—"

4

"So," RANDY growled, "I've got the job of explaining to Mary Ann, eh? And without telling her the truth. That's hard, Wade. . . ."

Wade kept turning his round face from side to side to avoid meeting Randy's eyes. He couldn't look into them—not now, not any more.

"Tell her part of the truth, then," he said. "Tell her Oren's got some kind of a hold on me—you don't know what. Lord God, I've been putting her off about that for more than a year now—ever since she told me she was going to have the twins—not that we knew it was going to be twins. I can't put her off no more."

"I won't lie," Randy said. "I've never stooped to that, Wade. But I'll try to arrange things. That's all I can do."

"You can see my point, can't you, Randy?" Wade pleaded. "I'm Mayor of the town now, head of the local branch of the Knights of the White Camellia. Folks say I've got a chance to run for Governor, come next election. I can't give all that up, Randy—I can't!"

"I see," Randy said slowly. "You've got two choices, boy. You can kill Oren Bascomb, or submit to him. You choose to submit; that's your business. But tell him not to cross my path. I'd as soon shoot him as I would a rattlesnake—no, sooner."

"On what basis could I kill him?" Wade burst out. "They hang folks for murder. Lord God, what excuse could I have? He don't even tote a penknife, let alone a gun. So it couldn't be self-defense. And you told me not to get excited. . . ."

"If you have to risk a stroke for any reason," Randy said, "this is at least a good one. I don't think life is important enough to be preserved by dishonor. But if you want to spend the rest of your life under perpetual threat of extortion, again I say it's your affair. By the way, how are Mary Ann and the twins?"

"Just fine," Wade said. "Lord God, Randy, how those youngsters can eat! I've got three nigger women wet-nursing them in relays. They're so big now Mary Ann can hardly pick them up. You can tell them apart now. Stone—he's the older, by about two hours, is darker. But both of 'em's got Pa's blue eyes. . . ."

"You mean to tell me," Randy laughed, "that Mary Ann insisted upon calling that child Stonewall!"

"Yep," Wade grinned sheepishly. "Stonewall Jackson Benton, and Nathan Bedford Forrest Benton. Still, Stone and Nat ain't half-bad names, and that's all folks are going to call 'em anyhow."

He stood up.

"Got to be going now," he muttered. "Randy—"

"Yes, Wade?"

"You won't breathe a word about what I told you to anybody, will you now? Not even to Ma. That was to get out, I'd be finished."

Randy stared at him, his gaze so level and still, that Wade's pale little eyes danced in his fat face, trying to avoid meeting it. But he could not. Randy's eyes drew him, held him.

"Lord God, Randy," he spluttered; "I didn't mean—"

"I know," Randy said quietly; "but I still think you ought to shoot that blackguard."

"And I told you I don't have no excuse to," Wade whined; "don't you see that, Randy?"

"No," Randy said coldly, "I don't. You could do it the very next time he lays a hand on Mary Ann. And he will, you know. Under the circumstances, you could hardly expect him not to."

"Oh, Mary Ann can take care of herself," Wade blurted.

Randy stood up then, towered up, his face granite, his eyes cold.

"Get out of here, Wade," he said. "Get out before I really lose my temper. You heard me—get!"

"All right, all right—I'm going!" Wade Benton said.

Randy stood there without moving for a long time after he had gone. Then he turned slowly back to his desk.

You poor bastard, he thought; you poor, fat, whining, womanish bastard! Lord God, where on earth did Tom Benton get a thing like that?

He reached for his hat. No use hanging around the office, he thought. This good weather means mighty lean pickings for an old sawbones. Might as well go on home for a while, and then go look in on Mollie Murphy. Poor thing, I'm afraid she isn't long for this world. . . .

As if in answer to his thought, the door burst open, and Tim Murphy stood there, trembling, his eyes bloodshot and wild.

"Doctor Randy!" he got out, "you've got to come! Mollie's took bad! 'Pears like she's going to die!"

"All right, Tim," Randy said. "You go wait in the buckboard while I get my things together."

"Oh, Lord, Doctor Randy, please hurry! She's suffering something awful!"

"Wait outside, Tim," Randy said sternly.

"Yessir, Doctor," Tim Murphy said.

So it was that Sarah was alone in the house when the stranger came. She heard his light, diffident knocking on the door, and swore with great force and feeling. Another one, she thought. Another poorwhite devil, or no-'count nigger come to beg Randy to drop everything and come. And he's killing himself by inches, the poor old thing. Dear Lord, after I finally got myself a good man—it's his very goodness what's going to take him away from me. Oh, stop it! I'm coming. . . .

But when she opened the door, the strange young man stood there.

"You're Mrs. McGregor, I presume?" the stranger said.

Sarah stood there, staring at him. It was not merely his use of that word, 'presume,' which Sarah had never heard spoken, as a part of living speech, before in her life, though she knew what it meant; it was more: a hint of foreignness, the faintest trace of an accent that clung to his speech, so that the words were precisely, correctly spoken, pronounced with exactitude in a deep, well modulated voice, wonderfully musical, the lilt of them was wrong, and the tune. Beyond this there was something else, that strange, dreamlike feeling of having stood and looked into this same face before, oh, many, many times before, of having watched these same lips move, shaping words, having looked into these eyes—that, no. The eyes were strange, she realized suddenly, and it was this which convinced her she had never seen this young man before.

"Yes, I am," she said, "but you've got the advantage of me, sir. Who might you be?"

"I am Clinton Dupré," he said simply. "I suppose you've heard of me?"

"Yes," Sarah's voice sank to the barest husk of a whisper. "My God, but you're like—"

"My father. Yes, I am. You must find it terribly strange that I call upon you. . . ."

"As a matter of fact, I do," Sarah said; "but come on in. I don't aim to hold Tom's sins over your head, young man. I'm glad you did come. Reckon we've got right smart to talk about, you and me."

He smiled then, and she saw one of the ways that he was not at all like Tom Benton. He was actually much handsomer, and his smile was something to see, lighting the dark eyes his mother had given him, transforming his whole face, making it boyish and sunny, without any of what Sarah had called Tom's poison-meanness at all.

She led him into the parlor and sat there looking at him in frank and open curiosity. What she saw both pleased her and made her sad. Mighty fine, she thought, mighty fine. So Tom did have it in him after all. That means that Wade's my fault. Never knew that Lolette Dupré well, but she must have been a better woman than I am, to get a son like this. . . .

"I hope you'll forgive me, Mrs. McGregor," he said; "but my father invited me out to Broad Acres to visit you two—the week before—he died. I told him I'd come; but things—his death chiefly, and after that, the war—got in the way. . . ."

"You fought, didn't you?" Sarah said. "What was your regiment?"

"I'm sorry, Ma'am," Clinton said; "but it was the Fourth Massachusetts."

"Union Army, eh? Don't worry about that, Clint. It's 1870, now. Besides, I don't care what side you were on, if you fought like a man and a soldier. That would be all Tom would ask of you. Were you decorated?"

"Yes," Clinton said, "three times, Mrs. McGregor—and promoted to Captain on the field. Guess I was a reckless young fool. . . ."

"You must have been in it right from the first," Sarah said.

"As a matter of fact, I was—though not as a soldier. I was only seventeen the first year—too young, though I was big enough to get by if I had thought of it. But at seventeen, Ma'am, I was the authorized correspondent for five French newspapers, including *Le Soir*, itself. I was the only American they could find who spoke and wrote French. I've finally broken myself of thinking in French; but I still speak and write it better than I do English. . . ."

"I thought you talked sort of funny. You lived abroad, didn't you?"

"In France—practically all my life. I went through a year and a half of the war as a newspaperman. Then I joined up. I'd seen too many battles, had boys I'd grown fond of killed before my eyes. And, again I don't mean to offend you, Ma'am, I hated slavery. . . ."

"So did I," Sarah said grimly. "Go on—"

"Did you, Ma'am? That's strange. Besides, in the Lycée in Paris, my best friend was a black boy named Antoine Hébert—from Martinique. He was a brilliant student, a fine athlete, and a wonderful fellow generally. That made it sort of personal. We talked a lot about slavery in Paris. He told me some terrible stories of the days when his own people were slaves. I felt like I was doing it for him. . . ."

"I see. Why do you say Ma'am, like a Southerner, Clint?"

"Picked it up in New Orleans, I guess. Then a lot of those mid-Western farmboys I knew in the army said it, too. I don't really know. But I had to see you, Ma'am. My father loved you so. My mother, with all her faults, never permitted herself to say an unkind word about you. She said that you were a wonderful person—that sometimes she wished you weren't so she could have taken my father away from you. . . ."

"She tried hard enough," Sarah said dryly. "How is she, Clint?"

"Dead, Ma'am. She died in 'Sixty-five, just before the end of the war. I think she just didn't care to live. She was too unhappy. She neglected to eat or take care of herself. She caught a cold, and died of double pneumonia within a week—"

"God rest her soul," Sarah said. "I'm sorry, Clint. . . ."

"Thank you, Ma'am. In a way it was the best thing. My mother was sick and nervous and unhappy for years. She was—difficult, Ma'am—"

Suddenly, impulsively, Sarah put out her hand and laid it over his strong, brown wrist.

"Call me Mother Sarah, won't you, Clint? I'd like you to. In a way, you're my son, now. Any son of Tom's would have to be mine, too. . . ."

He stared at her, a long, slow time.

"Thank you for that—Mother Sarah," he said.

"Good! Now we're friends. What are you going to do now, Clint?"

"Start a newspaper—here in Benton's Row, if I can, Ma'am. My mother left me a good bit of money, but I'd like to do something useful. A newspaper can be a powerful force for good, Mother Sarah. Besides, as little as I've seen of this place, I love it here. I don't know why, but everything about it intrigues me. I feel I can recapture the life I should have had with my father—and didn't. . . ."

"Fine," Sarah said. "You can stay here with us. I've a spare room."

"Thank you, Mother Sarah, but I'd rather not. I'd be an embarrassment to you. After all, I do look rather like my father—"

"His spitting image," Sarah said, "only better-looking. Stay for a while anyhow—till you find yourself a proper place."

"But, Ma'am, your husband . . ."

"Was Tom's best friend, and fair doted on him. Heck, Randy would be delighted."

"Then I will stay," Clinton said. "Mother Sarah—"

"Yes, son?"

"There's one more thing I guess I ought to tell you. My sister, Stormy, is in New Orleans. She's married to a Yankee General turned carpetbagger. They came down on the same boat I did."

"Lord God!" Sarah whispered.

"I asked her if she were coming to see you. She said: 'Oh, you tell Ma I'm here. She'll drop by some time when she's in New Orleans.'"

"That's Stormy all right," Sarah said bitterly. "Dear Lord, what did I ever do to deserve such a child?"

"I'm sorry, Mother Sarah," Clint said. "By the way, I'd like to meet Wade and his wife, if it's possible. When I asked about you down in town, they told me he was running the plantation now, and that you lived here."

"'Course you can," Sarah said. "Tell you what: I'll send Buford, our nigger houseboy, to ask Mary Ann to come here for supper tonight. You can ride over to the store and ask Wade yourself. Know where it is?"

"Why, yes—I passed it on the way here. But I didn't know my brother ran it. Strange, isn't it, to have a brother you've never seen. . . ."

"A half brother," Sarah corrected grimly. "And I wouldn't go claiming kin with Wade too quick, Clint. He's kind of prickly, that boy. But you'll get used to him, I reckon."

"I hope so," Clinton smiled. "Now, Ma'am, if you'll excuse me, I'll go over there."

"All right, son. But hurry back, won't you? Kind of nice to have somebody to talk to. Reckon I spend too much time by myself."

"Yes, Mother Sarah," Clint said gently, "I'll hurry back."

She went out on the veranda with him. He had scarcely ridden half a block when she saw Randy coming home. He came from the same direction in which Clint was riding; and as he passed the young man, he stared at him, half in recognition, half in puzzlement.

Sarah waited until he came up to the house. He climbed down from the buckboard, his face gray with weariness and misery, and she knew without thinking about it, that another of his patients was dead.

"Who," he drawled, "was that handsome youngster who just left here? Appears to me you're picking 'em kind of young these days, Sarah—"

"Tom's boy," Sarah said; "by Lolette Dupré. You knew about that, I reckon. . . . Not that you'd ever tell on Tom."

"Yes," Randy said, "I knew. No wonder he looked so familiar! By God, but he's like Tom."

"Very much," Sarah sighed. "Come on in and let me fix you something to eat—"

"Don't want any," Randy growled. "That poor bastard, Murphy . . ."

"I know," Sarah said. "Come on, Randy, you've got to eat. There'll be others you can save."

"All right, Sarah," Randy said.

But when Clinton reached the store, he found it closed. He stood there a moment, looking at it. Guess he's gone home, he thought. Doesn't matter really. I'll ride out there and present myself. It's not very far, and anyone hereabout can direct me. . . .

He remounted, whistling the tune of *Lorena*. He was then still a very simple and cheerful young man.

Some four hours later, Randy woke up from a deep and refreshing sleep. He felt much better. He had made peace with himself over his failure to save Mollie Murphy's life. It had been a thing beyond human science, a thing that could only have been staved off, not cured. And what above all had been lacking, the missing factor which could have kept her alive was simple compassion. And this, Randy realized with sad acceptance, was, in any time, rare almost to the point of nonexistence.

He got up and looked for Sarah. He found her in the kitchen, her eyes both worried and wrathful.

"That Buford!" she said; "I sent him out to Broad Acres with a message more than four hours ago. Bet my bottom dollar it's Cindy again! Buford's gone plumb crazy over that little wench."

Randy smiled.

"Reckon we'd better get them married, and hire Cindy as your maid," he said. "That way, we'd be able to keep Buford around."

"Ain't a bad idea," Sarah said. "Cindy's kind of flighty, but she's a neat little thing. I could learn her some sense. But I'm worried about Clinton, too. He's been gone just as long and he promised to hurry back."

"I'll ride out toward Broad Acres," Randy said, "and see if I can't find both of them. You seem quite taken with that boy, Sarah."

"I am. He's a mighty fine boy, Randy. Kind of a son I wish I'd had. You ain't too tired?"

"No; I'm fine, now," Randy said.

It was, by the time he got there, already too late, though he did not realize it then. He had merely the vague feeling, all the time he talked to Mary Ann, that something was wrong—a hint of tension—a certain inquietude, which he dismissed, at first, as imaginary.

"I'll take Buford back with me," he said to Clinton; "and you, young fellow, can ride alongside. Sarah's expecting you for dinner."

"Doctor Randy!" Mary Ann said sharply, "Mister Dupré has accepted an invitation to dine with me!"

Her voice, Randy thought, was odd. A trifle high, and a little breathless. Too many worries, he decided; maybe she needs a sedative. . . .

Then he saw her face.

"Very well, child," he said slowly, "I'll explain to Sarah. Where is that burr-headed black jackass?"

"Out on the back steps talking to Cindy," Mary Ann said. "I let him, Doctor Randy. The poor boy is sure lovesick."

"All right," Randy said, "I'll go get him." He paused, looking at them.

"Good appetite, children," he said. "Can we expect you for supper then, Mister Dupré?"

"Yes, Doctor," Clinton said, "thank you very much."

The two men shook hands. Doctor Randy looked past the tall young man to where Mary Ann stood. She was turned half away from them, staring out of the window. He sighed.

Then he went out back and found Buford, sitting there holding Cindy's small brown hands in his own enormous black paws, looking for all the world like a moonsick calf.

"Come along, Buford," Randy said.

"Aw, Doctor Randy!" Buford protested.

"Take him, Doctor Randy, suh," Cindy laughed; "he sure is one pest!"

"Buford, you heard me!" Randy said.

"Aw, all right then," Buford groaned, "I'm coming. . . ."

The two of them walked around the house and stood before the veranda.

There is a fatality about this house, Randy thought. It was born out of the whirlwind and destruction, and built upon violence. I think that happiness will always be a stranger here. . . .

"Marse Tom's boy," Buford muttered; "his spittin'-image!"

Randy didn't answer him.

"You poor bastard," he said aloud; "you poor, poor bastard. God help you now."

Buford stared at him.

"He might be a woodscolt, all right," he said. "But ain't nothing poor 'bout that boy of Marse Tom's, Doctor Randy. He's mighty fine. . . ."

"I wasn't talking about him," Randy said. "Damn your black hide, come on!"

5

"Lord God, Oren," Wade Benton said, "ain't you never going to be satisfied? We got stores in Gahagan, Coushatta, and Pleasant Hill as well as here. A cottonseed mill, too? Lord God!"

"Told you I aimed to get rich," Oren said, "and when I said rich, I meant rich—not halfway."

Wade looked at him. Randy's right, he thought. I should shoot this son of a bitch. Only I ain't built that way. Lord Jesus, why wasn't I born with a little guts?

"Fastest growing industry in the State," Oren said blandly. "Use the pressed seed for fodder and fertilizer. Two dozen uses for the oil, and more being found out every day. Hell, Wade-boy, we'll be millionaires!"

"If you want to be a millionaire," Wade said dryly, "you ought to turn scalawag and go round kissing niggers. Get yourself elected, and then you'd have the whole blamed State to rob blind, 'stead of just me."

Oren opened his dark eyes wide.

"Now looka here, Wade," he said, his tone the perfect counterfeit of injured innocence, "how come you think I'm robbing you? Fact is, it's my ideas what's made us all the money. I runs the plantation good, bringing you a fair profit. I talked you into opening them supply stores, which have made you a mint. You know damned well wasn't for me you wouldn't have a pot to do you know what in. Ain't that so?"

"It is, and it ain't," Wade growled. "I do all the work in the stores: buying, selling, bookkeeping, supervising the managers in the other towns, and you don't do a damned thing, yet you collect half of the take— before expenses, Oren. You're getting rich all right, but I ain't. After I pay off those thieving managers and the Yankee supply houses, I do just a little better than breaking even. Same thing with the plantation. These days, a man can't get rich growing cotton. But I could live, wasn't for you. Broad Acres don't even break even most of the time. I have to keep it going with the little bit I get from the stores. Wish to hell you'd go into politics—get you off my back then."

"No," Oren grinned. "I take a long view of things, Wade. Them folks up North going to git tired of sending down troops ever' time we kill a couple of dozen niggers and whips a carpetbagger. And no party based on nigger support can last in the South. Man what gits rich that way, is going to fall that way, too, when them carpetbaggers is drove hightailing it back to their stinking mill towns up North, if he ain't lynched to boot. 'Sides I'm for the white man, first, last and always. But owning a cottonseed oil mill would be a mighty fine thing. Me and you would be partners as usual. Hell, I'd even be willing to share the expenses."

"That way," Wade mused, "there might be a chance. Only there is one thing you don't seem to have figured, Oren: Where in hellfire would I get the money to build a factory? It would cost a hundred thousand dollars if it cost a cent—maybe more."

Oren grinned.

"Your sister, Stormy," he said, "spends that much money a year for clothes. Last time I was in New Orleans, folks wasn't talking about nothing else but that ball she gave at the Saint Louis Hotel. Hundred and fifty invited guests, two orchestras, sixty waiters, damn near a ton of food, and enough wine to keep even the Republican legislature drunk a year. Know how much it cost her, Wade-boy? Twenty-five thousand dollars, folks say, what with every lady getting a piece of expensive jewelry as a favor, and every gentleman a bottle of sixty-year-old brandy brung over special from France. For one ball, boy. And she gives them regular."

"Stormy wouldn't give me a red copper," Wade said. "Always has been bad blood 'twixt the two of us."

"I know that. But that there old Yankee General she's married to—seventy if he's a day, has got control of the lottery. Lord God, Wade, that there Louisiana lottery takes in twenty-eight million dollars a year! And bad blood or no, that old pirate is hauling away a sight too much folding money for us not to git our fingers on a part of it."

"I agree with you there," Wade said; "but how, Oren? You tell me that?"

"I don't know yet. All I know is I got to be introduced to your sister. She is one cool-headed woman from all I hear tell. Gal like that, I kin talk to. Show her a point or two for mutual benefit."

"Look, Oren, I have never been inside my sister's door. So how in hell-fire you expect me to introduce you to her?"

"Well, now, there's your ma. She's been pining to see your sister, but she's too proud to call first. Suppose we fix something up. The twins' birthday ain't far off. Be two years old sometime next month, won't they? Give a big shindig and invite your sister. I'll kind of rally round as master of ceremonies till I see my chance."

"She won't come," Wade said. "You don't know Stormy, Oren."

"Then I got another idea. I'm going down to New Orleans next week end—how about your writing a nice, sweet note to your sister, and letting me deliver it, personal? Then I could try persuading her. I'm right smart good at persuading folks."

"Don't I know it!" Wade groaned. "All right, Oren. Maybe if this scheme of yours works out, I might have a little something to leave my boys."

"Sure you will, Wade-boy. A mighty heap, too. Yessir, a mighty heap," Oren Bascomb said.

The mimosa was in bloom in the yard. Two bluejays scolded there, making the air raucous with their ugly voices. Mary Ann looked up at them. It was no use trying to drive them away and she knew it. Jays didn't know what fear meant.

In their double carriage, the twins slept. They weren't much trouble. Except for their habit of smashing everything they could get their hands on, toddling over and pulling the cloths off tables laden with dishes, tearing pages out of books, upsetting inkwells, and wiping intricate designs on the walls with their smudged fingers, they were no trouble at all. They never cried or were sick. Except the one time that Stone hit Nat in the head with a hammer, she had never had to call Randy for them. They, she thought fondly, are completely bloodthirsty little savages; but they aren't like their father. Nat didn't even cry much when Stone hit him. Nothing weak about my monsters, no sirreebobtail!

She saw Oren walking away from the house, and sat very still, trying not to attract his attention. But it was no good, and she knew it. He came over to her.

"How you doing, Honeybunch?" he said in his lazy drawl. "How about you leaving them two cannibals with their overstuffed pa and taking a li'l' run down to New Orleans with me this week end?"

I ought to go with him, Mary Ann thought savagely. It's a pity I despise him so—because it would serve Wade right if I did something like that. It sure Lord would!

"How would you like for me to tell Doctor Randy that you're still pestering me?" she said.

"Wouldn't like it a-tall," Oren grinned. "That man sure got himself one bad temper! But it's kind of sad to have to go running to your pa-in-law, your step-pa-in-law at that, with something your husband ought to settle hisself—now, ain't it? Lord God, it ain't even no fun for me to make love to you in front of old fat boy's face no more, 'cause he don't even bat an eye!"

"Go 'way from here, Oren," Mary Ann said sullenly.

"Sure, Ma'am," Oren mocked; "but one of these days, you gonna see the advantage of having a man instead of a nothing. I mean permanent, not on and off like that pretty bastard half brother of Wade's."

"Oren, I'm warning you!"

"Yes'm. One of these days you're going to shoot me with that pretty little toy you totes. Only, you ain't. 'Cause I don't aim to force you, Honeybunch. I'm just going to wait around for one of them hot June nights, with a big moon shining through the cheniere, and the whippoor-wills a-calling, and you a-laying there trying to sleep and can't 'cause you's a natural woman and ain't no good woman can do without—that. Listening to that fat hog in the guest room where you done put him, laying there snoring, whilst you toss, and turn, and twist. . . ."

"Oren!" Mary Ann grated.

"I'm going, Ma'am," Oren said; "I'm going right now!"

He's not human, Mary Ann thought bitterly. How could he know so much? But I couldn't have put into words the way I spend my nights any better myself. The Good Book says that as a man thinketh in his heart, so is he. Reckon that applies to women, too. If that's so, I'm going to bust hell wide open when I hit it, 'cause what I think about every time I catch a glimpse of Clint would scorch the paper if anybody tried to print it! And a glimpse is all I catch. Lord Jesus, how come those Hendersons had to come back from Mississippi just now?

Wade came around the house leading his horse. He had not mounted, because he always stopped to look at the twins before riding back to the store. Whatever the relationship between him and Mary Ann now, this one bond held them. They both adored the twins. Since their birth, Mary

Ann had slept in the nursery with them, not even pleading ill health or making any excuse whatsoever. She had said very simply: "I just don't love you any more, Wade. And that's one thing that requires love. When the boys are big enough, I'm going to leave you. In the meantime, I'd thank you to forget all about me. I'm just a stranger in your house. You're free. You want another woman, you have her. Believe me, I won't lift a finger, or say a word. I just don't care—that's all."

Wade had stood there, staring at her a long time. But in the end, all he said was: "As you like, Mary Ann."

It had been two years now; but he hadn't taken another woman. He was cursed with a certain gift for introspection—even for realism. Though he knew quite well, it would not have been difficult to find a mistress, he also realized that, being what he was, both physically, and morally, it would have been his reputed wealth, and undeniable social position which drew a woman to him. Since he had neither vanity nor self-love, he realized the obvious impossibility of anyone's loving him. In all those two years, he had not so much as sought out a prostitute to relieve whatever natural hungers he might have had. And he did not even pride himself upon his chastity, for, as one of the inevitable results of his obesity, the fires of sexuality flickered but feebly within him. He never recognized his gluttony for what it was: an attempt to substitute an immature pleasure for a mature one. He made fitful efforts at self-control, but given his lack of anything remotely resembling willpower, these forays at exercise and diet seldom lasted two full days.

He was one of the most completely unhappy young men who ever drew the breath of life. He thought often and darkly of suicide, but his physical cowardice, his horror of blood and pain prevented his doing anything about it. He thought much more frequently of killing Oren Bascomb, and thus ending the perpetual threat under which he lived. He devised numerous schemes for murder, in which the deed itself would be disguised as accident; some of them almost brilliant, and having in his rural world and the then infantile state of the science of criminology, a real chance for success. But they all required the things he lacked: courage, force of character, firmness of will. So he did nothing, existed, rather than lived, held on, endured, suffering all the time that marvelously exact duplication of hell which is forever the lot of the weakling born into a world requiring above all other things, strength.

"How are they?" he asked.

"Just fine," Mary Ann said.

He peered at her, curiously.

"You don't look happy," he said.

"I'm not," Mary Ann answered him.

He stood there as though considering her statement. Then he smiled a little.

"That there Jane Henderson's a mighty pretty girl, ain't she?" he said.

162

"Heard down in town that her brother Ashton's done withdrew his objections to her and Clint getting hitched."

Mary Ann didn't answer him.

" 'Bye now," he said, and climbed into the saddle.

"Oh," he said, "I nearly forgot. We're giving a party on the twins' birthday. I'm inviting my sister, Stormy, and General Rafflin. Ma and Randy, of course. Think I'll stop by the newspaper, and ask Clint to bring Jane."

He touched his crop to the brim of his hat, and rode off, toward the gates.

Mary Ann sat there without moving. Her eyes stung, suddenly. They felt as though she had sand in them.

"Oh, damn you, Wade!" she whispered. "Damn you to hell, and back again! God damn your nasty, cruel soul!"

Stormy reached for the bell cord above her bed and gave it a vigorous pull. Then she sat back against the silken pillows and surveyed her bedroom. The furniture was all gilt Louis XVI, delicate and fine, brought at great expense from France. On the walls were a Corot, a Fragonard, and a David—authentic works of the masters, and she had the papers to prove it. The crystal chandelier which tinkled in the breeze from the open windows was an exact duplicate of those which hang in the hall of mirrors at Versailles, and had at one time graced the salon of a villa belonging to a mistress of Louis XV. The wallpaper of this so very French bedroom of hers, was a deep, vivid green, and had, additionally, the curious property of killing any insect which reposed too long upon it, since the color was achieved by a chemical combination having a strong base of arsenic.

A very pretty mulatto girl came in and stood there waiting. She was clad in a uniform of light gray, with a stiffly starched and ruffled white pinafore apron and cap. One of the advantages of General Byron Rafflin's great age, was that Stormy could indulge her love for beauty even in the selection of her domestics. All servants in the house were the lightest colored mulattoes, quadroons, even octoroons, that Stormy could find, and the handsomest. There was even in this madness, much method. The servants added to the attractiveness of her house—at least among the younger men, whose wives prudently sought out the ugliest Negroes available in order to limit the natural proclivities of the Louisiana male, who, over the years, has consistently produced more mixed-breed offspring than the inhabitants of any other State in the Union.

"Take these things away, Seraphine," Stormy said, waving an indolent hand toward the breakfast set of finest Meissen.

"Yes, Madame," Seraphine said; "but you sure don't eat nothing, you. You ain't hardly touched your *brioche*, yes."

"I know," Stormy said. "I'm never hungry in the morning; you know that. Besides, I like having the finest figure in New Orleans."

"You sure have that, yes!" Seraphine laughed. "You look like a girl. How old you really are, you, Madame?"

"That," Stormy said, "is none of your affair, Seraphine. If I were to tell you that, it would be all over New Orleans before dark. Now get out of here and draw my bath . . ."

"Yes'm," Seraphine grinned. "I do it right now, me."

The minute the girl was gone, Stormy leaped from the bed, throwing back the brocaded silk coverlets, so that the heavy silk sheets showed, and crossed to the mirror. She bent close to it, examining the corners of her eyes, the flesh at her throat, seeing the tiny, almost invisible lines that were beginning to form.

Damn that girl, she thought. Why did she have to remind me? Nearly thirty! Lord God, I wonder—

She stepped back and yanked the gossamer wisp of a gown over her head and stood there naked before the mirror. She looked at her reflection slowly, and with great care. Then she smiled. Her body was perfect. Except for the fact that her breasts were a trifle fuller, it had not changed since she was seventeen years old.

She picked up the gown and put it on again. Then she frowned.

Lord God, but I'm bored! she thought. I have everything: all the money that old brigand I married can wring out of human hopes and desperation, pretty clothes, servants, the finest house in town, lovers. . . .

She sat down on the edge of the bed. That was the crux of the matter: even the lovers bored her now. The whole thing lacked the spice of danger, of excitement. General Rafflin, a man nearing eighty, was content to have his glittering, ornamental young wife as a showpiece—in the same category really as his exquisite furniture, old masters, and the finest equipage of matched grays in town. He made no demands upon her, sleeping soundly and happily in his own walnut-paneled, Tudor-style bedroom, while Stormy repeatedly added to the number, shape, and convolutions of the horns she placed upon him in the green and rose bedroom scant yards away.

Out of respect for him, because he was very gentle and kindly toward her, she half-heartedly concealed her numerous affairs from him. But she knew quite well it didn't really matter to him, and in a way, that spoiled things.

Not much fun deceiving a man who doesn't care, she thought. That is, if I really am deceiving him. I doubt it. I'm just another possession of his— like a piece of jewelry to be shown off before his ancient New Jersey cronies to make them envious. Since he's incapable himself, what I do with other men doesn't bother him. He closes his eyes to it. And I kind of hide it from him. Sort of a game with rules we both respect. As long as I don't proclaim his cuckoldry before the world, it doesn't trouble him. . . .

But there was more to it than that. The other aspect to the matter was the lovers themselves. Gerald Metroyer. Lucien Sampoyac. Murray Randolph. Ashley Davis. André and Henri Aubert. Georges le Blanc. Saint-Just Beauregard. Thomas Chandler. . . . The list was endless. On the whole there were more Creoles than Americans, because she had found them better lovers. The Americans were too brusque, violent, poorly controlled.

And those perfumed Creoles are just too damned artistic sometimes, she thought. Wish I could find a man who could combine American brutality with French control—I guess there isn't any such animal. Chattering, glittering popinjays, all of them! Lord God, I'm bored!

There was in this a thing she never suspected, a dark, hidden root component of her being. Her lovers, one and all, had an invisible, invincible rival—her subconscious memory of her father. Even adolescence, that time of rebellion, had not shaken his ascendancy over her. By then the plastic mold of her being had been too firmly set—and the first impressions, her infantile memories of him, towering dark and gigantic above her, the boom of his laughter, the fear that appeared in the eyes of other men at his frown, though pressed down below the level of conscious thought by the newer memories, the weight of years, lived in her still. There had been no one else like him since; there never would be. He had beaten her cruelly, but she recognized the justice of her punishment. And behind that remained the other images, warm and undiminished, of herself striding through the woods with him, seeing his deadly marksmanship, his centaur-like bearing on a horse, his infinite pride in and approval of her, the looks that came over the faces of women at the sight of him, their mouths slackening, growing moist, a hint of panting getting into their breathing. There was, of course, a certain amount of distortion, a loving exaggeration in these her memories of Tom Benton; but both the distortions and the exaggerations were very natural things repeating in her the source materials out of which men have always created their legends, valuable in themselves, because without the ancient, majestic father-image, man would have had to endure the terrible centuries bereft of the saving myth of God.

She was sitting there, lost in reverie, when Seraphine knocked again on the door. She glanced quickly at the gold and china clock on the mantel, and frowned. Barely ten minutes had gone by. It was quite impossible for the girl to have heated her bath water to the degree she liked it, perfumed it, laid out fresh underthings, towels, and all the intricate luxuries of her toilette. No, she decided, it must be something else. One of the boys, maybe. Damn his soul, anyhow, whoever he is; they all know very well I don't receive until afternoon. . . .

"Come in, Seraphine," she said crossly. "What is it?"

"A man," Seraphine said, thrusting her head through the doorway. "Says it's important, him—that he's got to see you right now, yes!"

"Which one is it?" Stormy said. "Damn it all, Seraphine! How many times do I have to tell you I don't see anyone before noon?"

"Ain't nobody we know, Madame. He's a strange gentleman, him. Never seen him before, me."

Stormy half turned and stared at the maid speculatively.

"Tell me, Seraphine," she said, "what's he like?"

Seraphine grinned. She knew her mistress' tastes.

"Mighty fine, him," she said. "Dressed to kill, but kind of country-fied. . . ."

"Doesn't interest me," Stormy said. "You know I can't abide bumpkins!"

" 'Scuse me, Madame," Seraphine said, "but this one's different, him. It's sort of hard to explain why. He's real ugly; but, Madame, it's the real exciting kind of ugliness—the kind what makes a girl look and wonder. Time I saw him I thought: Madame's going to like this one—he's twice the man of all them pretty boys she's always got around her, yes!"

Stormy went on looking at the girl. Then, very slowly, she smiled.

"Send him up here, Seraphine," she said.

Oren Bascomb had a kind of instinct for the differences between women. He had been mistaken in Sarah, who had lived too long, and too hard to be deceived by him. But he was almost entirely correct about Mary Ann. Sooner or later, he knew, out of weariness, boredom and desperation, she would fall into his hands. That she would never love him, he also knew; but it didn't interest him. He had not one ounce of sentimentality about him. He failed to see what difference it made whether a woman loved or hated him as long as he was able, finally, to enjoy her body. He rather preferred their hatred to their love, which had the bad habit of becoming cloying and too demanding. But to take a woman in spite of her dislike, to make her submit both to his prowess and the humiliating admission of her own animalism, was to him the quintessence of delight. It was an attitude of mind similar to the one Tom Benton had had, expressed almost in the same words: "I like 'em a mite bitchy," but grosser, in fact, as the man himself was cruder, lacking the deep vein of sensitivity which Tom had had to fight all his life.

Now, seeing Stormy in the big bed, her black hair spread out on the rose-silk pillows, a slow smile lighted his eyes. She was staring at him with cool appraisal, her blue eyes, startlingly light beneath the heavy black brows she had inherited from her father, searching his face in speculation, interest, and amusement.

Damn my soul! he thought happily, here she is—the woman I been looking for all my life. Pure bitch and bitters all the way through! Soft as cream on the outside but harder than a ten-penny nail inside. Look at that gawdamned mouth! Big and red and wet—Lord Jesus, that there nightgown's made out of window glass! Damn my soul! Damn my wicked, ever loving soul. . . . But aloud, all he said was:

"Howdy, Ma'am. I'm Oren Bascomb—overseer on your brother's place."

"How do you do, Mister Bascomb," Stormy said coolly.

"Got a little message from your brother. Here it is." He crossed to the bedside and gave her the note, taking the opportunity as he did so to peer down the low-cut vee neck of her gown, which made very little difference anyway, since he could see through the gossamer silk almost as clearly.

Stormy saw the look, but made no effort to cover herself.

"You like what you see, Mister Bascomb?" she said icily.

"Sure Lord do, Ma'am," Oren grinned. "Just checking to see if my eyes was deceiving me . . ."

"Well," Stormy demanded, "are they?"

"No'm. Except for being kind of blinded by the sight, they ain't told a word of lie. Lord God, Miz Stormy, a build like that is a sure Lord, Simon-pure miracle! You ought to charge admission and that's a fact."

Stormy studied him—lounging there, his dark eyes filled with insolent delight, the whole of him so gangling, homely, rawboned, and yet so shamelessly cocksure, that for the life of her she couldn't help smiling.

She patted the edge of the bed.

"Sit down, Mister Bascomb," she said. "You know, I think I'm going to like you."

"Ma'am," Oren said; "I'll be most humbly grateful if you do—no matter how little."

"Humbly!" Stormy laughed. "You haven't an humble bone in your body, Oren Bascomb, and you know it! Now shut up and let me see what my fat, swinish brother has to say."

She looked up again after a couple of minutes.

"A birthday party, eh?" she mused, "for his brats. Tell me, Oren"—she was making no attempt to go back to formality now—"tell me, are they like him?"

"No'm," Oren laughed. "From all I hear tell them two bloodthirsty little cannibals is just like your pa. Tough! Lord God! Let 'em alone for a half a hour the whole house is plumb wrecked. I'm crazy about 'em, myself. Had any kids I'd want 'em like those two—grit in their craw and no mistake!"

"Good," Stormy said. "Ordinarily I wouldn't consider going within one half mile of that fat swine; but I would like to see Ma. And Clint is going to be there. There's a man for you, Oren! I'm sorry as all get out he's my half brother."

"Then you'll come?" Oren said.

"I haven't said so yet. Tell me one other thing, Mister Oren Bascomb. Are you going to be there? Ordinarily overseers aren't included in family gatherings."

Oren grinned at her.

"I ain't no ordinary overseer, Ma'am. Me'n' Wade's old war buddies. I was at Briar Creek when he—"

"I know," Stormy said. "And you can skip the lies, Oren. I know very well, and I don't give two hoots up a hollow stump how many Bibles you swear on, that that story you made up for Wade is the damnedest lie you ever told in a lifetime of lying. Anybody pointed a gun at Wade—pointed it, mind you, let alone fired it, he ran like a rat. Or knelt down and cried and begged. One or the other—and I don't care which!"

167

"Ma'am," Oren grinned, "you ain't being fair. You're downright misjudging your brother. . . ."

"Rubbish!" Stormy said. "So you'll be there, eh?"

"Yes'm," Oren said.

"Then I'll come. Now get out of here and let me get dressed. Tell Seraphine to come and help me as you pass."

"Yes'm," Oren said again, then: "First time in my life I ever admired to be a lady's maid . . ."

"Good-bye, Oren," Stormy said, and put out her hand.

Oren took it and stood there, holding it. He resisted the temptation to jerk her forward into his arms.

"I," he said, "got me a mighty sweet little whitewashed cottage down in the south section—long ways from the big house, Miz Stormy. I'd sure admire to have you see it. Got roses growing round the door. But I ain't got no pink silk sheets, Ma'am."

Stormy looked at him. Then she smiled.

"That doesn't matter, does it, Oren Bascomb?" she said calmly; "I rather think it's the man that counts, isn't it?"

Oren threw back his head and laughed aloud.

"Lord Jesus, how fine you put it!" he chuckled. "Be seeing you, Miz Stormy."

"Yes," Stormy said; "I rather think you will—at that. . . ."

Riding out to Broad Acres the day of the party, Clinton Dupré was morose and sad. He kept glancing at his fiancée, trying actually to find some basis for the mood that gripped him; but there was none—nothing tangible, just this faint malaise, this brooding sense of impending disaster.

Jane Henderson was, as Wade had said, a very pretty girl. She had her father Davin Henderson's white-gold hair and soft blue eyes. She was also very sweet and very gentle, but at that moment, perversely, Clint hated her with all his heart.

I'm a fool! he thought angrily. She's a lovely girl—any man on earth would be proud. . . .

"Clint," Jane said, "let's not go up to the house just yet. There's a place down on the river I'd like to see—the spot where my father's house used to stand."

Clint looked at her wonderingly.

"But my father owned all the land hereabouts," he said.

"Finally. After he had stolen this section from Dad. Didn't you know that?"

"No," Clinton said. "But then I didn't know my father. I met him for the first time—consciously that is, because I must have seen him when I was very small; but I don't remember it—just before he died. And strangely enough, I liked him. I hadn't thought I would; because, in a way, he had treated my mother very badly. But there was something fine about him. I don't know what it was; yet . . ."

"I can understand that," Jane said. "Even Dad was much less bitter toward him afterwards. You see, if your father hadn't sent Zeke Hawkins to burn our barn, we would have stayed here and been poor all our lives—merely because Dad loved the beauty of his little place. As it was, Dad acquired much better lands in Mississippi, and with mother to drive him on, by the time the war came we were quite rich. Funny thing, too—Mother and Dad had been childless for years; but as soon as they settled in Mississippi in 'Forty-four, they started having children. My oldest brother, who was called Davin after my father, was born the very next year. He—he was killed in the war, you know. Then Ashton came along in 'Forty-seven, and I was born in 'Fifty-two. All that helped Dad feel better about it. Of course we lost all the money during the war, but it's nice to have had it."

"My father engaged in barn-burning?" Clint said. "You know, Jane, for some reason, I can't quite believe that. Doesn't seem like him . . ."

"He did though. The cotton in that barn was all that stood between Dad and bankruptcy. Your father knew that. He had been pestering Dad to sell our place, offering him fantastic prices and when Dad refused, he sent that roughneck to burn us out. Then Henry Hilton took over and sold your father this place. Of course that was after your father got better; because Dad had shot him."

"Good Lord!" Clint said; "I don't know a thing about my family history, do I? I'm sorry, Jane—I didn't know there was bad blood between our families. Is that why Ashton was against our engagement?"

"Partially," Jane said. She looked at him and smiled. "There were a lot of other things, too. You look so much like your father, that everybody expected you to act like him, too. But you've been so nice you've won Ashton over. Then there were the circumstances surrounding—your birth. I convinced Ashton we couldn't rightly hold that against you—you neither chose your parents nor the way you were conceived. But the biggest thing, Clint, was—and is—that newspaper of yours. I'll admit you've whacked away at the carpetbaggers and scalawags just as hard as you have at the Knights of the White Camellia and the Ku Klux Klan. You say you're an independent; but Clint, your sheet does seem a mite too friendly toward Negroes even to me."

"I can't help that," Clinton said; "I feel sorry for the poor devils. And I must tell the truth as I see it. You must bear with me, Jane."

She looked at him—a long, slow look.

"I don't have to bear with you, Clint," she said; "you see—I love you. That kind of arranges everything, doesn't it? Or it will—when we really are together."

They sat there a long time, on the veranda of the abandoned cottage, looking at Davin Henderson's view.

"Now I understand your father," Clint said; "that is worth anything a man can give to keep it. It's ever so much more valuable than cotton or corn, or any of the tangible things, isn't it? I think sometimes that all the good things of life are like that: strangely untouchable, Jane. They have no market value, cannot be bought or sold—or even owned. The things that God keeps for Himself and only shares with us a little: trees, and streamers of moss, the slant of sunlight, the blue of the sky, and the river running down there talking to itself, saying the only things that really matter, the things we seek all our lives to know and somehow never learn. . . ."

"You're strange," Jane whispered. "Sometimes you scare me when you talk like that. What could a river say that we couldn't learn?"

Clint smiled at her.

"The river, and the wind, Jane," he said in his deep, quiet voice. "They've always whispered things to me, but I could never quite catch the words. The tune I knew; but the words were strange. If I could catch them once, I'd know it all—the 'why' of things—what we were born for, I mean, where we came from, where we are going. Maybe even what life is, and death—and the hereafter, if there is such a thing. But that's not given unto man, my dearest, because then he'd become one with God, and man no longer. He'd have to be driven out then, branded, crucified. . . ."

"Lord God, Clint, don't talk like that! You give me the shivers!" Jane said. "Come on now, we're going to be late."

"I'm going to ask Mary Ann to sell us this place," Clint said. "Just for the house, Jane. It's in surprisingly good shape. A little painting and patching here and there, that's all. We wouldn't need the land. I'm no planter, God knows, and the paper will take care of us well enough."

He was aware suddenly of how she was looking at him, of the expression on her face.

"Always Mary Ann," she said slowly, "never her husband. It's his land, isn't it? But he doesn't count to you, does he, Clint? He doesn't even exist, does he?"

"Sorry," Clint said shortly. "You're right. We'd better be going now. . . ."

"I," General Rafflin said pompously, "have become thoroughly Southern since I've been here. You understand, Doctor, that I don't engage in politics. I'm a businessman pure and simple. . . ."

"But you did play politics, General," Sarah said tartly, "and you won your point, even if it did take barn-burning, twisting railroad tracks around trees, and laying waste farmland to do it. Guns settle things sometimes what ballots can't, don't they?"

"I was a soldier, Ma'am," the General said, "serving my country just like your husband served his. I wasn't fighting to free the black man. As far as I was concerned, you could have kept him in slavery forever. It's all he's fit for, anyhow. What I wanted was simple, that we should remain one great nation, instead of dividing into two weak ones, forever hostile, and both inevitably falling prey to England or France or Spain. Whatever your reasons, what you people down here wanted to do was suicide—for both of us . . ."

"You're right, General," Randy said.

"Of course, I am!" General Rafflin thundered. "But, Ma'am, I want it clearly understood that I neither support nor condone the follies of Radical Republicanism. I'm no hypocrite. It astonishes me to hear people crying for rights and privileges for the Negro down here that we don't grant him up North. Look at the facts: In fourteen Northern States, not counting the slaveholding States like Kentucky and Maryland which did not secede, Negroes are not allowed to vote at all. In New York, at first, they could only vote if they had a certain amount of property, a provision which did not apply to whites. And since 'Sixty-nine, the blacks have not been allowed to vote at all in that state. In only five States of the Union is the Negro allowed to vote freely. We don't receive him in our homes, fraternize with him, marry him or anything else. A nigger, Ma'am, begging your pardon in advance for the strong language, is damned well a nigger up North. Then what is it that makes him so different down here in the hands of the same men who killed him in carload lots in the New York City draft riots during the war?"

"What you're saying, General," Clint said quietly, "is merely that inhumanity and barbarity have no geographical limits. If you expect men to fight and die, as black troops have in every war this country has ever engaged in, if you expect men to uphold even the elementary duties of citizenship, you've got to give them all its rights, including the ballot. It's a strange way of reasoning to compound wrongs by geography and expect them to add up into rights. They won't. And the murderous swine who burned that Negro orphanage in New York City with twenty-three colored children in it, don't improve the smell of their brethren in New Orleans in 1866, Bossier, St. Landry, and St. Bernard in 1868, nor any of the other places in the South which have made Negro killing a favorite outdoor sport. Perhaps I'm obtuse, but I fail to see the justification, if any, in what you're saying."

"Lord Jesus!" Wade got out, his voice shrill, womanish; "pa would never have permitted such talk in his house; and by heavens, neither will I, Clint! I don't care who killed how many niggers, nor where. Kill 'em all, I say! Kill every black son of a bitch ever born—or you'll end up seeing the day when one of them can marry your sister!"

Clint looked at his half brother, steadily.

"So," he smiled, "what's wrong with that, Wade? I rather think that would be my sister's affair, if she wanted to. Don't you, Stormy?"

Stormy smiled wickedly. Any situation permitting her to torment Wade was a pure, unalloyed delight to her.

"Yes, Clint," she drawled, "I do. I've seen some mighty fine-looking big buck niggers, Wade—all man, brother mine. But you wouldn't understand that, would you?"

"Lord Jesus!" Wade shrieked.

"This," Stormy said, "is a bore. I think I'll take a ride around the old place. It's been years since I've seen it. Mister Bascomb, would you be so kind as to show me around?"

"De-lighted!" Oren grinned. "Excuse us, folks?"

Sarah stared at her daughter, a frown creasing her forehead. Then it cleared. Let her go, she thought, all she's going to do here is cause trouble. . . .

"Kill 'em all!" Stone piped from the floor where he had been playing with his gifts. "Kill sonsabitches!"

"Kill sonsabitches!" Nat echoed.

Sarah stood up, wrath in her gray eyes.

"You see!" she said. "Now I'm purely going to lay down the law! The next person, man or woman, who brings up niggers, politics, or religion can be excused, with my blessing. And that includes you, General, much as I respect your years, and appreciate how good you've been to my daughter. So there!"

"You're right, Mother Sarah," Clint said, "I freely apologize."

"And I, Ma'am," General Rafflin said. "A social gathering is hardly the place for such a discussion . . ."

"I beg your pardon, Ma," Wade growled.

"Good!" Sarah said. "Now, Mary Ann, how about that ice cream and cake?"

"Right away, Mother Sarah," Mary Ann said, and stood up.

Clint looked at her. Then, at that moment, his eyes were naked.

"Can I help you, Mary Ann?" he said.

Mary Ann hesitated, glancing at Jane.

"Go right ahead, Clint," Jane said; "don't mind me."

Sarah stared at the girl, suddenly. Of them all, only she had caught the edge in Jane Henderson's voice.

"Oh, I can manage," Mary Ann said.

"Why, Mary Ann," Wade sneered, "where are your manners? You don't mean that you're going to deny your—friend—the chance for a little private chat?"

Mary Ann's brown eyes blazed.

"Of course not!" she snapped. "Come along, Clint!"

Clinton got up and followed her.

In the kitchen, a Negro youth ground away at the ice-cream churn, while Luella added the final touches to the frosting of the cake.

"Ready, Lou?" Mary Ann demanded.

"'Bout ten minutes mo', Ma'am. You go back with yo' guests. I call you soon as hit's done."

Mary Ann turned to Clint.

"Let's take a walk, Clint," she said; "I don't want to go back in there, now."

"All right," Clint said; "but I don't like this, Mary Ann. The way Wade spoke, you'd think . . ."

"And Jane," Mary Ann said bitterly. "Come on outside, Clint."

They walked in the orchard behind the house. Mary Ann did not speak at all.

"What's the matter with him?" Clint said irritably. "What have I ever done to him? He never misses a chance to say something unpleasant."

He stopped talking, seeing her standing there, the sunlight flooding through the peach trees, lighting her auburn hair, her brown eyes, and glittering through the great tears, hot and bright and sudden on her face.

"Don't you know, Clint?" she whispered. "He does. And you're a mighty heap smarter than he is. . . ."

Clint stood there. There was an interval of no-time, everything alive, everything moving coming to a dead halt: the blue flies fixed in midair; the jays' mouths frozen ludicrously open, but no sound emerging; the breeze itself that had stirred the peach trees miraculously still, a no-time in which nothing moved or breathed or spoke.

Then Clint broke it.

"Yes," he said, his voice very deep, and far off, and sad, "I know. . . ."

They stood there, like that, looking at each other. They did not so much as touch hands, or fuse mouth to anguished mouth. They stood, under the peach trees, and were silent.

"We'd best be going back now," Mary Ann said.

"Right," Clint muttered, and in that single word, compounded all there is of death and hell.

First in the morning, before it was light, Stormy awoke. She looked about the room, then at the bony form of Oren Bascomb, sleeping peacefully at her side. She yawned, luxuriously.

Damn! she thought; I meant to get back to the house before midnight. Well, this has done it—no help for it now. . . .

She got up quickly, and started to dress. But quietly as she moved, Oren woke up and grinned at her.

"About that cottonseed oil factory," he said; "you really think . . ."

"Forget it, lover," Stormy laughed. "Why should you break your neck making money for Wade when you can have it all for yourself? You come down to New Orleans in two weeks. By then I'll have it all fixed: a job, no, a position, in the lottery company. Inside two years you'll be a millionaire. Folks are always going to gamble; that's one sure thing; surer even than death and taxes . . ."

He lay there on his side like an elongated scarecrow, staring at her.

"How," he said, "do I know you'll keep your word, Honeybunch?"

Stormy came over to him. Then she bent down and kissed him, hard.

"You're worried about that," she said, "after last night? Lover boy, in order to keep my hot little hands on you, I'd get you ten jobs!"

"Well," Oren grinned complacently, "wimmenfolks always allowed I was right pert good."

"You, lover," Stormy said, "are the best—absolutely the best in the world."

She kissed him once more, very thoroughly. Then she straightened up, smiling.

" 'Bye now," she said. "Be seeing you—in New Orleans. . . ."

She had no fear of waking General Rafflin. The old man slept hard and late. But the thing she feared most was exactly what happened to her: Sarah met her in the doorway.

"Before you open your mouth to say it," her mother said, "I'll admit I ain't got no right to blame you. It's in your blood—from both sides, Tom's and mine. But right or no, I'm still mistress of this plantation, and I don't aim to have no shooting or killings on it no more. So I'm telling you, Stormy, get off my place. Get off and don't never come back. And I hope I never see you again as long as I live!"

Stormy smiled at her.

"You got guts, ain't you, Ma?" she said. "All right, have it your own way. Now will you please, Ma'am, step aside and let me get some sleep? Lord God, but I'm dead!"

It was almost exactly one year after the birthday party, in the spring of 1873, that Clinton Dupré belatedly announced his forthcoming nuptials. He made the announcement in the Benton's Row *Gazette*, his own newspaper, setting the day for a Sunday some weeks from the date of that issue. And that same evening, Wade Benton came home from the store and tossed a copy of the newspaper into his wife's lap without a word.

Mary Ann sat very still for a long time after she had read it. Then she got up very quietly and went in to supper with her husband. She ate very little. Neither of them talked. After supper, with the help of Luella, she bathed the twins and put them to bed.

She heard Wade in the bedroom, busy with his regalia; when he came out, he was clad in the flowing white robes of the Knights of the White Camellia, and carried his ghostly helmet under his arm.

She stared at him, but she did not speak.

"See you in the morning," he said, and was gone.

Mary Ann did not answer him. She waited very quietly until he had ridden away, then she bathed and dressed herself with some care. Then she went across the yard until she came to the big gates. She stood beside them, looking down the road. She stood there, almost without moving, for two hours. At last, she turned and started back toward the house.

In the three-room flat above his newspaper offices, Clinton Dupré sat before his desk staring at the announcement he had put in the paper.

I've done it now, he thought. Couldn't put Jane off any longer. No reason to. She's lovely, and sweet, and fine. I have no excuse. My father died like a dog, in shame and dishonor, because he could never let other men's women alone. Well, I've maintained my honor—whatever that is. I haven't been near Mary Ann in a year. Something to be proud of, I guess—but I am not proud. . . .

He took a long pull at the bottle of bourbon that stood on the desk. It was nearly empty. He had been drinking since early that afternoon.

Not proud, he thought darkly, savagely, in the hot whiskey haze. What is the price of pride, and the measure of honor? What are they worth? Count the knots twisted in my guts, add up the splintered slivers of glass I drag into my lungs with every breath I draw. Plumb the depths of this hunger that devours all other hungers so that I have not finished a simple meal in a year. Lay by the heels this thief of time, this killer-brigand who has murdered sleep and stolen all my nights. How many dawns have I sat here and watched come up out of the river? How many miles have I walked by night with only the wind, and the proud, unspeaking ghosts of my honor for company? Honor, honor, honor—what's honor to me, or I to honor, that I should weep for her?

He got up and strode about the room, weaving a little now, feeling the tears, hot and salt and unashamed upon his face.

"And so I leave you, Mary," he murmured, "leave you bound to a swine, a man without courage or pride or decency or—honor. That word again! 'Dear God, I could be bounded in a nutshell, and count myself master of infinite space, were it not—' for my honor!"

He threw back his head, and laughed loudly, savagely. Then all the laughter died within him. He stood there, unmoving, his arms outflung, bound upon the invisible cross upon which his love, his pride, his honor had crucified him, until the titanic fury inside of him tore him free, and he whirled, his hands tugging at the door, swinging it open furiously; and took the stairs four at a time, running, going down. . . .

Mary Ann had almost reached the house when she heard the hoofbeats. She stopped still, waited. He burst through the gate in a cloud of white dust, rolling behind him, drifting down the wind. He jerked the horse to a halt, sawing savagely at the bit. Then he was out of the saddle, running toward her. And quietly and simply and finally, she held out her arms to him.

"I knew you'd come, Clint," she said. "God, yes—I knew you'd come!"

6

Wade stood there, tapping the page of the newspaper with the end of his riding crop.

"Know anything about this?" he growled.

Mary Ann looked at him.

"If you'll stop hitting the paper long enough for me to read it," she said, "I'll tell you."

Wade took away the crop.

"The discussion which took place yesterday afternoon between Mister Ashton Henderson and your editor was settled amicably and to the satisfaction of both parties," she read. "This discussion, which was of a private nature, did not warrant any of the excitement it seems to have caused. The editor regrets to have been, even by error, involved in anything which allegedly threatened the peace and tranquillity of Benton's Row. He wishes to take this means to assure his friends, and all other citizens of good will, that such an event will never occur again. To those who bear him ill will, he can only state, with sincere sorrow, that they can have as much trouble as they want, as often as they ask for it." It was signed, "Clinton Dupré, Editor."

Mary Ann looked up.

"How," she said evenly, "do you expect me to know anything about this, since not a word of it makes any sense?"

"It makes sense, all right," Wade said. "Clint rode out to the Hendersons and broke his engagement with Jane. When Ash came home, he found her in hysterics. Seems your name was mentioned—at least by her."

"Then she has a dirty mind," Mary Ann said. "Go on—"

"So Ash went gunning for Clint. He went to Tim's first and had himself quite a few. Tim saw the gun in his belt, and anyhow everybody could see he was wrought up. Tim refused to serve him any more. Asked him kindly like to give up his gun, saying he wasn't in no state to tote one."

"So?" Mary Ann said.

"Ash allowed he'd damned well tote a gun if he wanted to, and what's more he aimed to let a little daylight into a trifling skunk who'd been playing fast and loose with his sister. Somebody got the idea of sending for Martha Bevins—you know, the girl what Ash has been courting. But, by then, it was too late—Ash had gone. More than fifty men followed him out of Tim's. Every step he took, the parade grew. When I come along, there was more than a hundred milling around in front of the newspaper office."

"Then what happened?" Mary Ann said.

"Ash went upstairs. We waited—maybe ten minutes. Then he come down again and pushed his way through the crowd. Everybody waited some more, till Clint opened a window and said: 'You can go home now. I'm in a perfect state of health. Next time, don't send a boy to do a man's job.' Then he shut the window again. . . ."

Mary Ann stared at her husband.

"You said my name was mentioned," she said.

"When I started back for the store," Wade said, "I found Martha Bevins in front of Tim's. Being a decent girl, she couldn't go in. She asked me kindly to go get Ash out of there. I went in and got him. He didn't give me no trouble until I got him out on the sidewalk. He just stood there a-crying and a-cussing. Then he looked me up and down and spat almost on my feet. 'Mister Mayor,' he said. 'Fine mayor what can't even take care of his own wife!' "

"So?" Mary Ann said.

"So I asked him what he meant. He said: 'Your wife's the cause of this.' I asked him who says so. 'Jane,' he told me, 'and believe me, she knows!' "

"Still say she's got a dirty mind," Mary Ann said flatly. "Lord God, Wade, what did happen in that office?"

"Nobody knows 'cepting Clint and Ash. And ain't neither one of them a-saying. But what I want to know is how deep you're mixed up in all this?"

Mary Ann looked at him. Then, very slowly, she smiled.

"That," she said calmly, "is one thing you'll never know, hero. Your supper's ready. If you want to eat, you'd better go get it."

He stood there a long time, looking at her.

"If I thought—" he growled.

"But you don't think," she said. "Do you, hero? 'Cause if you did, you might have to do something about it. Cheaper not to think so, Wade—or you might find yourself coming up against a man—and that would likely bring on one of your fits. Mustn't get excited, you know."

"God damn it, Mary Ann, I—"

"Your food is getting cold," Mary Ann said.

That night, she heard again the shuffle and limp of his step as he came down the hall, the tap of his cane. She had left the door open a little, and she saw, as he paused before the door, the white of his regalia. Then he went on down the hall and out the door.

She lay there without moving. There was bitter warfare inside her mind. What she wanted to do, and what she had to, were two different things; not only this night, but for many nights to come.

Dear God, she prayed, let Clint understand. I can't come tonight, Clint —I purely can't. . . . Wade stopped before my door and made good and sure I knew he was going out. He never does that. He overplayed his hand. Lord, but men are stupid! Ten to one he's waiting out there in the cheniere for Clint to come or for me to pass so he can follow me. . . . He'd never have the guts to stand up to Clint; but then, he wouldn't have to. All he'd have to do would be to give the word to those murdering cowards in dirty nightshirts, and they'd kill Clint for him. So I can't go— I just purely can't.

She lay there, starkly, terribly awake, the moonlight slanting across her face.

Suppose he comes here, looking for me? He could. Clint ain't scared of God nor the Devil. Then Wade would know. Lord God, don't let him come. . . . Keep him away, God. . . . I'm scairt they'll kill Clint and then I wouldn't have nothing to live for—not nothing a-tall. . . .

She heard the grandfather clock in the hall sounding the hour. She lay there very still, the slow drift of time crawling along her nerves. She wanted to scream but she couldn't do that either. There was nothing she could do but wait.

At three o'clock in the morning, she heard Wade's limping footstep come up the hall. He stopped before her door, stood there. She heard the door creak as he pushed it open. She closed her eyes, tight. But she couldn't control her breathing. That, nor the beating of her heart.

He stood there, looking at her. Through the open door she could hear the big clock ticking. It grew louder, louder. Then Wade sighed, just once, deeply, and went out again.

I'll have to get word to Clint, she thought; got to let him know what the trouble is . . . but how? Can't send a note by one of the niggers. Wade would know about that in half an hour. Niggers just can't keep secrets. Nothing on earth they love more than tale-bearing. Go down there myself, the whole blamed town would know it the minute I went in the office, especially with Ash Henderson talking like that in front of folks. But there's got to be some way. There's just got to. . . .

But it was after four in the morning before the way came to her finally. And it wasn't even a good way, at that. It had too many elements of risk in it. It left entirely too many things to chance. She would have to try it, though; there was no getting around that. . . .

The next morning, when she drove into town, she took the big surrey instead of the small buckboard, taking Luella and the twins along with her. Caleb put the double perambulator in back and drove the matched roans himself. She stopped first at the store.

No point in having Wade find out from somebody else I'm in town, she thought. This way, somebody tell him they saw me talking to Clint I can say it was purely accidental—bumped into him in the street. And it sure Lord won't look romantic with a nigger woman and the twins along. Main thing will be to get that note to Clint without Luella seeing it. Don't think she'd tell on me; but what she don't know, she can't tell. Better that way. . . .

She pushed open the door, and went into the store. Wade was sitting behind the counter, his face white as death.

"You going by Ma's?" he said before she had a chance to speak.

"Yes," she said. "Lord God, Wade, what's the matter with you?"

"Had another attack this morning. Real bad this time. Pain something terrible round my heart. Mary, go over there and ask Randy to stop by here. I'd go myself, only I don't feel up to it. . . ."

"All right, Wade," Mary Ann said. "But I've got the surrey outside. Brought the twins and Luella in with me. Caleb's driving. If you want, I can take you over there."

"Good," he said; and started to get up. Then he crashed back again, even his lips white now.

"What is it?" Mary Ann said.

"My leg!" he whispered. "And my arm! Lord God, Mary Ann, I can't move them!"

"Caleb!" Mary Ann called through the doorway.

The two of them got him into the surrey. He lay back against the seat, groaning. The twins stared at him.

"Papa hurt?" Stone said.

"Papa's hurt, all right," Wade groaned. "Feels like I'm dead!"

Randy was out, making calls. But as he had only been gone a few minutes, Sarah sent Buford after him. Ten minutes later, he was back.

The two women waited in the parlor. They talked absently of the children, the weather, the crops. Then Randy came in.

"Is it bad?" Sarah said.

"Yes," Randy growled. "He's had a light stroke, complicated by his old war wound—just as I said he would. His left side's paralyzed. He may never use that side again, or he may. I'll know in two weeks."

"A stroke," Mary Ann said; "but, Doctor Randy, Wade's too young."

"Nobody's too young, child. Wade's got high blood pressure, as I told you, brought on chiefly by overeating, but also by worry. I'm going to starve the living hell out of him. He's got to lose most of that blubber, or—"

"Or what, Doctor Randy?"

"The next one may paralyze him completely. Or kill him, which would be preferable to my way of thinking."

"The next one?" Sarah said. "Then you think . . ."

"There'll be another one? Almost certainly, Sarah, unless we prevent it —if we can prevent it."

"Lord God, Randy, you make it sound so hopeless!"

"It is," Randy said grimly. "Look, both of you, that boy is going to die. In two weeks, three weeks, three months, three years, maybe even five —I don't know which. I could keep another man in the same position alive almost indefinitely, but not Wade. Especially not Wade."

"Why not Wade, Doctor Randy?" Mary Ann whispered.

"He's got a thing on his mind and his conscience that's eating him alive. I can make him lose weight, for a while, and that will help. But the minute I turn him loose, he's going to start eating again, because he hasn't the will power not to. But even if I could keep him on starvation rations for the rest of his life, and I'd have to—I couldn't control that blood pressure unless he finally got his mind at ease."

"Do you—do you know what's troubling him, Doctor Randy?" Mary Ann said.

"Yes, child, I do. But I'm honor bound not to tell it unless he gives me permission to. Even so, the only thing that would do any good would be for him to tell it himself. Sort of like the Catholic confessional. That would do him a world of good. But you mustn't press him, either of you. He's got to do it of his own free will for it to have any effect. . . . And Sarah . . ."

"Yes, Randy?" Sarah said.

"We'll have to keep him here for the next two weeks. To take him out to Broad Acres in a jolting wagon might kill him. Mary can stay here, too, if she wants to. Or she can come every day to visit."

"I'd rather do it that way," Mary Ann said quickly. "I wouldn't inflict my two cannibals on anybody."

"Lord, no!" Randy said. "You keep those noisy little beggars out of here, child. Wade's got to have quiet."

"Can I see him now, Doctor Randy?" Mary Ann said.

"I think not. I gave him something to make him sleep. When he's stronger, I'm going to lay down the law to him. He'll have to resign from being Mayor, and from the Knights. The store—all right, as long as he sits down most of the time. And he has to stop worrying."

Mary Ann stood up.

"I'll have to be going," she said. "Those little savages have probably driven Lou mad by now. Have to take them home."

"I must say that for a woman with a husband at death's door," said Sarah tartly, "you're mighty cheerful. Still, I don't reckon Wade would be much of a loss to you."

"Mother Sarah!" Mary Ann said.

"Oh, get along with you, child. You haven't been happy with my son, and I know it. Don't reckon any woman could be. He's a mighty poor specimen, even if he is mine. You don't have to pretend in front of me. I can't abide dishonesty. But you be careful, you hear. Won't do, to get the whole town talking."

"Yes, Mother Sarah, I'll be careful," Mary Ann said.

She went out into the street. The note didn't make sense any more, but she had to see him. She had to. Mother Sarah's right, she thought: there's no point in being dishonest—especially not with yourself. I wouldn't care if Wade died. I feel sorry for him now, but I wouldn't care. I'd be free then and Clint . . .

She walked along with Luella, who pushed the twins in their big pram. They sat bolt upright and stared at the world. A woman stopped, clucking and cooing. Stone regarded her coolly.

"Silly ol' woman," he said clearly.

"Ol' damfool," Nat said.

"Oh, Lawdy, Miz Mary Ann!" Luella gasped; "listen to them chillun!"

"I heard them," Mary Ann said sadly. "Sorry, Ma'am, but they ain't had no home training."

"I'll say they ain't!" the woman said.

They passed in front of the newspaper office, moving very slowly. There was no sign of Clint.

Oh, damn! Mary Ann almost wept. It's my one chance and now he ain't here!

But a block further on, when she looked back, she saw him coming after them. He was almost running.

"I was tied up," he explained; then bending close: "What happened to you last night?"

"Shake hands with me, Clint!" Mary Ann whispered.

He looked at her, his brows crawling upward. Then he smiled.

"How do you do, Mrs. Benton?" he said, and put out his hand. "Please forgive my bad manners."

"It's no matter," Mary Ann said, seeing the little start as he felt the folded paper cool and crisp in his palm.

He started to draw away his hand, but she tightened her grip. He could feel the tension in her arm, drawing him closer.

"Tonight," she said between set teeth. "Midnight. The old Henderson Place, as usual. Pay no attention to that part of the note."

She was aware that Luella was staring at her. She dropped his hand.

"Sorry," she said aloud; "I'm a little upset, Mister Dupré. My husband is very sick."

"So?" Clint said; "I'm sorry to hear that, Mrs. Benton. What's the matter with him?"

Lord God, Clint! she implored him inside her mind, relax! Surely you know enough about niggers to realize how smart they really are. It takes brains to play-act and pretend to be dumb the way they do. Luella's one of the smartest women I ever met; use your own voice, Love. Be natural—the way you're talking now, so stiff like, she'll guess in a minute!

"He's had a stroke," she said quietly; "he—he may lose the use of his left leg."

"Too bad," Clint said gravely. "When did it happen?"

"This morning," Mary Ann said.

"No objection to my running a little item about it in the paper, is there, Mrs. Benton? After all, the state of the Mayor's health is of public concern."

"No objection," Mary Ann said.

"Good. I'll check with Doctor McGregor for the details. Good day, Mrs. Benton."

"Good day, Mister Dupré," Mary Ann said.

They moved off.

"Lord, Lord!" Luella laughed; "that man sure do talk fine! What's the matter with him, Miz Mary Ann? He drunk?"

"No," Mary Ann said shortly.

"Just said that to be polite," Luella grinned. "Knowed all the time he warn't drunk. Not with likker, leaseways. Lord God, Miz Mary Ann, how you do knock 'em dead!"

"Luella!"

"Sometimes I feels right sorry for whitefolks. Lord, Lord! Handsome man like that—was me, I'd forgit I was married so damn fast!"

"Luella, for God's sake!" Mary Ann said.

"Yes'm, Miz Mary Ann," Luella chuckled. "All the same, you's a young and pretty woman—and now you's saddled with a sick husband. Let slip a chance like this—tell me, Ma'am, howcome whitefolks so smart some ways—and otherwise so dumb?"

"Luella Benton, if you don't shut up, I'll—"

"Yes'm, Miz Mary Ann," Luella said.

That evening, Mary Ann unlocked the cabinet containing the elderberry wine. She drank half a glass, and left the bottle on the table. Then she went out in the yard with the twins.

Luella'll think I forgot, she thought gayly. She can't resist that wine. By midnight, a cannon shot couldn't wake her up. Strange—all my life I've been a decent woman, when the chips are down my mind could hide behind a corkscrew. Reckon women are just born crooked. Wonder why? Maybe it's 'cause we ain't got the strength to fight and be direct like men. Always have to figure ways and means. . . .

The twins were wrestling happily. Since they were exactly the same size and strength, these contests usually ended in a draw. They were hard and masculine and thoughtless, but they weren't cruel. Person strong enough is hardly ever cruel, Mary Ann thought; that's a sign of weakness—like Wade. . . .

At three years old, they were as big as most children are at five. They were beginning to lose their babyish awkwardness. They could run fast and far, and throw rocks with deadly aim. Now they stopped their wrestling and streaked away behind the barn. Mary Ann heard the rooster squawking, and started to get up. But before she could do that, the rooster came flying from behind the barn, completely denuded of his tail feathers.

The twins ran after him, whooping. The tail feathers were stuck in their long hair.

Mary Ann smiled. Indians again. Well, anyhow, when I cook that rooster, I won't have to pluck him. By then he'll be as naked as a jaybird. . . .

She heard Luella's voice from the kitchen, the full, rich contralto soaring up in one of the spirituals.

"No—body knows—the trouble I see!

"No—body knows, but Jeeesus!"

The words were sad; but not the tone. Luella sang happily, gayly. Bless that elderberry wine, Mary Ann thought.

It took a long time to get dark. Mary Ann had to bathe the twins and put them to bed herself, for by that time Luella was useless. She sat in the kitchen, giggling to herself.

"Yes'm," she said happily, "I been in the wine, Miz Mary Ann. Your own fault, Ma'am; you knows my weakness. How come you didn't lock it up? Just purely can't stay away from that wine. Just purely can't!"

Mary Ann held the bottle up to the lamp. It was three-quarters empty.

"Here," she said; "you might as well finish it, Luella. But take it to your room—or else I might have to put you to bed, too."

"Thank you, Ma'am!" Luella laughed. "Lord, Lord but you's the best, Miz Mary Ann! Don't never want to work for nobody else!"

"Nobody else would put up with you," Mary Ann said. "Get along with you now."

She lingered in her bath. It was hard to keep from thinking, but she had to. So easy to shock a man—even Clint. Go running to him and throw myself in his arms like a crazy woman again he's going to get disgusted. But God, it's hard not to think. . . .

After she was dressed she went down the hall to Luella's room. Luella was asleep, the bottle cradled in her arms. Mary Ann took it away from her. It was quite empty.

She left the house by the back door. She walked very slowly. It was long before midnight. It was a summer's night and warm; but she shivered all over like someone half frozen. She had to hold on to herself to keep from running. She couldn't do that. She didn't want to get to the old Henderson Place all hot and mussed and sweaty. And above all, she mustn't think.

She was passing the pigpen now and she saw how the fence barely hung there so dilapidated that one good push from the hogs inside could knock it over. She seized upon that—this one trifling detail to fill her mind to erect a barrier against the thoughts she couldn't, dared not let break through into consciousness. . . .

Look at that fence! That's one thing Oren was good for. He kept the place in tiptop shape. This new man, Nelson, ain't worth the powder and shot it would take to blow him away with. But I'm glad Oren's gone. Lord God, but he was a pest. . . . I wonder if Mother Sarah knows about that? She must. She goes down to New Orleans often enough. Hasn't Stormy any shame—making a public scandal like that? Going everywhere with that scoundrel, kissing him in public! It seems to me that she'd—

She stopped dead.

I should talk. The only difference between Stormy and me is she's brave. She just don't give a damn about people and what they think. But me, I'm scared stiff. If somebody was to find out, I'd purely die. . . .

She moved off, walking faster now. She was into the cheniere, going faster all the time, when the enormous black shape came upon her. She opened her mouth to scream, but then the moonlight fell upon his face.

"Buford!" she got out; "Lord God, you gave me a start!"

"Miz Mary Ann," he said; "you know how it is. You been in love. I got to see her, Ma'am. I just got to!"

"All right, Buford," she said, "go ahead. But control yourself. If you give that child a baby, I'll—"

She stood there, frowning.

"Wait," she said; "I'll bring Cindy in tomorrow. And Doctor Randy and I will arrange the wedding. That is, if she's said yes. Has she, Buford?"

"Yes'm," he said happily. "Day before yestiddy. Us was fixing to ax you tomorrow."

"Good. Go on, then. But, remember—control yourself!"

"Yes'm, Miz Mary Ann," Buford said. "God bless you, Ma'am!"

She moved off, through the cheniere. Fine chance he'll mind me, she thought. Niggers ain't got no self-control a-tall. Better get those two married right away. First thing I know he'll get Cindy with child and . . .

She came to a halt, her eyes enormous in her small face.

"Lord God!" she breathed. "Dear Lord Jesus!"

Then, very slowly, the dilation of her pupils softened, and the corners of her mouth moved upward into a smile.

I wouldn't care, she thought. I wouldn't care. Care? Lord God, I'd be glad!

Then she was off again, running hard down the shadowy path.

The Spanish moss caught the moonlight, and made filigrees of silver. Fireflies winked in the oak dark, like sudden bright stars. They could hear the river talking below. It talked in dark voices, very quietly.

They leaned out of the window and looked at the river. It had a swarth of moonsilver across it, and on both sides of that, the dark.

"I'm sorry he's sick," Clint said. "That changes things. It was bad enough before, but now—"

"Don't talk!" Mary Ann said.

He stopped, looking at her.

"Clint—" Mary Ann said.

"You want to?"

"I want to. With you I always want to. Afterwards we can talk."

The soft rustling sounds. The crisp, drifting sounds. The coolness. The sudden freedom.

"The encumbrances of civilization," Clint said.

"Don't talk!"

"No," Clint said. "Not here. Over there—in the moonlight, where I can see you. . . ."

"You like seeing me? Does that make it—better?"

"God, yes!" he said.

They looked down upon the river, slow coiling in the moonlight.

"Clint," she said, "tell me what happened between you and Ashton Henderson."

He looked at her.

"What do you want to know that for?" he said.

"I have to know, Clint. Ash gave Wade the idea I was mixed up in it."

"Good God!"

"That's why I passed you that note. I thought sure we were going to have to stop seeing each other for a while. And we would of, wasn't for Wade's getting sick. Go on, tell me."

"Ashton paid me a little call," Clint said quietly. "He came storming into my office like a wild man, waving a pistol. Ordered me to draw so he could shoot it out with me. I told him I couldn't do that, since I don't even own a gun."

"And then?"

"He didn't believe me, of course; since in this benighted land, a gentleman puts on his holster along with his pants. I opened my coat and showed him. He pointed to my desk drawer. I opened that, too."

"So then, being a Henderson, he couldn't shoot you, eh, Clint? Thank God it was him, and not one of those common, low-bred folks."

"That was about the size of it. He just stood there, swearing the air blue for about a minute. Then he turned around and went back down the stairs. After that I went to the window and exchanged a few mutually complimentary remarks with the mob. But I think now, it would have been better if I had had a gun."

"Why, Clint?"

"Oh, I wouldn't have fired on him. I swore I'd never kill again, not even in self-defense. But perhaps I'd be out of this now—and you'd be free of all the worry and trouble I've caused you."

"Lord God, Clint!" she said, "don't talk like that! Don't even think like that!"

"I," Clint said, "am my father's son. I only want what I can't have, what I have no right to. There's a kind of dark fatality in us, Mary. We must go down to destruction, because what we could have, we don't want, and what we do want always belongs to somebody else."

"I don't belong to him!" Mary Ann cried; "I don't! I don't!"

"You've borne his sons. You're his wife. You can't be free of him because the only way you could would lay a damnation upon your house, and upon your children."

"Clint," she said; "if I gave him grounds—would they take the twins away from me?"

"Yes," he said, "if it came to divorce. But it wouldn't come to that. I'd have to meet him, Mary. And I couldn't fire on him. I swore that when the war was over I'd never kill again. . . ."

"Then you'd be killed," Mary Ann said.

"Very likely. I couldn't refuse to meet him, you know."

"Oh, no!" she said, "oh, Clint, no!"

"Perhaps he wouldn't even challenge me," Clint said slowly. "People have all but stopped dueling, nowadays."

"He wouldn't," Mary Ann said bitterly. "He'd shoot from ambush, or put those hooded cowards on you. He hasn't the guts to fight."

"I'm not thinking about that. I'm only thinking about how you'd be crucified afterwards. That's why I'm going away, Mary. Before I really harm you. Before I make you the target of every dirty, vicious tongue in the whole damned parish!"

She stared at him. She opened her mouth to speak, but she could not.

She stood there, looking at him until the trees, the moon, the river dissolved in the scalding haze of tears.

"Don't cry, Mary," he said; "for God's sake, please don't cry!"

She shook her head.

"Cry," she said; "I didn't know what crying was until I met you, Clint. I thought it was something you did with your eyes. I didn't know how it felt to cry all over, outside and inside, each time something kept me away from you. Now I know. I get sand in my throat, and cockleburs in my lungs, and a black thing in my middle that twists my insides between its hands until I can feel them giving away, tearing . . . That's what loving you has taught me, Clint. So don't tell me—"

"Mary, for God's love!"

"Not to cry. I'm going to go on crying until the day I die and even after that if there is any afterwards. You'll never be free of me, Clint. You'll hear me in the wind and the rain, and maybe you'll even almost see me in the night sometimes, wringing my hands and crying. If that's what you want, Clint Dupré, then go!"

He looked at her.

"If," he whispered, "there were only some way. . . ."

"There is. Just waiting, Clint. He's going to die. Doctor Randy says so. Maybe not right away. Maybe in three years. Five at the most. Because to stay alive, he's got to be careful in a way he can't be careful. He can't get excited, and he can't eat too much. And he just ain't got the will power not to. He's had these attacks for years, but now they're getting worse. I can wait, Clint—like Mother Sarah waited for Doctor Randy. I've waited for you all my life, so a few more years won't kill me."

"I'm still going away," he said slowly. "I can't go on doing this, Mary. I can't stand it: the lying, the sneaking, the pretense. I've never felt this way about anybody before. I won't go on dirtying it this way. I'm proud of loving you, Mary. I want to walk with you on my arm, for all the world to see. I want to say to them: Look you beggars and blackguards, she's mine! See what I have!"

"And what have you?" she said sadly: "A little old funny-looking girl with a turned-up nose with scads of freckles on it, and a big, wide mouth. . . ."

"I have an angel. I have a love that's a kind of a glory. I know other men have loved other women as I love you—that is, my mind knows it. But my heart won't believe it. It's like we invented it—as though, between us, we created love. And I cannot shame that, Mary. I can't hide it. Don't you understand that? Can't you see?"

"I see all right. I see you're already tired of me. . . ."

"Oh, Mary, for God's sake!"

"I'm sorry, Clint," she said. "I'm being plain selfish, that's all. It's best for you to go away. If you stay here, there'll be nothing but trouble. This way, I can write you—tell you about things. You mustn't answer me,

though. That would be too dangerous. And one day, I'll be able to say: Come back to me, Clint. You can now—oh, Love, you can!"

"I'll be waiting for that," Clint said.

She looked at him.

"And I'm waiting now," she said. "For us to stop wasting time. We have so little of it, Clint, and we throw it away, talking. . . ."

"God, yes," he said, "so little, little time. . . ."

Wade lay on the big bed and stared at the ceiling. Going to fool them, he thought. Sitting around with long faces, waiting for me to die. Ma and Randy, anyhow. Mary Ann's face sure Lord ain't long. She'd be glad, I reckon. But I'm going to fool them. I'm going to git up from this damned bed. I'm going to walk again. And that business about her sleeping in the nursery is going to stop, too. I'm going to stick around to see that neither Clint nor Oren gits her. Pa got hisself killed and Randy stepped in almost before he was cold in his grave. That ain't a-going to happen to me. Oren ain't around no more; but Clint is. Have to take care of that. Git up from here I'll have myself a necktie party with that bastard half brother of mine as the guest of honor. Only reason the boys ain't took care of him now is 'cause they know he is my brother. But brother or not, he'll have to go. Thought once, I'd just ride him out of the parish on a rail; but I can't do that now. Got to make it permanent. When I pass on, I sure Lord don't aim to leave him behind. Him nor Oren neither one.

Funny how knowing you ain't got long to live changes things. Didn't dare hit out at Oren before. But now he and Clint done give me something to live for—like this, I can't stay alive long; but I'm going to hang on long enough to finish both of them, so help me God. . . .

I don't understand it, Randy thought, sitting by that same bed, two weeks later; but if there is any one factor that upsets medical theories, it's the human mind. Two weeks ago, I wouldn't have given a plugged picayune for his chances, but look at him now! He's going to get up from there. He's going to regain partial use of that leg, as much as he had before, perhaps, with those ligaments shot away. And all because he wants so badly to live. Why? That's completely incomprehensible. If I had his life, I'd throw it away for a laugh or a song. A livelihood gained by robbing the poor and the helpless, a wife who all but hates him, a marriage which, if not already decorated with horns, soon will be. Good Lord! What manner and species of man are you anyhow, Wade Benton?

He looked at the younger man with something very nearly approaching admiration for the first time in years.

I thought you were yellow all the way through. But this is a species of courage, isn't it? I suppose no man is all of a piece. All you have to do, really, is to find the mainspring of his being, what it is that makes him tick. Crowded far enough, even a rat will fight. But what crowded you that far, boy? Was it Clint? Did this thing between him and Mary Ann push you down far enough to find out you are a Benton, after all?

"Well, Randy?" Wade growled.

"You're fine, boy. You can be up and about in another week."

"Then I'm finished with these attacks?"

"No. Truthfully, you'll never be well, Wade. All the rest of your life, you're going to have to be careful. You've got to resign from the Knights, give up being Mayor. The store, maybe, if you stay seated most of the time, and don't get excited. And you've got to keep your weight way, way down."

"And if I don't?" Wade said.

"You'll die. Or you'll be totally paralyzed. Take your choice. Far as I can tell, you've got a mild form of thrombosis, brought on by high blood pressure. What I mean is it's mild so far. But thrombosis never stays mild unless you do something about it. Overweight and high blood pressure go together. That's one of your troubles. The other is that you have too much on your mind. You're too young to have hardening of the arteries; but there's one other thing which behaves almost the same way—"

"What's that?" Wade said.

"Bad nerves. Worry. A guilty conscience. Call it what you like. I'm sure it's that, though; because you recover. When an artery is partially closed by hardening of the walls, it never relaxes. But an artery half closed by a nervous spasm does open again. If it does it soon enough, the clot may dissolve, or enough blood can flow around it to relieve the pressure on the motor sections of the brain. Then the functions come back; never as strong as they were before, but enough. . . ."

"That's why I mustn't get excited, eh?"

"Yes. Get worked up and an artery will block again. Stay worked up and the clot formed will become too massive to dissolve in time. Result, permanent impairment of the faculties: speech, hearing, locomotion; then paralysis; then death. You see?"

"I see, all right," Wade said; "but I ain't going to let it happen."

"Good. That way, you'll be fine. I know it's not pleasant to be a semi-invalid; but it's a hell of a lot more pleasant than being paralyzed—or dead."

"Right. When can I go home, Doc?"

"Oh, day after tomorrow, I reckon," Randy said.

Mary Ann sat under a shade tree in the yard. Her face was very white. From where she sat, she could see the door of the house and part of the way into the hall. She sat there, watching the doorway, waiting for Wade to come out. She hoped he wouldn't come out, so she could put off what she had to say to him a little longer.

Her mind counted very slowly: A month and a half since Clint left. A month to the day since Wade came home and found Oren out here, pestering me again. In a way that was a good thing, because it'll keep

Wade from being too sure. That Oren! Wonder what the devil he'd been up to? Told me he'd been back in the parish for three weeks, and I'll be blessed if anybody had seen hair nor hide of him. Up to some mischief for that lottery company again, I reckon. Let's see—it's been two months since that first night I met Clint at the Henderson Place, and a month and a half since the last time. Every night for two whole weeks and now—

And now, I'm sure. Reckon I was sure right from the first. I took the danger of that into consideration right from the beginning—ever since I bumped into Buford that time. Lord God, I had children for Wade. And Clint's a man. Couldn't expect to spend two whole weeks with him without—this happening. Well, it's happened, and I'm glad. The only bad part about it is what I've got to do now. . . .

She sat there a long time, but Wade did not come out. I'll go in and talk to him, she thought; but she didn't move. She couldn't make herself do it. It was too hard.

Tonight then, she decided. Yes—better tonight. I've got to. Can't put it off any longer. Any more time and even he'll know better, stupid as he is. But I hate it. Wasn't for the twins, I would have gone with Clint—wasn't for them, I would have gone. . . .

That night, she sat before her mirror, brushing her hair. The face that peered back at her was the face of a sacrificial victim. I'm numb, she thought; I'm numb all the way through.

She got up very slowly and went down the hall. She moved stiffly with a trance-like motion until she came to his door. She pushed it open and stood there.

"What do you want?" he growled at her.

"I—I've been thinking about the way I've treated you," she said. "Reckon your getting sick gave me time to think. I—I'm sorry, Wade."

"So?" he said.

"After all, you are my husband, and my children's father. . . . What I'm trying to say is—I've come to be your wife again, Wade."

He stared at her, and his eyes were bleak.

"All right," he said slowly, "come on. . . ."

He lay there, looking at her, lying with her eyes closed, in the crook of his arm. Better this way, he thought bitterly; this way I'll never be sure. I couldn't stand being sure. It would kill me, I reckon. Clint's gone, and Oren's back in New Orleans. So she's come back to me. Because she's lonesome and needs a man? Huh! Bet my bottom dollar in seven or eight months she'll be telling me she fell down or took a cold bath or some other reason to explain why the baby come so quick. I'm a sick man. I can't go traveling round gunning for polecats. No, better like this. Now there's an outside chance that she might be telling the truth.

He lay there a long time, thinking about it. Not only that night, but for many nights, until finally, worrying it over in his mind had dulled the edges of it, until finally he came almost to believe what he needed to believe, until he thought he had dominated it.

But that spring day in 1874 when Sarah placed the tiny red bundle that was Jeb Stuart Benton in his arms, it was back again, this thing he would have to live with.

He stood there, holding the infant, seeing the masses of inky black hair curling damply over the tiny head. He stretched out a clumsy finger, and pushed back one eyelid. Jeb wailed—a thin, piping sound. But Wade had had time enough. Jeb's eyes were black as night.

"Here, Ma," he said, "take it."

"It's a mighty pretty baby, son," Sarah said uncertainly. "Looks just like Mary Ann."

"Take it, Ma!" he screamed at her, "or 'fore God, I'll . . ."

She leaped forward, her arms encircling the child.

"Wade, you wouldn't!" she breathed.

"Oh, wouldn't I?" he screeched; "you better keep this little bastard out of my sight, then!"

Then he lurched forward, throwing all his weight on his cane, hobbling heavily, painfully forward until he reached the door. He jerked it open, and went out without a backward glance.

Sarah stood there, holding the baby. Then she turned to the bed, her gray eyes speaking fire.

"Here!" she snapped; "take your child, Mary Ann!"

Mary Ann put out her arms.

"Yes," she said; "I'll take him, Mother Sarah. After all, he is mine. There's no doubt about that. You're all mine, aren't you, Jebbie? Yes—all, all mine!"

7

WADE BENTON sat on the veranda, holding a bowl of hominy grits in his lap. He had eaten very little and that little very slowly, because, two years ago, in the early summer of 1878, he had had another quite serious attack. It had left him with a partial paralysis of the facial muscles which made talking and eating difficult. At first he hadn't been able to talk at all; and they had kept him alive on liquids forced through his set teeth with a straw; but the paralysis had slowly receded until now by the late summer of 1880, it had reached the point where no further improvement could be hoped for; that is, until he could speak with a thick, blurred voice, and eat only very soft foods.

To everybody's astonishment, Randy had been delighted by this development. He had come to regard the task of keeping Wade alive as a personal challenge; he fought stubbornly, ceaselessly against new attacks. He sent to the medical centers of the North, to Scotland, and even to Germany for every new study made on the subject of cerebral thrombosis, becoming in the process of guarding the flickering flame of Wade Benton's entirely useless life, one of the foremost specialists of the day upon this and related disorders. His reason for being pleased with the continued impairment of Wade's facial muscles was very simple:

"Heck," he told Sarah, "it's going to keep the boy alive. I've been trying every way I know to get him to eat sensibly, but he always back-slides. Now he's going to have so damned much trouble eating at all that he's got to stay thin. His blood pressure will come down, which is all to the good. This way, he may live out his full span, if we can keep him from getting excited. . . ."

But Randy had reckoned without Wade Benton. Although he did lose weight, he did not lose enough, for, by the simple expedient of demanding the richest custards, sillabubs, floating islands he managed to keep himself comfortably plump, and his blood pressure hovering around two hundred.

He sat there, that summer day of 1880, and ate the cold, thick grits without relish. He hated grits, but he had now a renewed interest in keeping alive. Going to balk him yet, he thought savagely, him and Oren. What the devil he have to come back for?

Out in the yard, the twins were banging away happily with their light shotguns at a row of bottles set up as targets. At ten, they were bigger than most boys of fourteen, and had all the Benton force and competency. Beside them six-year-old Jeb watched. He didn't own a gun, largely because Mary Ann wouldn't permit it. He was tall for his age, and very thin; but he was a beautiful child. Sarah had early succumbed to his grave charm, so that he was no longer a bone of contention between her and Mary Ann. As for his mother, she made no secret of the fact that she adored him.

Jeb lived, then, in a strange and confusing world. From the man he called father, he had only harsh words, rebuffs, icy silence. He was saved from physical cruelty, now that Wade stayed at home, and let Mary Ann keep the store, only by reason of the fact that Wade was now incapable of using force. But he suffered from this rejection as only the sensitive can. He would have loved Wade with all his boyish heart, had he been permitted to; thrown off, he could only double his worship of his mother, and welcome with pure delight his few visits with Randy, whom he idolized.

He had, from all this, the exact conditions which go into the makings of a poet. Petted and spoiled by his mother, roughed over regularly by his brothers, rejected by Wade, the only element of stability in his life was his grandmother's calm, steady love, combined with her firm sense of discipline. From Randy, he had all too rarely what he needed most: fatherly companionship.

So he grew up grave and thoughtful, with a puzzled look nearly always in his enormous dark eyes. But there was something more in his make-up, a quiet strength, that not even his love for beauty and his dreamer's mind could entirely hide. Mary had found that out one day, when she had been holding him in her arms, a practice which at six he was already beginning to resent, at least when she did it in public.

"You mustn't do that, Mama," he said; "I'm too big now."

"I see," Mary Ann said, and turned him loose. "Tell me, Jebbie, what do you like best?"

He considered the question.

"You," he said dutifully.

"Oh, I don't mean people," Mary Ann laughed. "What kind of things do you like best of all?"

"Butterfly wings," he answered gravely. "And—and rainbows. Stars, too. And candleflies. Spanish moss—sometimes. . . ."

"Why sometimes?" Mary Ann said.

"'Cause it's dark sometimes and ugly. I only like it when it's pretty."

"You mean when it has sunlight in it?"

"Yes, Mama."

"What else?"

"Flowers and apples and—and a gun!"

"A gun!" Mary Ann said. "Do you like to kill things?"

"No. But a gun's pretty, too. A shiny gun. Besides, it makes a nice noise."

Mary Ann frowned. He is a Benton after all, she thought sadly; I had forgotten that. . . .

"Can I go now, Mama?" Jeb said.

"Yes, Love," Mary Ann whispered, and her voice was very sad.

"Lemme try it, Stone," Jeb begged. "Bet I can shoot good, too!"

"Aw, you're too little," Stone said. "This here gun'll knock you plumb over. Then you'll go running to ma. . . ."

"He can't," Nat pointed out; "ma's down at the store. 'Sides, he ain't so bad, Stone. He don't cry half as much as most kids."

Wade put down his bowl with trembling hands. There was a malicious glint in his pale little eyes.

"Let him try, Stone!" he called, in his thick, blurry voice. "He's got to learn, some time."

Jeb looked at him in pure astonishment. Help from this source was the last thing on earth he expected.

"Go ahead, boy!" Wade called; "try it!"

Stone gave him the gun. Happily he leveled it. Then, without seeming to take aim, he fired first one barrel, then the other. Two whiskey bottles crashed into iridescent showers of powdered glass.

The twins stared at him incredulously.

"Do that again!" Stone demanded. "Bet it was a fluke!"

192

Nat passed him over his own gun. Although the fowling pieces were both small and light, being little bigger than a twenty-caliber rifle, they dwarfed the little boy. Yet Jeb lifted it without apparent effort. He was very thin; but now, as he aimed Nat's gun, Wade saw that his thinness was all wiry strength.

This time, he fired more slowly; but the results were the same. Two more bottles disappeared into showers of glass.

The twins looked at each other. Simultaneously, they nodded.

"He can shoot," Nat said gravely. "Now we have to take him with us."

"All right," Stone said; "but 'possum hunting first. Target shooting's one thing; hunting's another. He do all right, we'll take him after coon, then fox. Have to try him first, though."

Jeb stared at his brothers. He was beside himself with joy.

"You really going to take me?" he breathed.

"Yep," Stone said, "tonight."

He had suffered at his brothers' hands, but not because they were cruel. They were simply Bentons, which meant they were hard and rough and thoughtless, and impatient with anything small and weak. They didn't dislike their baby brother; they had merely, up to now, considered him a pest. But they were eminently fair: that he could shoot changed things considerably. And being entirely sure of themselves, this revelation of his skill caused them neither anxiety, nor jealousy. They were, in fact, at that moment, rather proud of him.

"He'll do," Stone said; and Nat nodded in sage agreement.

On the veranda, Wade sat back in his chair, and his thoughts were black and bitter.

The little bastard's all right, he thought. Took me ten years to learn to shoot like that, and he does it the first time. Clint, then; not Oren. Still, it don't prove nothing. Oren's a hell of a fine shot, too; and can he ride! Trouble is, that damn little woodscolt don't look like neither one of them. Could even be mine, though I doubt it. Mine, he could of took after pa a little; but then, if he's Clint's, he could of took after pa just the same. Hell of a thing. 'Side from that godawful birthday party, that time, ain't nobody ever seen Mary Ann so much as speak to Clint; far as I know; but Oren—

The thing that he was remembering, the root and fount of his confusion, existed for him only in the gray distortions of a sick memory. He had never discussed it with Mary Ann, had, in fact, never so much as mentioned it to her, so he had no way of knowing the truth of it; had had therefore to judge only by appearances, thereby condemning her, who was guiltless of this one thing at least, and condemning himself, too, to a disastrous retreat out of the saving grace of ignorance, into a wilderness of half knowledge, of conflicting beliefs, which was, for him, far worse.

He had come home in the surrey, propped up on pillows, that time of his first serious attack, some weeks after Clint's disappearance in the fall of 'Seventy-three; and as Caleb had driven him into the yard, he had seen

Oren Bascomb standing under the oak tree, holding Mary Ann quiet, and unresisting, in his arms.

Until then, he had been sure that if she had a lover at all, it was Clint; but seeing that, his bitter inclination to read all human actions in terms of planned deceits told him how easily the very fierceness of her dislike, of her scorn for Oren could be the best of all concealments; that even Clint, himself, had been perhaps for a deliberate false spoor laid down to throw him off the trail.

Worse, through his connection with the Knights of the White Camellia, he, alone of all the family, had been aware of how long Oren had been in the parish; now, counting backward from the date of Jeb's birth, it fitted with damning exactitude. Of course, Clint had been in Benton's Row during the same period; grounds for suspicion existed in the fact that he had left precipitately directly afterwards; but he had seen her with Oren, and no one had ever seen her with Clint. Which proved nothing. He knew that. What he did not know, the sole factor he lacked to clarify his thinking, was that Oren, seeing the surrey long before Mary Ann had, had deliberately put his arms around her, knowing that he, Wade, must see it; and she, being grown up now, being mature, had already so perfected her defenses that she no longer needed to struggle. She had merely said quietly:

"Don't be tiresome, Oren; you should know by now that won't get you anywhere."

Whereupon Oren released her; but too late. The damage had been done.

Wade picked up the bowl again, fighting against the shaking in his hands. The grits were cold; but he ate them doggedly. Going to need all my strength, he thought; going to need every damned bit. . . .

Clint now. He's been back in town for more than a month in connection with that damyankee education fund for the niggers. Hear tell he helped organize it. Well, he's going to git hisself a surprise. Now that there schoolhouse is finished, we're going to take care of him! Can't have this damned foolishness about educating niggers. Teach a nigger to read, and you ruin a good plowhand—and that's fact. Take care of that horsefaced Yankee witch he brung with him at the same time. Hell of a name: Prudence Crandall-Hyde. We'll teach her some prudence all right. . . .

He stared at the boys without really seeing them.

Yet, Clint's been here a month. In all that time, he ain't been near the store. He called on Ma and Randy—still does right frequent. But he don't so much as look at Mary Ann. Means he ain't interested—or he's being double careful. Lord Jesus, how I'd like to know!

He looked up in time to see Floyd Nolan enter the gates. Nolan was the present titular head of the Knights; but he consulted regularly with Wade, took orders from him, was, in actual fact, no more than Wade's lieutenant. It pleased the Benton in Wade to know that even in his semi-invalid state, sitting on his veranda, he was able to control the entire parish as effectively as he had when he had ridden at the head of his men. This seeming lust for power was, in him, far from the simple thing it appeared.

He needed to rule men and events not for any tangible benefits accruing to himself, but to make up for his illness, both actual and spiritual. He could say to himself: "Weakest man in the Knights could push me over with one finger, but I control 'em, damned if I don't. It's what's between the ears that counts, not muscle. And I've got that all right. . . .

He was not entirely wrong. His enforced idleness had given him time for scheming; his association with Oren Bascomb had given him both the taste for it, and the practice. And in that community of simple men, a schemer did not need to be polished to be effective. He sat there smiling to himself, waiting for Nolan.

"Howdy," Nolan said. "That there school, Wade—"

"Has been running a full week. Every nigger what can is going—from pickaninnies to grandpas. That what you come to tell me?"

"Lord God!" Floyd Nolan said; "ain't there nothing you don't know?"

"Precious little! Think it's about time?"

"Hell, yes," Nolan spat. "Don't throw the fear of God into them niggers soon, they'll be completely out of hand."

"Good. Tonight, then. Now, Nolan, do me a favor. Go 'round back and tell Caleb to hitch up my buckboard. I'm going into town with you. Doc Randy won't let me ride a hoss no more. But I wouldn't miss this show tonight for nothing in the world."

"All right," Nolan said. "Boys be glad to have you. Give 'em a mite more sperrit. . . ."

Nolan drove the buckboard, with his own horse tied behind because the chronic shaking in Wade's hands which had also been a result of the last attack, made even this simple task quite difficult for him.

"Leave me off at Doc Randy's," Wade told him. "I'm about due for a check-up."

"Right," Floyd Nolan said.

The first thing Wade saw when he entered the yard was Buford's wife, Cindy, sitting under a shade tree, reading a story to their four-year-old son. Wade stopped beside her, leaning heavily on his cane.

"Mister Wade," Cindy smiled. "Howdy, sir. I'll go tell Doctor Randy . . ."

"No," Wade growled; "go on with your reading. I want to hear you. Ain't never heard a nigger read before. Go on, Cindy—read!"

"Yessir," Cindy said uncertainly. Little Fred stared at Wade.

"Go on, Cindy, I'm waiting," Wade said.

She started to read again, slowly. She read quite well, though she mispronounced some of the words, and had a tendency to halt upon each word like a child, augmented now by her nervousness, that made the reading jerky. Still, all things considered, it really wasn't bad.

"And Buford can read too?" Wade said.

"Yessir. Better'n me, sir. But then Buford's much smarter."

"Well I'll be damned!" Wade said helplessly. "No, don't get up, I'll just go on in."

He found Randy in the dining room, sitting over the remnants of the midday meal. Sarah was there, too. But what brought Wade to a dead halt in the doorway, was the sight of Clinton Dupré, standing by the fireplace, chatting easily, gayly with them.

Wade stood there a moment, thinking: Mustn't show my hand. Handle this like Oren would—play my cards close to my chest. Got a chance now to get this bastard brother of mine where I want him. . . .

He limped into the room.

"Howdy all," he said quietly.

The way they all stiffened pleased him. Randy and Ma know something, or think they do, he thought. Not that I'll ever git it out of them. Don't need to, though—don't matter much whether I know for sure or not. Tonight I'm going to git rid of this bastard for good and all. . . .

"Howdy, son," Sarah said.

Wade hobbled over to Clint and put out his hand.

"Glad to see you back, Clint," he said. "Staying long?"

"No," Clint said, as he shook hands, "I'm leaving day after tomorrow, in fact."

"That so? I must say you ain't showed much family spirit, boy. You been here more than a month and we ain't seen hair nor hide of you at Broad Acres. Not even at the store, which would have been more convenient for you."

"I've been—busy," Clint said.

"So I heard. How's your nigger school coming?"

"Just fine," Clint said. "I rather thought you wouldn't approve of the idea, Wade."

"I don't," Wade said bluntly. "Don't think book learning does niggers any good. Teach 'em to plow, and do mechanical work, I say. Besides, we got a State law now, providing for their education."

"I," Clint pointed out evenly, "have seen precious few signs of its operation, Wade."

"Give us time, boy. State's damn near bankrupt, you know. Reckon we've got to teach the niggers a little reading, writing and figuring. Don't object to that so much. What I do object to is having it done by outsiders. Makes misfits out of our niggers. Better to have them educated for their proper place in society by folks who make up that society. That's my whole bone of contention."

"Wade," Randy said warningly.

"Don't worry, Doc," Wade grinned; "I don't aim to git excited. 'Sides, world's big enough for differences of opinion now. I don't hold it against Clint how he feels about things."

"Good," Clint said; "I'm glad to hear you say that, Wade."

Wade smiled slowly.

"Look, Clint," he said, "why don't you ride over to the store with me after Doc Randy gits through with me? Mary Ann's been pining to see you. Feels right smart bad you ain't even stopped in to say hello."

196

"I didn't know that I was welcome, Wade," Clint said flatly.

Wade opened his little eyes, wide.

"Just because you and me had words the last time you was out to the place? Heck, boy, I don't hold grudges."

"Then I'll come," Clint said.

"Good," Wade said. "I'm ready, Randy."

"All right," Randy said coldly, "come along, then."

Riding over to the store, Wade kept up a steady stream of talk.

"Going to drop in on that school of yours, soon as I feel up to it," he said. "Must be a funny sight to see niggers trying to git book learning through their thick skulls."

"No," Clint said gravely. "As a matter of fact, it's rather pitiful. They try so hard; you'd think their lives depended upon it. Some of them, like Buford and Cindy, are remarkable, though."

"That so? Reckon they can't all be dumb." Wade turned his face sidewise, watching Clint out of the corner of his eyes. "You ought to see my twins, Clint," he said; "what boys! Ride, shoot, and hunt like men. The little fellow's coming right along, too."

"The little fellow?" Clint said.

"Jeb. He's six, now. Curious little critter: thin and dreamy. Lot different from the twins. 'Course pa had jet black hair; but Jeb's first Benton I ever heard tell of, who ever had real dark eyes—dark as yourn in fact."

Clint looked down a little, seeing Wade's awkward fingers trembling on the reins.

A child, he thought bitterly. A third child—a son. And this is the first I've even heard of his existence. Mary Ann never mentioned him in her letters—all those wonderful letters she begged me not to answer. Nobody in the whole time I've been here—that's natural enough, I guess, as far as the townspeople are concerned. Unless it happened to come up accidentally, they'd assume I already knew. But Mother Sarah, and Randy. . . . That's something else again—something deliberate. . . . Is it because they know, or suspect . . . ? Dear God! Dark hair and eyes. And she never told me—not even so much as a word. . . .

"I think it depends upon the mother, sometimes," he said quietly. "For instance, I'm a Benton—every bit as much of a Benton as you are, Wade, and my eyes are dark. If you insist upon blue eyes, you shouldn't have married Mary Ann."

"Reckon you're right," Wade said. "By the way, your ex-lady friend, Jane Henderson, married Barton Hendricks and moved away to Texas. But I reckon you knew that."

"No," Clint said, "I didn't."

"And her brother Ash and his wife have a little girl. Named her Pat—Patricia. Cutest little tyke you ever did see. But then them Hendersons always was mighty handsome folks. Well—here we are."

She got up very slowly, as they came in, and even from the doorway, he could see her face paling. She had to put one hand on the counter to support herself. But she recovered very quickly, and put out her hand.

"Howdy, Clint," she said quietly; "I'm bound to say that you sure Lord have neglected us."

"I—I've been busy," Clint said lamely.

"So I hear," Mary Ann said. "It's a fine idea, Clint; but I'm not sure it's wise."

"Why not?" Clint said. "The Democratic voters have approved of schools for Negroes. The Knights have disbanded. And since the Hayes election, everything the conservatives down here were fighting for has been won. No more carpetbaggers, Mary. 'The Good White People of the South,' like your husband, here, are in control again. So surely there won't be any trouble over a little thing like a school."

"There will be though," Mary Ann said flatly. "The Knights haven't disbanded at all. They just don't have to wear their robes any more. And the Democrats voted the way they did as a sop to Northern opinion. The few schools they've opened for the colored people are just put there to point at—so that they can say: 'Look what we're doing for the poor benighted heathen.'"

"That," Wade growled, "is a hell of a way to talk, Mary Ann!"

"And one day," Mary Ann went on, ignoring him, "they'll burn that school of yours, Clint."

"Oh, come now, Mary!" Clint laughed; "they've stopped that. People don't burn schoolhouses nowadays. Ten years ago, maybe, but not now."

"Now," Mary Ann said. "Benton's Row is ten, twenty years behind the times. The whole South is."

"Why do you hate it, Mary?" Clint said. "You were born here. Why do you hate the South?"

"I don't." Her eyes caught his, implored them, entreated. "I love the South. All of it, the beauty of it, I mean. There's a place down by the river I love most of all. Where the water makes a hook, and catches the moon in the bend, and there are fireflies and Spanish moss when the light is in it, and—"

Wade stared at her.

"You crazy or something?" he said in his thick, blurred voice.

"No. Just different from you, Wade. Clint understands me, I think. Don't you, Clint?"

"Perfectly," Clint said.

"Well I don't," Wade growled. "You drop in on that school every night, don't you, Clint?"

"Yes, I do—usually," Clint told him.

"Good!" Wade Benton said.

It was very dark in the pinewood and Jeb was having a hard time keeping up with the twins. He was afraid of the dark, but he didn't want them to know it. He ran behind them, hearing the hounds belling somewhere ahead, the sound deep, long drawn out, sad. It gave him the shivers, but he liked it. He was very tired and frightened, but most of all he was puzzled. The elaborate plans the twins had evolved to sneak him out of the house without his mama knowing it hadn't been necessary: for some strange reason, mama had not come home at all.

It was the first time in all his life that had ever happened. He had questioned the twins about it, but they had only shrugged. Whether mama came home or not didn't interest them. They were all Benton—nothing interested them but the business at hand.

"Let's stop here," Nat said. "The li'l' fellow's winded. 'Sides when they scent something, we'll know it."

"How?" Jeb said.

"They'll start bugling," Stone told him. "Different kind of a sound. Git real close, you'll hear 'em yapping. Then you'll know they've treed something. Silly to run after them all night, 'cause they run in circles anyhow, mostly. All right to stay here as long as we can hear 'em. Git too far away, we have to go after them again."

The three of them sat down on a fallen tree.

"Mama didn't come home," Jeb said.

"Don't worry about it," Stone said. "She's all right, kid. Probably stayed over at grandma's. She'll be home in the morning; you can bet on that."

"First time she ever stayed off," Jeb said.

They didn't answer him.

"Aren't you going to light the lanterns?" he whispered.

"Not yet," Nat said. "Not until we come up on something. If it's a 'possum, we light them and shine them in his eyes."

"Then what happens?"

"Then we climb up the tree, and catch him by the tail, and put him in the sack."

"Won't he bite?"

"Naw—'possums don't bite. They're too scairt."

They sat there, waiting. It was a warm night with many stars. There were fireflies in the trees. It was still and quiet and peaceful except for the sound of the dogs, mourning through the pinewood. The sound grew fainter, came back again. The dogs were quartering the wood, working it back and forth in long diagonals. They would cover every inch of it sooner or later. Jeb didn't feel afraid any more.

When the dogs changed their note, the twins didn't have to tell him. He was on his feet as soon as they were, running toward the sound. It wasn't far, but before they got there, the dogs started yapping.

"What is it?" Jeb panted.

" 'Possum or coon. Can't tell yet," Nat said.

They burst out into a clearing in the pinewood. There were three dogs, tumbling over each other in their eagerness, around the foot of a tree.

"Damn!" the twins chorused.

"What's the matter?" Jeb said.

They were busy getting the lanterns lit while they told him.

"That tree. Ain't much more than a sapling. Git halfway up and it'll bend over and—"

"Why?"

"Me or Nat's too heavy. Can't git nowheres near that damned 'possum."

They stopped suddenly, staring at him.

He opened his eyes wide. He was afraid two ways: He was deathly afraid of climbing that tree in the dark; but he was just as afraid of losing his brothers' respect. The tree was one thing; but he didn't have to live with the tree.

"All right," he said; "I'll do it."

"Good for you, kid," Stone said gruffly.

They gave him the sack. Then they boosted him up as far as they could reach. He grasped the trunk and started upward. It wasn't as hard as he had thought. But the higher he got, the worse it was. The tree swayed, and the unwinking little eyes stared down at him. On the ground, even the dogs were quiet now. Jeb climbed. There was a hollow in his middle that grew and grew. Sweat trickled down into his eyes. From the tree top the opossum stared down. The obscene little beast wrapped its scaly, ratlike tail around a branch and glared at him.

He stopped within reaching distance of the opossum. He hung there looking at it.

"Grab him, kid!" the twins called.

His hand shot out, grasping the tail. He jerked it loose from the branch, almost losing his balance. Then he dropped the little beast into the sack he had slung across his shoulders. It made no resistance. He clung to the tree trunk, shuddering.

"Good for you, kid!" Stone called. "Come on down!"

He felt good, suddenly; warm and good. He did not know it, but he had something the twins lacked. He was actually braver than they, because he knew what fear was—the meaning of it. But he didn't let it stop him.

The twins would go on, all their lives, performing prodigies of valor; but they would never know the special triumph of doing a thing that is agonizingly impossible, but doing it anyhow, conquering both the object, and, at the same time, one's own weaknesses, frailties, fears. It was a very good feeling.

He started downward, groping with his feet for the branches below him. He missed the first one, slid sickeningly downward until his left foot jammed hard against a stop limb. He hung there, dizzily; and it was then he saw the glow.

"Fire!" he yelled. "A whopping big one!"

"Where?" they cried.

"That—a—way!" he called, pointing.

"Come on down!" they roared.

He came down, sliding, scraping his hands and knees, ripping his clothes, his fears gone, forgotten, the excitement and wonder working within him like an intoxicant, heady and wild.

They snatched the sack from him as soon as his feet touched ground. "Git going, kid!" Stone barked; "you lead!"

He ran ahead of them in a whooping broil of sound: the dogs bounding around him in all directions at once, it seemed to him, giving tongue, making a symphony of mournful music wonderfully fitting, a thing of rushing speed, and hound bugling, and the hammer of running feet, earth muffled. The twins could outdistance him, but they hung back, letting him lead; and he, running easily, freely, felt neither fear nor weariness, but only the glory of leadership, of being now on a plane with his brothers, a man, truly, among men.

They burst out into the clearing; and crashed to a halt against an invisible wall of terror: stopped almost physically by the heat blast against their faces, standing there goggling at that inferno; the roll and boom and cackle of flames that soared upward, boiled up, drowning the stars in a wash of savage red.

The men on horseback sat there watching it, and a little beyond them, their father, his round face orange red in the fireglow, sitting in the buckboard, trembling. Then Jeb saw it. He caught at his brothers' arms, jerking them, pointing, unable to speak, beyond now, even the utterance of sound.

The big Negro came out of the fire, all his clothes, even the woolly hair on his head blazing, the whole of him burning like a torch. He was carrying something in his arms, something that writhed and moaned. He stopped, knelt, and lay her down very carefully. Then he came on again, without haste, making no sound at all, no cry, nothing, just moving like that toward the riders, walking, coming on.

Jeb found his voice.

"It's Buford!" he shrieked; "Lord God, it's Buford!"

Then all the guns spoke at once.

"Come on," Stone said, "take his arm, Nat. That ain't fitting for no kid to see."

Clint lay there, holding Mary Ann in the crook of his arm, puzzling idly in the warm lassitude of contentment over how bright the room had suddenly become. Strange, he thought; there's no moon. . . . Then he saw the glow was red.

He leaped to his feet, spilling her abruptly out of his arms.

"What is it, Clint?" Mary Ann said.

"Fire!" he breathed. "The school! It must be the school—come on!"

"Like that?" Mary Ann smiled.

"Oh, damn!" Clint swore, and began yanking the clothes onto his fine, big body.

But the Henderson Place was too far from the school. By the time they got there, only the fallen rafters smoldered stubbornly, surrounded by a crowd of bayou people who talked in whispers, or did not talk at all, standing there like that staring at the two objects on the ground from which the smoke still rose, until the wind changed and they got the smoke, and the smell full in their faces; and they, all of them, breaking out and away from there, made a path through which Clint and Mary Ann came.

The riders were gone by then, and the buckboard. Only the weeping, red-eyed schoolmarm, her gray hair hacked off by the riders in grotesque tufts, her spectacles broken, her clothing singed, was left to tell them how, after she and her pupils had been ordered out of the schoolhouse and the building set afire, Cindy had missed little Fred. Not knowing him safe in the arms of another woman, she had dashed back into the fire. It mounted too quickly, the kerosene they had flung through the windows had done its work too well, so that when Buford reached her, it was too late—too late for both of them.

"He put her down and went after them," the teacher whispered. "They shot him—all of them. But it was a mercy, the way he was burning." Her voice, speaking, was flat, level, dead; little more than a whisper, it carried better than any shout, was, to them, listening, more terrible than any scream.

"Clint," Mary Ann said, and laid a hand on his arm.

He shook it off, savagely.

"Don't touch me!" he said. "But for you I would have been here. I would have prevented this, or stopped it, or died trying. But for you."

"Clint!" she said again.

He looked her up and down slowly. Then he turned to Miss Crandall-Hyde.

"Come," he said, "we'll take you home, now. . . ."

When Mary Ann got back to Broad Acres, she wasn't crying any more.

I'm through crying, she thought; I've cried enough for all the rest of my life. . . .

Through the open door of the bedroom, Wade heard her. He had been lying there, trembling. He was afraid. He had seen it, and he was afraid the way he felt would bring on another attack. Then he heard her.

"Mary Ann!" he called. "Where the devil have you been?"

She stepped into the bedroom. She stood there, looking at him. She didn't say anything. She just stood there, like that, looking at him. Then she turned and went out of the room. He heard the door of the guest room open and close, the crash of the big bolt being slammed home.

"Oh, good Lord!" Wade Benton said.

8

"You are a fool, Oren Bascomb!" Stormy said. "Couldn't let well enough alone, could you? You had to have it all!"

Oren grinned at her.

"Now, Baby," he said, "don't take on so. Some mighty nice places for a fine, upstanding young couple like us up North—that is, after we come back from abroad. Always did have a hankering to see London and Paris."

Stormy looked at him coldly.

"I'm not going with you, Oren," she said.

He straightened up then, stiffening out of his habitual lazy slouch for the first time in years, his dark eyes wide.

"But, Baby-doll," he began.

"You listen to me, Oren," Stormy said quietly. "You've been with the lottery company long enough to know how it operates. You're not dealing with General Rafflin alone, now. The whole damned organization is going to be after you."

"So?" he said; but his tone was less sure.

"I got you this job nearly nine years ago. In that nine years, you've become one of the richest men in the State—legitimately, if anything connected with gambling can be called legitimate. But you weren't satisfied. General Rafflin, for all his being older than God Almighty, is nobody's fool. You, Lover, have embezzled in the past three years nearly a cool million dollars. Do you deny that?"

"No," Oren said boldly. "Going to steal—steal big, I say. This way I can buy myself out of most anything they try to bring against me. Git the right connections, I can buy off extradition from most any foreign country."

"If you ever get to a foreign country," Stormy said flatly. "I'd lay you ten to one you'll never leave Louisiana alive, if I had any way to collect the bet."

"What the devil do you mean?" Oren snarled.

"Simple, my sweet. The Mafia. Ever heard of them?"

"Of course," Oren said uneasily; "but what have them murdering guinea bastards got to do with this?"

"Plenty. Ever wondered how a man like Giovanni Maspero ever got elected to the Board of Directors of the company? They've bought their way in, or forced their way in—and believe me, Lover, the Black Hand plays for keeps. They aren't even interested in that chicken feed you've stolen. They don't care if they get the money back or not. Oh, they'll go through the motions all right. My dear, beloved, antediluvian husband is downtown right now, swearing out a warrant for your arrest. But you won't be arrested."

Oren brightened.

"Then I don't see . . ."

"Let me finish, Lover. A trial would be much too embarrassing to the lottery company, what with the Governor bringing pressure against it now. Oh no, you're going to be allowed to skip. . . ."

"Why don't you skip with me, Sugar-pie?" Oren grinned. "You'n'me together could . . ."

"Because, my sweet, I don't relish being found in a back bayou with my nose, mouth and ears notched like a sow's, and my dainty throat split from ear to ear. That's what's going to happen to you, Love—with a few variations I can safely leave to your imagination."

"Stormy, for the love of God!" Oren whispered.

"Which is why I'm not going with you. As I said, they aren't really interested in the money. To them, it's small change. But they're very much interested in having a shining example of what happens to little blackguards who cross them on exhibition as a warning to anyone else who might get ideas in the future."

Oren stood there, staring at her.

"What am I going to do?" he said. "Tell me that, Stormy!"

"Skip, Lover-boy," she said calmly. "Right now. Move fast enough and far enough, you might have a chance. I doubt it, but it's worth a try."

"Lord God!" Oren whispered.

"Another thing: don't head directly North. They'll expect that. And wherever you go, stay away from big cities—any place having a sizable Italian population is likely to have the Mafia. Don't write me. I wouldn't get the letters anyhow, and they'd trace you through them."

She put out her hand to him.

"Good-bye, Oren," she said.

"Lord, but you're hard," he got out.

"No," she said, "I'm not, really, Oren. If you do get away, remember there's only one thing you're good for. Stick to that, Lover—some woman will always take care of you."

"Stormy," he pleaded.

"Good-bye, Oren," Stormy said.

Riding northwestward toward the Red River parishes, Oren Bascomb had plenty of time for thinking. Traveling on horseback was agonizingly slow, but they would be watching the steamboats and the railroads. Besides, a lone horseman didn't have to keep to the main roads—or, for that matter, until he reached the bayou country, to any roads at all. The lottery company and the Mafia were going to have one sweet time tracing him, he reckoned.

His brain worked slowly, clearly, under the starlight. Ain't a-going to skip alone, he thought. When I do light out of this State, sure Lord be easier to git through as an old farmer traveling with his wife. Fine idea. I'm noted for my clothes. But in overalls and a straw hat, and enough flour in my hair. . . . Better wait on this beard, though. In two weeks, it'll be just right. Git myself a ragged carpetbag. Then me and my wife going North to Cincinnati. Country folks on a holiday. . . .

Only trouble is, you can't rightly tell 'bout Mary Ann. Clint skipped a year ago. Got out of the niggers that they quarreled. Said she cried for days. Ought to be ripe for the plucking by now. She don't care for me nohows, but I can persuade her. Tell her I'll take her to him if necessary. . . .

Don't have to worry about old Fat Boy. He's still too scairt I'll rat on him. Fat fool! What difference would it make now?—sixteen years since the end of the War. Folks done plumb forgot that war. He's half dead, anyhow—out of politics and still he's scairt. Hope he stays that way. . . .

He rode on, doggedly.

Be there tomorrow, about noon, I reckon. Find my chance to sweet-talk Mary Ann, then light out. Shouldn't be hard. Couple o' times I seen her looking at me like she'd like to find out what a real man is. Course there's a better than even chance that Clint's already taught her. Clint or somebody—'cause that last kid sure Lord ain't Wade's. . . .

He pulled up the horse and moved a little way off the path.

Got to sleep. Too damned tired. Ain't seen a sign of them knifing Black Handers yet. Reckon they're still watching steamboats. Hell, if necessary, I can buy a wagon and drive North. They'll never think of that!

He took down his saddle roll, and spread the blanket out, placing the rest of the things under his head. Then he pushed the revolver a little way under them, ready at hand.

Going to miss Stormy, he thought; she were right pert good. Lord God, but I'm tired!

Mary Ann looked up from the letter she was writing. Jeb was standing there watching her out of his enormous dark eyes.

Poor little fellow, she thought. He saw Buford die like that. The twins admitted that he was with them. But he's never said a word. You'd think he'd forgotten it. Maybe the shock drove it completely out of his mind. . . .

She put out her hand and stroked his face.

"Run along outside and play, Jebbie," she said, "until Mama finishes her letter. Then we'll go into town and post it—would you like that, son?"

"Yes, Mama," Jeb said.

"Where are your brothers?" Mary Ann asked him.

"Gone hunting."

"Wouldn't they take you with them?" she asked him.

"Yes, Mama. I can shoot better than either of them. . . ."

"Then why?" Mary Ann said.

"I didn't want to go, Mama."

"Just as well you didn't," Mary Ann said cheerfully. "Now we can have a trip into town all by ourselves. Have you seen your papa?"

"No, Mama—not since this morning. He was walking down by the pig-pen, feeling the fence."

"I know. Reckon I'll have to repair that fence myself I ever want it done. Run along now, son; I'll only be a few minutes."

"Yes, Mama," Jeb said.

Mary Ann sat there studying the half-finished letter. Then she picked up the pen again. Her hand raced over the paper, pausing only to dip the pen in the inkwell.

"You know, my Love," she wrote, "that I have long since forgiven and forgotten your harshness to me the night of the fire. Why do you continue to mention it? It is true I lured you away from your business; and it is true that you let yourself be lured. You feel that you behaved less than the man, by blaming me for it; but Clint-love, that has been the role of women, ever since Eve!" She stopped, smiled. Then she began to write again:

"You say you'll come for me and Jebbie. But that, Love, is hardly wise. I'll meet you in Memphis. I've waited this long, and now, at last, I'm sure; the twins are all Benton—they will always be able to take care of themselves. Besides they will forget me before I'm entirely out of sight. But Jebbie needs me, and he needs you even more. He will be so glad to have a father. . . ."

She paused, reading what she had written. Then the pen raced on.

"I wonder how we can explain to him. He is such a serious child—so much older than his years. I guess we can just say: Look Jebbie, this really is your father—see how much you look like him? He'll accept that—he believes anything I tell him—so why not this, since it is the truth?"

She stopped, the point of the pen digging into the paper, and sat there, staring at the shadow that had fallen across it.

"Lord God! Damn my wicked soul, but I do have luck!" Oren Bascomb said.

Jebbie wondered who the tall man was. He didn't like him; he was sure of that. In spite of the fact that the tall man had given him peppermint candy almost as soon as he had gotten off his horse, Jeb was sure he was a bad man. He rubbed his head where the tall man had patted it. He didn't like the way the man's hand had felt, so bony and cold.

He was sorry he had told the man his mama was in the kitchen. He was sure she wouldn't like the tall man either. Better go and see if she needed him—if the tall man bothered her, he'd . . .

He moved toward the screen door. Then he saw his papa coming up the path from the pigpen. He was glad of that. He didn't like his papa very much, but the tall man wouldn't dare bother his mama with his papa about, that was one sure thing.

He peered through the screen door and his black eyes opened wide. His mama was fighting with the tall man. She was trying to get something away from the man—a piece of paper. The letter she had been writing, Jebbie guessed.

"Let her go!" he cried; "damn you, let my mama go!"

Then he turned and saw that his papa was coming very fast, hopping on his cane. But he didn't come to the screen door. Instead he came up to the side window. Jebbie saw that his face was very red.

Mama was crying now. He heard her say: "Give me my letter, Oren! Confound you! Give it to me!" But after that she didn't say anything else, because his papa smashed in the windowpane with the barrel of his pistol and started shooting.

Jeb saw the funny expression come over his mama's face. The tall man turned her loose, and she fell down on the floor and lay there without saying anything at all.

The tall man started toward the window, yanking at his hip pocket as he came.

"You fat fool!" he said, "you've killed her! God damn your soul you can't even sho—"

Then his papa shot again very fast, five more times so fast it sounded like one sound. The tall man bent over just like he was bowing to papa, but he went on down and lay on the floor beside mama, making a whimpering little noise in his throat, then the noise stopped, and Jebbie couldn't hear anything at all except the beating of his own heart.

He didn't move or speak. Then his papa came around the side of the house, hopping very fast on his cane, and shoved him roughly aside. He waited until his father had yanked the screen door open, and gone inside, then he came back again to the door.

He could hear his papa crying. He could see what his papa was doing, but he didn't understand it. Then he saw the top part of his mama all white with the blood on her, and he went away from there, running. He didn't stop until he was completely out of breath. And even after that, he kept on running and crying and stopping when he was out of breath and starting again until he came to his grandma's house.

John Brighton came back out of the bedroom, and closed the door behind him.

"You ain't touched nothing?" he said. "That's just how you found 'em?"

Wade nodded silently.

"Reckon you was within yore rights, Mister Benton," Sheriff Brighton said: "still folks are going to think you went a mite far—killing yore wife, too. A hosswhipping would of been enough, to most folks' way o' thinking. . . ."

"Didn't aim to kill her," Wade choked. "Lord God, John—you know how my hands shake! That was an accident—I was shooting at him. . . ."

John Brighton looked at him.

"Yep," he said, "only one bullet hit her—that's right—in the back. All the rest of 'em in him. That bears out what you was saying. Reckon any man would of done the same thing, coming in here and finding 'em in yore own bed. . . ."

Wade stared at the sheriff, tears penciling his fat face.

"Can't you keep that part quiet, John?" he said. "Mighty messy, specially since I got growing boys. . . ."

"Nope," John Brighton said. "It's yore defense, son. Justifiable hom-icide. You ain't even going to be tried. Coroner's jury going to hand down the unwritten law and that'll be that."

"Oh, God!" Wade Benton said.

"What I can't understand," the Sheriff drawled, "is that windowpane broken in the kitchen—and them few spots of blood on the floor. 'Pears to me somebody tried to wash 'em up and didn't do such a good job."

"I broke that window, John," Wade whispered. "Cut my hand bad, doing it—see? That's what made them spots. They had locked all the doors. I had to break that window to git to the catch to open it."

"I see," John Brighton said. "Funny there warn't none of the house niggers around. . . ."

"My—my wife had give 'em the day off," Wade muttered; "reckon all this was planned, John."

"Must of been," John Brighton said. "Reckon that explains everything. Now, Mister Wade Benton, I hereby arrest you, and, considering the cir-cumstances, release you into your own custody. Have to go through the motions, you know; folks expect that. That about covers everything, I expect. I'll send the undertaker out after 'em. . . ."

"Yes—thank you, John—thank you kindly," Wade Benton said.

"Got here mighty quick, didn't you?" Sarah said tartly.

"The minute I read it in the papers," Clinton said. "I was coming any-way. I was just waiting to hear from Mary Ann. . . ."

"Well, you won't hear from her now," Sarah said.

"Sarah, for God's sake!" Randy said.

"He admits it's happened before!" Sarah stormed; "he's come right here in my house and claims Jeb as his child—though how anybody can tell what particular man any of her children belong to under the circum-stances is more than I can see!"

Randy looked at his wife.

"She's dead, Sarah," he said quietly. "I think we can afford a little Christian charity now . . ."

"She led my son a dog's life!" Sarah said, "and him at death's door. One man after another and . . ."

Clinton stood up. His face was white under his tan.

"That's enough, Mother Sarah," he said quietly. "I can allow for your feelings as a mother. But I think you should have some consideration for mine. I loved Mary Ann. I would have married her if I could. I begged her for years to divorce Wade. She chose to stick by her bargain—her very bad bargain, begging your pardon, Ma'am. You know Wade was cruel to her. You know as well as I do, what kind of a man your son is. All I'm saying is that I want my son. I don't want him brought up by his mother's murderer."

"Murderer!" Sarah got out. "Randy, for God's sake! You going to stand there and let him . . ."

"Clint," Randy said sternly, "I must ask you to apologize for that."
Clinton looked at him.

"Very well," he sighed, "I do apologize out of deference to a mother's feelings. But I don't think I've spoken unjustly. May I see Jeb, please?"

"Yes," Randy said tiredly; "come along, Clint. . . . Strange—so far, the poor little fellow has refused to talk about it. . . . He saw it, you know."

"I know," Clint said. "Maybe he'll talk to me."

The boy walked with Clint in the garden, and his dark eyes were very still and grave. Seeing them there, together like that, Randy was sure. The resemblance between them was very strong.

Clint talked to the boy, and little Jeb listened. Suddenly, very shyly, he put his hand into his father's.

"I like you," he said; "I wish I was your boy."

Clint blinked his eyes very fast, and coughed a little.

"You're going to be," he said. "Tell me, son—you saw what happened, didn't you . . . ?"

"Yes," Jeb said.

Clint looked at him, considering how to put the question. Randy stood there watching them. Then he turned and went back into the house.

"Randy," Sarah said, "I'm sorry. Don't reckon I've been fair."

"You haven't," Randy said; "When you've seen as much human frailty as I have, you learn to forgive, Sarah."

"You've learnt that, haven't you, Randy? Even mine. Must have been hard listening to me talk like that about that poor, dead child, when you remembered what I was when you met me."

"You," Randy said, "were a woman, Sarah. Always a good one—sometimes even a great one. It's not whether a person does evil in God's sight—we all do, Sarah. It's why he does it, and what he does afterwards. What you did that one time, you've made up for with a lifetime of good."

"Thank you for that, Randy. Maybe poor Mary Ann would have too, if she'd got the chance."

"Sarah," Randy said.

"Yes, Love?"

"Mary Ann hated Oren Bascomb. I know people—I know when they pretend dislike to cover up. She wasn't pretending. She really hated him."

"I know," Sarah whispered. "What is the answer, Randy?"

"I wish I knew," Randy groaned; "Lord God, how I wish I knew!"

"Grandma," Jeb said, pushing open the door, "Uncle Clint ran away." They stood there, staring at him.

"Jebbie," Sarah whispered, "did you talk to him before he left?"

"Yes, Grandma," Jeb said.

She put both her hands on his thin shoulders.

"Jebbie-love," she said gently, "what did you tell him?"

"I told him about mama," Jeb said.

"What about your mama?" Randy said.

"What—what happened to her," Jeb said, then he started to cry.

"Please, Jebbie," Sarah said; "grandma knows this is hard. But could you tell us, too?"

"Yes'm," Jebbie gulped. "Yes, Grandma. . . ."

"Tell us, boy," Randy said.

"Mama was in the kitchen, writing a letter. Then—that man came. I—I looked through the screen door. . . ."

"Yes," Sarah said; "yes, darling?"

"The man was fighting with mama! He took her letter—she was trying to get it back. . . ."

"In the kitchen?" Randy said.

"Yes. Then papa broke the window with his gun. He started shooting and mama—and mama . . ."

His words dissolved into wild, formless sobbing.

"In the kitchen," Randy said to Sarah, "in the kitchen, Sarah!"

"I heard," Sarah wept. "Jebbie, please—what happened after that?"

"Mama fell—down. The—the man started running toward papa and yelling at him—and then—papa shot him, too. . . ."

Randy picked the boy up and sat him on his knee.

"It's all right, Jebbie," he said gently. "Your mother's in heaven. She's watching over you right now—"

"No, she's not!" Jebbie wailed; "She's not! She's not! She's dead. She was all over with blood! I saw it when papa carried her into the bedroom!"

"When papa carried her into the bedroom . . . ?" Sarah whispered. "But, Jebbie—"

"I saw it!" the boy shrieked; "when papa took off her dress!"

Sarah looked at her husband. There was death in her eyes.

"You'd better get out there, Randy," she said; "you still might be in time. . . ."

Randy stood up.

"No," he said; "for a bastard like that, I wouldn't lift a finger, Sarah!"

"Randy," Sarah said, "he's my son. And Clint is Tom's. For both of them, Randy. For Tom's sake—not for mine. . . ."

Randy looked at her.

"All right," he said; "I'll go. But for your sake, Sarah. Only for your sake."

He came pounding into the cheniere outside the big gates. He had almost reached them, when Clinton rode out into his path.

"You—you didn't?" he got out.

"No," Clinton said. "He wasn't armed. Neither was I, at first. I had to stop in town and buy a gun."

Randy looked at him.

"You were waiting?" he said.

"Yes. I gave him until sunset to come out. Then I'm going in after him."

Randy put out his hand.

"Give me that gun," he said.

Clint shook his head.

"You know what he did?" he burst out. "He killed them in the kitchen! They were fully clothed! Then he—"

"I know," Randy said. "Give me the gun, Clint."

"No! He dirtied her before the whole damned world to save his miserable hide. I'm sorry, Randy, but he's going to pay for that."

"I agree," Randy said. "That's why I want your gun."

Clint stared at him.

"I don't see—" he began.

"Listen," Randy said tiredly. "You go in there and you kill him—or he kills you, and what have you proved? That Mary Ann was not shot in the very act of adultery, as he claims—or merely that she had still another lover? That's all people are going to think if you kill him. Don't be a fool, boy. I'm going in there and bring him out, and he's going down to John Brighton's office and sign a full confession, clearing that poor girl's name. . . ."

"They'll hang him," Clint warned.

"He wouldn't live that long. In his condition, the fear of it would kill him long before. Better that way. Come on, give me your gun."

Slowly Clinton drew it out and passed it over. He smiled, crookedly.

"Thanks, Randy," he said; "I was about to break my most sacred oath. And Wade's not worth it."

"No," Randy said, "he's not. Now, we'll wait. If he doesn't come out in half an hour, I'll go after him—alone, Clint. He won't fire on me. I'll go before dark so he can see who I am."

"All right," Clint said.

Wade sat in the kitchen with the revolver in his hand. He's coming, he thought, Clint's coming. . . . And I can't hardly lift this damned thing any more. . . . Can't rightly aim with this here shaking . . .

He peered toward the big gates.

Didn't think of that damned little bastard! Had plumb forgot he was there. . . . I kilt Mary Ann—kilt his ma. Lord Jesus God Almighty! Didn't mean to kill her, You know that, God; didn't mean to—just these damned trembling hands couldn't aim straight, couldn't . . .

He laid the revolver down on the table and got his thickened fingers around the whiskey bottle. He forced it upward, level with his mouth. The whiskey ran down his chin, soaked his shirt . . .

"Damn!" he wept. "Can't even drink no more!" Planned it so good, too —got rid of Oren. Nobody'll ever know now—nobody but Randy. Had to tell him. . . . Can I help it 'cause I was born without guts? Briar Creek— Lord Jesus, ain't I paid for it? Had to run that day—just had to—man

would of been a fool to stay there and fight the whole Yankee army. . . .
But they was fools, those boys, fools and heroes, and they was smarter'n
I was 'cause dying is quick, and dead they didn't have to wake up night
after night in a cold sweat, like I do still. . . . I can hear 'em, screaming
with them Yankee bayonets through their guts, and cussing me with their
dying breaths for leaving 'em. . . . Didn't have no luck that time—wasn't
for that sharpshooting sentry, I'd of got clean away—then there wouldn't
of been all this business about Oren blackmailing me. . . .

He tried the bottle again. This time some of the whiskey went down
his throat.

Pa, too. Cussing me with his dead eyes. Ratted on him, too. Told
Louis Dupré 'bout Babette—got my own pa killed. Didn't meant it, Pa.
Sure Lord didn't. You know that—you know—Pa! Don't stand there like
that a-glaring at me! Lord God, Pa—don't . . .

He got up from the table, hobbling backward toward the door, leaving
the revolver where it lay. He went down the back steps, favoring his
bad leg.

"Pa," he whispered. "Pa, I was young and crazy jealous and anyhow I
didn't mean it. . . . You understand that, don't you, Pa? Pa, you're
dead. Don't you know you're dead, Pa? Close your eyes, don't glare at
me like that, Pa for Jesus' sake Pa don't—don't—"

He was running now, a crazy hop-skip, a wild, lurching hobble, down
the path.

"Pa! Don't follow me! Pa, you're Clint and you're gonna kill me—staring like that—she's dead, Pa! She's dead lying there so white with the
blood all over her. And I loved her so. . . . But I kilt her Pa like I kilt you
like I kilt them boys at Briar Creek, like I—"

He stopped still. The sun went out suddenly. Then it came back again,
swinging dizzily in the sky. His father was gone. He was alone, leaning on
the fence by the pigpen, under a blood-red sky that came down closer,
closer until it was all around his head like a blanket, roaring in his ears
like a surf tide. He went down, feeling himself going, and the fence
crashed in under his weight.

He lay there, breathing hoarsely, while the red went out of the sky and
the sun steadied into its accustomed place. Then he saw the first of the
thick gray shapes come grunting toward him. He started to put down his
hands to push himself up, but nothing happened. He looked at his
hands, seeing them there: thick, inert, useless. He tried moving them,
concentrating with a fury of will upon each finger, then upon his toes.
His eyes, rolling in a face that was motionless, too, rested finally on the
gray shapes, a yard away, moving in. He screamed then—all the more
terribly for the fact that he made no sound.

"I'm going now," Randy said; "don't follow me, Clint."

"All right," Clint said. Then they both heard the guns.

Randy looked at him. Then he jerked his head in the direction of the sound. "Come on," he said.

They whirled the horses around the house, and went hammering down the path. They pulled up together and sat there.

The twins were firing into the herd. They were both crying, and their tears had made streaks through the powder black on their faces. But they kept on shooting into the milling, screaming hogs.

Then Randy saw it.

"Dear God!" he whispered—and gave Clint back his gun. The two of them sat there on the horses and emptied their revolvers into the herd, firing until the last beast was dead.

Randy got down from the horse. He took off his coat and laid it over the thing on the ground.

"Come, Clint," he said, "help me pick him up. . . ."

"Too much," Clint whispered; "not even he—"

"Give me a hand," Randy snapped; "the twins—"

"All right, Randy," Clinton Dupré said.

Book Three

LUCIFER'S FALL

1

I'M OLD, Sarah thought; I'm too old and they won't let me lie down like a body my age ought to have the right to. . . . Reckon I'm a fool. I should give up and let them manage without me. But they can't. They're going to have to one day soon; and that's a fact. I know them too good, and that's what keeps me going; I know every time another damned Benton is born, people should run for cover. If there ever is any more of them—Roland don't seem to be in any hurry to start a family. He's been married since right after the Armistice and not a word about a child. Funny he ain't come home yet. War's been over six months and he's still abroad. Maybe he's 'shamed of that there foreign woman he married. . . .

Can't be that, though. Jeb and Patricia said she was a sweet little thing from one of the very best families over there. Poor things—Hank was all they had. Reckon the main reason Jeb took that job in New York after all is 'cause everything around here reminds them too much. Won't be no more Duprés after them. Hank was the last, and I reckon Pat's too old now for childbearing. . . .

She sat there on the veranda of Broad Acres that June morning of 1919, rocking in her chair. She sat very straight and tall, and her gray eyes were clear. She was ninety-six years old, and she could still get about after a fashion, leaning heavily on a cane, with her other arm supported by Buck, her Negro chauffeur-houseman. Every time she went into a store, which she occasionally did even nowadays, people accepted it as a matter of course that the clerks were going to stop waiting on them without apology and rush to serve her. Before the war, when she happened to visit the court while Jeb Dupré was pleading a case, the proceedings had ceased at once while everybody, judge, jury, lawyers, the criminal being tried, and all the spectators rose to say, "Howdy, Miz Sarah." She was almost never late to church, which was a good thing, because it was a known fact that the Reverend Reddings wasn't going to start services until she got there, which he proved one Sunday by sending one of the congregation all the way out to Broad Acres to see what the matter was when she miraculously didn't appear. When the young man got back with the news that Miz Sarah was kind of poorly, Reverend Reddings said:

"Friends, I reckon we ought to all go out there and cheer Miz Sarah up . . ."

So it was that that Sunday's sermon was preached from the veranda of Broad Acres, while the congregation stood around in the yard, and Sarah listened through the window. At the beginning of it, she called Cora Lee to her bedside, and by the time Reverend Reddings was intoning the final prayer for the health of this good and great lady whom the Lord in His infinite wisdom had seen fit to spare for so many years to be the guiding light and inspiration for the whole community, the serving girls had enough chicken fried for everybody, with potato salad and all the trimmings. Which wasn't hard, because Reverend Reddings habitually hammered away at sin, which he was against, the devil, whom he put behind him, and fire and brimstone, which yawned threateningly at the feet of all the spectators, for at least two hours. All in all, it was quite an occasion.

It had started to rain, a thin driving mist, but she didn't move. Jeb and Pat would come for her. They had promised and that was that. The idea of giving up her monthly visit to the cemetery, of not indulging in the quiet worship of her dead, because of such a thing as bad weather, never even occurred to her. It was her chief interest in life now, this ritual of going the third Sunday in each month, and walking among the tombstones, the many tombstones bearing the name "Benton," and communing in quiet and peace with the revered dead. She didn't even think about going back into the house. She had too many things on her mind. She had not become unclear with age. She remembered everything in chronological order and never got things mixed up as some of her contemporaries did. Only she hadn't any contemporaries to speak of. They had all drifted down the dark river into the mists and the silence.

"Make him come home, Lord," she prayed silently; "don't he know that's all I'm waiting for—to know there's going to be more Bentons to trouble the world? Got to make sure of that. Can't have them finished like the Duprés. . . ."

No, that would be unthinkable to her; that the strong strain, that the heady, hard violence of Benton maleness should no longer set their iron tread upon earth—that the passion in them, the wild sweet delirium they so easily evoked in response to their clarity and their force should cease, should vanish from out of life and time was more than unthinkable—it was insupportable.

Buck came around the house now and stood by the edge of the porch a yard from where she sat. Out of her great need, she asked him again although she knew already exactly how he would answer her.

"You saw Roland abroad, didn't you? When you were in the army, I mean."

"Yes'm," Buck said.

"And this here French girl he married?"

"Yes'm—tell the truth, Ma'am, I only saw her oncet, and it was real dark. But from what I saw, she was really something."

There was a warmth to his tone that nettled her, arising as it did out of this black boy's memory of a woman who, however foreign she might be, was, after all, white. Certain dim memories stirred reluctantly into life: the whispered reports that had passed from man to man upon the A. E. F.'s return from France about the peculiar response of the French, and more especially of Frenchwomen to Negroes, dim not because they were not recent, even current; but because she had dismissed them completely the first time she had heard them, with an outraged snort, as being plainly beyond belief.

"Did you," she snapped, "know her before?"

"No, Ma'am!" Buck's tone was so shocked that her ugly, half formed suspicion vanished at once, disappeared as though it had never been. But he was talking again, rushing into speech: "It was only cause I took Mister Roland home to Miz Stormy's up there in Passy that I saw her. She was staying with Miz Stormy at the time. I come up on Mister Roland by accident—he was sick and I . . ."

"You mean he was drunk," Sarah said clearly.

"No'm—sick. More sick than drunk anyhow," Buck insisted. "That was right after Mister Hank got kilt—and poor Mister Roland was half out of his mind. He was pitiful, Ma'am—the way he talked didn't make much sense a-tall. Anyhow, he told me how to git up there, so I took him—and this French lady opened the door and said: "Okay, soldier, I'll take care of him now.""

"Apparently," Sarah began, but the word was muffled. She put her hand to her mouth and then said loudly, clearly, in the toneless voice of the partially deaf: "Damn these store-boughten teeth!"

Buck let a chuckle escape him.

"What you laughing at, Buck?" she snapped.

"Nothing, Ma'am," Buck said.

"Apparently," Sarah went on serenely, as though her thought had not been interrupted, "she did just that."

"Did just what, Miz Sarah?" Buck said.

"Took mighty good care of him," Sarah said.

The big Packard drew to a stop in the yard and Jeb and Patricia Dupré got out of it. They were a very handsome couple in their early forties. They were well dressed, and calm, moving toward her with easy grace so

that anyone seeing them would have said, "Lord, what a fine looking pair
. . ." That is until he saw their eyes. Their eyes were terrible.

" 'Lo, Grandma," Jeb said, and bent to kiss her cheek.

"Howdy, son," Sarah said fondly.

Jeb bent down to help her up, and Buck ran around to the other side.
Together they got her to her feet, with some difficulty, not because she
was heavy, but because both of them handled her as though she were
made of infinitely fragile, unimaginably precious rare old china.

Patricia gave her the cane and Jeb started helping her down the stairs.
He smiled at her, and a light came into his sad, dark eyes. He was forty-
five years old, and Sarah adored him. To her, he was still the same thin,
dreamy, beautiful child she had shared with Clinton, his father, ever
since . . .

But she didn't like to think about that. There were so many things
she didn't like to remember.

"Grandma," Jeb said, "you're still the most beautiful woman in the
whole blamed world."

Sarah started to make a joke, but then she saw that he meant it.

"Next to Pat, eh son?" she said.

"No. Next to no one," Jeb said gravely. "Pat's lovely now. Maybe she
will be for many years to come: but she won't look like you do at ninety-
six . . ."

"I pray God," Pat said sharply, "that I won't live that long!"

"Oh, it ain't as bad as all that," Sarah said. "Go on, boy, flatter me
some more. I like it."

Jeb smiled, sadly.

"I reckon," he said, "a woman never does get really beautiful until she's
old. By then, her beauty's real, because it's the reflection of her soul. If
she has refused to get bitter, and gone on loving folks like you have,
Grandma, in spite of everything—then the beauty inside of her shines
through like a light. And that's the only kind of beauty that counts."

"You always did talk real pretty, Jeb," Sarah said. "Even as a child! Got
it from your poor pa. He had a way of talking that could charm a jaybird
off a branch."

"Yes," Jeb said quietly; "only I never think of him as 'poor' pa. He'd
been a sick a long time. And lonely, too. Besides, he was sixty-five when he
died. That's quite a respectable age."

"Lord God," Sarah breathed. "That's one of the troubles of being nigh
as old as Methuselah. Don't seem possible that if Wade had lived, he'd
be seventy-five years old by now. Him and Clint. And Stormy's seventy-
six! Reckon I'm just a freak of nature, Jeb. Ain't nobody supposed to live
this long."

"You are," Jeb said. "Come on, let's get a move on, Grandma. Time's
a-wasting!"

Sitting beside Patricia, Sarah took out her spectacles and adjusted them.

She could see Pat's profile now, its exquisite lines marred by the tight hold she was keeping against the revelation of her grief and pain.

"Why don't you two have another child?" Sarah said flatly. "You aren't too old—'bout forty-three, aren't you, Patricia? Heck, I've known women to have babies till they was fifty."

"Granny, please!" Patricia whispered; and the anguish was there, vibrant in her voice.

"Shame to let the Dupré strain die out—or the Hendersons. Look, child, I know you're grieved. Terrible thing to lose an only child. But you should have had more of them in the first place. Handsome young couple like you . . ."

"Oh, Granny, we tried!" Pat said desperately; "it wasn't our fault we had only one child. I wanted six! That's why I know it's no good now. If I couldn't have babies in my twenties and early thirties, I can't expect to do any better old as I am now."

"Never can tell," Sarah said serenely; "sometimes when a body wants a thing bad enough. . . . Would be nice to have a little mite in the family again. Bound to be pretty, specially if it took after the Henderson side. . . . I remember Davin Henderson, your grandpa, mighty well. Aside from being a mite thin, he was one of the handsomest men I ever did see. . . ."

God, oh God! Patricia wept inside her mind; I can't stop her. I have to let her ramble on like that. She's so old—so old. And such a sweet old thing, really. . . . From the depths of her broken spirit she summoned up a wan ghost of a smile.

"Here we are," Jeb said. "Wait, Grandma! Buck and I will help you down."

They trooped into the cemetery with Jeb supporting Sarah, and the colored boy, Buck, walking a little bit behind. He was a very nice, quiet boy. Sarah knew that because she had brought him up. She had, in her lifetime, brought up two generations of orphans, and both times the children had been of the two races: Wade's sons, Stone and Nat, and Buford's Fred at the same time; and now Roland, Stone's son; the last legal bearer of the Benton name; and Buck, Fred's son.

And Hank, too, halfway, she thought. I done what I could to help Jeb and Pat bring him up right. He was a fine boy. Maybe there's some excuse for automobiles 'cause they take you a mighty heap further and faster than horses. More comfortable, too. But airplanes was plumb an invention of the devil. The good Lord never meant for folks to go a-flying through the air. Roland's fault. He led Hank into that flying business. Should of never let him go abroad—then he couldn't of got into that there Lafayette Escadrille. . . .

Bentons are just too wild, she reflected bitterly. White or black they always have to get themselves killed off by the worst way a body ever heard of. Reckon Hank topped 'em all, though. First one I ever heard of who got killed by falling ten thousand feet straight down. . . .

Then she hobbled forward, leaning on Jeb's arm and her cane, toward the family plot. It was laid out in the form of the letter H. On one side were the Bentons and the other was reserved for the Duprés. Though the Benton side was nearly full, the Dupré side was all but empty, having but a single grave in it, which proved nothing except, perhaps, that the Duprés were less violent than their kindred.

But the cross bar of the capital H was the grave of the one man who was neither Benton nor Dupré, but who lay among them by common consent, continuing thus, even in death, the role he had played so faithfully in life: the link, the conciliator between those two often warring clans, born as they were of the same blood. Beloved of them both, Randy McGregor slept here the long sleep among the graves of the proud, intractable Bentons, and the equally proud, but quieter and more sensitive Duprés. It was as he had wished it, he, who had fathered no sons, but who had been more than father, guide, counselor to many, becoming thus in essence, clan chieftain, sage, leader of men who, fearing nothing that breathed, yet bowed in deference to his higher courage, sensing in it something superior to their own, though they knew not what it was.

It was Sarah who expressed it, without knowing how much more her words held bound in their simplicity than lay upon the surface:

"He was a good man," she said; "wasn't many like him . . ."

The others held back, watching her. They knew the pattern, and they made no attempt to alter it, would have, in fact, resented alteration, for this was ritual, now, made sacred by repetition, so that any change would have struck them as blasphemy.

First to the grave of Tom Benton, himself, the man who had ridden out of the sunset seventy-eight years ago to alter in the small span of eighteen years the life of the little community caught between the river and the bayou so completely that it was beyond conception that it would ever escape his stamp, his brand, the mold into which so violently he had forced it, pausing there in silent prayer for the soul of this turbulent man who had much need of prayer. Then, one by one, down the other Benton graves: Wade, Tom's son, of whose death, and the manner of it, no Benton ever spoke, nor any Dupré either, bound up as were both the families in it, so that not one of the younger generation yet knew its connection with the most rigid of their tribal tabus, the fact that pork was never served on any Benton table, a tabu so strictly enforced that now the townspeople honored it, with the result that Roland Benton had never tasted pork in any form in all his life. A little apart from him, his wife, Jeb's mother, lay; for Sarah's strict sense of justice prevented her from having Mary Ann laid by Wade's side as was customary; and propriety forbade burying her in the Dupré section, next to the place where Clinton, now, since 1904, also lay, which was just.

But for the twins, Wade's sons, one single grave sufficed: Stone had slept under the dreaming grass since that day in 1894 they had brought his broken body in, lifting the overturned buckboard off it; of Hope, his wife and Roland's mother, there was no sign. She lay in the graveyard of a Massachusetts 'Hospital' labeled thus by courtesy among the Bentons, though they, some of them at least, must have known it was, in sober fact, an institution for the insane. Nor did his brother Nat, almost his image, have here his resting place. Only a polished metal plaque recalled his memory. For he had been buried at sea.

Then Sarah turned and pointed toward the second plaque inscribed: "Sacred to the memory of Fred Douglass, faithful Negro servant to the Benton Family, who died gloriously atop San Juan Hill in defense of his Country. 1876-1898."

Buck drew himself up stiffly before this tribute placed in honor of his father among the mighty dead. He didn't remember his father or his mother. He had been a year old when Fred was killed in action. And his mother, a high yellow girl, had departed with the drummer of a showboat band before his second birthday, leaving him to be cared for by Miz Sarah.

That Fred's death had been somewhat less than glorious was another thing that Sarah never mentioned. Partially out of a profound belief that no violent wrenching of a human soul out of life is ever glorious, and partially because from Nat's letters she knew the exact circumstances of his death, she never spoke of it. That the first Benton to die in battle was black, did not bother her. She was far above that peculiar littleness of soul. But what did bother her was the manner of it.

Nat had written from the field hospital where he lay, sweating his life out through every pore, "I'm very sick, and they're shipping me home next week. Maybe that's why I don't understand it. All I know is a skinny nigger boy named Fred Benton went up San Juan Hill in the very vanguard. He went up and he got to the edge of the trench with a group of his buddies when a piece of a shell from the American artillery hit him in the back. Those artillerymen killed more of our boys that day than all of the Spaniards put together. And when Lt. Colonel Teddy Roosevelt came storming up that hill every tooth and eyeglass gleaming, that skinny nigger boy Stone and I used to take turns kicking in the tail was already lying in the bottom of the trench, bleeding to death. Only they patched him up as well as they could and started him back down the hill on a stretcher, but it wasn't any good, because the whole division only had three ambulances. And when they got him down here, they laid him on the ground, not because he was black, Grandma, but because they had nowhere else to put him. They were doing the same thing with the wounded white boys, too.

"We've just gone through the worst-managed, worst-fought, maybe even the most dishonest war in our history. I say that because I'm sick and that makes me too sad, maybe; but also because Fred was wounded in line of duty by American artillery fire, and finished off by American Medical Corpsmen who didn't know their posteriors from an excavation.

"I'm tired. I don't understand it. He never had anything but a hard time from me and Stone, and all the world except you, Grandma. Why did he do it? Why was he brave?"

She had received the letter and the notification of Nat's death aboard that hospital ship the yellow journals transformed within a week to 'Horror' Ship. He had been killed by the same things that killed Fred: bungling, inefficiency, the crass stupidity implicit in the very idea of settling human disputes by mass murder. But she had the answer to that last question he had asked; and she said it now, standing beside a skinny gingerbread-colored boy in the cemetery in the rain:

"He was a Benton, too." That, to her, explained everything.

They went then to the section reserved for the Duprés. There was but one grave in it, so far, that of Jeb's father, Clinton. Of course, there had been other Duprés; but they were not of Benton blood. Besides, the first of them, Louis, had been hanged for killing Tom Benton; and Clinton's mother, Lolette, whose name had been given him because she had had no legal right to bear his father's, lay in the Saint Louis Cemetery in New Orleans. In New Orleans, too, in the Cemetery of Saint Vincent de Paul, lay the almost unmarked grave of another Dupré whom neither Jeb nor Hank had ever heard of. But any number of sporting gentlemen could have given them a rather complete account of Babette, Clint's mother's sister, who for so many years had enjoyed the unique distinction of being listed in *The Blue Book* as the "Queen of the Madams of Storeyville." That was another of the many things that Sarah never told them.

"He was a real nice boy," Sarah said aloud, standing by Clint's headstone. "You look like him, Jeb—only you're better looking. But his life was sad. . . ."

It had been, too—the rest of it, after Mary Ann's death; but out of that sadness had grown the Dupré fortune, so that today they were far wealthier than the Bentons had ever been. Having left only the child, Jeb, having only this living reminder of the love that had cost three lives in a single afternoon, Clint had centered all his affection upon the boy. Nothing had been too good for Jeb. And being possessed still of a considerable portion of the fortune his mother had left him, as well as the ownership of two newspapers, one in Benton's Row, and the other in Memphis, Clinton had set out to see that Jeb had it all, everything in the whole world.

Young as he was at the time of Mary Ann's death, Clinton never married, did not, men swore in awed wonder, ever again so much as look seriously at another woman, bending thus all his energies, and his not inconsiderable talents to the task of making money. With these, and the great advantage of a comfortable sum to start with, he plunged into publishing, controlling a string of journals in New Orleans, Natchez, Baton Rouge, Memphis, Minden, Shreveport, and several other towns. With the money thus gained, he financed a cottonseed oil plant, a lumber concern, a turpentine and related products works growing out of the lumber business and sawmill, branched out naturally into papermaking, until, at his death in 1909, he was a millionaire many times over. But, as Jeb had said, he died of loneliness and fatigue as much as from the pneumonia which finally killed him.

But for Sarah, Jeb might have grown up spoiled, a typical example of too much money, paternal indulgence, and the purposelessness of a man too rich ever to need concern himself with the problem of gaining a livelihood. Sarah, however, supplied the discipline, guiding him with the same stern, loving hand that she did his half brothers, Stone and Nat Benton, making, for that matter, precious little distinction even between them and black Fred Douglass Benton, orphaned by the schoolhouse fire that had killed his parents about the same time.

So Jeb had grown up unspoiled, completed his education at the Sorbonne, traveled widely on the continent, and returned at last to marry Patricia Henderson of that Henderson family with whom the Bentons had been warring for two generations, and promptly fathered another Benton-Dupré, giving him, in fact, both names, Henry Benton Dupré, which his boyhood friends and later the family reduced to merely Hank.

But the full name was there on the newer, brighter bronze plaque before which Patricia stood now weeping, quietly, hopelessly, with absolutely unbearable grief:

"In Loving Memory of Second Lieutenant Henry Benton Dupré, of the Ninety-Fourth Pursuit Squadron U. S. Army Air Corps, Born April 2nd, 1895, Killed in Action, June 10th, 1918, in the air, above the Villeneuve Sector, while fighting gloriously against overwhelming odds. In his death he honored his country, his family, and himself."

The words were taken from the letter Patricia and Jeb had received from Hank's squadron commander. From his almost brother, Roland Benton, who had witnessed Hank's death, there had been no word. He had merely, being a Benton, avenged it.

Standing there, in the soft drip of the water from the trees, for the rain had stopped now, looking upon the graves of her own offspring and Tom's, and also upon Tom's descendants in which she had no share of blood, Sarah began to form it in her mind, this thing which a lifetime of living with them had given her; and when she had it at last, she said it:

"Reckon there's some people just naturally born to trouble the world, to stir it up out of its sleepy ways. They come along, and nothing's the same any more. They cause a mighty heap of crying, and hurtfulness and even the shedding of blood. It's been hard for me, specially since the Bentons got the bad habit of getting themselves killed off, and leaving their babies for me to raise. I've done that twice now, with Wade's children, and afterwards with Stone's. Even the Benton niggers got the same bad habit. But I'm too old now; and I'm too tired. All I can do now is hang on like I promised Roland I was going to, till he gets back. I'm asking the Good Lord to spare me that long; and maybe a little while more—long enough to see Roland's first child, if he ever has one. Don't reckon I can die content until I know there's going to be some more Bentons in the world. . . ."

She paused, and a smile lighted her frail, beautifully wrinkled face, etched by time, by her own goodness, her enduring strength into something very fine under its halo of white hair.

"It's been hard. But don't misdoubt me: I wouldn't of missed it for nothing in the world. Come on, you-all, we got to be going. Cora'll have dinner ready by now."

In the car, on the way back out to Broad Acres to celebrate the tribal custom of always eating Sunday dinner there, Patricia said:

"No word from Roland yet? When they're coming, I mean?"

"Roland don't write," Sarah said; "but Stormy told me they were having to go through a mighty heap of red tape trying to get that child into this country. Hope I'm going to like her. It'll be strange having a foreign great-granddaughter-in-law . . ."

"Oh you'll like her all right," Jeb said enthusiastically; "Athene's absolutely adorable!"

"Think I will, Pat child?" Sarah said; "can't take a man's word for it—men are such fools when it comes to a pretty face."

"Yes," Patricia said. "She is the sweetest little thing, as kind as the day is long. At first I didn't think she was pretty because she's so—so French. But after I got to know her I saw she was more than pretty—she's actually beautiful—all the way through, Granny, if you get what I mean."

"I do," Sarah said. "That makes me feel a heap better about it."

"She and I got along famously," Pat said. "I'd heard a lot about her the first time Jeb and I were in Paris on the way to his job with the Red Cross in Switzerland. But I didn't meet her until we came back to France about a month after the Armistice. Then I saw what she was like. She—she'd met Hank, you know. She came up to me and kissed me, as though she'd known me all her life, and said: 'He was so very nice, your son. I loved him, too. He was like my brothers.' And I didn't find out until after the wedding, until Stormy told me, that she had had all three of her brothers killed in action, and her husband, too. She hadn't been married a month when that happened—like, like Hank, Granny, shot down in flames."

"Don't, child," Sarah said, and put her arm about Patricia's shoulders. "You've cried enough, I reckon."

"They're still at Stormy's?" Jeb said harshly.

"Yes," Sarah said.

"That's good. Stormy has a lovely old house in the Passy section—a real *Hôtel Particulier* with a garden. I was very happy there when I stayed with her when I was studying in France."

"Granny," Patricia said; "why won't Aunt Stormy come back home?"

"She was mixed up in a scandal she really didn't have nothing to do with," Sarah said. "A man she knew, a friend of hers, embezzled a lot of money from the lottery company. Since she'd gotten him the job in the first place, the newspapers claimed she helped him do it. But they couldn't prove it. And they were wrong. Stormy was wild and wicked and meaner than old hell, but she weren't dishonest. I know that."

"That's why she went abroad in the first place?" Pat said.

"Yes. She left in a huff; and she's been living in Paris ever since, except for that six-months visit she paid us in 'Ninety-four. Wouldn't come home for General Rafflin's funeral. Reckon he wouldn't have minded much if he had known. Never seemed to mind anything else she did, which was plenty. Old man like him, marrying a girl young as Stormy was when they got hitched, knows what to expect, I reckon. Went right ahead and left her so much money that it would take her more than the rest of her life to count it. She moves with the best over there. The Metroyers introduced her all around, since she'd been a friend of theirs in New Orleans."

"She sure does," Jeb said. "She dragged Athene over to meet Roland the day he arrived. Athene's family dates back to François I; she's a noblewoman, you know, Grandma—a Viscountess."

"That's so?" Sarah said; "never did have much faith in European nobility—mostly no good from all I heard tell. But I won't hold it against her, long as she's nice."

"Oh she's all right," Pat said; "and Roland's lucky. I was worried sick that he'd get too involved with that other one."

"What are you children talking about?" Sarah said.

"Oh just a girl Roland used to know," Pat said quickly. "Seems she tried to hook him, but he was smart enough to get away. Don't worry about it, Grandma."

"I won't," Sarah said.

They had turned into the yard before they saw the taxi. Roland stood beside it, while the driver unloaded the bags. Nothing that any of them had told her had prepared Sarah for the way her great-grandson looked. She took off her glasses, polished them, put them on again. It did no good, the tall young man who stood there was wraith thin, emaciated almost skeletal. She could not have recognized him but for his eyes, those terrible Benton eyes of blue ice, staring at her with the dead-level steadiness she remembered not only from him, but from his father and great-grandfather, but with something else in them now, something new, that was bad, very bad, the worst thing in the world, although she did not know what it was. Even his hair was different, being no longer the dark honey-blond color which he alone of all her descendants had gotten from her, but thickly gray thatched, the temples already snowy, so that although he was only twenty-six years old, he seemed immeasurably older than Jeb who was nearly twice his age.

He came toward the car, moving awkwardly, slowly, tiredly; and the girl followed him. He stuck his head in through the window.

"Grandma," he said huskily.

"Roland," she wept. "Roland-boy. Lord God, Roland!"

He opened the door and all but lifted her out. The girl came forward shyly.

"Grandma," Roland said, "this is Athene."

Sarah stood there, staring at her. Athene was a small girl. She was tiny, beautifully formed, exquisite. What held Sarah there was her coloring. She had never even asked about that, assuming that being French the girl must fit her provincial Southern conception of a 'greasy foreigner'—dark hair, olive complexion, oily skin; but Athene du Bousquier Benton was none of these. She was as fair as a Scandinavian with silvery blonde hair, cut, Sarah saw, with growing wonder, almost as short as a boy's, and eyes of a shade between blue and green. She wore a simple suit, whose singing perfection of cut, matchless chic, and skirt that stopped short eight inches above her ankles revealing the loveliest pair of legs that anyone in Benton's Row had ever seen, were to earn her the undying enmity of every woman in town the moment they saw it.

"Well, child," Sarah said helplessly.

"Enchanted, Madame," Athene whispered; then: "May I please kiss you, *Grandmère?* I want to—oh so very much!"

"Of course, child," Sarah said, and gathered her into her arms. And it was over, then and there, all the anticipated difficulties, all the strangeness, all the fear.

They sat on the veranda after the dinner was over, and talked.

"Yes," Athene said, "I met Roland at the house of your very *gentille* daughter, Madame Rafflin. She is a *Grande Dame*, absolutely formidable, and from the day she met me she was planning to capture me for Roland. It was not, you comprehend, *Grandmère*, a thing difficult to do. The first time I saw him I had the most horrible fear because I was already engaged to a very nice boy—also a *pilôte*—and your Roland was so very handsome and gay and charming and wonderful and formidable I was afraid."

"You married this boy you were engaged to, didn't you?" Sarah said.

"Yes, *Grandmère*, I married him—and we had one week end for a honeymoon—and he was called to the front. He had to fly an *avion* that only the *bon Dieu* and my prayers kept in the air at all. It was all we had in those days. And one day he encountered the great *Capitaine* Boelcke mounted on a machine like a falcon with a machine gun on it while my poor Raoul had only a little pistol he carried strapped to his side . . ."

She bowed her head a long moment.

"I am sorry," she said, when she straightened up, "but he was a very nice boy. And it is not pleasant to think that he had to jump because his machine was in flames."

"Don't," Patricia said, her voice shuddering up out of her throat, shredded upon her breath, torn; "please, Athene!"

Athene jumped up and ran to her, embracing her, and crying, "I am so sorry!" she said. "I am a pig and a selfish beast! I had forgotten."

"It's all right," Patricia whispered. "It's all right, dear."

Jeb sat there, staring at the floor.

"Look, Roland," he said heavily; "I never asked you this before. But could you tell me about my boy?"

Roland stared at him, and his blue eyes splintered into slivers of ice, so that Jeb watching it, turned away his head.

"No," Roland said, and that was all he said, just that one word, 'no'—without explanation, without even inflection, so that after he had said it the silence was almost tactile.

Athene stood up.

"This is very bad," she said; "we have spoiled things with sadness. It is spring now—and Louisiana is lovely, more lovely than I imagined anywhere could be—let us be happy—let us all be happy, please."

"You will do, child," Sarah said. "Looks like my boy did all right for himself; yessir—I think you did just fine, son."

"Thank you for that, Grandma," Roland said.

But in the predawn hours of that same night, Athene and Roland lay beside one another starkly awake, staring out into the darkness. Athene was crying.

"She asked me if I were *enceinte*," she whispered. "She wants so much that your family go on—that you should not be the last, my Roland. And I—I wish it, too! I want children—many children but I told you that—and you said you also wanted them."

She came up on one elbow, staring at the outlines of his form in the darkness.

"Why won't you love me, Roland?" she whispered. "In *le bon Dieu's* name, tell me why?"

He lay there, staring at the ceiling.

"Wrong word," he said flatly; "not won't. Can't."

She put her head against the hollow of his throat, and her small arm across him.

"You lie, Roland," she said dreamily. "Remember the night of the Gothas? The night that nice black man brought you home?"

She raised up, holding herself above him with her two hands pressed into the pillow beside his head.

"Is it that you require an air raid to excite you?" she said bitterly, "or can you only make love with girls with whom you are not married—like that *sale* Martine!"

"Athene," he said wearily, "what woke you up?"

"You—you were beginning to make noises. I was afraid you would scream again and wake *Grandmère*. . . ."

"That's it, Athene," Roland said.

"What is it, *mon coeur?*"

"The noises—don't you see, *Ange*, it's the same thing? It's a thing inside me. I do not remember when I awake that I cried out or why. But it is the same thing. And when I dominate it—we will be all right."

She smiled then, put her fingers into his hair, ruffling it, laughing. Her moods always changed like that, mercurially.

"I will not wait," she teased; "I will take a lover. I will take your Uncle Jeb for a lover, because he is such a beautiful man."

"Not beautiful, Athene—handsome. We only say beautiful of women . . ."

"Then you are wrong. He is beautiful and you are beautiful. But it is you whom I love. You, *mon brave type*, my tired old cabbage, my ancient pair of shoes."

She bent down and kissed his mouth. She kissed him a long time. Then she pulled away and stared at him.

"Roland . . ." she whispered.

"No, Athene," Roland Benton said.

2

JEB DUPRÉ stood there watching his wife packing their clothing. The other things, the furniture, the dishes and glassware were already packed. Their winter clothes were already gone, Jeb had shipped them to New York nearly a month ago. They themselves should have been gone long before. It was a good thing that Martin O'Conner was both a friend and an understanding man. It had been easy to explain to him the impossibility of their leaving before Roland arrived. It wouldn't have been right to leave anybody as old as grandma in the hands of the slovenly and careless servants who were all one could get these days. When he had been a boy, the Negroes had been comparatively unspoiled; but now—

Nor could they ask Grace, Hank's widow, to go on taking care of her. Grace Bradley Benton was a young woman—she had a right to a life of her own. He'd heard that she was seeing a lot of that Nelson boy these days. Harvey Nelson wasn't a bad sort, for all that his folks had been both Yankees and carpetbaggers. Still, Jeb reflected bitterly, she sure Lord got over her grief fast. Moved back with her own folks the day after we arrived—

He didn't need the job in New York. There was not, never had been any question of the money involved. Although he had gained the reputation of being one of the most brilliant lawyers in the State, he had gained it at the cost of his personal popularity, by taking the cases of impecunious poorwhites, and Negroes, his sole criterion for accepting a case being his belief that the accused had been unjustly treated. Since to be a pine-barren cracker or a black in the South meant that a man lived in a constant state of injustice, Jeb had never lacked cases—most of which he won; but rarely gaining a red copper from any of them. These two things his father, Clinton Dupré, Tom Benton's illegitimate son, had left him: a perhaps overdeveloped sense of justice, of moral indignation, and the money which afforded him the luxury of indulging his crusading spirit. The only reason, then, that he had accepted the position of Executive Vice-President of the O'Conner Enterprises, Inc. was to escape the thousand constant reminders of his son with which he was surrounded in Benton's Row. In this point of view Patricia concurred. If they were to have any kind of life at all, it would have to be somewhere else.

They had met Martin O'Conner in Switzerland, where they had gone in 1916 in pursuit of one of Jeb's causes, taking care of French and Belgian orphans brought into the tiny neutral state by the Red Cross. O'Conner, who had given not only a large part of his personal fortune but his own services to the work, had been in charge of the bureau in which Jeb was placed. The moment he had heard Jeb's fluent idiomatic French, he made Jeb his assistant; and the deep respect which the two forceful, brilliant men held for each other ripened into real friendship. More than that, Mary O'Conner became equally fond of Patricia, and the friendship of the executive's wife has never been an inconsiderable factor in American business affairs.

"Jeb, darling," Patricia said, "don't stand there looking so fierce. It doesn't help you look any more like an executive. Besides, you don't have to change—I like you as you are."

"Like me?" Jeb said, making an effort at gayety. "Heck, woman, all this time I've been laboring under the illusion that you loved me!"

"Sometimes, once in a while," Pat said. "I married you, didn't I?"

Jeb looked at her, and his dark eyes were somber.

"Yes," he said quietly, "you did."

"Jeb," Pat said, "don't think about that. I married you because I loved you. I was pretty brazen about it, I think—chasing you all the way down to New Orleans. I'm glad of one thing, though. . . ."

"What's that?" Jeb said.

"That Stone—died while we were on our honeymoon. Hadn't been for that, you never would have believed me. You'd still be thinking that I came to you because I'd lost all hope."

"Hadn't you?" he said, and the little note of anger was there in his voice.

"No. I did it because I was finally sure I loved you," Pat said.

"Sorry," Jeb said, and smiled. "Reckon I'm just naturally crazy as far as you're concerned, Pat. Else I wouldn't still be jealous of a dead man. Anyhow, now we can go. I'm sure glad Roland's back. I can stop worrying now. The war seems to have sobered him up a lot. He'll behave himself now. . . ."

Pat shook her head gloomily.

"He won't," she said. "He's Stone's son, remember. And you were brought up with Stone, so you ought to know."

He looked at her, his eyes dark and questioning.

"Stop looking at me like that!" she said. "It's insulting. I was never Stone's mistress, since you insist upon knowing. Also, since you insist upon picking a quarrel with me—it was his fault I wasn't, not mine. I would have been, if I had had the chance. Now get out of here, and let me finish this packing, or we'll never get up to New York in time!"

"Pat!" he said, and his voice was stricken.

She came over to him and put both hands on his shoulders.

"I'm sorry, Jeb," she said. "I'm a very honest woman, only sometimes I talk too much. That day you stormed out of the house swearing I'd never see you again, I knew I didn't care what Stone did—that I'd been an awful fool. I started to cry. Then I decided that wasn't any good either. So I came after you. And I've never been sorry—not for a minute. Besides, Jeb, we're middle-aged people now. A man forty-five years old shouldn't act like a child. And I'm a grown woman. I don't moon over a ghost. We Hendersons aren't icebergs, you know; and a ghost is entirely too insubstantial for me!"

He smiled at her, but the smile was sad.

"Get on with your packing, then," he said; "I've a few more papers to clear up. If you want me for anything, I'll be in the study."

Heaven deliver us from an oversensitive man! Pat thought, and turned back to the valises.

He had, of course, no other papers to finish. All he had, actually, was the necessity to remember it all again, to sort it out, to try to analyze it. He sat before his desk in his study, and took a Sweet Caporal out of the mahogany box. He did not light the cigarette at once, but remained there, like that, gazing off into space, the unstruck match cupped in his hand, allowing himself to drift backward in time, back to that summer of enchantment.

At that time, the summer of 1892, the magical one, he had been only eighteen years old. He had come home for the long vacation from the exclusive private school for rich men's sons in New York City to which Clint had sent him. He had not been back in Benton's Row a week before he accidentally encountered Patricia Henderson in the street. And that was the end of it, the finish of the various directions his life might have taken. From that moment, it was settled, though he did not know it then.

He stopped dead, open-mouthed, staring at her.

"I could love you," he groaned. "To tell the truth I already do!"

For more than half that golden summer they were sweethearts—for two whole months of magic. Sitting there in his study, so many years later, Jeb realized that there had never again been a summer like that one, nor could there ever be. . . .

It was so—so innocent, he mused. Yes, that was it—and that's one of the things a man can rightly weep for: the loss of innocence, the blight that falls so soon upon all trusting, believing, faith. . . . I remember the first night I kissed her—near the end of summer. Lord God, how clumsy I was! And she cried. . . .

He struck the match, lit the cigarette, drew in deeply, exhaled, the smoke veiling his face.

I must have apologized a hundred times. Then she stopped crying and looked at me like a mischievous little water nymph and said: "I was just crying 'cause I'm happy, Jeb. Go on, kiss me again."

But those were the days no man can keep, that he can only cherish inside his heart. And they had ended badly, for in late August, his half-brothers Stone and Nat Benton had come home from Virginia. It was a hot month, and Stone was bored. So he amused himself with little Patricia Henderson, took her buggy riding, teased her, made outrageous love to her, in banter, in jest, though she did not take it so. Then, suddenly, it was done. Stone disappeared for two weeks, and came back to Benton's Row with Hope Crandall on his arm.

When he heard from Nat the story of his brother's marriage, Jeb rushed over to the Henderson Place. When he knocked on the door, and had been announced, he heard Pat's voice sounding clearly from the bedroom:

"Tell him to go away. I don't want to see him!"

And he, being himself, and young, turned and walked away from there. He went straight to his father's office. Clinton was sitting behind his desk, reading some reports. He took off his glasses and looked at Jeb.

"I want to go away, Dad," Jeb said. He had started to call Clint "Dad" when he was eight years old, in order to distinguish him from Wade, whom he had called papa.

"Far away."

Jeb was gone two years. He spent those two years in Paris, living with his Aunt Stormy in her lovely old house in Passy. He read for the law. He fancied himself a man of the world. He made his conquests among the little midinettes, minor actresses, barmaids, and daughters of concierges. He was a remarkably blasé, sophisticated young man. He knew wines, and the best years of their vintage. He could order a meal like a true gourmet. He had at his tongue tip all the latest patter of the art world.

When, in 1894, he came home again, it was not, in truth, of his own free will, but because his Aunt Stormy had succumbed at last to her homesickness, her desire to see her aged mother one last time before she died. And trying to oppose Stormy's wishes was like trying to oppose the hurricane that had given her her name. They sailed from Le Havre late in March, and arrived in Benton's Row the first of April, some weeks after Patricia Henderson had come home, from Oberlin College, announcing flatly that she wasn't going back. "Expelled," the gossips whispered, at first, then said it aloud as the weeks wore on and everyone saw what she was doing.

Patricia Henderson, riding boldly by daylight through the streets of Benton's Row in Stone Benton's buggy, married as he was, and the father of a year-old son, crowded the latest atrocity in Cuba out of men's consciousness, becoming a topic of conversation far more exciting to the townspeople than even the ever approaching war with Spain.

The good Baptist Ladies paid a call upon Ashton Henderson. He showed them the door.

"My daughter is a Henderson," he said. "And Hendersons ain't responsible to you. They're responsible only to their own consciences and to God. We ain't obliged to live the way your dirty minds think we ought to. Long as we're doing right, we don't have too much truck with appearances. Good day, ladies. Next time tend to your quilting bees and your good works, and don't go poking your noses into what don't rightly concern you."

But, afterwards, he spoke to Pat about it.

"You behaving yourself, girl?" he said gruffly. "Don't want to have to take a pistol to that boy. Be a pity, him with a young child."

"I always behave myself, Papa," Pat said; "I like Stone. If he were free, I'd marry him. But he's not free, and I'm not a fool. I don't intend to ruin my life like that Lolette Dupré did. Right now, he claims to be awful unhappy with that frozen Massachusetts witch. I feel sorry for him. If he divorces her, or she dies, I'll marry him. But I won't be any man's mistress—not even Stone's."

"Folks are talking," Ash growled. "Sometimes you got to avoid the appearance of evil."

"To heck with them and their talk! I like Stone. I like being in his company. But if he hasn't done anything more than complain about how bad his life is by Christmas, I'm leaving. Six months, Papa. And in the meantime, don't worry about your girl . . ."

Even out at Broad Acres, Jeb heard the talk. He worried over it for a week, then put the question to Nat:

"Is this thing serious?" he said. "Are they having an affair?"

"Damned if I know," Nat growled. "I don't think so. Stone's having trouble with his wife. I think he'd like to divorce her and marry Pat. But there ain't but two grounds for divorce in Louisiana: desertion and adultery. Either way, Hope gets Roland. And that's what's got Stone hooked. He's crazy about that kid. Ain't the faintest chance of pinning anything on Hope. She doesn't even want to sleep with Stone, let alone another man. And she's still in love with him after her peculiar Yankee fashion. So if anybody causes a divorce, he'll have to. Make a mighty big mess if he does. You know how strait-laced folks are hereabouts . . ."

"What—about Pat?" Jeb whispered.

"Pat's a lady. You ought to know that. She'll marry Stone if he gets himself out of this. But she's not going to help him, and start her life out under a cloud. And I don't think she's fool enough to accept backstreet living. But you can't tell about a girl when she's in love. . . ."

"Nor a man," Jeb said miserably. "Come on, Nat, let's ride down to Tim's and have a drink."

"Right," Nat said.

When they entered the building, Nat clutched Jeb's arm, and pointed to the glass doors of the tea room.

"Lord God!" he whispered; "look at that!"

She moved among the tables, clad in the trim black uniform with the frilled white apron and cap that Tim insisted upon for his waitresses. Her red hair was drawn up in a chaste bun on the back of her neck.

Even now, twenty-five years after that day, Jeb could remember all of it, the gray-green of her eyes, her lips full, a trifle pouting, the way she walked, the combination of small details that changed the aspect of a beauty really exquisite, made it something else. In repose the girl could have sat for a painting of a Madonna by a pre-Raphaelite master; but the moment she raised her heavy-lidded eyes and looked at them, the first time she moved half a yard, that illusion was gone, completely destroyed, and another had taken its place.

"Ought to be a law," Nat breathed, "against a woman like that ever getting out of bed!"

"She'd probably kill a man in half a night," Jeb observed blandly; "I know that type."

"Oh death," Nat grinned, "where is thy sting!"

Nat must have waited around all evening until she came out, Jeb mused, thinking about it now, so many years afterwards. It's a pity he didn't have more sense; but then I don't suppose it would have made any real difference. . . .

He was right. It wouldn't have. In the next few weeks Benton's Row was rocked by excitement as profound as even the wave of feeling that swept over it four years later at the news of the sinking of the *Maine*.

Tim's receipts from the tea room tripled, quadrupled. For the first time since he opened it, the majority of its clientele became male. Even the number of women patrons increased. They came out of curiosity to see 'that awful creature,' as they called her.

Red, herself, was overwhelmed with invitations to go driving, picnicking, boating, by all the town's young blades. There were bloody fights over her; but she, driven by the same instinctive shrewdness that had made her resist all Big Belle's offers to make her number one girl at the Parlor House, realizing even then that her indisputable assets were worth far more than they could possibly command in that mass market—realizing that, and also that the road into which Belle and so many others were trying to drive her, led only one way, down; while she, in the very back of her brain had the idea, the desire, and the ambition to go up, to become indeed, mistress of this town, live finally in a great white house under the oaks, receiving the same women who now sneered at her—conducted herself with such circumspection that Tim was able to say very truthfully to the Baptist Ladies who came, demanding that he fire her:

"On what grounds, ladies? She's a good, hard worker, and honest as the day is long. You talk about the men staring at her and fighting over her; but tell me the truth—have any one of you heard one breath of scandal attached to her name? She behaves herself. All my girls do, or out they go, and they know it. That girl, since she came here, has conducted herself with more propriety than certain other young ladies from some of our best families, whom I wouldn't dare mention by name. I always try to be obliging, but I can't fire Saralee just because some of the younger bloods in this town haven't any self-control. It just isn't fair."

Nor could they budge him from his stand.

At Jeb's elbow, the telephone jangled. He picked it up.

"Yes?" he said; "why yes, Grandma. Pat's packing right now. Of course we'll come by to see you before we leave. Yes, Grandma. Sure thing, old dear, we'll write every week—come back to see you on vacations. Don't worry your pretty head about it—'bye now, Sweetheart—'bye."

I don't like to leave her, Jeb thought gloomily. Roland is as wild as Nat and Stone were then—I wonder how Stone got to Red? Everybody else failed. But that Stone was a true magician when it came to women— I remember how easily he charmed Pat. And afterwards—Red. He sat there, holding the stub of his cigarette, thinking about it.

He had gone driving several times with Pat that summer of 1894, not as often as he would have liked; but often enough, because, as she told him later, Pat was already gradually bringing herself to the point of a final break with Stone. She already knew it was no good; that Stone would never leave his wife so long as he was bound by his love for his child; but she couldn't quite bring herself to do it—for Stone, more than even Nat, had that magical quality of Tom Benton's, complete assurance, combined with vast animal vitality, and a kind of charm all the more appealing because he was totally unconscious of it.

During those drives, Jeb had come to grips with himself; and weeks before the final explosion, he was already sure. He loved Pat Henderson. He was going to marry her if it were humanly possible—which made the situation all the more maddening, to be balked thus by a man who could not have her except in a way that Jeb was prepared to die to prevent any man from accomplishing.

She laid a gentle hand on his arm the night he asked her.

"Please, Jeb," she said; "I can't—not now. I like you very much. Sometimes I think I love you. Then he comes along and—"

"And I'm gone, pouf, like that," Jeb said.

"Wait, Jeb. Listen to me. I've got to have time. Time to get this craziness out of my system. It wouldn't be fair for me to come to you with a divided heart. I'll tell you this, though—if I ever do marry anyone, it'll most likely be you."

"Thanks," he said bitterly, "thanks for nothing, Pat."

He turned the sorrel from her house and drove away to have it out with

his half brother, without troubling to reckon the danger involved in beard-
ing a Benton, knowing in his heart that this was one of the things he had
to do, if he wanted to be able to go on living with himself.

Hope, herself, opened the door.

"No," she said, all the enormous dignity of her New England ancestors
implicit in her tone, "he's not here, Jeb."

"Have you any idea—" Jeb began.

"You might try the Hendersons," Hope said quietly.

So, Jeb thought, you know, too. I should have known you would. There's
no escaping it. . . .

"No," he said, thinking that in this at least he could comfort her, "I just
came from there; I just took Pat home from a drive."

"Then I haven't any idea. Won't you come in, Jeb? Perhaps he'll come
back. . . ."

"No, thank you. If I don't run into him tonight, I'll stop by tomorrow
morning."

"As you like, Jeb," Hope Benton said.

But he did find Stone that night, becoming thus the first person in
Benton's Row to know what soon everyone knew, the basis for the feud
between the twins that threatened, before the unpredictable element of
chance entered into it, to end in the death of one or the other of them—
and this at his own brother's hand.

He came back to Broad Acres, not by the big gates, but by the bayou
road that led past the old Henderson Place, crumbling into ruin and
decay now; and heard, almost as an echo, an answering whinny to the
sound his own horse made. He pulled the sorrel up, and got down, going
on foot toward that house in which he himself had been conceived, although he did not know that then. And, as he came up behind it, he saw
Stone's buggy, the horse hitched to one of the crumbling fences.

He hung there dizzily, feeling something inside him ripping, something
bursting inside his heart, and the pain surging upward into his throat on
a rush of brine and fire.

Pat didn't go inside her house, he recalled savagely. She was still
standing there when I left. Waiting—for him. This is the end of it. I'll go
back with Aunt Stormy. And maybe, one day, when I'm a hundred years
old, I'll forget. . . .

He turned back toward his own buckboard. He had almost reached it,
when it came to him that he actually did not know it was Patricia in that
house with Stone. He turned in a wild surge of hope, and came back, running, making no effort to move quietly, pounding up onto the veranda,
calling:

"Stone! Stone!"

There was the sound of someone moving within. Jeb put his hand on
the door, shook it furiously, crying:

"Open, damn you! I know you're in there!"

The door crashed open. Stone stood there in the light of the risen moon, clad only in a pair of trousers, his feet bare. His hand shot out, catching Jeb by the shirt front, and the muscles of his arm knotted, lifting the younger man clear of the floor.

"You dirty little sneak!" he spat. "I've got a good mind to—"

Then he saw that Jeb was looking past him, over his shoulder, oblivious to danger, or to fear. There was an odd expression in Jeb's eyes, and after a moment, Stone saw that it was joy.

"Put me down, Stone," Jeb said softly; "I'm sorry I broke in. You see, I thought—it was Pat in there."

Looking at his watch, as he drove away from there, Jeb was surprised to see it was only eleven o'clock. Tim's bar at the Central Hotel would still be open, and every anguished nerve in his whole body cried out for a drink.

At the bar he joined his half brother.

" 'Lo, Nat," he said.

"Hiyuh, kid," Nat said morosely. "What're you drinking?"

"Bourbon. But it appears to me you've had enough."

"Ain't drunk," Nat muttered. "Ain't drunk a-tall. Just sick, kid. All my life I've been able to take my women or leave them. But not now. Lord God, not now!"

"What the devil are you talking about, Nat?" Jeb growled.

"Red. Was just a game at first. Thought I'd take her out a few times, have myself some fun—a little roll in the hay, and that would be that. Only, it wasn't. . . ."

Dear God! Jeb thought.

"I'm hooked. Can't get her out of my system, kid. I got to have her for keeps."

"God, no!" Jeb whispered.

"I'm going to marry her, kid. Going to marry her and make a decent woman of her. I know it'll damn near kill Grandma, but I can't help it."

Jeb stood there, holding the whiskey glass between his hands. It was neither the time nor the place to reason with Nat, and he knew it.

"Let's go home, Nat," he said. "We can talk about it tomorrow. Things will look a lot different by daylight."

Nat reached over, took Jeb's untasted drink from between his hands, and tossed it down at a gulp.

"It'll never be any different," he said.

And it wasn't. Even now, in this year of Our Lord, 1919, twenty-five years afterwards, Jeb didn't know the why of it. He knew, in a general way, and that only in part, what had happened. Of the people who knew more of it, only Stormy Benton was alive to tell it, she, and perhaps the woman, Red, herself; but no one in Benton's Row knew where Red was, or had even heard whether or not she was alive or dead.

By late fall, everybody in the Row knew about it: that intense, terrible rivalry of two brothers over the same woman, fought out with cold ferocity, though, in sober fact, one of them had no right to her; nor, perhaps, even the other, for no man has a right to his own destruction.

Jeb was caught in the very middle of it. He was arbiter between his brothers, cursed at, and berated by them both; torn, at the same time, by the spectacle of Patricia's helpless grief, having to watch the object of his adoration suffer from an emotion she was powerless to control, kept from him, who had every right to her by this insane barrier of feeling, watching this thing mount up, until even the love the twins bore one another was no longer enough, and Death, himself, stood between them, spectrally waiting.

It was too much for him finally. He had to get out of it, had to change something, had, in fact to end this hiatus in his existence, begin once more to live. He rode to the Hendersons; but Patricia was not there. He whirled his horse and pounded down the bayou road. Long before he reached the old house, he met her coming back, riding side saddle, her face whiter than the moonlight, paler than dead dreams or lost hope.

"You were with him," he snarled at her. "God in heaven, Pat, I—"

She shook her head.

"No," she said; "I wasn't. *She* was."

They sat there, like that, on the horses, looking at each other.

"Pat," he whispered.

"Yes, Jeb?" she said tiredly.

"Marry me," he said. "Now—tonight. I'll take you away from here. New York, Paris—anywhere you want. I'll be good to you. I don't care what you've done. . . ."

"No, Jeb," she said. "Not now."

"Why not?" he spat.

"If I married you tonight," she said quietly, "it would be for the wrong reasons. When I do, it will be for the right ones: when I'm really free to love you, Jeb. Let's not talk about it now. I'm sick, and hurt, and terribly confused. . . ."

"I'll never ask you again," he said flatly.

She smiled at him; but he saw the tears on her face, bright in the moonglow.

"Then I'll have to ask you," she said, "when it's time. Come, Jeb, be sweet and ride home with me . . ."

He turned the horse about and came up alongside her.

"Very well," he said; "let's go. . . ."

A week later, he was in a saloon on the edge of Storeyville in New Orleans. He was dimly aware that there was a woman with him; but he couldn't remember what her name was, or how she'd got there. He didn't even know what she looked like. He kept peering at her owlishly, but her face kept blurring off into blobs of color, suspended somewhere in the haze of cigar smoke.

" 'Nother drink, Cookie?" she kept saying to him.

He'd never really been drunk before. Tipsy, yes—in Paris, particularly. But not like this—never before for a whole week like this. He didn't especially like the feeling; but it was better than not being drunk, than being alive, cold sober, and having to remember Pat's face in the moonlight, with the tears on it, crying for his half brother. He couldn't get her face out of his mind; it kept getting between him and the shapeless, painted blob of the woman. He could see it now. It was very close to him. He could see the tears in her eyes. And he didn't want to see her face. He couldn't bear seeing it. He shook his head to clear it. But when he stopped shaking his head and opened his eyes it was still there: it, and all the rest of her, too.

"Get rid of the whore, Jeb; I'm here," Pat said.

They were married the next night, after she had nursed him through one of the most formidable hangovers in recorded history. They had a two-day honeymoon on Pat's money, for Jeb had gone through his by then. Finally that was all gone, and Jeb wired his father for more.

Four hours later, the answer came. Jeb tore open the yellow envelope. Then Pat saw him stiffen, his lips go completely white.

"What is it?" she whispered.

He couldn't answer her. He passed the telegram over.

"Hundred dollars waiting, reception desk," she read. "Come home at once. Stone is dead. Your Dad."

She stood there, holding it.

"Jeb—" she got out.

"Yes, Pat?"

"You won't mind if I cry? I've got to, Jeb; I can't help it."

"No," he said. "Go on and cry, Pat. Cry for both of us. I—I loved him, too. . . ."

He had put it together from bits and snatches gathered here and there. His father told him how his Aunt Stormy had rung the doorbell loudly in the middle of the night, then marched grimly into the house, saying:

"You'd better come. Stone's down on the bayou road, with the buggy and a horse on top of him. I think he's dead."

"Good God!" Clint whispered.

"You'd better phone that fool Doctor whatever you call him. And some other men, too. I tried to move him, and I couldn't. You're going to need quite a few to get that horse off him."

"What happened?" Clint said.

"Runaway. She was driving. That red-haired witch, I mean. I followed 'em. I meant to give 'em both a piece of my mind. I know from hard experience that that kind of peccadilloes mean nothing but trouble for all concerned."

"Come into the study and phone for me," Clint said. "That'll give me time to get dressed."

"All right. Clint—there's one more thing I'd better tell you. I couldn't see too well, but I'd swear my dying oath she threw away those reins."

"Why?" Clint got out; "Name of God, Stormy—why?"

"I don't know," Stormy said; "I've been a female all my life, and I'll be damned if I can tell you what goes on inside another woman's mind."

"I asked her to marry me," Nat told him. "She said she'd give me her answer tomorrow. I knew she'd been going out with Stone; but what could I do? You can't kill your own brother, 'specially not when you've been as close as Stone and me. . . ."

He looked at Jeb, his eyes dull with pain.

"I put it to her," he whispered; "she just laughed and said: 'Don't worry, Nat—I'm going to marry a Benton, all right. Just as soon as I can figure which one—' Now she's gone. She wasn't killed. I found pieces of dress on the briars, like she'd gone through that wood in a hurry. I even got the dogs. They went plumb to the railroad tracks. Then they just ran back and forth, yelping. She's gone. But I'm going to find her, by God. And when I do—"

But it was Pat who explained it best, who formulated what was to him, at least, the most acceptable explanation:

"She loved him. She looked hard; but she wasn't. Not that hard, anyway. There is a man somewhere, some time who can reach any woman—any woman at all. . . ."

Jeb stood there, looking at his bride.

"He must have broken with her. He was a pretty decent sort at heart. He'd decided to give her up. For Nat's sake, most likely. Or maybe even for the sake of Hope and little Roland. Anyhow, something happened inside her heart and mind. She forgot all her schemes to marry a rich man, especially a Benton. She plain forgot and let herself be a woman, hurt and rejected, and blazing mad. Then she whipped that horse. Lord God, Jeb, one of the men with your dad told me he'd never seen such marks on an animal in his life. . . ."

"She murdered him," Jeb said.

"No. Not deliberately. She was just crazy mad. If she thought about it at all, I think she intended to die with him. Poor thing. . . ."

"You pity her?" Jeb said.

"Yes. Her and every woman born in sorrow, I pity her, and I'm grateful to her; because she gave me—you."

"She? Good God!"

"Yes, Love. She did it the night I came upon Stone in a buggy with her, pawing at her like a drunken beast. The same night you asked me to marry you. I couldn't then. It took me nearly a week—then, one morning I woke up, and I was free. It felt like a mountain had been lifted off my heart. I wanted to laugh, to sing, to cry. Then I got up and flew over to your house. Your dad told me you had gone to New Orleans, and I said: 'Oh, my God, I'll never find him, now!' "

"What did dad say?"

"He sort of grinned at me. Then he said: 'If I were a young lady looking for a young man whose heart I'd just broken, I'd make a tour of the saloons. He's probably drunk as an owl.' And you were, too! Only I didn't expect to find you with one of those horrible creatures. Tell me, Jeb, what was she like?"

"I don't know," Jeb said honestly; "I just looked up and there she was. . . ."

"I don't believe you," Pat said tartly.

"Any more than I believe there was nothing between you and Stone," Jeb said angrily. And there it was, in the open, the quarrel that had stayed with them for twenty-five years, that might even have destroyed their union but for little Hank's almost unseemly haste in appearing on the scene one year and five days almost to the hour that they started on their honeymoon.

He got up from his chair, and started for the stairs. There wasn't any more to it, not any more that he had been there to remember. All the rest was history told by others: Hope's startlingly swift decline into illusion, into madness—swift that is, until, upon talking to the Negroes, his father learned how long it had gone on before, starting, actually, upon the first night of her marriage to Stone, when that all-male Benton had insisted upon exercising his husbandly prerogatives in spite of her quivering terror, thus inducing what the little doctor in far-off Vienna was already beginning to call Trauma. Her condition improved, after a time, but deteriorated with the agony she suffered giving birth to Roland, and afterwards fluctuated with the alternations of tumult and quietude that were quite normal in any Benton household. Stone's death, of course, was the thing that caused the irreparable damage to her delicate mental equilibrium—

Nat vanished, to reappear only in uniform, home on leave, on his way, finally, to Cuba and death. And finally, Sarah insisted, old as she was, in her seventies, then, upon taking care of the orphaned Roland. "I won't be lonely, then," she had said; "besides, I know boys."

The only Benton left, Jeb thought, as he climbed those stairs. Except me—and I don't count. Hank would have been the one to carry on. Never thought what it would lead to when I took him down to see that first air meet in New Orleans—when was it? December, nineteen—nineteen ten. Hank was fifteen. That was what started it—Roland sneaking off to Marblehead and Newport News all during his years at college learning to fly. Missed his own graduation to test a new type of machine for Tony Dexter. . . .

Hank was never anything but Roland's satellite. Followed him into the

jaws of death itself. Only Roland came out again, and my boy didn't. . . .
He had to die, and in a way so bad that Roland won't even talk about
it. . . .

He came into the room, just as Pat snapped the last bag shut. She
whirled as he entered, and came close to him.

"If I may quote Athene," she whispered, "let us be happy, Jeb. Let
us be happy—please!"

3

"YOU'RE GOING to do it, Grandma," Roland Benton said. "Just like you
told me when I left. You're going to live to be a hundred—maybe more."

"Don't count on it, boy," Sarah said loudly. "I don't care much no
more. I just told you that so's you wouldn't be so worried. You'd come
back from Harvard the end of February, remember, and there it was
nigh onto the first of May, and you was still hanging around 'cause you
didn't want to go way and leave me. You was dying to get to France—
mainly 'cause you wanted to study some more of that flying foolishness—I
know that now. So I told you I had decided to live to be a hundred, smack
dab up to 1923, and that I'd took it up with the Lord. And you believed
me, 'cause you knew anything I set my mind on doing, I always managed to
do. So you went and got caught over there by the war. . . ."

"You also told me to be careful of Frenchwomen, too—remember?"
Roland grinned.

"That I did," Sarah snapped. "Should of known, seeing as how you're
a Benton, you wouldn't take my advice. But then, all I knew about them
then was what I read in books. And I never realized they had girls like
Athene over there. Kind of a daughter I always wished I'd had. Really
sweet. Yep, boy, you done yourself proud that time. . . . I'm glad 'cause
there's just one thing I'm waiting for now."

"What's that, Grandma?" Roland asked her.

"To see one more Benton come into the world," Sarah said.

Roland looked away from her, out over the sun-washed yard.

"There's some things a body hasn't any control over," he said. "Some
people never have any children."

"Bentons do," she snorted. "Only one I ever heard tell of who never
had no kids was your Uncle Nat—and he never even got married, poor
boy. You sure you're doing your part?"

He turned, stared at her.

"Why do you ask me that, Grandma?" he said.

"I'm a plain-spoken woman. Maybe too plain-spoken, but I have to tell the truth as I see it. That girl don't act like no satisfied wife, and that's a fact, Roland Benton."

Roland didn't answer her. He stood up, looking toward the big gates. "Here they come now," he said.

Grace Dupré's Ford T came rattling into the yard, drew up before the house and stopped in a furor of coughing and shaking. Grace all but fell from behind the wheel, and collapsed on the porch steps, overcome with laughter.

Athene climbed sedately down out of the car, and stood there staring. at her.

"Is it that I have done something really terrible, Grace?" she said.

"Roland!" Grace hooted; "she's priceless! She's absolutely priceless! Where on earth did you find her?"

"Paris," Roland said. "What's she done now?"

"She has sent Doc Meyers seven cases of near apoplexy—maybe more. When she walked in the door in *that* dress with her hair cut like that, Harriet Major dropped her cards on the floor. Lord it's cute—I'm having mine cut just like it tomorrow!"

"Doggoned practical," Sarah said, "hot as it gets down here. When I think of all the years I've wasted a-brushing and a-brushing with my mouth half full of hairpins . . ."

Athene looked from one of them to the other with big, wondering eyes.

"Was I brusque with them?" she said; "I did not mean to be—but they seemed to find everything I said shocking."

"It was when they got around to their favorite subject, 'How I manage my husband' that she really floored them. Know what she said? And in that cute little trick accent of hers that keeps them hanging on every word: 'But of course I do not manage *mon* Ro—land; that would be unthinkable. If he could be managed I could not love him, because then he would not be a man at all, but a thing, and it is very difficult to love a thing, *n'est-ce-pas?'* And when she said 'a thing' I kept lining them up in my mind: little old Henry Tolliver with his skinny legs and little round potgut, old man Major wheezing along, fatter than a brood sow—and . . ."

Athene came up to Roland and took both his hands in hers.

"You have not shame of me, my heart?" she said. "I would not have you have shame for anything in the world. . . ."

"No," Roland said. "No, little pigeon. You only gave them what they had coming to them a long time. I'm proud of you."

"Then," Athene laughed, shaking her small, bright head, "I do not care a fig for them! They are only droll types and of no importance at all—"

Cora came waddling out on the veranda.

"Dinner's ready," she said; "y'all better come'n'git it, 'fore hit gits cold."

Seated at the table, Roland saw Athene looking at the food with wide-eyed dismay. He did not blame her. If, in sober truth, the best that can be said for most American cooking is that it is mediocre, any adjective short of "abominable," applied to the culinary art of the Deep South, becomes a kindness.

She tasted a little of everything, then pushed her plate away.

"What's the matter, child?" Sarah said hopefully, "feeling squeamish?"

"No," Athene said, "I hope I do not again seem brusque, *Grandmère*—but this dinner is unfit for human consumption . . ."

"Dad-blame it, child," Sarah snapped, "if these vittles ain't fit to eat, I like to see what is!"

"Tomorrow I will prepare *déjeuner* for you, *Grandmère*," Athene said firmly, "if you will be so genteel as to keep those *negrés incroyables* out of the cuisine and let me attend to everything."

Grace leaned over close to Roland.

"Do you know what?" she whispered. "She's right. This is lousy food!"

Roland smiled; but he had already moved out and away from there, the question of food providing the bridge over which his mind sped backward in time to another lunch, five years ago now, to the day of his arrival in Paris, in 1914, in May, before the world had become unalterably changed; that day of enchantment in which he had met both Athene—and Martine.

On the boat train coming down from Le Havre to Paris, that long-lost day, Roland could feel the excitement mounting within him. Everything was heightened, everything pleased him.

Even the uproar at the Gare Saint Lazare pleased him. He was delighted to find he could understand every fourth or fifth word of the conversation of passersby. He realized at once that his grandaunt, Stormy Benton Rafflin, was not there to meet him; so he pushed his way out of the doors and engaged a taxi.

The driver exercised the immemorial privilege of taxi drivers: that is, hearing the thick accent, he promptly took Roland the long way, for which Roland forever afterwards blessed him; for on that drive, he found the second great love of his life—Paris.

It all delighted him, all of it. It meant something, was indicative of something, of how far the tribe of Benton had come, perhaps, that Roland could give way to the feeling that the cool, serene beauty of Paris called up in him, even to the limited extent he did give way to it. Tom Benton, at the same age, would not have understood his own responses, would, in fact, have been both puzzled and angered by them. But Roland, descending from the cab, laughed aloud and said:

"You're one hell of a fine old town, aren't you? Something tells me that you and I are going to get along just fine!"

"*Comment?*" the taxi driver said.

Roland tried to explain it, but it was beyond his powers. The two of them laughed together, and the old pirate was so touched by so much youth and good humor that he only charged Roland double the usual fare, instead of triple, as he had intended to. Roland tipped him extravagantly, and went up to the house.

A maid in crisp black and a stiffly starched white apron and cap opened the door.

"M'sieur?" she said, then: "Ah, but it is certainly the grandnephew of Madame!"

Roland stared at her. She was, he decided at once, absolutely stunning.

"M'sieur?" the girl repeated, calmly.

"Benton," Roland said.

"M'sieur will have the goodness to follow me," the girl said.

That, Roland thought, does not take goodness, *bébé*. In fact, his mind added as he watched the sinuous motion that served her for a walk, that's the last damned thing on earth it does take. . . .

He followed her through rooms crowded to the point of congestion with furniture, lovely old pieces individually but obscured by the French conviction that if a thing is good, two are at least twice as good, so that Roland's bewildered eyes could not rest on anything long enough to decide what it looked like.

She stepped into a small room and announced him, and he heard the crisp, decisive voice of his grandaunt snap:

"Send him in, Martine! We've been waiting for hours."

The first thing he saw when he entered the small salon was his grandaunt. At seventy-one, Stormy Benton Rafflin was a true *Grande Dame*, complete with lorgnette, black ribbon about her sagging throat, and a formidable hairdo. Her white hair still bore traces of its original black, and her face, which had weathered into granite, showed force, decision, clarity. She had still the figure of a woman half her age, and her gown was completely *à la mode*.

"So," she said; "you're Roland. You're a Benton, all right—except you have mother's hair. Hmmn—you'll do. Handsome rascal, isn't he, Athene?"

Then Roland saw who the second person in the salon was: She was a girl of no more than nineteen, he guessed; blonde, exquisite, chic rather than beautiful; but so very artfully, perfectly Parisienne that the whistle his lips formed almost escaped them.

"I'm waiting to be introduced, Auntie," he said.

"All Benton," Stormy laughed. "Very well. Mademoiselle Yvonne Athene Josette Langeais, Vicomtesse du Bousquier, may I present my nephew, Roland Benton?" She turned to Roland: "She's free at the moment and can show you about . . ."

"Great," Roland grinned. "I can't think of anything nicer than being shown about by so lovely a guide."

"It will be a pleasure," Athene said prettily; "but I will only be here a month. *Mon fiancé* takes his *brevet* at the *Ecôle d'Aviation Militaire* at Pau next month, and of course I must be there to wish him luck."

"Your *fiancé*?" Roland said. "Oh, damn!"

"But it is natural to have a *fiancé*, is it not? You must have one in America, is it not so?"

"It is not so," Roland said. "I've never had much time for girls—that is, up to now. But," he added, speaking very rapidly out of the side of his mouth, "this *fiancé* of hers is going to have one hard row to hoe from now on, Auntie."

"I'm with you, boy," Stormy laughed, "all the way!"

"What does it mean, all this so very rapid talk?" Athene said.

"Nothing," Stormy said, "except that you're having your usual effect upon the male of the species, Athene—come on, you two, sit down. I'll have Martine bring apéritifs. I'm starved."

She pulled the bell cord, and Martine appeared so fast that Roland was sure she had been listening outside the door.

"Bring the Martini *rouge*," Stormy told her, "and the Cinzano. Oh yes, a Pernod, too. . . ."

"Yes, Madame," Martine said.

"I do not like this girl," Athene said when Martine had left the room. "I do not understand why you keep her, Madame."

"Why not, child? She has to work somewhere, and she's a good maid. Of course she looks like a seasoned *poule* and probably was; but I fail to see what difference that makes as long as she does her work and doesn't bother me."

"*Maman*," Athene said primly, "would never permit such a creature inside our house."

"Clarice," Stormy said, "has your father to contend with—and your brothers. They're men, and what's worse, Frenchmen. I don't have that problem."

Athene smiled.

"Ah, but you have now," she said. "You have him."

"I," Stormy said flatly, "will break his head if he tries any tricks. And throw Martine out of the house."

Martine came back with the bottles and glasses on a tray. Stormy poured the sweet red Martini for Athene and Roland, and a *pastis* for herself. It was the first time Roland had ever tasted the popular French apéritif. It tasted exactly like the cough syrup his Grandma had given him as a child.

"Your *fiancé's* a flyer?" he said. "That's wonderful. I'd like very much to meet him. You see, I am too."

"You mean to tell me you risk your neck in those crazy things?" Stormy said.

"Yes," Roland laughed; "but then I've an awfully tough neck, Auntie. Please, Mademoiselle, tell me all about it."

It was, all in all, a day of pure magic. They were like children, fresh and happy and innocent walking hand in hand. Athene was better than a professional guide, because she pointed out the sights to him with love and pride, as well as a marvelously exact knowledge of their history.

They had supper at the Café de la Paix, with violins playing about their table. They came out into the starlight, and Athene looked at her watch.

"Oh," she gasped, "I did not know it was so late! Get me a taxi, quick. *Maman* will be furious!"

As soon as they were seated in the taxi, Roland put his arms around her. She brought her hand up against his chest.

"No, M'sieur Ben—ton," she whispered. "Oh, no—please!"

But when he kissed her, she did not struggle. She kissed him back, very simply and softly and sweetly.

"This is very bad," she said quietly; "I have never kissed anyone beside my Raoul before. I have very much shame now. All Americans think we French girls are very bad, *n'est-ce-pas?*"

"I," Roland said solemnly, "think you're wonderful."

"I regret that. You are too handsome and too impetuous, and I have been away from Raoul too long. I think I must go back now. I think I must not see you again."

"God, no!" Roland said.

"Then you must be good. It is too bad that all strangers read only Maupassant and Flaubert. I do not know one girl like the creatures in their *romans*. I am engaged to Raoul. I am going to marry him. I love him very much. It is only that you are very handsome and very charming and I am a silly little *Française*, who is sometimes a little weak. But it means nothing. *Est-ce-que tu comprehends ça*, Roland?"

"Yes," Roland said; "I understand very well."

But she had called him both "tu" and Roland in the same sentence, and his heart was singing so loudly that he wondered if she could not hear the sound.

That night, he chatted for two hours with his aunt about family history, about Paris, about Athene. Then he went to bed, taking a bottle of red wine with him. The door opened and Martine came in.

"You rang, M'sieur?" she said.

Roland lay there and a slow grin lighted his eyes.

"Come here, Martine," he said.

"No," she said, "not here. If monsieur cares to honor me with a visit, I live on the Rue des Saintes Pères, number thirteen, just behind the Quai Voltaire. I shall be at home tomorrow night. And I shall be alone. *Bon soir, M'sieur*. Sleep well."

The next day, he spent the entire day with Athene. They covered widely separated sections of the city. First in the morning, they went up to the top of the Eiffel Tower, and Roland chose what he wanted to see. So they started at Les Invalides, motored to Notre Dame, climbed the hill of Montmartre, and visited Sacre Coeur. All day long Roland was silent, preoccupied. Even during a marvelously well cooked lunch at a small Montmartre restaurant, he said scarcely two words. And he ate almost nothing.

Athene sat there watching him, her blue eyes big with wonder. Suddenly, impulsively, she put out her hand.

"I regret this," she whispered; "I—I do not wish to make you suffer, Roland. For when you suffer, I suffer also and this is a very grave thing, you comprehend. I am promised. But, *le bon Dieu* knows, there is great confusion in my heart now. I—I think about you too much, and I am afraid—"

"Don't be, *chèrie*," he said morosely; "I'm nothing to be afraid of . . ."

"Yesterday, you weren't; but today you are. Yesterday you were nothing but a gay, handsome—oh so very handsome—stranger, who was mad and gay and impulsive; but today you are another thing, something I do not comprehend. And I have fear because the madman of yesterday did not trouble me; but the way you are today, I want—"

"What do you want, Athene?" Roland said.

"I want to comfort you. And when a woman desires to comfort a man, that is grave. It can lead to so many things. . . ." She stood up, suddenly, abruptly.

"Come," she said, "let us go. Tonight I will ask *Maman* and you can take me dancing, and we will be very gay."

He stood up.

"No," he said; "not tonight, Athene. I can't."

"Oh," she said, and the disappointment was mirrored clearly in her eyes. "Very well then—where do you want to go now?"

"Doesn't matter—just anywhere," Roland Benton said.

That night, when he had climbed the stairs of number thirteen, Street of the Sainted Fathers, Martine said calmly, "You see my room, M'sieur. You see how I live—"

"Well?" Roland growled.

"M'sieur is very handsome. I could, I think, grow quite fond of him. But such fondness is a luxury I cannot afford. M'sieur is very rich. If he is sufficiently kind, I might learn to be sentimental again. I'm not sure I can. It's been a long time since I've felt anything but hatred for men—"

"Why?" Roland said.

"All men are beasts, I learned that when I was twelve years old. But you, M'sieur, could be kind, I think . . ."

"What the devil do you want?" Roland said.

She kissed him very slowly, lingeringly, expertly.

He tore away from her.

"Name it!" he spat. "God damn it, Martine, name your price!"

"Very little, M'sieur Roland. A little flat in a *beau quartier*—with lights and water and a kitchen and a bath. Pictures on the walls. Big window through which the sunlight can come. A few pretty things to wear. It would cost you rather less a month, M'sieur, than one *grand diner à deux* at le Tour d'Or with Mademoiselle la Vicomtesse. And M'sieur will have the only other key."

A little less than a month later, on the twenty-eighth of June, he was lunching alone. Stormy was having lunch with a number of other *Grandes Dames* of the Cercle d'Art. Martine was serving him. She looked almost happy. The little flat on the Rue Lord Byron had changed her.

She put his lunch on the table, and bent over the back of the chair, with both hands about his neck.

"M'sieur is so very good," she whispered.

Roland smiled, and turned in his chair to kiss her. He felt her stiffen, and turned back again.

Athene stood in the doorway. Her face was very white. Her lips moved, but she did not speak. Then the tears were there, hot and bright and sudden, in her eyes. She whirled; he heard the staccato click of her heels in the hallway, running. They clattered on the stairway, going down.

He slammed the chair back, tore after her. But she had already reached the street. He ran after her, dodging through the crowd, not even realizing the strangeness of there being a crowd at such an hour on that quiet, residential street.

He caught up with her, took her arm.

"Let me go!" she cried; "you must not touch me! You come from that —from that—and touch me! Ah no, M'sieur, your hands they are dirty, I think!"

"Athene," he pleaded; but the bawling news vendor cut him off.

"Archduke Franz Ferdinand of Austria and his Empress assassinated at Sarajevo! Austria hands ultimatum to Serbia! M. Poincaré advises calm!"

She stopped dead, her face working.

"What does it mean?" Roland whispered.

"War," Athene du Bousquier said.

"Harvey's coming by for me at seven," Grace said; "so I might as well stay here until then. I told him I'd be here."

"Going to marry him?" Roland said.

"I—I don't know yet. He's very nice; but he's not—Hank. But then, nobody could be, I reckon. Roland . . ."

"Yes, Grace?"

"Why don't you ever talk about the war? Not about Hank. I know how you feel about that and I don't want to hear about it. Don't think I could stand it anyhow—But just the war itself, what it was like, I mean." You'd been fighting two years—nearly three, when we got into it," Grace said. "Why did you do it, Roland? Why did you join the Foreign Legion?"

"Because they wouldn't let me in the Air Corps," Roland said. "The Legion was more elastic—they welcomed crazy foreigners."

"But why did you fight at all? Was it all because of Athene?"

"No," Roland said; "it was because I got mad. I saw the first air raid in September of '14. I was walking up the Champs with Athene and a woman was killed right before our eyes. It made me so mad I tried to

248

join the Air Force—I was already a pilot, you know; but they wouldn't let me in. So I joined the Legion.

"Grandma's right—I was spoiling for a scrap, Grace," he said. "You see I was already in love with Athene, and she was already engaged to a French pilot. Nice guy, too—I met him afterwards. And nothing I tried worked. She wouldn't have any part of me."

"That is not true," Athene said; "I was so very confused, *chèrie*. I had believed myself to be in love with Raoul—and now I was spending all day and all night doing nothing but dreaming of Roland, which was very grave. I made up speeches how I was going to give Raoul back his ring and ask him to understand that the heart of a woman is, after all, a very foolish thing. But when I saw him again, he had already been called up—and I could not do it. It seemed such a little thing to give him, just a little happiness in the face of all the risks, all the dangers he would have to face. And I am glad I did because we had a week end for a honeymoon, and afterwards if you add up all his permissions until 1916, they came to less than a month."

"And I," Roland said, "was going through hell all that time because you were too bloody kind-hearted. Reckon the only thing that kept me from being killed was grandma's prayers, because I sure Lord didn't know what I was doing more than half the time."

"You had your *sale* Martine," Athene said tartly.

It was hot, even on the veranda. Athene and Grace went down to the end of it and sat in the swing. They swung back and forth, chattering like a couple of magpies. Roland sat on the porch steps near Sarah's big rocker. She was already beginning to doze off and he was glad of that because now he wouldn't have to talk to her.

At Aunt Stormy's he had found Jeb and Patricia Dupré, who had stopped off to see Stormy, on their way to Switzerland.

Just before noon Roland, clad in his blue uniform of a *soldat deuxième classe*, came into the *salon* with a second young American. He was tall, with a thin face plentifully supplied with freckles under his red hair. He was ugly with that humorous ugliness that is so much more attractive than mere good looks.

"Hello, everybody," he said.

"This," Roland said, "is Quentin Longwood, better known to everybody as Mono, because he's obsessed with the idea that all aircraft should be monoplanes."

"Did you," Quentin snorted, "ever see a biplane bird?"

"What on earth is he talking about?" Pat said.

"Nobody knows but him," Roland said, "and I'm not sure he knows, either. Well, Auntie—what about putting on the feedbag? We're starved."

"Your manners," Stormy said, "are as atrocious as ever. Very well, come along."

The meal, despite wartime shortages, was excellent. No one talked very much.

"We will have coffee in the *petite salon*, Martine," Stormy said. "Come on everybody—"

"Tell me," Jeb said, once they were seated again, "what made you join the Foreign Legion, Roland? I've always contended it was because you'd fallen in love with Paris."

"That was part of it," Roland said, "but mostly it was because of Athene—"

"Athene?" Pat said.

"The girl I'm in love with," Roland told her. "Fat lot of good it does me, though. She's married to a French pilot. Quite a decent chap, too. I've met him—"

"You mean," Stormy said dryly, "he *was* a decent chap, Roland."

Roland whirled in his chair.

"What the devil do you mean, Auntie?" he said.

"He's dead," Stormy said. "I had a letter from Athene last week. He was shot down above Verdun. His squadron mates identified the man who killed him. It was Captain Boelcke. Athene seems proud of that. I don't see what comfort she gets out of it—"

"Boelcke," Quentin said, "is the greatest ace in the German Air Force. No wonder she's proud."

"Good Lord, Auntie!" Roland said, "now I've got to get down to Pau! So Athene's a widow—Good Lord God!"

They all heard the clatter of the coffee cups on the tray.

"What's the matter with you, Martine?" Stormy said. "You've spilled the milk! Go get some more. I've never seen anything so clumsy."

But Pat was staring at the girl's face.

"Those Bentons!" she murmured; "those damnable Bentons!"

Sarah was leaning back in the rocker, her mouth open a little, snoring gently. From the porch glider, Athene's silvery laughter pealed out, and Grace joined her. Roland smiled at them, and retreated once more into his memories.

Poor little Martine. She'd had a rough life. But I never could have married someone like her. Didn't even dream she was hoping for that. She was good for one thing—the best at that—absolutely the best I've ever met. The hell of it is that the only way a woman gets to be that expert is by lots of practice. Shop-worn goods. We Bentons may be the world's greatest whoremongers, but we don't marry them.

There was just one more time after that—that last leave we had when we'd finished our brevet at Avord on the Nieuports. Mono and Bertie Nichols—poor devil—and me. Just before they sent us down to Pau for acrobatics and gunnery.

"Yes, that was the last time with Martine. Didn't even see her again until 1918 right after—right after I murdered Hank. There's no other way to put it—I murdered him and that's what's given me this sickness which has ended all my hunger for life so that though I am married to an angel, warm and generous and loving, I don't want to—no, that's not true—I cannot. This black sickness blocks me. Funny, I was never like this before. Take that last time with Martine, for instance. . . .

That last time, the first week of October, 1916, was their last 'permission' in Paris before having to report to Pau, which was by then the goal of all Roland's hopes. All through his training at Juvisy and Avord, he had kept a map hanging over his bed with Pau ringed in red ink and an arrow pointing out Athene's home village of Bousquier, seventeen kilometers away. That was where Athene was, he was sure. After her husband's death, it would have been only natural for her to go back there. But, in spite of that, when he got that last permission, without going to visit his Aunt Stormy at all, he went straight to the little flat on the Rue Lord Byron that he had provided for Martine.

And that had been the last time, the very last time, the end of Martine. For after that, flying out of Pau, he had made a faked forced landing at the Bousquier chateau and seen Athene again. Every other leave from then on until the war ended he had spent with Athene, never seeing Martine any more except that one time—that one terrible time—

After I had murdered Hank, he thought bitterly.

The girls were laughing again; but something about their laughter caught his attention. Athene's was clear, soaring, silvery; but Grace's laughter had a darkness in it, an undertone of pain.

"What are you laughing at?" he said.

"I was telling Grace, *chèrie*, about that time we met Hank on the Avenue de l'Opéra and he tried so very hard to explain to me the complicated business of how he and you were related, *mon cher*. Do you remember that, Roland?"

"Yes," Roland said, smiling, remembering it, one of the good times, one of the best, that day in the spring of 1918 when he had seen Hank Dupré again for the first time since the war began. He had come out of the Café de la Paix with Athene on his arm; and it was there, standing on the Avenue de l'Opéra, trying vainly to signal a taxi, that Hank Dupré caught up with them.

They sat in a little café near the avenue, and talked. Hank told them about Grace, showed them her picture.

"I shall look forward to meeting her," Athene said, "when Roland brings me to America after the war. But in the meantime you must be careful and do not get killed. It is bad to lose a nice husband whom one loves—I know. . . ."

"Oh, I'll handle the Boche all right," Hank said. "By the way, Roland," he continued, "Buck's over here, too. He's with a colored labor battalion."

"Best place for him," Roland said; "the black brother doesn't make a good soldier. No guts."

"Oh, I don't know," Hank said; "they say Buck's father was a hero in the Spanish-American War."

Roland snorted contemptuously.

"Were you there?" he said.

"Tell me about your *Grandmère*," Athene said. "Roland makes her sound—enchanting."

"She is enchanting. She married Roland's great-grandfather, the first Benton, and she's kept the family going ever since. And that was a job! The Bentons are the wildest, craziest, most wrongheaded folks that the Lord God ever blew the breath of life into. That is, if He did. I've always suspected that the Devil had a hand in it—"

"You Duprés aren't any saints," Roland said.

"I include us among the Bentons," Hank answered.

"But if you are Duprés, how can you?" Athene asked him.

Hank and Roland stared at each other.

"Go on," Roland grinned; "tell her—you started it."

"The Duprés," Hank said slowly, "are Bentons. You see, we all had the same great-grandfather. Old Tom Benton didn't always behave himself. He was already married to grandma, when he met my real great-grandmother, Lolette Dupré. So, of course, we had to be called Duprés."

"This is very confusing," Athene said; "you mean that you are all—illegitimate?"

"Only my grandfather, Clinton Dupré," Hank said, his face getting redder all the time; "after that, all the rest of us were the product of quite proper weddings, except—"

"Except?" Athene prompted.

"My father, Jeb. There was a little mix-up between Roland's grandfather and mine over—oh, good Lord, Roland, how did I get into all this?"

Roland was choking with laughter.

"What he really means, *chèrie*," he said, "is you're looking at the first Dupré in history who isn't a bastard—not in the literal sense, anyhow—"

Athene smiled.

"I have changed my mind," she announced primly. "I shall not marry you, Roland. For if your family is so very terrible, what would our children be like?"

"Fat chance you've got of getting away, *mon ange*," Roland said fondly. "And speaking of kids, how many would you like to have?"

"About twelve, I think," Athene said seriously. "For then, if there is another war, it would be very difficult to kill them all. . . ."

It was the noise of Harvey Nelson's big Buick roaring into the yard that woke Sarah up. She sat there blinking a little, squinting her gray eyes against the light.

Harvey bounced out of the roadster and came forward at a run.

"Roland," he roared. "You old son of a gun! Heard tell you were back. Been itching to get a chance to talk to you, boy; a fellow doesn't get a chance to talk to the greatest living ace, next to Rickenbacker, this country produced, every day in the week. Tell me, boy, just how many Germans did you shoot down? Know you were credited with fifteen or so; but I read that newspaper story where it said your score was probably more than fifty, 'cause you wouldn't report 'em. Said all your victories were reported by the other fellows in your squadron."

"Not all," Roland said; "I reported the first eight. . . ."

"But you did get more, didn't you, boy? Be a sport, tell me, how many was it?"

Roland stared at him, seeing the little blue eyes behind the thick lens of his glasses, the mouth slack and greedy, waiting for this thing which would enable him to bask for an hour in reflected glory, tonight, or to-morrow at Tim's saying, "Got it straight from old Roland, himself—him and me are like this, you know—twicet as many as Rickenbacker, more'n Lufbery and Frank Luke put together—yes sir, home-town boy, I tell you. . . ."

"I don't know," Roland said; "I didn't count them."

"Why, Roland?" Harvey gasped. "Name of God, why? You could of had every doggoned medal in the books. . . ."

Roland looked at him, his eyes steady, unwavering, so dead still, ice hard, that Harvey reddened to the roots of his hair.

"Oh well," he blustered, "reckon you had your reasons."

"Yes," Roland said, "I had my reasons."

"I see," Harvey said; but his tone was completely baffled. "I'd better warn you about something, Roland. The Mayor and a committee will probably come out here some time next week to ask you to be the principal speaker at the opening of the airport. They're naming it Dupré Field —after Hank."

"Oh my God!" Roland Benton said.

4

THAT NEXT day, for the very first time in her long life, Sarah tasted veal cutlets in a white wine sauce, with mushrooms, which it took Athene four full hours to prepare, stirring constantly over the lowest possible flame; and with that a *Quiche Lorraine* and side dishes of vegetables cooked in butter at very low temperatures, and very quickly, so that for the first time in ninety-six years, Sarah found out what some of the things she had been eating all her life actually tasted like; tiny, golden brown potato puffs, and afterwards, for dessert, an assortment of pastries as light, delicate and flaky as Athene's imaginative skill could make them.

Sarah tasted it all tentatively, then ate a good deal more than any woman her age had any business to.

"Grace," she said to Hank's young widow, "fix a couple of plates—a little of everything here for Cora and June. I want those niggers to taste this. Yes, right now."

She sat there, tapping her cane on the floor. Athene watched her in puzzled dismay.

"Bring it out to the kitchen, Grace," Sarah said.

Athene sat there, staring at Roland, after they had gone.

"I am desolate!" she wailed; "I thought she was going to like it!" Roland caught her arm.

"Wait," he said; "listen—now—"

"Eat it!" Sarah's voice crackled from the kitchen; "eat every blamed scrap of it! I want you stupid black wenches to learn what cooking—real honest-to-God good cooking—tastes like! And the next time Miz Athene tells you how to fix something—dad-blame it, you fix it thataway, or I'll have your hides! Do you hear me?"

"Yes'm, Miz Sarah," Cora and June chorused.

Athene jumped up from her chair, and ran around behind Roland's. She leaned forward, hugging him joyfully.

Later she took Roland's arm, and said to him:

"Come walk with me, *mon cher*, down by the bayou. I have a great envy to see the moon come up."

"All right," Roland said.

They went down the path together like children, that same path that Tom Benton had so often followed many years before, in pursuit of Lolette, coming out on the bayou's edge near where Louis Dupré's shack had stood on the pilings, gone, now, vanished, the last of its crumbling ruins blown away in the hurricane of 1912, the same storm that had also demolished the old Henderson house that had been the scene of so much of the long, tragic history of Bentons and Duprés—and stood there, watching the moon come up out of the bayou, filling half the sky, haunting the night birds into their wild, formless crying—pushing the dark back, illuminating the sky.

She stood there beside him, and her slim fingers on his arm quivered like violin strings; her voice, speaking, had the sound of flutes, trilling against his ear.

"Oh, Roland, *mon coeur, mon adoré, l'amour de ma vie*, do you not see that this is insupportable—that truly I die?"

"All right," he said harshly, "let's go back to the house."

"No!" she whispered; "no—not the house. . . . Here, here—with the moonlight on us—here where it is so lovely—Roland, please. . . ."

He drew her into his arms, feeling her mouth trembling upon his, hot and wet and sweet. . . .

But it was no good. His body would not respond to hers, not even to the incredibly lovely sight of her slim form silvered all over with moonlight, luminous and glowing; or, perhaps, even because of that: the perfection of line itself, the soft lift of breast, the singing litheness of hip and thigh, the hollow inverted-curve of her waist, becoming under that wash of moonlight a thing too ethereal, too lacking in the fleshly aspects of nakedness; that, and more, the thing that lived with him in the darkness, that came unbidden when he closed his eyes: the image of the Nieuport standing up on its nose on the tarmac, its wings crumpled around it, and the flames roaring straight up, shredding, skeletonizing that fuselage, while in the midst of them that figure writhed, crying. . . .

It was this that defeated him: that the damnable memory came always at the moment before the creation of life, as though, perversely, to block conception, itself, with this hideous combination of guilt and terror; but this time, happily for him, she understood how powerless he was to dominate his weakness; that the thing that lay between them was not the scar of his old encounter with Martine; nor even any diminution of his love for her, Athene; but something else again, a sickness of the spirit, a cancer devouring the very fabric of his soul.

He had tried; and he had failed. So she lay there in his arms like a moon-fairy, like a small, silver Diana breathed miraculously into life by some playful god, and comforted him.

"It is nothing, you comprehend, my dear," she whispered; "it is a kind of sickness of heart, and that can be cured. It is too bad I have not led a life of wickedness like that *sale* Martine so that I would know now all the secret arts and curious practices by which a woman tempts a man. Tell me, *mon* Roland, has the good *Docteur* Meyers the *diplôme* in *psychologie* also?"

"Good God!" Roland said; "you think I'm nuts?"

"But yes—of course you are crazy, my love. But you are also nice. So now we must cure the craziness and keep the niceness. . . . Does he?"

"I don't know," Roland said. "Good Lord, Athene—you don't mean you're going to him?"

"If you had the leg broken I would go to him would I not? This is much more grave. I have a natural envy to become to you what I was the night of the Gothas. Perhaps you should divorce me. . . ."

"Divorce you?" Roland growled.

"Yes, my poor old one. Then you could take me as a mistress. The night of the Gothas we were not yet married, and you were absolutely formidable. So if I must be *ta petite maîtresse*, and make *enfants illegitimes* of all our babies, I will do that. Is it not perhaps that you have no desire towards a mere wife?"

"You little idiot," Roland said fondly. "All right. Damn it all to hell, Athene, if Hugo Meyers can do me any good, I'll go to him."

"No," she said seriously; "let me go first. Perhaps he will give me something to make me beautiful. Or perhaps he will make for me a rendezvous with an old sorceress of the swamps who will give me a love philter . . ."

"Athene, for God's sake!"

"But I must make jokes, *mon coeur*. That is better than crying, is it not so?"

"Yes," Roland said; "it is better than crying. . . ."

She went the next morning, driving the little Chevrolet roadster that Sarah had bought them. She knew how to drive, for among other things, she had had to drive ambulances before the end of the war. It was while she was in Doctor Meyers' office that the Mayor's committee came.

Roland was on horseback, with Buck riding along with him, a precaution that Sarah insisted upon, since Roland had occasional spells of dizziness—when the two cars came into the yard.

"I don't make speeches," he said coldly; "and the war is one thing I prefer to forget."

"But Roland," they protested, "you and Hank was raised together. You flew in the same outfit and . . ."

Roland looked at them, his eyes steady, dead level, still.

"Good day, gentlemen," he said, and rode away from there.

He and Buck cantered their mounts through the pinewood.

"So you came back, after all," he said to Buck. "Thought you said you were going to stay in Paris. . . ."

"I tried to," Buck said sadly; "but they wouldn't let me."

"Not even that nigger-loving son of a bitch of a captain you were so buddy-buddy with?" Roland mocked.

"Cap'n Ross? He would of, but it wasn't in his hands. 'Sides, Mister Roland, you shouldn't hold hard feelings against him. After all, you jumped him. And he wasn't doing you no harm. All he was aiming to do was to get what he paid for."

"I," Hugo Meyers said heavily, "didn't study psychology or psychiatry, Mrs. Benton. It's true I went to school in Vienna; but my knowledge of those subjects is rudimentary at best. Still, I'm going to have a whack at this. Amazing! A Benton—Lord God, that's the last thing I would have ever believed. . . . I don't want to talk to Roland just yet. I want to interview Mrs. Sarah, without letting on to what I'm driving at. You, of course. And Grace Dupré. It'll make a picture. I've a hunch that you're entirely correct in your belief that this business is connected with Hank's death. You say he won't talk about it. But from all the psychiatry I picked up around Vienna, that's precisely what we'll have to make him do—talk it out of his system. I'll do all I can, Mrs. Benton. . . ."

"And I shall be eternally grateful to you if you do," Athene said.

Hugo Meyers was a man of warm human sympathies, and keen intelligence. The problem intrigued him, lifted him out of the humdrum routine of his usual practice. To be called upon to aid the beautiful princess in distress—and she's pretty damned near a princess at that, he thought, a viscountess, I hear tell—the exceedingly astonishing nature of her distress, considering her indisputable attractiveness, and the fact that she was married to the last of that line whose amatory prowess was a local legend, all this excited him, gave new zest to his rather sad existence.

He worked at it as hard as he had ever worked at anything in his life. But by the end of the month he had come up hard against a blank wall, through which the only means of penetration rested in the cooperation of Roland Benton himself. That wall was whatever had happened on June 10, 1918.

He knew certain pertinent facts: On May 5, Roland Benton, Quentin Longwood, and Bertrand Nichols had been transferred from Escadrille M.S. 156 of the French Corps d'Aviation to the Ninety-fourth Pursuit Squadron of the United States Army Air Force—at their own request; Roland, at least being influenced, Doctor Meyers was sure, by his knowledge that Hank Dupré was a pilot in that squadron. They had been able to perform this double miracle, considering how the military mind usually works, by reason of the fact that the story of their valor both as individuals and as a team, had preceded them; and also because of the extraordinary circumstance that the officer in charge of such transfers was a son of a Confederate officer who had fought in the same company as Randy McGregor in the Civil War, while he, the officer, himself, had slogged through the heat and dust and insects and weariness of the campaign in Cuba side by side with a young sergeant named Nathan Forrest Benton. So their transfer went through in three months, which was probably a world's record for getting this kind of action out of any army whatsoever.

On June 10, Bertie Nichols had been killed in action, shot down in flames above the lines. And on the completion of that same flight, Hank Dupré had crashed in landing his shot-up machine, and died, because, being already badly wounded, he had been unable to get out of it before it burned.

Those were the bare facts. But what did they mean? What was the significance of them, as related to Roland Benton? That was where Hugo Meyers met his blank wall.

"I can't talk about it," Roland said; "I mean it—I really can't."

And nothing Doctor Meyers could say would budge him from that stand.

But Hugo Meyers was a patient man—a man with great persistence. He came at last to the edge of the bayou on that frosty morning of February 6, 1920; which too, became an important date in the history of the Bentons, perhaps the most important of all, for it was then that the balance was swung in favor of their continued existence among men. But before that, Doctor Meyers had collected from Sarah, Athene, Grace Dupré, even from Patricia by mail from New York, three little vignettes so astonishing that they troubled his scientific conscience; but so completely in agreement that in the end, he had humbly recorded them.

Some time during the night of June 10, 1918, Athene du Bousquier had awakened in her bare little room in the nurses' quarters of the American Hospital at Neuilly. She was surprised to find that her face was wet with tears. She lay there in the darkness, crying, and she could not stop. It's Roland, she thought; *cher bon Dieu*, please don't let it be—it's only a dream I've had, a nightmare, is it not so? *Chère Sainte Vierge*, help him; he's all I have now—the bravest and the finest and the best. . . .

She put up her hand and took down the rosary which hung above her bed. She began to tell the beads very rapidly, saying the Ave Marias first:

"Hail Mary, full of Grace, the Lord is with Thee. Blessed art Thou among women, blessed is the fruit of Thy womb, Jesus. Holy Mary, Mother of God, pray for us now, and at the hour of our death—Amen. . . ."

And after that the Pater Nosters. But it was no good. She lay there fingering the beads until the dawn came graying in from the east, over the sleeping roofs of Paris, and her eyes were so swollen from crying she could hardly open them.

At the same hour of the same night, halfway across the world, Grace Dupré heard a sound coming from Sarah's room. She had been living at Broad Acres, at Hank's request, ever since they had come back from their brief honeymoon. She had taken wonderfully good care of the old woman, and had learned to love her with the same devotion that all the Bentons and the Duprés did. So now, hearing the sound, she ran robeless and slipperless down the hall and pushed open the door.

Sarah was on the floor, kneeling beside her bed. She knelt there, praying.

"Save 'em, Lord," she said loudly, clearly; "save both my boys. Don't ask me to make a choice between them. You wake me from my sleep and you tell me one of 'em's going to die—and then You leave me not knowing which one. It don't matter, Lord. I love 'em both. They're both my boys. . . ."

"Mother Sarah," Grace got out; "What's the matter? Dear Lord, you frightened me! Have you been dreaming?"

Sarah turned her ancient, regal head.

"Amen, Lord," she said; then: "Help me up, child."

Grace's voice was shrill now, edged with terror.

"What is it, Mother Sarah?" she said; "what did you dream?"

"Didn't dream," Sarah said flatly. "Was lying right here wide awake when I saw it—"

"But what did you see?" Grace whispered.

"An airplane—on fire and falling. Just like a shooting star. It was a little bit of an airplane and there wasn't but one man in it. Couldn't see who it was. But it was one of my boys—"

"Roland—or—Hank," Grace said.

"Don't know. Help me into bed like a good girl. That's a dear. Now don't go worrying your pretty head. Just an old woman's bad nerves, I reckon. Besides, I've already took it up with the Lord. . . ."

Grace Dupré went back to her room. But she didn't sleep. She sat by the window, listening to the cry of the night birds. Then the dark began to run out of the sky, and the birds of dawn started twittering. Grace didn't move. She sat there, staring down toward the river, where the mists had caught the sun.

Before the sun was up, Patricia Dupré came down the stairs of the Hotel Beau Rivage in Geneva, and walked along the Quai du Mont Blanc. Lac Leman was shrouded in haze, and the lake steamers tied up along the *quai* ready to receive the morning passengers for Lausanne, were ghostly white in the mist.

It was still cold in Switzerland, so she pushed her hands deeper into her fur muff and walked faster. Jeb was still sleeping, poor dear. Being assistant director in charge of the financing of more than three hundred French orphans was a task, especially since O'Conner left nearly all the work for him to do. Still, it was a good task—one that needed to be done. . . .

She wondered how she was going to like living in New York, after the war was finally over. She hadn't known very many Yankees, but Martin O'Conner, Jeb's boss, was very nice. He and Jeb had gotten on famously from the beginning. But it was Jeb's indisputable abilities, not his winning personality that had made O'Conner offer him the position of Executive Vice-President of O'Conner Enterprises, Incorporated. Martin O'Conner liked Jeb, liked him—and that counted in business—but he was, after all, a hard-headed business man.

It wasn't a question of money. Clinton Dupré had left Jeb more than they would ever need. It was rather, Patricia suspected, her own gentle needling of Jeb about his impracticality which had made him accept the post. No more 'causes' after this. She wondered if that were really such a good thing.

She crossed the Rue du Mont Blanc at the foot of the bridge, and walked along the Quai des Bergues, until she came to the little footbridge that led to her favorite spot in all Geneva—the little island nestling half under the Mont Blanc bridge. The flowers were already blooming there despite the cold wetness of the spring weather. She walked out to the island and sat on a bench under the willow trees. Only then did she permit herself to think of her son.

I hope he's all right. Roland's with him now—and he's very experienced, one of the great flyers of all times, the papers say. He'll take care of Hank. He'll—

She saw the swans move out from under the bridge. They were creatures from fairyland in the morning mist. They came silently drifting down the lake toward her, proudly, serenely, their plumage unimaginably white, reflecting a reverse image of their passage palely in the water.

She sat there, watching them. Then one more came drifting down the lake, far behind the others. She stiffened, staring at him. For this one was blacker than night, than—death, the words formed unbidden in her mind, his form slowdrifting, somber, funereal. . . .

It's only another swan, she told herself. Only a black swan. . . .

But she got up from the bench, and started running, wildly, toward the hotel.

"Is it," Doctor Meyers wrote. in his journal, "that under the stress of unbearably strong emotions, the barriers of distance break down, and they, those about to die, force their last agonized message through, triumphing by sheer will over the physical world? But all four women agree upon the time, hours before Hank Dupré died. Yet Mrs. McGregor, the oldest of them, the closest, therefore, to the invisible world of the spirit, *saw* his death. We know so little. What is time? Can it be bent; are there flaws in its flow, permitting the coexistence of the then and the now, and perhaps, even, when we have learned how, the still to be? This is unscientific nonsense. I know that. But I believe these four women; what's more, I know, against my better judgment, against my reason, against a lifetime of scientific training, that what they said is true. . . ."

So, by such a route Hugo Meyers arrived at February 6, 1920; at his curiously fateful rendezvous with Roland Benton.

The first red streaks of dawn were there now, in the sky, reflected like blood upon the black and silver water. The reeds made a forest of spears, silhouetted against the burning east. There were specter shapes, formed of the morning mists, rising above the bayou. Roland got up, stiffly, his breath making small puffs of fog, and all the dogs came up at once, heads lifted, waiting. He slipped the shells into the chambers, snapping the barrels back into place, scanning the sky, waiting. Then he saw the first black vee coming in very high and fast, wheeling far out over the marsh, then riding in upon him to the far, thin sound of honking.

He brought the shotgun up, and held it to his shoulder. As they swept in, he caught the leader in his sights, leading him just enough, touching the trigger, hearing half consciously the gun crash, and he, not even waiting to see the first bird fall, swinging upon the next, firing, seeing it halted suddenly by death, plummeting downward, trailing a scattering of plumage through the still, frosty air. The retrievers plunged in, oblivious to the cold. When they came back again, he took the dripping bundles of feathers from their mouths, and stuffed them into his game bag, thinking, It's doubly murderous to kill a thing that flies.

Then he said it aloud, savoring the words:

"It is doubly murderous to kill a thing that flies."

"Why, Roland?" Hugo Meyers said quietly, from where he had stood for nearly five minutes now, a yard behind the last Benton; "why is it doubly murderous to kill a thing that flies?"

Roland stood there, looking at him a long time, and the Benton eyes were veiled. Then they cleared, and he said it:

"There's something pure about flight, Hugo. The very idea, I mean. We —we've been trying to do it, for hundreds of years. And ten years after we'd done it finally, ten short years after all the years of hoping, praying, dreaming—to break away, Hugo—to be free—to soar—do you understand me?"

"Yes," Hugo said, "go on."

"We fouled it. We made of it an instrument of murder. To blast open the bellies of babies. To cut down women in the streets. To kill each other even—a flyer killing another flyer, can you conceive of anything more horrible?"

"Strange," Doctor Meyers muttered, "I never thought about it like that. . . ."

"Yes, yes!" Roland said; "like that! The men who had learned to mount up, to hurdle the mountaintop, to lose themselves in the bosoms of cloud; the men who had left the dirt and smells and littleness, Hugo, the first men in human history who were free—really free up there where you can see how small the world is, measure the littleness of human vanities— these men in the space between 1903 and 1915, say, had already learned to blast each other down out of the clean air, leaving the stink of fabric and oil and human flesh burning as an offense in the very nostrils of God!"

He held the Doctor there with those eyes of his, dead level, sure, until finally the blaze went out of them. Then he said it again, like a litany or a prayer:

"It's doubly murderous, Hugo, to kill a thing that flies. . . ."

"Sit down, Roland," Hugo Meyers said quietly. "Sit down and tell me about Hank. You can now, you know."

The light came back into Roland's eyes then, the splintering of blue ice into the harsh planes and angles of pure grief; then it smoothed into a glow, into disbelief dying, into, finally, what was pure wonder.

"Yes," Roland said, "I can, can't I? How did you know?"

"I don't know," Hugo Meyers growled; "but anyhow I knew. . . ."

"We came up off the 'drome at fourteen hours," Roland said. "I was leading, with Hank and Mono as my wingmen—"

"Mono?" Doctor Meyers said.

"Quentin Longwood. We called him Mono because he insisted to anybody who would listen that all the aircraft of the future would be monoplanes without struts or flying wires. He's right, of course, but it'll take a long time. . . ."

"Go on. Sorry I interrupted you . . ."

"Bertie Nichols was above and behind Hank, and Tom Cartwright was covering Quentin, making the same kind of a vee that ducks and geese make, you understand, Hugo, and then I turned eastward toward the lines. . . ."

As he told it, he made Hugo Meyers see it: a mixed flight of eight dark-gray Albatross D 5's and ten black Fokker triplanes of Jasta Seven screaming down upon them.

Roland had fought in the air for two years, but this was a thing he had never been able to dominate, which could not in fact, be dominated, this awful suddenness with which death came. He had not seen the enemy aircraft. He had searched the whole sky, and he had not seen them. Swearing, he yanked the stick right and left, waggling his wings. Then he eased back on the stick so that the Nieuport's nose rose imperceptibly, the crosshairs of the gunsight climbing the fuselage of the D 5, until the round, helmeted head of the German pilot appeared in them; then his thumb clamping down on the trigger button atop the stick, and the tracers leaping out, the enemy pilot jerking in his seat as the steel-jacketed thirty calibers tore into him, slumping forward, coughing his life out in a thick red tide that obliterated his instruments before his quick-fading sight, the weight of his body, lifeless now, slamming forward against the control stick, the Albatross going down, straight down.

He saw, as he pulled up, that Hank was onto another Boche, and that Bertie and Mono had already sent two more down, flaming. Even as he watched, in that curious relative suspension of time, Hank got a long burst into the D 5's tank, and the Albatross blew up, scattering pieces of dark gray debris all over the sky. The whole action had taken, actually, a shade under thirty seconds. The Fokkers of Jasta Seven were gone.

"I regrouped the flight and saw I had only four machines left. Tom Cartwright, the new man, the youngster who had arrived two days before at the front, was gone. Then I saw the Fokkers again. They were down almost to ground level pinning hell on a French observation balloon."

Down below, the ground crew was frantically trying to haul the fat balloon down; but the lead Fokker got in a long burst with incendiaries, and a solid sheet of flame broiled skyward, with the remainder of the sausage dropping below it like dirty rags. Roland shook his head. He had far too much respect for Jasta Seven Fokkers to lead four Nieuports against ten of them.

He saw the parachutes of the balloonists blossom out, wondering for the hundredth time, when if ever, someone would adapt the bulky life-savers for use in planes, thinking of the dozens of boys he had known personally whom a 'chute could have saved; then, against his will, he was already screaming downward, because at that last possible instant he had seen the Fokkers sliding down, taking turns at machine-gunning the parachutists. From the way they hung beneath the shroud-lines, he was sure they were already dead, but the Fokkers rode on in upon them, penciling the air with the white crisscross of tracers, with their targets jerking like macabre marionettes under the impact of the slugs.

Roland got the leader in his sights, and sent him down, burning. Then, as he dove upon another, his guns jammed.

"I cleared the jam, and turned back; but I was already too late. Mono was going down in a flat spin; but at the last minute he pulled out of it and started for home trench-hopping. He got the hell shot out of him, but he made it. Then off to my left, I saw Bertie. He was flying straight and level, under perfect control, Hugo, only he was trailing a sheet of flame from his nose to his stabilizer, and fifty yards out beyond that.

"He—he climbed out of the cockpit, Hugo. It was the damnedest thing to watch. Then he reached back into that hell inside the cockpit and found the stick, and slipped her beautifully, blowing the flames out and away from him; but one of the Fokkers caught him across the middle with a burst. His feet slipped off the wing, but he was still hanging on to the rim of the pit, by one arm. Then he got his other hand up to his face, put his thumb to his nose, and wiggled his fingers at me. Then he let go, sprawling out on nothing, Hugo, going down. . . ."

"Take it easy, boy," Hugo said; "you don't have to go on with this. . . ."

"I want to—in fact I've got to," Roland said. "There weren't but two of us left, then—me and Hank. And there were eight Fokkers, because somebody, Mono or Hank, had gotten another one. I signaled for Hank to get the hell out of there. . . .

"Then because he was still green, and scared—anybody who tells you he wasn't scared is a whorehopping son of a liar, Hugo; I used to get out of the cockpit and throw up—he forgot the ten thousand times I'd told him you couldn't powerdive a Nieuport Twenty-eight. . . ."

"Why not?" Hugo said.

"Because the fabric wasn't stitched onto the upper wing right. No matter how many more stitches you had your rigger put in, the fabric would still burst on that top wing in a vertical power dive. Hank's machine and Bertie's and Mono's and mine all had twice the stitches they came with; but a square meter came off of Hank's top wing when he shoved that stick all the way forward. After the war was over they found out they'd sewed them in the wrong place. I saw d'Avoville wring a Twenty-eight out at le Bourget and everything stayed together; hell of a lot of good that did Hank and all the other good flyers they killed."

"That was the first mistake he made. The second one was when we were over our 'drome, and he forgot that after you've throttled back a *monosoupape le Rhone*, you have to gun it with extreme caution. . . ."

Hugo shook his head.

"Greek," he said; "pure Attic Greek . . ."

"I could explain it, but it would take too long. Put it this way, Hugo, every time you slowed up that motor, it slung raw gasoline into its own cowling. Then when you opened it up to get more speed, the exhaust flames hit the raw gas—and you'd catch fire five times out of five if you weren't damned careful. . . ."

"Who the hell," Hugo roared, "ever accepted a machine like that for service?"

"Nobody," Roland said. "The French rejected them after the first test. Then some glory-hungry blockhead in our Procurement Command started yowling for planes so we could shoot down the whole damned German air force, which being Americans, and therefore God's chosen race, was going to be easy for us. We had to have Spads, hundreds of Spads right away. Only the French were catching hell supplying Spads to their own crack Escadrilles—the Spad being the only decent aircraft they ever produced—so they couldn't do it. So our swivel-chair heroes swore they'd take anything they could get, down to and including 1914 Voisin pushers, and still lick the hell out of the Boche. . . ."

"Aren't you being a little bitter, son?" Hugo said.

"I am bitter. So they sent us over the lines in Nieuport Twenty-eights which were sweet little busses to fly; but which killed so many of our own pilots, including Raoul Lufbery, Hugo, that the boys swore the German General Staff had awarded both the Iron Cross, and the *Pour le Mérite* to the bloke who designed them. . . . But I reckon we couldn't argue considering the fact that the country in which the airplane was invented never put one single aircraft of totally American design and manufacture into the air in the whole damned war. . . ."

"You still haven't told me about Hank," Doctor Meyers said.

"I went down to the treetops to protect Hank," Roland whispered; and the pain was there now, naked in his voice.

"Then we . . . we started home."

He was back with it again, living it. He had fought off the whole Fokker patrol, crossing and recrossing Hank's tail, taking their fire, seeing his wind screen fly into splinters, his oil gauge disappear in a splurge of broken glass and oil, his goggles hanging halfway down his face where a grazing tracer had cut the strap, doing things with a Nieuport that no Nieuport could do, making that mass of steel and spruce and fabric respond to his naked will.

It stayed with him, its wings and fuselage seamed with bullet holes, crossing the noses of the Fokkers so close they had to turn out, charging them and firing head on, until the lines were behind them and their 'drome almost in sight. Then his guns jammed again, just as he saw a Fokker straighten out of a turn above and behind Hank, the muzzles of its machine guns winking, the tracers penciling their white trails through the air toward Hank's cockpit, reaching their mark, so that Hank went into one half-turn of a spin before yanking his Nieuport out of it twenty feet above the ground and heading for home. Roland's right gun was still jammed tight, but with his left he sent the Fokker plunging headlong into the ground, and then followed Hank's sinking plane to the 'drome where it made the field only to dissolve into a roaring whoosh of flame.

Mono, standing by the *piste*, saw the two planes coming in, Roland's

264

plane staggering through the air, holding together by a miracle, and Hank's a flaming torch, but still under control, landing too fast with only half an upper wing to support it, touching down, bouncing, then going up on its nose with the flames roaring straight back, enveloping the cockpit; and Roland standing up in his still moving machine, jumping before she stopped, hitting the tarmac running straight toward the wreck of Hank's Nieuport, and he, Mono, knowing the tank was going at any second, knowing that Hank was beyond human help, cut Roland off, tackling him, pulling him down; but he, with that strength that comes from utter desperation, struggling to his feet hammering at Quentin with both fists, got free and five yards closer to the Nieuport before Mono pulled him down again. Close enough to hear Hank's choked, muffled, "God, oh God, oh God—" coming out of the fire; and he, rising to his knees, got his service Colt out and aimed it with great care; but Mono knocked his arm up so that the bullet plowed into a hangar roof; and then the tank blew.

That was all of it, the whole story, except the part he did not tell Hugo, how he, with two hours of daylight still left, borrowed, or more truly stole another plane and went out alone hunting for Jasta Seven. He did not find them. Instead he ran into another unit, on the very first day they were trying out their new Fokker D 7's, and plunged headlong into a flight of twenty-five of the most nearly perfect pursuit planes produced in the whole history of flight up to that time, and came out of it alive, saved by the fact that they were too many, that much of the time they had to hold their fire to keep from hitting each other; that they were not yet familiar with their machines' almost limitless possibilities; and by something else, luck, chance, a silver dome of thundercloud into which to dive, disappearing from their sight in the cool white blanket of mist, by these, and perhaps even by a girl lying on a bed in a hospital barracks, fingering a rosary and crying, by an old, old woman, in far-off Louisiana down on her knees in prayer.

No, he did not tell Hugo that, nor the story of the leave they forced him to take, after they found him passed out cold in the cockpit upon landing, without a scratch on him. Twenty-four hours later he was in Paris, stopping at every other bistro to toss down another *fin*, although the inside of his stomach felt as if it had vitriol in it now.

He came out of the last one, staggering a little. There was on the *trottoir* ahead of him a soldier walking with a girl. Roland didn't even look at the soldier. He just started running toward the girl, knowing with absolute certainty that only one person in Paris walked like that, seeing her moving through the silvery luminosity of the mist-veiled moonlight, the soldier holding her arm, the two of them making silhouettes walking, but he, running after them, was already sure.

"Martine!" he called; and she turned. But the soldier with her turned, too, and Roland saw that he wore the uniform of the American army with the fortress insignia of the Engineers.

"The lady's busy, Captain," the soldier said.

"I didn't ask you," Roland said flatly; "Martine, in the name of—"

"Run along, Reb," the soldier said, in the nasal twang of a New Englander. "Go on—blow; get lost. . . ."

"You bastard," Roland said, and bored in.

"Stand back, Johnny Reb," the soldier grinned; "that war's over. Take it easy, chum. . . ."

"I'm no chum of yours," Roland spat, and came on in, swinging.

The soldier dropped Martine's arm, feinted with his left, pivoting on the ball of his foot, leaning with the beautifully timed, perfectly executed right cross, and the sky fell on Roland Benton's head.

When Roland came out of it, they had already moved off, fifteen yards down the sidewalk. He got up, doggedly shaking his head and started after them. The soldier turned again and faced him, saying patiently:

"Go home, Captain. Get some sleep. I haven't a damned thing against you, personally. Just leave us alone. But keep this up and you're going to get hurt. . . ."

"Son of a bitch," Roland whispered, and swung.

The soldier stepped inside his swing and put a left jab into his stomach, doubling him up, drawing his right back to finish it, when the colored soldier stepped in between them.

"Leave him be, Cap'n Ross," the colored soldier said; "I know him. He's a friend of mine. . . ."

"You sure have some damned peculiar friends," Captain Ross said. "Okay, Buck, just keep him quiet. Take him wherever he's going. Don't see how you colored boys ever stood it—can't teach them a damned thing— not even in Paris—come on, *bébé*—"

"You're strong," Martine laughed, "so very strong! I like for a man to be strong, eh *mon cher?*"

"You can say that again, *bébé*," the red-haired Captain said.

Buck stood there, supporting Roland, while he held his middle and threw up in the gutter.

"Take it easy, Mister Roland," he said. "Oughtn't to go picking fights with strange Cap'ns. That one there is the light-heavyweight champeen of the whole division—been fighting in the ring since he was fourteen years old. You did fine, considering . . ."

Roland looked at him. His belly felt like it had been sawed in half.

"That girl," he grated; "she—"

"Oh, I wouldn't worry about Martine," Buck said calmly. "Everybody knows about her. She ain't nothing but a whore. . . ."

"Jesus!" Roland breathed.

"Look, Mister Roland, take it easy. Ain't no call to git yourself upset over nothing. You just got to change your way of thinking, leasewise while you're over here. As Cap'n Ross said, this here is Paris, not Louisiana. You ain't exactly top dog over here, if you'll 'scuse me for saying it. So play it cool—it's just for the duration. When it's over you can go back to Benton's Row and be Mister Big, sit on the front porch with your feet on the bannisters, and whip yourself a nigger every morning for breakfast. . . ."

Roland looked at Buck.

"And you?" he growled.

"Oh, me?" Buck said. "I ain't never going back, Mister Roland. You see, over here—I been free—"

They moved along the *trottoir* toward the *quai*, Buck holding Roland up. It was a long way to the Rue Raynouard, and there weren't any taxis; but Buck hailed a horse-drawn delivery wagon, and after a long discussion, and the payment of two hundred francs (Roland's, not Buck's), they moved off along the *quai*, going finally across the Pont d'Iena into the Trocadero, and out the Boulevard Delessert into Raynouard.

Roland slept peacefully all the way. When Buck roused him, he climbed down by himself. The ex-prizefighter had rendered him a service by making him rid himself of the cognac and the food which his weakened stomach would never have been able to handle. He felt lightheaded and weak; but other than that, he was all right—until he tried to walk. Then he staggered so dizzily that Buck put an arm around his shoulder again.

The bell rang a long time. Then the light in the hall came on, and a slim figure in a nightgown and robe opened the door. Too slim, and too young to be his Aunt Stormy.

"It's okay, soldier, I will take care of him now," Athene du Bousquier said.

"I always stay here with your Aunt Stormy when I get my permissions," Athene said, as she knelt beside the bed, bathing his swollen face. "You see, I have not any longer any relatives in Paris. The last of my cousins left with the shelling of the city by the long-range gun they call *la grosse Berthe*; and now—"

The sound rode in upon them, shrill, demented, terrible.

Roland sat up, staring at her.

"It is only the *alerte, mon coeur*," she said; "it means that the Gothas have come again. I knew they would; always do when there is a moon. But now we must put out the light. . . ."

"Stay," Roland said thickly.

"Yes," Athene said; "I shall stay. I will come to you, for I have seen the way that you will die. And you must not die without having been mine— without my having also been yours. This is just and no longer grave; for *le bon Dieu* has taken from us the long years of life. But He cannot take everything from us, can He, Roland?"

"No, Athene," Roland Benton said.

But later in the darkness, she heard him crying, his voice choked saying: "Those Goddamned Fokkers. Hank, I tried. Bertie's dead, too—Bertie's dead, Hank, because only the Boche know how to build aircraft and these murderous crates they give us. . . . Hank, I tried. You know I tried, Hank. Only a Nieuport isn't good enough. Nothing we've got is good enough, and then Mono wouldn't let me shoot you and stop you from suffering like that, Hank-boy. He wouldn't let me, so you died and Bertie died and Tom Cartwright died and I who killed all three of you stay alive with my half gut and my Benton pride—dear God!"

First in the morning, Stormy Benton Rafflin opened the door of the guest room, and found them there, locked in each other's arms, their faces in sleep soft and peaceful and innocent, like the faces of children. She stood there, looking at him. Then she went out again, and closed the door very quietly behind her. Old as she was, Stormy had not forgotten her youth.

"I was born in Stuttgart," Hugo Meyers said heavily; "this war has made me sad—that Belgian business, the submarines, the bombings—and this thing you tell me about machine-gunning the parachutists . . ."
Roland looked at him.
"Both sides did ugly things, Hugo," he said. "Evil or good is not the exclusive possession of any one nation. I'm sitting here now because of one decent German, a Bavarian chap named Otto von Beltcher. After I got back from the leave in Paris they made me take, because I was cracking up, I found they'd finally given us Spads. On a Spad you had a chance, because it was a good, sound aircraft. So I managed to live until the cease-fire, mostly by running like hell. I wasn't scared, that is, not any more scared than I'd been all the time; but I'd promised Athene I'd come back to her. I had an obligation to keep my word. She'd suffered enough. And now that I knew she loved me . . ."
"I quite understand," Doctor Meyers said.
"Anyhow, I met Otto von Beltcher on the morning of November 10, Hugo—one day before the Armistice was to be signed. I was flying alone at twenty thousand feet, when he came walking up on me in a spanking new Siemens-Schuckert D-Four, all white except for the wingtips and the tail, which were painted blue. And I had had it. I knew better than to try to run, because those D-Fours could almost literally fly rings around a Spad. That's what we were up against during most of the war, Hugo, that immense technical superiority of German engineering. So I fought him. He was as good a flyer as I was, and his machine was so damned much better. We started that combat at twenty thousand and finished it at treetop level, with him sitting there on my tail with me lined up perfectly in his sights. I remember yelling: 'Shoot, you Hun bastard and get it over with!' "
"And then?"

"I looked back, and he wasn't there any more. I looked around for him, and there he was just off my left wingtip, with not five meters separating our wings. I could see his face clearly. He was the beefy type, with a red face, and he had pushed up his goggles, and was sitting there, grinning at me. Then he saluted me, and pulled that little hornet up in a corkscrew spiral that would have pulled the wings off of even a Spad. I just sat there watching him go. He was out of sight in three minutes, heading toward his own lines. . . ."

Hugo Meyers rubbed his hands together, trying to warm them.

"Thanks, Roland," he said.

"That's not the whole story," Roland said. "I knew where he came from, because of the blue wingtips and tail on his machine. Those were the colors of Udet's Staffel, the Bavarian Blues. So when the shooting stopped at eleven o'clock that next morning, I flew across the lines and landed on their 'drome. Otto and I, and all those boys I had been trying my damnedest to kill a few days before got drunker than coots together. Fine fellow, Otto. He was an engineer before the war. Reminded me a lot of Mono, though they didn't look alike. . . ."

Doctor Meyers stood up. "I'll walk you home," he said. "I've got the picture now—I think. You blame yourself for the death of Hank and Bertie. But I'll be blessed if I see why."

Roland laid the opened shotgun across the crook of his arm.

"When I was put to the test, Hugo," he said, "I failed. There are many kinds of courage. We Bentons have always had plenty of the wrong kind. I shot down in all probability damned near as many aircraft as Richthofen or Rene Fonck—I truly don't know how many, because I'd formed this complete mental block against counting them. But it isn't a thing I'm proud of. But when it came to the right kind of guts—the kind which allows a man even to run away with honor, if need be, I failed."

"Maybe I'm thick; but still . . ."

"Those parachutists were dead, Hugo. There wasn't a damned thing that any of us could do for them. But I acted with childish anger, instead of with the sober judgment of a man. I took four murderous crates, of a type which had been known to come apart in the air while flying straight and level at cruising speed, down against a crack outfit mounted on some of the most wickedly efficient fighter aircraft ever designed, into an action which could have been avoided, and under the circumstances should have been. . . .

"Men die in war. Sometimes they die badly, and sometimes, well. Those balloonists' deaths were an act of murder—all right. But men always die with complete impersonality. For me to make a personal issue of it was the act of a child. And having done it, to involve the rest of my flight in it was an act of idiotic criminality. I should have gone down alone—or hunted up that Fokker group when I had enough men behind me to tangle with them on something like even terms. As a result, Bertie and Hank were killed—by my hand, as surely as if I had held a pistol to their heads . . ."

"Tell me one other thing, Roland," Hugo Meyers said; "when did this business of—of impotence start. Athene says you weren't always like that. . . ."

"After we were married. We went up to the hospital at Neuilly to see Mono—he'd got the hell shot out of him by a flight of Fokker D-Eight monoplanes, a week before the Armistice, largely because he was so busy admiring the sight of full cantilever, tapered monoplane wings, unsupported by either struts or wires, which nevertheless stayed on, that he didn't fire a shot. And we ran into my old Colonel from M.S. 156, Colonel d'Avoville. He was there visiting a wounded pilot. He invited me to come to le Bourget to see the new machines that we would have gotten if the war had lasted long enough. So we had lunch with him, and went. . . ."

"And?"

"And a test pilot pulled the wings off a Nieuport monoplane right before our eyes, fought it down with half a wing left, and crashed fifteen yards from where we were standing. He burned to death. Like Hank. That did it."

"I see," Doctor Meyers said. He was turning it all over in his mind. And when he had it, he said it. He turned upon Roland, his round face working.

"You damned arrogant son of a Benton!" he roared. "This is what's eating you? This is why you've deprived that poor child of the right of being a wife? Mister Roland Benton God. Judge, jury and executioner. If I were young enough and strong enough to lick you, I'd kick your behind so hard your tailbone would break your back teeth!"

Roland stood there, staring at him.

"Did you design those bloody machines? I ask you, did you?"

"No," Roland said, "but—"

"Did you order anybody to fly them? No, by God! All you did was to take them down into a fight where you were outnumbered more than two to one. You fought in the air for two years. Tell me, you arrogant bastard, didn't you ever fight against greater odds—you, yourself, alone?"

Roland frowned.

"Why, yes—several times. A week before we were transferred, I dropped into a flight of Pfaltz'—eighteen of them, shot down the leader and got clean away. But I was flying a Morane Saulnier, which was so tiny that they couldn't see me, and was faster than anything the Germans had. And besides it was my neck. . . ."

"Think, boy. Your only mistake consisted of acting upon a very normal human impulse, one of the nobler ones at that—a sense of outraged justice. If you want to accept the responsibility of that mistake, all right. But as for your friends getting killed, you have to at least share that guilt with that poor bastard of an engineer who didn't know how to design an aircraft whose wings would stay on, that wouldn't keep from catching fire in the air and so on—and I feel sorry for him because the ghosts of the boys he killed by his helpless ignorance must haunt him. I say helpless, because there didn't exist then, and only halfway exists now, a true science of aeronautics. It's like medicine—God, the numbers we murdered before we half learned what we're doing. . . ."

"Well," Roland murmured, "maybe—"

"Maybe, hell! You have to share it with him, and even more with the— what did you call him? Oh, yes! With the glory-hungry swivel-chair pilot who accepted for American boys aircraft which the French, who at least knew a little something about airplanes, had condemned. You haven't even mentioned that other poor boy who was killed—Tom something or other—because he died in a more routine fashion. But damn it to hell, Roland, no man's death is routine to him and to those who love him. Any man who joins the army in wartime accepts at least in principle his own death. But I cannot accept your right to abrogate what are after all the privileges of fate, destiny, God. . . . The unbelievable cheek it takes to decide that you, you, Roland Benton caused anybody's death—even, in the final analysis those of the German pilots you killed. You were just an instrument; and they, I insist, damn it, were dead the minute Austria handed that ultimatum to Serbia, just as Hank, Bertie Nichols, and that other boy were dead the instant that Congress declared war.

"You bloody Bentons have always ruined yourself by your pride. And you're the worst of the lot. Come off of it, Roland! Start living, boy. If you have to do something to appease your overdeveloped conscience, why don't you take a job with an aircraft company, and give them the benefit of your experience, so that the next generation of fighter pilots won't be killed by their own machines? That's constructive thinking. The past is finished. All you've got is the future. Use it. . . ."

Roland stood there, looking at him, and his eyes were very clear, and very peaceful.

"Thanks, Hugo," he said.

"Don't thank me," Doctor Meyers snorted. "Thank God!"

5

By the time they got back to the house, Athene was sitting by the fire-place, listening to Sarah's endless retelling of the history of the Bentons:

"I was the most mixed-up young woman you ever did see, child. Tom's poison-meanness had got me real disgusted with him; but, I realize now, I was still in love with him. And there Randy was—a-looking at me with those big, sad eyes of his'n. . . ."

The door opened, and Roland and Doctor Meyers came in.

Athene looked up, seeing Roland's face with the firelight flickering over it. She started to kiss him, and it was then that she saw his eyes.

"Roland!" she breathed. "Oh, my love. . . ."

"You'll excuse us, *Grandmère*—Docteur?" she said; "I wish to have a little word with my husband. . . ."

"Of course, child," Sarah said.

Hugo Meyers didn't say anything. He just sat there, staring into the fire and smiling.

Outside in the hall, Athene caught both Roland's hands. She went up to tiptoe, peering into his face.

"Yes," he said quietly; "yes, Love—I'm cured. . . ."

"Oh!" she breathed, and kissed him. She stepped back, staring at him. Then she laughed gayly—like a child.

"Come!" she said. "Oh, Roland, come!"

"But it's daytime," Roland protested mildly.

"That makes nothing!" she laughed; "it will be night and again daytime and again night before I turn you loose! A week, perhaps! Ah, but what a tired old cabbage you're going to be, *mon* Roland—come!"

Then she was off, down the hall, laughing, holding on to his hand, dragging him along behind her.

"Now what on earth has got into those children?" Sarah said.

"Youth," Hugo said. "Leave them be, Mrs. Sarah. . . ."

But it was the very next afternoon that Quentin Longwood came.

He got down from the truck that the beefy, red-faced man in the ill-fitting clothes was driving, and came hopping toward the veranda on two canes, looking for all the world like some curious, elongated species of bird. Roland stood up at the sight of him, and Athene, too; neither of them recognizing him at first—and everybody there, Sarah, Grace Dupré, and Harvey Nelson, to whom Grace was now openly engaged, jumped at Roland's deep-voiced roar:

"Mono! You old son of a penguin! Lord God, Athene—it's Mono!"

"Had the damnedest time finding this place," Quentin grinned. "People seemed to think I was crazy or something because I didn't already know where it was. 'Th' Benton Place? Oh, I reckon you mean Broad Acres—Miz Sarah's place. Right down the road a piece, young feller.' Only trouble was I didn't know 'a piece' meant ten miles!"

Athene came down the stairs and kissed him on both cheeks, and the two of them helped him up the stairs where the others waited.

"Grandma," Roland said, "this is Mono—I mean Quentin Longwood. He was my wingman—"

"Howdy, son," Sarah said. "Mighty pleased to make your acquaintance I'm sure. But I have to admit I ain't got the faintest notion what a winging is. . . ."

"That," Roland laughed, "is the best description of Mono I ever heard.

A wingding is exactly what he is. This, Mono—is Hank's—wife, Grace. . . ."

Quentin sobered instantly.

"Your husband, Mrs. Dupré," he said quietly, "was the best—absolutely the best in the world. A fine flyer—an officer and a gentleman. I'm going to be proud all my life that I knew him—even for a little while. . . ."

"Thank you," Grace whispered. Then she put her face against the sleeve of Harvey's coat and started to cry.

"Oh, I am sorry—" Mono began; but Sarah cut him off.

"It's all right, son," she said; "that kind of a cry never did a body any harm. Who's that feller out in the truck? Kind of cold to leave him sitting there. . . ."

"Lord!" Mono said; "I forgot all about Otto! You know Otto, Roland. Von Beltcher, from Udet's Staffel, the one who—"

"A German?" Athene said, bristling.

"Yes," Roland said; "but a hell of a fine fellow, Athene. I fought him the day before the Armistice from twenty thousand feet down to the ground. And he beat me, had me dead to rights under the muzzles of his guns like a sitting duck—and didn't shoot. He told me afterwards that he'd long ago found that any further slaughter was useless. . . ."

"Then," Athene said, "I will even forgive him for being a Boche. Go bring him in, *mon cher*. . . ."

Otto von Beltcher climbed down from the truck. He was fat, and very red, and his sparse blond hair was cut Prussian fashion.

"I cannot English very well yet speak," he said in his heavy Bavarian accent; "but I am very glad to see you, Herr Benton. . . ."

"Likewise," Roland laughed. "I never expected to see you again, Otto. By Jove, this is a mystery! I remember I gave Mono your address—but I certainly never dreamed . . ."

"A common interest, Herr Benton. Quentin came to Germany to learn something of our methods of aircraft construction. He could not have come to a worse place. Under the treaty of Versailles, we are forbidden the building of any machines above a certain power; but since he is from a *sehr* rich family, he managed to get me out of Germany. We have spent the last six months in the Fokker plant in Holland. I think I may say now we have gained a sufficiency of knowledge for our plans. . . ."

"If they've got anything to do with aircraft, count me out," Roland said. "But come meet my folks."

He led Otto up the steps.

"Everybody," he said, "this is Otto von Beltcher, the damn fine fighter pilot who—" and again he told the tale. When he was done, Sarah put out her thin, spidery hand.

"I want to thank you, Mister von Beltcher," she said, "from the bottom of my heart. Roland's the last Benton left. And—" she shot a sidewise glance at Athene, "looks like there ain't a-going to be no more. You staying in this country long?"

"Oh, Otto's taken out his first papers," Quentin said. "He's going to be an American citizen, Mrs. Benton. . . ."

"Good," Sarah said. "Finest country in the world—'specially since you Yankees have started to get civilized—a war is a war, I reckon; and we have managed to settle down and live real peaceable with the Northerners even though they sure Lord tore up the countryside hereabouts right smart. Lot of ex-carpetbaggers have stayed down here and developed into proper Southerners, take Harvey's folks, for instance. . . ."

"Why, Grandma!" Grace said sharply; "you shouldn't—"

"Ah, leave her be," Harvey grinned. "It's the Bible truth, so why shouldn't she say it? My grandpa came down here and stole everything that wasn't nailed down—bless him. Wasn't for him I couldn't even afford to think about marrying you, Hon. . . ."

"So I don't see," Sarah went on with the blandness of the partially deaf, "why we can't get along with the German people. Done a lot of good in the world, music and medicine and suchlike; and I reckon they've got the fighting and killing out of their systems for a while. . . ."

"Gottseidanke," Otto said. "That is one thing I have never had, Gnädige Frau. I joined the Flieger Staffel because I wished to learn at first hand of the problems confronting the pilot himself. We engineers exist too much in the realm of theory. We have many ideas which we wish now to try if we your support can gain. . . ."

Athene was on her feet at once, facing him.

"I," she said; "had three brothers, M'sieur. Before the end of 1917, they were all dead, and also a very nice husband, whom I loved. This is a thing I cannot hold against you, personally, you comprehend, because you seem *bien civilisé*. But if you lead my Roland back to this stupidity of flying which serves only to kill people, and adds nothing to the dignity and the beauty of living, I shall hate you!"

"Then," Otto said in perfect French, "I shall be desolate, Madame. I should much prefer that we be friends—"

Athene smiled and put out her hand.

"We are friends," she said, "because you did not kill my Roland when you could have. But if he ever flies again and is killed I shall search the world over for you, and I shall kill you. I swear it . . ."

"How about me?" Mono grinned. "I'm in on this, too—"

"And also you," Athene declared. "There is nothing in life more precious to me than *mon* Roland. I have yet a million, million kisses to give him—and *aussi toutes les nuits d'amour de toute le reste de ma vie*—which is a thing I can say only in French because I have no wish to shock *Grandmère* and Grace as terribly as I would if they could comprehend the meaning of that phrase. They are very sweet, but they are *Américaines*, with that kind of prudery which is very charming; but also completely *inutile*. But I am a *Française*, and when we love, we love totally with a jealousy immense that not only does not support other women, but also anything that will separate the object of our desire from us—including *avions*. You see, Quentin? You have well understood this which I have said?"

"Perfectly," Mono grinned.

Under the cover of the general laughter, Mono caught Roland's arm and whispered:

"C'mon, boy—I want you to see what we've got out in that truck."

Roland stood up.

"You'll excuse us, everybody?" he said.

"No," Athene said tartly; "I shall not excuse you, my love. If you must go look at the detached pieces of *avions* that Mono has probably in that *camion*, I shall go with you."

"You're perfectly welcome to come along," Quentin said, and took her arm.

There were in the truck many steel tubes, several propellers, and a crated aircraft engine. There were other boxes containing instruments, fabric, wire, wheels, copper tubing—all the hundreds of things that go into the construction of a plane.

Athene saw Roland's eyes kindle. Oh no! she wept inside her mind, oh Roland—no.

"Look, Athene," Quentin said; "I want you to help us. You say that aircraft kill people—that, unfortunately, is true. But for better or for worse, we've got them—so the thing to do is to make them stop killing people—right?"

"I will not listen!" Athene said furiously. "You will attack me with logic and in the end I will be forced to agree, for one cannot understand logic. Yet dying is not something of logic, but entirely of feeling, and if you get my Roland once more to fly airplanes that is what he will do—die! You cannot ask that of me, Quentin, you cannot."

"No more flying, Mono," Roland said gravely, "I promised her. . . ."

"Oh for God's sake!" Quentin said, "who said anything about flying? Otto can test it once we get it built. He's a better pilot than you anyhow; he beat you, didn't he?"

"Nor that tactic either, Quentin!" Athene said.

"Oh, all right," Quentin laughed; "I guess I was slipping him the old needle. But really, Athene, we lugged all these things down here because mainly we wanted the benefit of Roland's experience in the first place. They're having a competition at Dayton next fall and all the big manufacturers are going to submit pursuit planes—the winner to become the official fighter plane of these United States. I'll wager there'll be three thinly disguised Spads, and one or two modifications of the S. E. 5—and maybe, if we're lucky, a fair imitation of the Fokker D 7. And more kids are going to be killed in aircraft whose wings won't stay on, which are tricky to fly, a beast to land and . . ."

"And you, of course, have the answer to all these problems?" Athene said.

"No," Mono said honestly, "but I've at least the answer to more of them than the average crate builder. Roland, listen to me—I talked to your Uncle Jeb in New York. Told him what I planned to do, and why I planned to do it. For Hank, Roland. We owe him that much—him and Bertie. Damn it all, I think it'll please them up there where they are to know that three guys who don't need the money, don't even want it—hell, boy, we'll give this little sweetheart of a plane we're going to build to the government!—are working like blazes to see that the next batch of crate jockeys have machines whose windmills don't conk out, whose wings don't come off, which don't spin when you turn left, and can be landed without stalling at a nice, slow speed. When I got through, your uncle said: 'Count me in on it, Quentin. I want to be part of this. I'd be very happy if you'd let me supply the financial backing.' Money is the one thing I don't need, but I cut him in, because I could see how much it meant to him."

He turned to Athene.

"You don't mind his *building* an aircraft, do you? Especially if I promise you I won't even let him put his hand inside the cockpit?"

Athene looked at Roland.

"You wish to do this, my heart?" she said quietly.

"Yes," Roland said; "if we can give the next group of pilots a plane that won't kill them before the enemy does, it'll be a good work, Athene."

"Then do it, *mon coeur*. And I will help. I will sew the fabric onto the wings. It will be very pretty. I shall put lace around all the edges—"

"Good God!" Quentin Longwood said.

It proved to be, for Roland, what physicians in a few more years would be calling occupational therapy. He slept soundly and he did not dream. His behavior towards Athene remained, to her intense delight, that of a normal young husband. Life, for both of them, that spring of 1920, became a thing of enchantment, with almost nothing to darken it.

By the end of August, they had the little monoplane finished. It had cost Quentin a fortune in tools, parts, and all of them hundreds of hours of labor. It was a very beautiful little craft, having a strong family resemblance to the Fokkers.

Athene came out to the field and watched Otto make the first flight. He put on a masterly exhibition of acrobatics, and landed with his fat, red face split in an enormous grin.

But Athene was looking at Roland. She could read the deep longing in his eyes.

"You wish to fly it, *mon cher*?" she whispered. "Then do so, for I can not stand to see you suffer so from wanting to. But give me time to go home, get into bed, and put three big pillows over my head. Then fly it, but carefully, my heart. Don't do these wild sillinesses like Otto—"

"You really don't mind?" Roland said.

"Mind? I shall die a million deaths until you are out of it again. But my so foolish heart cannot deny you anything you really want. So fly it, my Roland, and the good God save you while you do!"

She turned then, and fled, wildly, toward the house.

And nothing happened. Roland and Otto continued to fly the little fighter for three weeks. During that time, they continually made improvements in the streamlining, going to fantastic lengths to cut down parasitic resistance, smoothing everything, fairing everything into the sharklike contours of the body, until, except for those struts, she looked like a winged projectile. They talked about nothing else, thought about nothing else, so that morning of September 25, Roland failed to even guess at the significance of the attack of violent nausea that Athene had.

He gave her some bicarbonate of soda and went out to the airfield. But when Athene failed to pay her morning call upon Sarah, the old woman came to her room, and studied her greenish tint with undisguised joy.

"You better go see Doc Meyers," she cackled. "How long has this been going on?"

"About two weeks, but never before so *dûr*," Athene said. "Oh *Grandmère*, is it perhaps that I have now a *bébé?*"

"Yep. Think so. Get up and get dressed, child. I'll have one of the niggers drive you in. . . ."

Athene bounced out of bed and hugged her, fiercely. She skipped around the room in her nightdress, singing. She wouldn't let anyone drive her into town. She drove herself, sending the little Chevy roaring through the gates.

Sarah sat on the veranda, humming to herself. She was very weak and very tired. But she was completely content. It's been a good life, she thought peacefully, a mite too long, and a heap too strenuous; but mighty good for all that. Make it a boy, Lord. Maybe you're tired of dealing with Bentons; I'm tired, too; but You shouldn't of tangled 'em around my heart like this. I couldn't come home to You in peace if there wasn't none of them left. . . .

Out on the field, they had finally taken the struts off the little monoplane. It stood there, the high parasol wing held to the fuselage only by two sets of short, thick, enormously strong N braces, just ahead of the wind screen. Except for the landing gear, she was utterly clean. Roland stood there with the others looking at it. Then he picked up his helmet and goggles and started walking toward the wickedly beautiful little machine, moving very slowly. . . .

It's been such a long time, Sarah thought, so blamed long since Tom came riding down that little rise and stopped just about right over yonder. Wasn't no veranda to set on, then. I just stood in the doorway and looked at him, with old Jonas standing behind me with the gun. . . .

So long ago—hard to remember how it felt now. A body changes, getting old. I was hard on my children, trying to keep them from sinning the way I sinned. Now I can't even call to mind how it felt, all the burning and the aching and the freezing—the old devil inside a body powerful enough to make me drive a good man away from his religion and his God and send him down to death alone. . . . Funny. I can remember my babies, how they looked, how fat they were, how they cried, and was sick and needed tending, nights. But I can't call 'em to mind, growing—I don't even know that old woman over there in France looking nigh onto as old as I do, who is my daughter. Wade, now—I can picture him 'cause he died young —poor sniveling weakling that he was. Funny I can call to mind, Clint, Tom's yardchild, because he lived long enough for that to be almost now. Clint was a nice boy, for all that he took Wade's wife. But I was took, too —only that ain't the right way to put it. Nobody ever took a woman from anybody else till long after she's been drove away by meanness, by neglect, by not getting what she was born for. . . .

Almost happened twice with me, but that Randy was such a gentleman. No trouble remembering him. Strange—him and Tom are the only two what just pops into my mind clear as one of them moving pictures down at the Nickelodium the minute that I think about 'em. Poor Randy. Poor, sweet, kind, good Randy. That was one good thing the Lord God gave me—the life I had with him. Reckon living with Tom was a kind of punishment for all my sins—but it was good, too; more'n half the time it was good. . . .

The twins, now. Can't rightly call them to mind except I know they had that Benton look. Don't even remember what Roland's ma looked like, that cold Yankee woman. Poor thing, she had a hard row to hoe, being married to Stone. Never no luck in this family. Stone dead underneath that buggy, killed by that awful creature he got mixed up with—wonder what did become of her? Reckon nobody'll ever know—and Nat dying of fever in Cuba in that Spanish war. . . .

So many wars, all with Bentons in 'em. Tom going down to Mexico in 'Forty-five with Randy; and Randy and Wade in 'Sixty-five, and Nat in 'Ninety-eight along with our nigger boy, Fred. Lord God, even our niggers caught that bad Benton habit of getting themselves killed off. Buford and Cindy in the schoolhouse fire, and Fred on top of San Juan Hill. Then this last war, the worst war of them all 'cause they thought up so many devilish mean ways of killing folks: poison gas, and submarines to blow the bottom out of ships, and airplanes to drop bombs on cities full of women and old folks and babies. . . .

Reckon I done lived too long. That last one made four wars I've seen— no, five, if you count the Philippines as a separate one. I've lived to bury two husbands, a son and his wife, two grandsons of my own and the wife of one of them, and a son of Tom's what wasn't mine. Spent my life raising orphans 'cause Bentons always was too reckless to live long enough to see their own children grow up. The Dupré side didn't do much better, though—none of them left except Jeb—and he's grieving himself to death over poor little Hank. 'Cept for that boy mostly they died in bed though;

not with knives in them and under buggies and having heart attacks in pig-pens—Lord God, what a family.

Wouldn't of missed it for anything, though. The Bentons was always kind of special. Maybe they could never live peaceable, but they sure Lord kept things moving. A body got plumb wore out living with them, but they warn't dull—them nor the Duprés neither. Funny, for all them being fullblooded Bentons, too, they always was quieter. Reckon that there Lolette must of been a softer kind of woman than I was. Don't recall I ever saw her. Must of, though—seems to me she and her pa came to the house building; but I don't remember her, nor that sister of her'n that got Tom kilt. Don't hold it against her, though; way I heard tell, it wasn't rightly her fault. That Louis Dupré was a mite crossed up on account of Wade's lies. . . . 'Sides, if it hadn't of been her, it would of been some other woman. . . .

She sat there very still, surrounded by her ghosts, while the morning sun mounted the sky.

Have to write Jeb and Patricia up there in New York, she thought; but I'll wait until I'm sure. . . .

She rocked a little, singing in a low, cracked voice a song popular with both sides in 1865:

> *The years creep slowly by, Lorena,*
> *The snow is on the grass again. . . .*

"Make it a boy, God," she prayed. "Make it a sweet, wild Benton boy!"

Roland gunned the motor, listening to its fullthroated roar as he warmed it up. He throttled it down, gunned it again.

He sat there, looking at that wing. Then, suddenly, decisively, his hand shot forward, chopping the throttle, killing the motor. He unfastened the seat belt, and climbed out of the machine. Mono came hobbling over to him.

"Something wrong?" he said anxiously.

"No," Roland said, and his voice, speaking, was the most peaceful thing in all the world; "I'm just not going to fly it again, Mono. Not this one, nor any other. Not ever. . . ."

Mono stared at him.

"Right, boy," he said at last; "don't. Thought for a minute there you'd lost your nerve; but it isn't that, is it?"

Roland smiled at him.

"No, Mono," he said; "it's not that. Maybe I've just come back again—back into the world. . . ."

The two of them stood there and watched as Otto took the monoplane up and wrung it out. He did everything, including a vertical powerdive from fifteen thousand feet, snapping the plane out of it brutally at five thousand, hauling the stick back so hard that he passed out momentarily when the forces engendered by that pullout reached nine times the normal force of gravity and still that wing held.

They were watching him land it, flaring out beautifully, fishtailing a little to kill the forward speed, when Athene came toward them, running.

"Oh, Roland!" she laughed; "I am so very happy! Docteur Meyers says—"

Roland smiled at her.

"And what are you 'so vairee 'appee' about now, little *cucú?*" he said.

She went up on tiptoe, putting her lips close to his ear, cupping her hand over the side of her face, whispering.

Roland stood there, staring at her, the hard Benton blaze gone from his eyes—forever.

"Is Hugo sure?" he said.

"Almost, *mon amour.* It will take a month to make certain. But he is confident, all the same. . . ."

He stood there, looking at her.

"Have you told Grandma?" he said.

"No," Athene said, still laughing.

"Then, let's go tell her now," Roland Benton said.